STORM FRONT

RICHARD CASTLE

STORM FRONT

A Derrick Storm Thriller

TITAN BOOKS

FOR MY FATHER

Storm Front
Print edition ISBN: 9781781167892
E-book edition ISBN: 9781781167908

Published by
Titan Books
A division of Titan Publishing Group Ltd.
144 Southwark Street
London
SE1 0UP

First edition May 2013

1 3 5 7 9 10 8 6 4 2

This edition published by arrangement with Hyperion.

This is a work of fiction. Names, characters, places, and incidents either are products of the author's imagination or are used fictitiously. Any resemblance to actual persons, living or dead, business establishments, events, or locales is purely coincidental.

Did you enjoy this book? We love to hear from our readers.
Please email us at readerfeedback@titanemail.com or write to us at
Reader Feedback at the above address.

To receive advance information, news, competitions, and exclusive offers online,
please sign up for the Titan newsletter on our website:
WWW.TITANBOOKS.COM

A CIP catalogue record for this title is available from the British Library.

Printed and bound by CPI Group (UK) Ltd, Croydon, CR0 4YY

CHAPTER 1

VENICE, Italy

The gondolier could only be described as ruggedly handsome, with dark hair and eyes, a square jaw, and muscles toned from his daily exertions at the oar. He wore the costume the tourists expected of his profession: a tight-fitting shirt with red-and-white jailhouse striping, blousy black pants, and a festive red scarf tied off at a jaunty angle. He finished the outfit with a broad-rimmed sunhat, an accessory he kept fixed to his head even though it was nearly midnight. Appearances needed to be maintained.

With powerful, practiced movements, he propelled the boat under the Calle delle Ostreghe footbridge. When he felt they were sufficiently under way, he opened his mouth and let a booming, mournful baritone pour from his lungs.

"*Arrivederci Roma*," he warbled. "Good-bye, *au revoir, mentre . . .*"

"No singing, please," said the passenger, a pale, doughy man in a tweed jacket, with a voice that was vintage British Empire boarding school.

"But it's-a part-a the service," the gondolier replied, in heavily accented English. "It's-a, how you say, romantic-a. Maybe we-a find-a you a nice-a girl, huh? Put you in a better mood-a?"

"No singing," the Brit said.

"But I could lose-a my license," the gondolier protested.

He rowed in silence for a moment, cocked his head directly toward the Brit, then resumed his crooning.

"*Assshoooooole-omio*," he crooned. "*Ooooo-sodomia . . .*"

"I said no singing," the Brit snapped. "My God, man, it's like someone is squeezing a goat. Look, I'll pay you double to stop."

The gondolier mumbled a curse in Italian under his breath, but the singing ceased. The moon had been blotted by clouds, giving him little light by which to navigate. He focused on his task, pointing the boat's high, gracefully curved prow toward the middle of the Grand Canal, then out into the open waters of the Laguna Veneta, a strange place for a gondola in the dark of night.

The currents were stronger here, and the flat-bottomed vessel was not well suited to the chop created by a stiffening breeze blowing in from the west. The gondolier frowned as the Campanile di San Marco's tower grew faint in the distance behind them.

"Where are we-a going again?" he asked.

"Just keep rowing," the Brit answered, his eyes surveying the darkness.

A few minutes later, three quick floodlight flashes split the night from several hundred yards away. They came from the bow of a small fishing boat that was approaching the gondola's starboard side.

"There," the Brit said, pointing to the right. "Go there."

"*Sì, signore*," the gondolier said, aiming the boat in the direction of the light.

Soon, they were alongside the fishing boat, a white fiberglass trawler. The gondolier took quick stock of its occupants. There were three, and they weren't fishermen. One was stationed on the bow with an AK-47 anchored against his shoulder, the muzzle arching in a semicircle as he scanned the horizon. One manned the wheelhouse, with both hands firmly planted on the helm and a handgun holstered on his right hip. The third, an egg-bald albino, was in the stern, apparently unarmed, and focused entirely on the Brit.

This would be easy.

The fishing boat's engine shifted into neutral and it slowly glided to a stop. Once the boats were stern to stern, a brief conversation between the Brit and the albino ensued. The gondolier waited patiently for the exchange, then it happened: a small, velvet bag passed from the albino to the Brit.

The gondolier made his move. The man with the AK-47 never saw the long oar leave the water and certainly didn't realize it was tracking at high speed in his direction—at least not until the blade was three inches from his ear, at which point it was too late. He dropped to the bottom of the boat with a heavy thud.

One down.

The man at the helm reacted, but slowly. His first move was to leave the wheelhouse and inspect the noise. That was his mistake. He should have gone for his gun. By the time his error began to occur to him, the gondolier had already dropped his oar and leaped onto the fishing boat, and was approaching with hands raised. The gondolier had a full range of Far Eastern martial arts moves at his disposal but opted, instead, for a more Western tactic, delivering a left jab to the side of the man's nose that stunned him, then a right uppercut to his jaw that severed any connection the helmsman had to reality.

Two down.

The albino was already reaching down to his ankle, toward a knife that was sheathed there. But he was also far too late and far too slow. The gondolier took one long stride, pivoted, and delivered a devastating back kick to the albino's skull. His body immediately went slack.

The gondolier quickly secured all three men with plastic ties he had produced from his pants pocket. The Brit watched in dumbfounded terror. The gondolier didn't even seem to be breathing heavily.

"All right, your turn," he said to the Brit, pulling another restraint from his pocket, all traces of his Italian accent suddenly gone. He was . . . American?

"Who . . . who are you?" the Brit asked.

"That's hardly your biggest problem at the moment," the gondolier replied, preparing to reboard the gondola. "Being found guilty of treason is a much greater—"

"Stay back," the Brit shouted, pulling a snub-nosed Derringer pistol from out of his tweed jacket.

The gondolier eyed the pistol, more annoyed than frightened. Intelligence had told him the Brit wouldn't be armed—proving, once again, just how smart Intelligence really was.

Without hesitation, the gondolier performed an expert back dive, vaulting himself off the fishing trawler and into the choppy waters below. The Brit yanked the Derringer's trigger, firing off a wild shot. The gondolier had moved too quickly. The Brit would have had a better chance hitting one of the innumerable seagulls in the faraway Piazza San Marco.

The Brit swiveled his head left, right, then left. He turned around, then back to the front. He kept expecting to see a head surface, and he fully intended to shoot a hole in it when it did. The Derringer was not the most accurate weapon, but the Brit was a deadly shot. Spies often are.

He waited. Ten seconds. Twenty seconds. Thirty seconds. A minute. Two minutes. The gondolier had disappeared, but how was that possible? Had the Brit's bullet, in fact, struck its target? That must have been it. The man, whoever he was, was now at the bottom of the lagoon.

"Well, that's that," the Brit said, returning the Derringer to his jacket and gripping the sides of the boat so he could stand and survey his situation.

Then he felt the hand. It came out of nowhere, wet and cold, and clamped on his wrist. Then came the agony of that hand twisting his arm until it snapped at the elbow. He bellowed in pain, but his excruciation was short-lived: The gondolier vaulted himself onto the boat and delivered a descending blow to the side of the man's head. The Brit's body immediately lost whatever starch it once had, slumping, jelly-like, into the gondola's seat.

"You should have let me sing," the gondolier said to the Brit's unconscious form. "I thought it sounded *lovely*."

The gondolier snapped restraints on the Brit, found the velvet bag, and inspected its contents. A handful of diamonds, at least two million dollars' worth, sparkled back at him.

"Daddy really ought to do a better job protecting the family jewels," he said to the still-inert Brit.

The gondolier stood. He lifted his watch close to his face, pressed a button on the side, and spoke into it.

"Waste Management, this is Vito," he said. "It's time to pick up the trash."

"Copy that, Vito," said a voice that sprouted from the watch's small speakers. "We have a garbage truck inbound. Are you sure you've finished your entire route?"

"Affirmative." The gondolier surveyed the four incapacitated men before him. "Only found four cans. They've all been emptied."

A new voice, one that sounded like it was mixed with several shovels of gravel, filled the watch's speakers. "We knew we could count on you," it said. "Good work, Derrick Storm."

CHAPTER 2

ZURICH, Switzerland

The robber was in the kitchen. Wilhelm Sorenson was sure of it. With his heart racing, he closed in on the swinging door that led to the room and paused, listening for the smallest sound.

Yes, he heard it. There was a faint rattling from one of the copper pots that hung from the ceiling. It was the robber, for sure. The chase would be over soon. The robber would be captured and brought to justice. *His* version of justice.

Sorenson moved like an Arctic fox crossing tundra until his hand rested against the door. Another noise. This time, it was a giggle.

He did so love their version of cops and robbers.

"Oh Vögelein!" he called. Little Bird. His pet name for the robber.

She giggled again. He burst through the door, jowls flopping, breathing heavily from the exertion. This was the most exercise he ever got.

She was already gone. He felt moisture pooling on his brow, watched as the droplets rolled off his face and splattered on the floor. He had taken a triple dose of his erectile dysfunction medicine a half hour earlier, and the pills had dilated just about every blood vessel in his body. Now the blood was roaring through him, flushing his otherwise pale face to near purple and cranking his internal thermostat so the sweat was pouring from him as if he were an abattoir-bound hog.

It was a good thing none of the board members could see him right now, to say nothing of the press: Wilhelm Sorenson, one of the richest men in Switzerland and one of the most powerful bankers in the world, dressed only in socks, boxers, and suspenders, with a costume shop gendarme's hat perched atop his head.

He had dispatched his wife to their chalet in the Loire Valley for a weekend of wine tasting with a group of lady friends, just what the old booze hound wanted. He had their mansion on the shores of Lake Greifen to himself.

Or, rather, to himself and Brigitte, the nineteen-year-old Swedish ingenue who had become the latest in a long line of Wilhelm's barely legal obsessions.

Their little tête-à-têtes were not, under the strictest interpretation of law, illegal; just immoral, adulterous, and intrinsically revolting. Truly, there were few things more abhorrent to nature than the sight of Wilhelm, a married man pushing seventy, with a mass of lumpy, flaccid flesh overhanging his underwear, chasing after this sleek, blond, gorgeous young thing.

Nevertheless, this was their little game. She donned whatever absurdly priced lingerie he had bought for her most recently—this time, a four-hundred-dollar shred of feather-trimmed pink silk acquired on a trip to New York—and raced around the house. She drank directly from a 450-euro bottle of Bollinger Vieilles Vignes Françaises the whole time. Five long pulls was enough to get her pretending to be drunk; ten would actually do the job, making her sure she could tolerate the feeling of him, grunting and sweating on top of her. Then she allowed herself to be caught, mostly so she could get it over with. It usually didn't take him more than about five minutes.

"Oh, *Schnucki!*" she sang out. Her pet name for him. It roughly translated to "Cutey"—making it perhaps the least accurate nickname in the history of spoken language.

11

She was nowhere in the kitchen. He followed the mellifluous sound of her voice into the living room, the one with the soaring cathedral ceiling and the commanding view of the lake. Not that its placid waters had his attention at the moment.

"I'm coming to get you, *Vögelein*!" he said.

He stubbed his toe on the couch, swearing softly. He had not been drinking. He could barely perform sober. Drunk he would never be able to rise to the occasion, even with all those little blue pills he had consumed.

The giggling now seemed to be coming from the hallway that led to the foyer, so he followed the sound. Yes, this would be over soon. The foyer had a sitting room off it, but otherwise it was a dead end. She would soon be his.

Then he heard her scream.

Sorenson frowned. She wasn't supposed to make it this easy. That wasn't part of the game.

No matter. He would get what he wanted, then send her down into the city with his credit card for a night in the clubs. That way he could get some sleep.

"I've got you now, *Vögelein*," he called out.

He rounded the corner into the darkened foyer and stopped. There were six heavily armed men dressed in black tactical gear. Their facial features were shrouded by night-vision goggles.

One of the men, the biggest of the bunch, had grabbed Brigitte by one of her blond pigtails and was pressing a knife against her throat. Her eyes had gone wide.

"What is this?" Sorenson demanded, in German.

The shortest man, a ball of muscle no more than five-foot-four, peeled off his goggles, revealing an eye patch and a face half-covered in the waxy, scarred skin left behind by severe burns. He brought a Ruger .45-caliber semiautomatic handgun level with Sorenson's gut.

"Shut up," said the man—Sorenson was already thinking of him as "Patch" in his mind—then pointed to the sitting room. "Go in there."

Wilhelm Sorenson was the top currency trader at Nationale Banc Suisse, the largest bank in Switzerland, with assets of just over two trillion in Swiss francs. He moved untold fortunes in euro, dollars, yuan, and rand every day with the push of a button. His bonus alone last year was forty-five million francs, to say nothing of what he made on his private investments. No one ordered *him* around.

"This is . . . this is outrageous," Sorenson said, switching to English himself. "Who are you?"

Patch turned to the guy holding Brigitte and nodded. The man jerked his knife hand, cutting a wide gash in the girl's throat. Her scream sounded like it came from underwater. She fell to her knees. Blood poured from her severed carotid artery. Her hand went to her neck, but it was like trying to stop flood waters with a spaghetti strainer. The blood burst through her fingers.

"I'm no one to be disobeyed," Patch said.

Sorenson watched in horror as the life bled from his plaything. He felt no concern for her, only for himself. The panic spread over him. He had given his security services the weekend off so he and Brigitte could have their tryst in private. He had a gun, an old Walther P38 his Nazi-sympathizer father had willed him, but that was locked upstairs in a safe. His phone was clearly not on his person, and in any event these guys did not look like they were going to let him make phone calls.

He was at their mercy.

"Please, let's be reasonable here," Sorenson said, trying to sound calm. "I'm a very wealthy man, I can . . ."

"Shut up," Patch ordered, raising the .45 so it was in Sorenson's face. "Move. In there."

Sorenson felt a gun barrel in his back. One of the other men had circled around him and was using his weapon to shove him toward the sitting room. He slowly allowed himself to be herded there. He assured himself these men were not here to kill him. He needed to keep his wits about him. You don't just *kill* a man like Wilhelm Sorenson. The repercussions would be too great. But this was clearly going to cost him a lot of money, to say nothing of a lot of embarrassment.

Sorenson took one last glance back at Brigitte, now facedown in a spreading pool of blood. How was he going to explain *that* to his wife? He had always been discreet with his little hobby, or at least discreet enough that he and the cow could pretend they had a normal marriage. Worse, Brigitte's blood had seeped onto the antique Hereke they had found in Turkey. It was his wife's favorite rug. Damn it. He was going to be in real trouble now.

When they reached the sitting room, Patch said, "There," pointing to a high-backed Windsor chair that had been a gift from the Windsors themselves. Working without wasted movement, two men duct-taped Wilhelm to the chair, unspooling great lengths on his ankles, knees, hips, chest, and back. Only his arms were being left free.

"Whoever is paying you to do this, I can pay you more," Sorenson said. "I promise you."

"Shut up," Patch said, backhanding him with casual viciousness.

"You don't understand, I—"

"Do you want me to cut off your lips?" Patch asked. "I'll happily do it if you keep talking."

Sorenson clamped his mouth closed. They wanted to establish dominance over him first? Fine. He would let them do it. When the two men finished securing Sorenson to the chair, Patch unzipped a black duffel bag and pulled out an unusual-looking wooden block. It was the base for manacles of some sort, with oval slots for both wrists and adjustable clamps that allowed it to attach to a flat surface.

Patch looked around for a suitable table and found what he needed in the corner: a hand-carved ebony table from Senegal that had been inlaid with Moroccan tile. The thing weighed several hundred pounds. It had taken two men and a dolly to get it in place when it had been delivered three years earlier, and it had not been moved since then. Patch lifted it alone, barely straining himself in the process. He positioned it in front of Sorenson, then affixed the manacles.

Patch nodded, and the men who had been working the duct tape each grabbed one of Sorenson's arms. Sorenson got the feeling they had done this before. Their every movement seemed practiced. They guided his arms into the manacles. Patch snapped the device down, then tightened it until Sorenson's wrists were immobilized.

Patch pulled a pair of needle-nose pliers out of the bag and studied them for a moment. Then, without further comment, he systematically yanked every fingernail out of Sorenson's right hand.

Sorenson screamed, cursed, pleaded, cajoled, threatened, whimpered, cried, and cursed some more. Patch was unmoved. He was focused on his task, no different than if he were yanking old nails out of a board. He paused just slightly between each digit to inspect the bloodied fingernail, then dropped it into a pouch on his belt. He loved fingernails. His collection numbered in the hundreds.

Sorenson's thumb had been a little bit stubborn. Patch had to take it in three pieces. He frowned at the sloppiness of his workmanship. He would not save this one.

He nodded. His men removed Sorenson's bloodied mess of a right hand from the manacle. Then Patch turned to the left.

"Now," Patch said. "Tell me your pass code."

Sorenson was on the brink of cardiac arrest. His heart was thundering at close to two hundred beats per minute. The pain had sent him into shock, so while he was sweating from every single pore, his body was ice cold.

"What . . . what pass code?" he panted.

Patch's answer was to yank out the pinky nail on Sorenson's left hand. The banker howled again. Patch calmly placed the nail in his pouch.

"Jesus, man, tell me which pass code," he implored. "I'll give it to you, I just need to know which one."

"To the MonEx Four Thousand," Patch said.

The MonEx 4000? What did they want with . . . It didn't matter anymore. Only the pain did. And making it stop. Sorenson rattled off his pass code without hesitation. Patch looked over at a man whose long, flaming red hair protruded out from under his night goggles. The man pulled out a small handheld device and punched in the combination of letters and numbers Sorenson had provided. The man's head bobbed down and up, just once.

Satisfied, Patch pulled the .45 out its holster and put two bullets in Sorenson's forehead.

WHEN SORENSON'S BODY WAS DISCOVERED BY HIS GARDENER that next morning and reported to the local authorities, it was approximately 3 A.M. Eastern Standard Time.

It was around four-thirty when the computers at Interpol, the international policing agency, flagged the crime, noting its similarities to murders that had been committed in Japan and Germany in the five days preceding this one.

Within the half hour, Interpol agents confirmed the computer's analysis and decided to implement their notification protocol. They began alerting their contacts across the globe, including American law enforcement.

The Americans dithered for an hour before deciding how to best handle it.

An hour later, at exactly 6:03 A.M., Jedediah Jones's phone rang.

Officially, Jones worked for the CIA's National Clandestine Service. His job title was head of internal division enforcement. Unofficially, his title's acronym was suggestive of his true purpose. His missions, personnel, and budget did not, in any formal account of the CIA, exist.

The man calling said he was sorry for phoning him so early on a Saturday, but the truth was that he need not have bothered apologizing. Jones had been jogging at four, at work by five-thirty. He considered that his lazy Saturday schedule.

Jones took his briefing, thanked the man, and went to work, yanking the levers that only he knew how to pull.

It took about an hour for Jones to get his people on the ground in Switzerland, Japan, and Germany.

Within about two hours, he began receiving their preliminary reports.

It was when he learned that the killer in Switzerland had worn an eye patch that Jones realized that his next course was now decided. There was one man in his contact list whose training, intellect, and tenaciousness were a match for this particular killer.

He reached for his phone and called Derrick Storm.

CHAPTER 3

BACAU, Romania

I t's the eyes that get you. Derrick Storm knew this from experience.

You can tell yourself they're just normal kids. You can tell yourself everything is going to work out fine for them. You can tell yourself that maybe they haven't had it too bad.

But the eyes. Oh, the eyes. Big, dark, shiny. Full of hope and hurt. What stories they tell. What entreaties they make: Please, help me; please, take me home; please, please, give me a hug, just one little hug, and I'll be yours forever.

Yeah, they get you. Every time. The eyes were why Storm kept returning to the Orphanage of the Holy Name, this small place of love and unexpected beauty in an otherwise drab, industrial city in northeast Romania. Once you looked into eyes like that, you had to keep coming back.

And so, having finished the job in Venice, Storm was making another one of his visits there. The Orphanage of the Holy Name was housed in an ancient abbey that had been spared bombing in World War II and was converted to its current purpose shortly thereafter. Storm had slipped inside its main wall, grabbed a rake, and was quietly gathering leaves from the courtyard when he saw a set of big, brown eyes staring curiously at him.

He turned to see a little girl, no more than five, clutching a tattered rag that may once have been a teddy bear, many years and many children ago. She was wearing clothing that was just this side of threadbare. She had brown hair and a serious face that was just a little too sad for any child that age.

"Hello, my name is Derrick," he said in easy, flowing Romanian. "What's your name?"

"Katya," she replied. "Katya Beckescu."

"I'm pleased to meet you."

"I'm here because my mommy is dead," Katya said, in the matter-of-fact manner in which children share all news, good or bad.

"I'm sorry to hear that," Storm replied. "Do you like it here?"

"It's nice," Katya said. "But sometimes I wish I had a real home."

"We'll have to see if we can do something about that," Storm said, but he was interrupted.

A woman dressed in a nun's habit, no more than four-foot-eleven and mostly gristle, approached with a stern face. "Off with you now, Katya," she said in Romanian. "You still haven't finished your chores, child."

She directed her next set of orders at Storm.

"I'm sorry, little boy, but we're not taking any more residents at the moment," she said, switching to English that she spoke in a rich, Dublin brogue. "You'll just have to run along now."

"Hello, Sister Rose," Storm said, dropping his rake and enveloping the nun in an embrace.

Sister Rose McAvoy smiled as she allowed herself to be semi-crushed against Storm's brick wall of a chest. She was pushing eighty, looked like she was sixty, moved like she was forty, and maintained the irrepressible spirit of the teenage girl she had been when she was first assigned to the orphanage many decades before, as a young novitiate. She always said she was Irish by birth, Romanian by necessity, and Catholic by the grace of God.

During her time at Holy Name, she had intrepidly guided the orphanage through the Soviet occupation and Ceauşescu, through the eighties' austerity and the 1989 revolution, through the National Salvation Front and every government that followed, and lately, through the International Monetary Fund.

Improbably, she had kept the authorities appeased and the orphanage alive at every stage. If ever asked how she had done it, she would wink and say, "God listens to our prayers, you know."

Storm wasn't sure what to think about the force of His almighty hand, but he suspected the orphanage's success had a lot more to do with Sister Rose's abilities as an administrator, fundraiser, taskmaster, and loving mother figure to generations.

It certainly wasn't because she had it easy. Sister Rose made it a point to take in the worst of the worst, the kids other orphanages wouldn't touch, the ones who had almost no hope of being adopted. Many had been damaged by neglect in other orphanages. Many were handicapped, either mentally or physically. Some ended up staying well beyond the time at which they were supposed to age out, their eighteenth birthday, simply because they had nowhere else to go and Sister Rose never turned anyone out in the cold. They were all God's children, so they all had a place at her table.

Storm had come across the orphanage years earlier, doing a job the gruesome details of which he made every effort to forget. Whenever he visited, he came with a suitcase or two full of large-denomination bills for Sister Rose.

Now they strolled, arm in arm, through the garden that Sister Rose had tended to as lovingly as she did her many children. Storm felt incredible peace here. The world made sense here. There was no ambiguity, no deceit, no need to parse motives and question whys and wherefores. There was just Sister Rose and her incredible goodness. And all those children with their eyes.

"Sister Rose," Storm said with a wistful sigh, "when are you going to marry me?"

She patted his arm. "I keep telling you, laddy, I'm already hitched to Jesus Christ," she said, then added with a wink: "But if he ever breaks it off with me, you'll be my first call."

"I eagerly await the day," he said. Storm had proposed to her no less than twenty times through the years.

"Thank you for your donation," she said, quietly. "You're a gift from God, Derrick Storm. I don't know what we'd do without you."

"It's the least I can do, especially for children like that," he said, gesturing toward the little girl, who was now chasing a butterfly across the yard.

"Oh, that one," Sister Rose said, sighing. "She's a pistol, that one. Smart as a whip, but full of trouble. Just like you."

Sister Rose patted his arm again, then the smile dropped from her face.

"What is it?" Storm asked.

"I just . . . I worry, Derrick. I'm not the spring chicken I used to be. I worry about what will happen when I'm no longer here."

"Why? Where you going?" Storm asked, his eyebrow arched. "Don't tell me: You're finally taking me up on my offer to run away to Saint-Tropez with me. Don't worry. You'll love it there. Great topless beaches."

"Derrick Storm!" she said, playfully slapping his shoulder. "You look like this big, strong man, but underneath it all you're just a wee knave."

Storm grinned. Sister Rose turned serious again: "The Lord has given me many blessed years on this mortal coil, but you know it won't last forever. When he calls me, I have to go. He's my boss, you know."

"Yeah. Speaking of which, you ought to talk to him about his 401(k) plan. I was looking at your—"

Storm was interrupted by a ring from his satellite phone. He glared at it, considered ignoring it. It rang again. It was coming in from "RESTRICTED," which meant he could guess its origin.

"Now, answer your phone, Derrick," Sister Rose scolded. "I'll not have you shirking your work on my watch."

Storm let two more rings go by, and then when Sister Rose scowled at him, he tapped the answer button.

"Storm Investigations," he said. "This is Derrick Storm, proprietor."

"Yeah, I think my lover is cheating on me. Can you dive into the bushes outside a seedy motel, take some pictures?" came that familiar, gravelly voice he had last heard in Venice two days earlier.

Jedediah Jones was one of the few people left in Storm's life who knew he had once been a down-on-his-luck private investigator, a decorated Marine Corps veteran turned ham-and-egg dick who actually did spend his share of time in just such bushes—if he was lucky enough to even *have* work. That was before a woman named Clara Strike had discovered Storm. They became partners. And lovers. And even though it ended badly, the lasting legacy of their relationship was that she had introduced him to the CIA and turned him over to Jones.

It was Jones who'd trained Storm, established him as a CIA contractor, and eventually turned him into what he was today: one of the CIA's go-to fixers, an outsider who could do what needed to be done without some of the legal encumbrances that sometimes weighed down the agency's agents. Jones's career had thrived with many of Storm's successes.

"I'm sorry, sir," Storm said, playing along. "I know you're hurt by what your lover is doing. But I don't take pictures of goats."

"Very funny, Storm," Jones said. "But joke time is over. I've got something with your name on it."

"Forget it. I told you after Venice that I was taking a long vacation. And I mean to take it. Sister Rose and I are going to Saint-Tropez."

Storm winked at the nun.

"Save it. This is bigger than your vacation."

"My life was so much better when I was dead," Storm said wistfully. He was only half-kidding. For four years, Storm had been considered killed in action. There were even witnesses who swore they saw him die. They never knew that the big, messy exit wound that had appeared in the back of his head was really just high-tech CIA fakery, or that the entire legend of Storm's death had been orchestrated—then perpetuated—by Jones, who had his own devious reasons for needing the world to think Storm was gone. Storm had spent those four years fishing in Montana, snorkeling in the Caymans, hiking in the Appalachians, donning disguises so he could join his father at Orioles games, and generally having a grand time of things.

"Yeah, well, you had your fun," Jones said. "Your country needs you, Storm."

"And why is that?"

"Because a high-profile Swiss banker was killed in Zurich yesterday," Jones said, then hit Storm with the hammer: "There are pictures of the killer on their way to us. He's been described as having an eye patch. And the banker was missing six fingernails."

Storm reflexively stiffened. That killer—with that M.O.—could only mean one thing: Gregor Volkov was back.

"But he's dead," Storm growled.

"Yeah, well, so were you."

"Who is he working for this time?"

"We're not a hundred percent sure," Jones said. "But my people have picked up some talk on the street that a Chinese agent may be involved."

"Okay. I'll take my briefing now if you're ready."

"No, not over the phone," Jones said. "We need you to come back to the cubby for that."

The cubby was Jones's tongue-in-cheek name for the small fiefdom he had carved out of the National Clandestine Service.

"I'll be on the next plane," Storm said.

"Great. I'll have a car meet you at the airport. Just let me know what flight you'll be on."

"No way," Storm said. "You know that's not the way I operate."

Storm could practically hear Jones rubbing his buzz-cut head. "I wish you could be a little more transparent with me, Storm."

"Forget it," Storm said, then repeated the mantra he had delivered many times before: "Transparency gets you killed."

CHAPTER 4

NEW YORK, New York

Soaring high above lower Manhattan, Marlowe Tower was a ninety-two-story monument to American economic might, a glistening glass menagerie that housed some of the country's fiercest financial animals. In New York's hypercompetitive commercial real estate market, merely the name—Marlowe Tower—had come to represent status, to the point where neighboring properties bolstered their reputations by describing themselves as "Near Marlowe."

Marlowe Tower was a place where wealthy capitalists went to grow their already large stake in the world. After parking their expensive imported cars at nearby garages, they entered at street level through the air lock created by the polished brass revolving doors, wearing their hand-crafted leather shoes and custom-tailored silk suits, each determined to make his fortune, whether it was his first, his second, or some subsequent iteration thereof.

G. Whitely Cracker V joined them in their battle each day. But to say he was merely one of them did not do him justice. The fact was, he was the best of them. His Maserati (or Lexus, or Jaguar, or whatever he chose to drive that day) was just a little faster. His shoes were just a little finer. His suits fit just a little better.

And his executive suite on the eighty-seventh floor made him the envy of all who entered. It was six thousand square feet—an absurd bounty in a building where office space went for $125 a square foot—and it included such necessities as a coffee bar, a workout area, and a multimedia center, along with luxuries like a full-time massage therapist, a vintage video game arcade, and a feng shui–themed "decompression center" with a floor-to-ceiling waterfall.

As the CEO and chief proprietor of Prime Resource Investment Group LLC, Whitely Cracker had won this palace of prestige the new old-fashioned way. He'd earned it—by taking an already huge pile of family money, then leveraging it to make even more.

Whitely Cracker was the scion of one of New York's wealthiest families—the Westchester Crackers, not the Suffolk Crackers—and could trace the origin of his name to 1857, with the birth of his great-great-grandfather.

The first in the line had actually gone by his given name, Graham. This, naturally, was before the National Biscuit Company came on the scene and popularized the slightly sweetened rectangular whole wheat food product. Graham W. Cracker had been a visionary who had made a fortune by luring Chinese workers across the Pacific to build railroads for substandard wages. That Graham Cracker gave his son, Graham W. Cracker Jr., seed money that he used to create a textiles conglomerate.

This set the pattern honored by all the Graham Crackers who followed: Each made his riches in his own area, then helped set up his son to make money in an industry befitting his generation.

Graham W. Cracker III struck it rich with oil refineries. G. W. Cracker IV—the popularity of the aforementioned Nabisco product had necessitated the use of initials—had been in plastics. And in keeping with the modern times, G. Whitely Cracker V, who used his middle name so no one confused him with his father, had become a hedge fund manager.

Yet while all this wealth and success might make them seem detestable, the fact was people couldn't help but like a guy named Graham Cracker. And G. Whitely Cracker was no exception. At forty, he was still trim and boyishly handsome, with but a few

wisps of gray hair beginning to blend in with his ash-blond coiffure. He smiled easily, laughed appropriately at every joke, and
shook hands like he meant it.

He coupled this effortless charm with a gift for remembering
names and a warmth in his relations, whether personal or professional. He was self-deprecating, openly admitting that his wife,
Melissa—who was adored in social circles—was much smarter
than him. And in a world full of philanderers, he was unerringly
faithful to her.

He was also endlessly generous to his employees, whom he
treated like family. He was a friend to nearly every major charity
in New York, lavishing each with a six-figure check annually and
seven-figure gifts when any of them found themselves in a pinch.
And if ever he was panhandled by an indigent, he kept a ready
supply of sandwich shop coupons—nonrefundable and nontrans-
ferrable, so they couldn't swap the handout for booze.

It was this last trait that led to one glossy magazine deeming
him the "Nicest Guy in New York."

Everyone, it seemed, liked Whitely Cracker.

Which made it all the more confounding that he was being
stalked by a trained killer.

WHITELY CRACKER WAS, NATURALLY, UNAWARE OF THIS AS HE
drove in from Chappaqua. He had kissed Melissa at 5:25 A.M. that
Monday, put on his favorite driving cap and driving gloves, the
ones that made him feel like a badass, climbed into his vintage
V12 Jaguar XJS, because he was in a Jaguar kind of mood that
day, and made the drive to Marlowe Tower, tailed several car-
lengths back by an unassuming white panel van.

That Whitely was a creature of habit made him surpassingly
easy to stalk. He liked to be at his office by 6:30 A.M. at the latest,
to get a good head start on his day. This was not unusual among
the kind of people who populated Marlowe Tower, some of whom
passive-aggressively competed with one another to see who could

be the first to push through the brass doors each day. The current winner clocked in shortly after four each morning. Whitely Cracker had no patience for such foolishness. What was the point of being absurdly wealthy if you couldn't set your own schedule?

By 7 A.M., he had dispatched a few small items that had built up overnight from markets in Asia and Europe, beaten back his accountant, the always-nervous Theodore Sniff, and retreated to his in-office arcade. Every super-rich guy needed some eccentricities, and classic video games were Whitely's. They soothed him, he said, but also focused his brain. He claimed to have invented one of his most lucrative derivatives while battering Don Flamenco in Mike Tyson's Punch-Out.

On this morning, he made sure Ms. Pac-Man was well fed. He burnished Zelda's legend for a little while. Then he switched to Pitfall!, where he amassed a small pretend fortune by swinging on ropes and avoiding ravenous alligators—oblivious that he had a real predator's eyes on him, albeit electronically, the whole time.

When he had finally satisfied his pixel-based urges, it was nine-fifteen, which meant it was time to turn his attention to his actual fortune. He left the arcade, smiling and waving at the employees he passed on the way, and returned to his office, where he settled in front of his MonEx 4000 terminal. He entered his password, the one that only he knew, and it came to life.

The MonEx 4000 had, in the last few years, become *the* preferred platform of the serious international trader, replacing a variety of lesser competitors. Faster and more versatile than its rivals, it provided access to all major markets, currencies, and commodities, seamlessly integrating them into one interface. Its operations were baffling to anyone unfamiliar with the bizarre language of the marketplace—its screen would appear to be something like hieroglyphics to a layman—but a seasoned trader could work it like a maestro.

Whitely Cracker made it sing better than most. He was legendary among fellow traders for his ability to keep up with a myriad of complex deals simultaneously. In the worldwide community of

MonEx 4000 users, many of whom only knew each other virtually, Whitely's virtuosity had earned him the nickname "the great white shark"—because he was always moving and always hungry.

This day was no different. Within a half hour of the opening of North American markets, he had already made twelve million dollars' worth of transactions, and he was just getting warmed up. He had just pulled the trigger on a 1.1-million-dollar purchase of cattle futures—he would sell them long before they matured four months from now, because Lord knows there wasn't space in the decompression center for that many cows—when the MonEx 4000's instant messaging function flashed on the top of his screen.

It was from a trader in Berlin to whom Whitely had just made an offer.

Selling short again, White?

Whitely's handsome face assumed a slight grin. His fingers flew.

Just hedging some bets elsewhere. Looking to shore up some significant gains. You know how it is.

The top of the screen stayed static for a moment, then a new message appeared.

Ah, the great white strikes again.

Whitely studied this for a moment, weighed the benefits of prodding the guy a little bit, and decided there could be no harm. He was offering the Berliner what would appear to be a solid deal. The guy would be a fool not to take it.

Don't worry. You're not my tuna today. Just a small mackerel. Maybe even a minnow.

Whitely enjoyed this, the jocularity of bantering traders. He liked the money, too. But the real benefit was, simply, the deal itself. He was an unabashed deal junkie. Buy low, sell high. Unearth an undervalued asset, snap it up. Discover an overvalued asset, sell it short. Big margins. Small margins. Didn't matter. The deal was his drug. Whether he made millions, thousands, or mere hundreds was immaterial. As long as it was a win. The high was incomparable. When he was trading, he was even more engrossed than he was when he played his video games. The hours just slipped by. The outside world barely mattered when he was trading.

He certainly didn't notice that his every move—and every trade—was being captured by three tiny cameras that had been hidden behind his desk: one in the bookcase, one in a picture frame, one in the liquor cabinet.

Each had a perfect view of every trade he offered and accepted. Each relayed its crisp, high-definition video feed to an office on the eighty-third floor.

On the other side of his desk, and littered in numerous spots throughout those six thousand square feet, there were more cameras and bugs. It helped that Whitely preferred such lavish furnishings: It made for more hiding places. His home in Chappaqua, his various cars, anywhere he regularly went—even his health club— were festooned with them. There was nothing he did, no conversation he had, that wasn't being monitored by a person well trained in the ways of killing.

Whitely was oblivious to it all, just as he was oblivious for the first three minutes Theodore Sniff spent lurking in his doorway midway through the morning. Sniff had been Prime Resource Investment Group's accountant since its inception. He did not have his boss's charm, and certainly lacked his good looks: Sniff was short, fat, *and* balding, the Holy Trinity of datelessness. His clothes, which seemed to wrinkle faster than ought to have been scientifically possible, never fit right. By the end of his long days at the office, his body odor tended to overpower whatever deodorant he chose. Even with a salary that should have made him

plenty attractive to the opposite sex—or at least a certain oppor-
tunistic subset of it—Sniff hadn't been laid in years.

His lone gift was for accounting. And there, he was genius,
capable of keeping a veritable Domesday Book's worth of accounts and ledgers at his command. Whitely leaned heavily on
this ability because, in truth, he couldn't really be bothered to
oversee these things himself. Whitely took pride in his instincts
as a trader, instincts that had built an empire. He could feel
changes in the marketplace coming the way the Native Americans of yore could feel the ground trembling from buffalo. But
keeping up with the books? Boring. Melissa told him he should
make more of an effort. He told her that's what Sniff was for.

Cracker was so loath to pay attention to the bottom line, he
even tended to overlook when Sniff was in the room. For Whitely,
a man ordinarily so attuned to his staff, ignoring Sniff was like a
congenital condition. There was seemingly nothing he could do
to stop it. The accountant was entering his fourth minute of standing in the doorway before he finally coughed softly into his hand.
Whitely did not look up from his screen. Sniff rattled the change
in his pocket. Nothing. Sniff cleared his throat, this time louder.
Still nothing. Finally, he spoke.

"Sorry to interrupt," Sniff said. "But it's important."

"Not now, Teddy," Whitely said. Whitely always called him
Teddy. Whitely used the name affectionately; he thought it brought
the men closer. Sniff never had the courage to tell his boss he ab-
horred it.

"Sir, I . . ."

"Teddy," Whitely said sharply, without taking his eyes off his
screen. "I'm trading."

Sniff turned his back and slinked off.

The camera in the far corner caught his dejected look as he
departed.

CHAPTER 5

LANGLEY, Virginia

Derrick Storm was a Ford man.

Maybe that didn't seem like a very sexy choice for a secret operative. Maybe, in a nod to the great James Bond, he should have gone with an Aston Martin, or a Lamborghini, or, heck, even just a Beemer.

But, no. Derrick Storm liked his Fords. He was an American spy, after all. And an American spy ought to have an American ride. Besides, he liked how they handled. He liked the familiarity of the instrument panel. He liked knowing that he had good old Michigan-made muscle at his command. When he was a teenager, his first car had been a non-operating '87 Thunderbird he bought off a buddy for five hundred dollars of lawn-mowing money and nursed back to glorious health. He drove the car all through high school and college. That had been enough to hook him. He had driven Fords ever since.

And, in truth, they were a much more practical choice for a man of his profession. Tool around in a Bentley just once and everyone notices you. Drive the exact same route every day in a Ford Focus and you might as well be invisible.

He kept Fords stashed near airports in many of his favorite cities. In New York, for example, he had recently purchased a new Mustang, a Shelby GT500 with a supercharged aluminum-block

V8—a spirited revival of an American classic. In Miami, he kicked it old school, going with a '66 T-Bird convertible, with the 390-cubic-inch, 315-horsepower V8. In Denver, he had an Explorer Sport, good for climbing mountain passes on the way to ski slopes.

In Washington, he kept a blue Ford Taurus. It was a staid choice for a town where ostentatious displays of wealth had been historically frowned on. But this wasn't just any Ford Taurus: It was the SHO model, the one with the 3.5-liter, 365-horsepower twin-turbo EcoBoost engine, the one capable of throwing 350 pounds of torque down on the pavement. Much like Storm himself, it was a car that looked ordinary on the outside but had a lot going on under the hood.

It also handled bends well, which made it nicely suited to the George Washington Memorial Parkway, which was where Storm found himself just after noontime on Monday. It was a route Storm traveled often, not only because its tight curves made it one of the more enjoyable roads to drive in the D.C. area, but because it led to CIA headquarters.

He slowed as he passed the oft-mocked sign that read "George Bush Center for Intelligence Next Right" and took the winding exit ramp. He passed through Security, parked, then stopped at Kryptos, the famed copperplate sculpture containing 1,735 seemingly random letters, representing a code that has never fully been broken.

"Some other time," Storm said, moving on to the CIA's main entryway, an airy, arched, glass structure.

There, he was met by Agent Kevin Bryan, one of Jedediah Jones's two trusted lieutenants.

"The hood?" Storm said by way of greeting.

"The hood," Bryan replied, handing him a piece of black cloth.

"Jones better have some seriously cool toys waiting for me."

"Toys?"

"Gadgets. Devices. Exploding toothpaste. Pens that are actually tiny rockets. Something. I know you guys have been holding out on me."

"We'll see what we can do. Meantime, the hood."

The hood. Always, they made him wear the hood. Even with all his security clearances, even with background check after background check, even with all the times he had proven his loyalty, he still had to wear the hood when he was being escorted to Jedediah Jones's lair, aka the cubby.

He understood. At the CIA, there's classified, there's highly classified, there's double-secret we'd-tell-you-but-we'd-have-to-kill-you classified.

Then there's the unit Jedediah Jones created.

It was so classified, it didn't even have a name. It was a kind of agency within the agency, one whose primary mission was to remain as invisible as possible. Its existence was not explicitly stated in any CIA materials. The allocations that funded it could not be found in any CIA budget. Its employees did not have files in the personnel office, nor could they be found on the office phone tree, nor did they appear on e-mail listservs, nor were their paychecks drawn from normal CIA accounts. Its organization chart was a running gag—Jones handed his people a takeoff of a famous Escher print, one where there was no beginning and no end. The names on the chart were all cartoon characters.

The architect of this domain—and the master of it—was Jones. He had created this shadowy cadre many years before and, with a seemingly innate understanding of how to manipulate the sometimes-stubborn controls of a federal bureaucracy, had since built it into the elite unit it was today. He did it with a mix of obeisance and threats. Everyone in the high reaches of the CIA seemed to fall into two groups: either they owed Jones a favor, or he had dirt on them.

With the hood on, the trip to the cubby always felt a little disorienting. Storm was led down a hallway to an elevator, which felt like it first went up, then down, then over, then up again, then down some more. It was like being on an elevator in Willy Wonka's Chocolate Factory, only it didn't smell as good.

By the time the ride was over, Storm was left with the feeling he was underground somewhere, but it was impossible to know for sure. The cubby had no windows, just an array of computers, wall-mounted monitors, and communications devices. They were run by a group of men and women known collectively as "the nerds," a term that was spoken with fondness and great respect for their abilities. The nerds had been pulled from a broad spectrum of public and private industry to form a cyber-spying unit that was second to none.

From the comfort of their high-backed chairs, the nerds could read a newspaper over the shoulder of a terrorist in Kandahar, monitor an insurgent's attempts to make a bomb in Jakarta, or follow a suspected double agent through the streets of Berlin. They also had access to virtually every database, public or private, government or civilian, that anyone had ever thought to compile. If it was on a computer that ever connected to the Internet, the nerds could eventually put it at Jones's fingertips. They just had to be asked.

As usual, Bryan removed Storm's hood when the elevator doors opened. Storm was greeted by a man who appeared to be about sixty. He wore an off-the-rack blue suit that draped nicely over his fit body. He was average height, with a shaved head, pale blue eyes and, at least for the moment, a wry smile.

"Hello, Storm," he said in his trademark sandpaper voice.

"Jones."

"It's good to see you, son."

"Wish the circumstances were better."

"You look great."

"You look like you need a tan."

"Sunlight's not in my budget," Jones said.

"You bring me here to small-talk?"

"Not really."

"Well, come on then," Storm said. "Let's get to it."

. . .

STORM FOLLOWED JONES INTO A DARK CONFERENCE ROOM. IN AD-
dition to Agent Bryan, they were joined by Agent Javier Rodriguez, Jones's other top lieutenant. Jones clapped twice and the
room was instantly illuminated.

"Really, Jones?" Storm said, raising an eyebrow. "The Clapper?"
Jones offered no reply.

"The most futuristic technology the world has never seen, spy
satellites that alert you when a world leader farts, databases that
could produce Genghis Khan's first grade report card . . . And
you turn the lights on with the Clapper?"

"The damn automatic sensor kept failing, and there's only one
electrician in the whole CIA with a high enough security clear-
ance to come here and fix it," Jones explained. "Plus, we like the
kitsch value. Sit down."

Storm took a spot midway down the length of a cherry-top
table with enough shine to be used as a shaving mirror. A motor
whirred, and a small projector emerged from the middle of the
table. Jones waited until the motor ceased, then clicked a button
on a remote control, and a 3-D holographic image of an unre-
markable middle-aged white man appeared, almost as if floating
on the table. Without preamble, Storm's briefing had begun.

"Dieter Kornblum," Jones said. "Senior executive vice president
for BonnBank, the largest bank in Germany. Forty-six. Married.
Two kids. Net worth approximately eighty million, but he doesn't
flaunt it. His investment portfolio is about as daring as a wardrobe full of turtlenecks. Autopsy noted among other things that
he double-knotted his shoes."

"And what misfortune befell him that he required an autopsy?"
Storm asked.

Jones slid the remote control to Agent Rodriguez, who resumed
the narrative: "Five days ago, Kornblum didn't show up for work,
didn't answer his cell phone, didn't answer his e-mail, nothing.
This is a man who hadn't missed a day of work in thirteen years

and never went more than two waking hours without checking in with someone. He was Mr. Responsible, so his people were concerned right away. When it was discovered his kids didn't show up at school and his wife had missed a hair appointment, the Nordrhein-Westfalen Landespolizei were dispatched to his home in Bad Godesberg. They found this."

Another projector emerged from the ceiling. Crime scene photographs started flashing up on a screen on the far wall. It was all Storm could do not to avert his eyes. The children, both in their early teens, had been killed in their beds, apparently in their sleep. Powder burns around their entry wounds suggested point-blank shots. Their pillows were blood-soaked.

The wife's body was found in the master bedroom. She had made it out of bed, but not very far, as if she had gotten up to investigate a noise and met her end quickly thereafter. Her body was faceup perhaps five feet away from the bed. Her eyes stared blankly at the ceiling. There were two crisp bullet holes in her forehead. Whatever bloodstains she'd left behind were hidden by the dark carpet on which she had fallen.

Kornblum was in a different room, one that appeared to be an office. He had been tied to a chair. His head was tilted back at an unnatural angle. Blood and brain matter were splattered on the wall behind him. There was no visible entry wound, but Storm figured it out: The killer had stuck the gun in the banker's mouth.

"Awful," Storm said. "And I assume Kornblum was tortured?"

"Correct," Rodriguez said. "All the fingernails on Kornblum's right hand were missing. So was the back of his skull, for whatever that's worth."

"Do we know what he was being tortured for?"

"Negative," Rodriguez said. "There was no sign of any robbery. None of his papers or files were disturbed. The local authorities were quite baffled. A home invasion crew usually at least goes for jewelry, if nothing else. They assumed Kornblum had screwed someone over in a business deal and this was some kind of revenge hit."

"What do we know about the assailants?"

"Crime scene techs found six distinct footprints in and around the house that they believe belonged to the intruders," Rodriguez said as pictures of boot treads flashed up on the screen. "There were no fingerprints, naturally. No hairs. No fibers. At least not anything useful that's come back so far. No surveillance cameras. No witnesses. The Kornblums lived in a large house that couldn't be seen from the road and was separated by some distance from their neighbors."

"Didn't they have any security system?" Storm asked.

"Yeah, but Dieter didn't put any money into it, so it was *Romper Room* stuff. The driveway was gated, but a two-year-old with tweezers could have hot-wired it. There were alarms on the doors and windows, but they were pretty easily defeated, too. The central monitoring was never tripped. It was a clean job."

"So nothing from the scene?"

"Nope."

"What about at work?"

"Kornblum's bosses weren't terribly forthcoming with the German authorities. Either that or German authorities weren't terribly forthcoming with our agents. Our guys were able to sniff out that Dieter did a lot of work in securities of varying sorts, but he also worked in currency, bonds, a bit of everything. It sounded like he had a pretty big job. He was a jack of all trades, if you'll excuse the pun. But as to something that could get him killed? We haven't really come up with anything yet."

"Is that all we know about Dieter Kornblum?"

"All that's worth saying right now, yeah."

More like it was all that Jones was willing to say. There was always a hold-back with Jones. Storm had come to accept this as part of working with the man. It was like being the frog who ferried the scorpion across the river. No matter how many times the scorpion promised otherwise, the sting was always coming. It was in his nature. That Storm was still alive was simply because he had grown adept at anticipating when it was going to happen.

Speaking of things he needed to anticipate . . .

"Do you have Clara Strike working this already?" Storm asked.

"No," Jones said. "Your girlfriend is otherwise deployed."

"She's *not* my girlfriend," Storm said, sounding a little too much like a petulant teenager.

"Fine. Have it your way," Jones said.

"Whatever," Storm spat. "Next."

Agent Rodriguez ceremoniously handed the remote control to Agent Bryan, who brought a new image up on the hologram. This one was an Asian man with rounded cheeks and a smooth, boyish face.

"Joji Motoshige," Bryan said. "President of global trade at Nippon Financial, one of the Big Four of Japanese banking. Thirty-seven. Unmarried. No kids. Notorious playboy. Pretty much every high-end strip club in Tokyo knew Mr. Motoshige. He'd show up with one girl on his arm and leave with two more. He didn't seem to bother with Japanese women, but he liked pretty much every other flavor. Argentinian. Ukrainian. Ethiopian. His girlfriends looked like a Benetton ad, but he never kept the same one for more than a few weeks."

"Commitment issues," Storm said, knowingly.

"Something like that," Bryan said. "He certainly had the money to afford the best. He had recently cashed in a stock option that netted him a hundred and six million. That was on top of the millions he had already made in salary and bonuses. But it still wasn't enough for him. His unofficial motto was 'Work hard, play hard.' He was legendary for being able to work a sixteen-hour day then hit the town until the early morning, sleep for maybe an hour or two, then go right back to his desk."

"I assume he did drugs to keep him going?"

"Not that anyone is aware of. Unless you count pussy as a drug. Women were his only vice and he chased them relentlessly. All he ever seemed to do was get laid and make money. Colleagues described him as indefatigable in both pursuits."

"I note you're using the past tense," Storm said.

"That's right. He lived in the penthouse of a sixty-story luxury condo, a real high-end place. Three days ago his housekeeper entered his place to do her usual cleaning. She came three times a week, and she was used to finding some pretty weird stuff—naked girls passed out on the couch, French maid costumes tossed about, erotic asphyxiation rigs, you name it. Instead, she found this."

An image of Motoshige's lifeless body appeared on the screen. His throat had been slashed in a neat line. The blood had poured down from the line like a scarlet bib.

"No gunshot wound?" Storm asked.

"It can be hard to find firearms in Tokyo, even if you're a criminal," Bryan said. "The Japanese just don't do guns like we do here in the Wild West. Plus, this was a high-density living situation. Someone might have heard a gunshot, even if it had a silencer."

"Right. High-density living situation. A luxury condo with, presumably, at least one doorman. So how did the perps get in?"

"From above. They rappelled down from the roof and cut a circular hole in his living room window. That was pretty much the only trace they left behind—well, other than Motoshige's body."

"How did they get up on the roof?"

"The Tokyo police are still trying to figure that out. There's a tower being constructed next door. It's possible they could have attached a zip line from one building to the other."

"Either that or we're looking for a crew that includes Spider-Man," Storm said. "I assume Mr. Motoshige was tortured as well?"

"Yep. He held out a little longer than Kornblum did. In addition to the fingernails on his right hand, he was also missing the fingernails on his left. There was also a slash mark on his face. That must have been what caused him to acquiesce to their demands: He didn't want his pretty face to be ruined."

"But I assume we have no clue as to what those demands may have been?"

"Nothing yet. We still don't know whether it was information or something tangible, like a document or a safe deposit box key or what," Bryan confirmed. "The Japanese authorities pretty much wrote off the whole thing as being an outcropping of Motoshige's overactive penis. They assumed Motoshige pissed off some girl's boyfriend or husband or brother and that he finally got what was coming to him. There were too many suspects to even begin to narrow it down."

"A husband or brother is going to rappel from the roof to kill the guy?" Storm asked.

"Our thought exactly. But apparently no one at Nippon Financial was pushing real hard for an investigation. The higher-ups at the bank were deeply embarrassed by Motoshige's lifestyle, and they didn't want to risk bringing any attention to this. They've managed to keep it hushed up in the media so far. Japanese culture is all about saving face and not acting in a way that disgraces your company. High level bank executives just aren't supposed to behave like Motoshige did. His bosses only tolerated him because he was brilliant at what he did. Like Kornblum, he had his fingers in a lot of pies. Anything that involved foreign transactions at Nippon was in Motoshige's domain. The guy spoke five languages."

"Ah, a real polyglot," Storm said.

"Since when do you know a word like 'polyglot'?" Jones teased.

"You've had me learn eight languages and you ask me how it is I know the word 'polyglot'?"

"Point taken."

"Anything else on Motoshige?"

"Nothing that struck us as relevant," Jones interjected. And again, Storm thought about Jones's wandering definition of what relevant actually was.

"Okay, so when do we get to the Swiss guy?" Storm asked.

"Right now," Jones said, taking ownership of the remote control. He clicked, and a picture of a fat, jowly man with a hooked nose appeared in a 3-D hologram.

"Yikes," Storm said. "Did someone make him take an ugly pill?"

"Wilhelm Sorenson," Jones said, ignoring the commentary.

"Chief currency trader for Nationale Banc Suisse, the third-largest bank in the world, asset-wise. Sixty-eight. Married. Two kids, both grown. Most of his assets were, naturally, in Swiss banks, and as you know they aren't very good about sharing information. But we do know he was a multi-multi-millionaire, and we also know he also had a weakness for women. Young women. The other victim at the scene was a seventeen-year-old runaway with a fake I.D. that said she was nineteen. She was wearing a bitty little piece of lingerie that left scant doubt as to the nature of the relationship."

Jones catalogued the details of the scene, ending with the missing fingernails.

"The Interpol computers didn't pick up the similarity of the crimes until the third iteration, but Sorenson's killing finally tripped their alarm bells," Jones said. "The local authorities botched the scene a little. Believe me, they were asking some hard questions of the wife, who was, quote-unquote 'out of town' on some kind of girls' weekend in France. But thankfully Interpol called our people, and they were able to move in. Sorenson had a fairly extensive external security system. So we were able to get these."

Several high-definition still photos of a six-man crew popped up on the screen. Five of them were men Storm had never seen before. One was a man he could never forget.

"Volkov," Storm said. "What happened to his face?"

"We assumed that was the remnants of your handiwork in Mogadishu," Jones said.

"There's no way he survived that explosion."

"There are three dead bankers who would beg to differ if they could still talk."

Storm shook his head slowly. It had been five years since he last tangled with Volkov. Not long enough. Five lifetimes wouldn't be long enough.

"Get him off that screen. I've seen enough of that face," Storm said. Jones complied as Storm went on: "So we have three dead bankers from three large banks in three different countries. At least two of them seem to have problems keeping their flies zipped. Are we sure the third wasn't also into the hanky panky?"

"We looked into that, but Kornblum was a total Boy Scout," Jones said. "There's not a single skeleton in his closet. And, believe me, we looked. He ought to run for the chancellorship with a record this clean. Not that he'd like the pay cut."

"Okay, what about links between the three men? Some kind of deal Kornblum, Motoshige, and Sorenson were involved in together? A trade they did?"

"Nothing we've been able to find so far," Jones said. "Kornblum had traded with Sorenson. And Motoshige had once offered a trade to Kornblum that didn't go through. But those deals were five and three years ago, respectively. It strains credulity to call that any more than a coincidence. These guys were all big players in what is a relatively small world of ultra-high finance. It stands to reason they might have had some incidental contact at some point. But that's all."

"What about a common associate between them?" Storm asked.

"Unfortunately, there are dozens," Bryan answered. "Like Jones said, these bankers are pretty clubby. They go to the same conferences, pal around with the same groups. If you start playing degrees of separation, you can link anyone in this world with anyone else in two steps or less. They all worked with a guy who worked with one of these guys, or who went to school with one of these guys."

"What about phone calls to the same numbers? E-mails to the same accounts?"

"We're working on that as we speak," Rodriguez said. "We'll let you know if anything pops."

Storm drummed his fingers on the polished tabletop. The three agents let him have a moment. Storm wondered how much of the full picture he was actually getting. What wasn't Jones parceling out? Who was he protecting? What other angle was he working?

"Of course, there's one connection we know they have for

sure: Volkov," Storm said. "Volkov is smart, but he isn't sophisticated enough to be killing bankers on his own. He's acting as muscle for someone. We can always try to work backward from there. Do we have any idea who might have hired him?"

Rodriguez glanced at Bryan and said, "Told you our boy hadn't lost a step during his time on the shelf. Twenty bucks."

Bryan shook his head as he reached for his wallet.

"You really bet against me, Kev?" Storm said, crossing his arms and faking an indignant stare.

"I've learned my lesson. I'll never doubt you again and . . . Oh, man, I'm out of cash. Javi, is it okay if . . ."

"No, no," Storm said. "My old man always taught me a debt must be paid promptly. I'll cover you, despite your lack of faith in me. Just remember you owe me. You owe me for this *and* Bahrain."

"Really? You're going to talk about Bahrain as if it's even in the same league as twenty bucks?" Bryan said.

Storm handed Rodriguez a twenty-dollar bill. "Just adding it to your tab."

Jones stared at them. "You ladies done?" he asked.

"Sorry. Continue."

"Good. To answer your question: Yes, we have a theory on who hired Volkov," Jones said. "We think it might be the Chinese."

"Why the Chinese?"

"We're still trying to piece that together," Jones said. "But one theory is pretty straightforward. China has the world's second largest economy, and they're pretty open about their goal of being number one. It's possible they're trying to create some kind of disruption in the financial markets aimed at undermining our economic stability."

"By killing foreign bankers? Why wouldn't they just kill American bankers?"

"That's the nature of global trade these days," Jones said. "Everything has become so interconnected, the most vulnerable parts of our financial system are actually located overseas. Plus . . ."

"What?"

"It's very possible Volkov isn't done yet," Jones said. "This might just be the beginning of something that's going to get bigger."

Storm nodded. He didn't need to be convinced of the depth of Volkov's evil. Even the man's name spoke to his nature: Volkov is derived from *volk*, the Russian word for wolf.

"Now, bear in mind, this is a delicate thing with the Chinese," Jones continued. "We're not just talking about some backward banana republic that's going to change dictators in three weeks anyway. We're talking about our most important, most sensitive foreign relationship, with a country that happens to be the most populous on Earth. And, oh by the way, they also have the largest army. We need more information on what the Chinese are up to, but we absolutely can't be caught snooping around. We need some . . . deniability."

"In other words," Storm said, "if I get caught, you'll deny you ever knew me and I'll spend the rest of my life in a prison shackled next to a bunch of Tibetan dissidents."

"Affirmative." Jones smiled.

"Charming," Storm said. "So what's my next move?"

"The Chinese finance minister is set to give an important speech to the European Union in Paris," Jones said.

"Yeah? So?"

"So one of our people tells us that the Chinese Ministry of State Security"—the Chinese equivalent of the CIA and the FBI, rolled into one—"has a joint covert operation of some kind going on with the Chinese Finance Ministry. A Ministry of State Security agent is now traveling undercover with the Finance Ministry. It makes sense that if this plot involving bankers has the kind of complexity we think it does, it would need to have Finance Ministry expertise—and State Security Ministry cunning. Our working theory—and, again, it's just a theory at this point—is that this State Security Ministry agent is the one who hired Volkov."

"What do we know about the guy?"

"Absolutely nothing. We're getting this from one of our double agents, who is getting it from a source he is only starting to cultivate, so it's all still a little shady at this point. The only thing we know for sure about this State Security agent is that she's not a guy."

"A female agent?" Storm said, his face involuntarily lifting.

"I knew you'd like that part," Jones said, sharing conspiratorial glances with Bryan and Rodriguez. "Our person on the inside told us she made a trip to Switzerland a few days ago."

"Switzerland. As in, where Wilhelm Sorenson was found murdered. Think that's a coincidence?"

"That's why you're going to Paris," Jones said. "Find her. Get close to her. Figure out what she's up to."

CHAPTER 6

JOWZJAN PROVINCE, Afghanistan

From the outside, it looked like there was no inside. That's what made it such a good hiding place.

Gregor Volkov had come across the cave complex during the early nineties, back when he was a young operative with the secret Soviet police force known as the Komitet Gosudarstvennoy Bezopasnosti, back when there was still such a thing as the KGB.

This was only a few years after the USSR had publicly given up on the folly of trying to tame Afghanistan—and a decade or so before the United States took up the same fool's errand. The Soviets still had secret operations in the country, even though it was clear they could not conquer it. In the vacuum created by the Soviet departure, many groups competed for power. It was a wild time in a wild place, which made it perfect for Volkov, the wolf. The Taliban were slowly taking hold in some of the cities, but out in the mountains, it was the same as it had always been. The notion that there even was such thing as a nation state called Afghanistan—or that the locals owed it some sense of fealty—was not commonly accepted. Political power was wielded behind the muzzle of a gun by whoever had the fortitude to assert it.

This kind of might-makes-right ruling structure appealed to

Volkov. When he found the cave, he knew the USSR was not long for this planet. In some ways, he was ambivalent about its demise. Mother Russia had weakened herself by taking on so many dependent children. It was better for Russia to cut the apron strings and pursue an empire without them. In the meantime, Volkov was also envisioning his own independence, one that involved a future as a freelancer. As the USSR entered its final spasms of dissolution—and order began to break down in the KGB—Volkov returned to this small crevice in the side of a mountain and made it his base of operations.

Through the years, he had turned it into an effective launching pad and a comfortable home. The entrance was only a few meters wide and well covered with trees. But inside, nature had burrowed out a generous labyrinth that led deep into the mountainside. Volkov had hired local laborers to help broaden parts of it, smooth out other parts, generally civilize it. Then he killed the laborers one by one, to keep them from talking about it.

From there, he installed a makeshift plumbing system, with clean water piped in from a nearby spring. He brought in generators to give him power and heat and stashed enough barrels of diesel fuel—stolen from the Red Army as it crumbled—to keep the lights on for many years. He replaced the empties one by one. He installed a few strategically hidden satellite receivers that allowed him to communicate with the outside world or, if he chose, just kick back and surf the Internet.

Volkov could come and go as he pleased, crossing the border from Turkmenistan via any number of mountain passes. He didn't have to worry about the authorities, because there were none. The only passport he needed was whatever automatic or semiautomatic weaponry he was carrying at the moment. The nearby villagers—who only knew he was somewhere in the mountains and only saw him when he came to town for supplies—lived in mortal terror of him. There was a warlord known to operate in the region. He did not bother with Volkov. There was plenty of room for

everyone, what with hundreds of square miles of basically unin-
habited mountain terrain. Besides, Gregor Volkov was not the
kind of man anyone wanted to pick a fight with.

He only brought his crew here when he needed something
done, and now he needed their help. And so, having successfully
completed their latest job in Switzerland, Volkov and his crew
had spent one wild night in Monaco, indulging their taste for
girls, booze, drugs, and gambling. Then they stole a Monex 4000,
broke it down into small enough pieces that it could be transported without detection, and then reassembled the pieces in the
cave, so that Volkov could attempt to turn this already profitable
job into something even more lucrative.

"Yuri, have you secured the link-up yet?" Volkov barked at a
young man with a mane of fiery red hair tied back in a ponytail.
Yuri's fingers were flying across a keyboard that was connected
to a computer that, in turn, remotely controlled the angle and direction of Volkov's satellite dishes.

"Yes, General, I'm just getting them now," Yuri answered.
General. Volkov insisted all his men called him General. He
believed that if the USSR had held together, he would have eventually risen to the top of the KGB, then switched to the military,
where he would have ascended to that rank and exerted his influence on the Politburo. That none of that ever came to pass did not
change Volkov's opinion that he ought to be addressed in that
manner.

"And you've got this terminal set up?" Volkov asked.

"Yes, General. I've been working on it, but I . . ."

"All right, let's see it then," Volkov interrupted, strolling across
the branch of the cave that served as his communications center.

The MonEx 4000, protected by a casing of beige-painted steel,
was the size of a footlocker and weighed several hundred pounds.
It looked not unlike a large server. Not all digital electronics had
yet shrunken down to handheld size, and this was one the complexity of which necessitated its ample dimensions. It fit on the

top of a table one of the crewmen had brought into the communications center.

"General, with all due respect, I don't understand why we're doing this," Yuri said.

"You don't understand what?"

"Our employer is paying us generously for each MonEx code we supply, am I right?" Yuri asked. Volkov had not told his crew how generously. He was getting a million dollars per code, but he told his crew it was a hundred thousand. Each member of the five-man crew thought he was getting a decent deal—ten thousand each, with the other half going to Volkov. If any of them suspected the split was, in fact, much less fair than that, none of them dared let on.

"That's correct," Volkov said, feeling his anger starting to grow. He did not like being questioned by an underling.

"So why don't we just keep supplying codes? A hundred thousand to kill a paper-pushing banker—it's good money for easy work, is it not?"

"Shame on you, Yuri. You think so small," Volkov said.

"How so, General?"

"Simple logic. If someone is willing to pay us a hundred thousand for a code, it must be worth more than that, yes?" *Especially when he's really paying us a million*, Volkov thought.

"But maybe it's only worth that much to him," Yuri countered. "Maybe, we should . . ."

"Yuri," Volkov said, grabbing the young man's ponytail and jerking it backward. Yuri's eyes grew wide as Volkov slapped a hand on his throat. "You are correct in that we may not be able to exploit these codes for our own purpose, in which case we will accept our bounty and move to our next job. But I would like to think optimistically. Don't you want to be an optimist, Yuri?"

"Yes, General," he choked out.

"In chess, a grand master does not just approach the game one way," Volkov said, tilting Yuri's head farther back. "He has many different strategies, all working at the same time. That way he is prepared, no matter what his opponent does. Do you understand this?"

"Yes, General."

"I waste my breath on you, Yuri. Just show me what you have," Volkov said, and released his grip, then subconsciously adjusted his eye patch, which had been knocked just slightly off center.

Yuri rubbed his neck. He did not relish what he had to say next.

"That's the problem, General. I don't . . . We don't . . . We don't have anything."

"What do you mean? The terminal was reassembled perfectly. We took pictures. I studied the schematics myself." The volume of Volkov's voice crescendoed to at least a mezzo forte.

"It's not that, General. I . . ."

"Is it the connection? I thought you said you had the satellites set up properly."

"Yes, General, I do. It's just . . ."

Volkov was now at forte. "Then what is the problem?"

"It's this," Yuri said, tilting the screen so it was directly facing Volkov.

The Russian's one good eye scanned back and forth across the text on the screen, his confusion growing with each passing second. It was not that the letters were unfamiliar—they were from the Roman alphabet, one Volkov had long ago been taught. It was not that the words were undecipherable—it was clearly English, which Volkov spoke fluently. But the screen, when taken in its entirety, was incomprehensible. Or at least it was incomprehensible to someone who had not received extensive training in the peculiarities of the MonEx's unique operating system. And neither Yuri nor Volkov had.

"You've entered the code properly?"

"Yes, General. I double-checked it twice."

"Then what's . . . what's this?"

"I'm just not sure," Yuri said.

"We must be able to . . . transfer funds out of this somehow . . . or . . . something."

"I've tried, General. As you can see, the func—"

"Get out of my way," Volkov ordered, gripping Yuri's shirt and using it as a handle to toss him roughly from the chair.

Volkov sat, tilted his good eye at the screen, and surveyed the keyboard. Surrounding the familiar QWERTY setup were rows and columns of buttons the purpose of which he could not even guess. He typed *transfer funds*. The screen lit with:

```
[INVALID COMMAND ERROR]
```

Access account, Volkov typed.

```
[INVALID COMMAND ERROR]
```

Show funds, Volkov tried.

```
[INVALID COMMAND ERROR]
```

With each error message, Volkov felt his blood pressure rising. He started experimenting by hitting the strange buttons along the side. Some did nothing. Others made random, odd-looking characters appear on the screen—or strings of letters that made no sense to Volkov. Then there was the baffling series of error messages:

```
[IMPROPER NULL FUNCTION]
```

Or:

```
[OPERATOR VOIDED TRANSACTION]
```

Or:

```
[INTERNAL CONSISTENCY CONFLICT]
```

Or, more simply and most frequently:

[ACCESS DENIED]

This was going nowhere. Volkov's anger only grew. The MonEx had not been easy to steal in the first place. It had been even more difficult to smuggle into this country and lug halfway up a mountain. He should be rewarded for this effort, not stymied by it. Volkov stood and snarled at Yuri.

"Sit back down," Volkov ordered. "How *dare* you shirk your duty?"

"But, General, I . . ."

"You said you could make this work!"

"I thought it was Linux-based," Yuri protested. "I didn't know it had its own operating system. I've been trying to find an instruction manual, but you need to have a licensing code and we don't—"

"Your excuses are feeble," Volkov shouted. He was at a full fortissimo.

"General, if you could please just give me a week or two to—"

"We don't have a week or two," Volkov sputtered. "We have a deadline."

And they did. Volkov's employer had been very explicit: Volkov had to deliver six codes, from the six bankers designated by the employer, all on a strict time line. If Volkov failed to deliver even one of them, he wouldn't get paid a cent. He could hardly ask for more time because he was trying to figure out how to use the codes for his own illicit purposes.

"General, I . . ."

"Your incompetence galls me," Volkov said.

"But, General, if—"

The remainder of the sentence never got out. Volkov yanked the Ruger from its holster, held it to Yuri's forehead, and depressed the trigger three times in rapid succession. Ribbons of crimson shot across the room, followed by flesh that had previously been attached to Yuri.

Two other members of the crew rushed into the communications center to respond to the gunfire. They stopped short when they saw that the flowing strands of red on Yuri's head were not, for once, merely his hair. Volkov passed by them and was on his way out of the room before he spoke.

"Yuri has decided to retire," he said. "Get him out of here."

"Yes, General."

"And when you're done with that, get packed," Volkov said. "We have another job to do."

"Oh," he added, looking at the MonEx, "and find me someone who knows how to work that machine."

CHAPTER 7

FAIRFAX, Virginia

D errick Storm crept through the late-afternoon shadows, approaching downwind from the southwest. His flight to Paris didn't leave until that evening. He had time for one quick mission.

The target house was a split-level ranch, built in the height of the Ugly Seventies and nestled in the heart of a typical East Coast suburban neighborhood. Other houses nearby had become tear-downs or candidates for additions. Not this one. It was essentially the same house it had been on the day the first owners moved in. It had been well maintained, but there was only so much nice landscaping could do to save the thing from its own basic dowdiness.

Storm moved with measured confidence. He was armed, one pistol strapped to his chest and another attached to his ankle. His intelligence on the interior of the target house was exhaustive. He knew its every crevice, from its three shag-carpeted bedrooms to its cramped kitchen to its four-shade aqua-and-white bathroom tile. He knew its vulnerabilities, its accesses and egresses, its partially obscured trapdoor. He knew how to shimmy up the storm drain and vault into one of the bedrooms on the second floor. The floor plan was practically implanted in his brain.

He stayed in what he recognized would be blind spots, invisible to any of the house's occupants. This was what Derrick Storm had long trained himself to do: to see without being seen, to slink without notice. He was stealth personified. He was like the wind, there but forever unseen. There would be no detecting him, not even as he circled to within striking distance of the house, moving from tree to tree, ever closer to the target.

The final twenty feet from his last hiding spot to the house was open terrain. This was the most perilous part of the job. He studied the house for signs of alarm and, seeing none, paused to gather himself. Then he performed a perfect cheetah sprint to the side of the house nearest the garage.

He stopped again, listening intently for even the smallest hint that anyone inside had become aware of his presence. There was none. The rhythms of the late afternoon in this neighborhood were unchanged.

Storm allowed himself a small glimpse around the corner. The garage was of the two-car variety, the kind with a single broad door covering both bays. There was a man inside, working on a car. An Orioles game crackled on an ancient Westinghouse radio, the soothing voice of Fred Manfra managing to overcome some seriously worn transistors.

Storm stayed pressed against the side of the house, waiting for his heartbeat to return to an acceptable range. There could be no mistakes in this operation. He needed total surprise, and he was sure he had achieved it. With one final . . .

"Jesus H. Christ on a popsicle stick, if you're going to sneak up on an old FBI agent, try not wearing those faggy Italian shoes, huh?" a voice from inside boomed. "How many times I gotta tell you, boy: rubber soles. You'll never go wrong with rubber soles."

Derrick Storm frowned, leaving his hiding spot and rounding the corner. "Hey, Dad," he said.

Carl Storm dropped the grease-stained rag he had been wielding and came around the car to grab his son in a bear hug. Like his son, Carl was solidly built. He was a shade under six feet, and even though Derrick had his old man beat by at least three inches—at six-foot-two and a solid 230 pounds—he still felt small in his father's embrace. He hoped he always would, but he knew otherwise. There was no hiding that Carl had lost some of his vitality in the last few years. His skin was getting that papery, old man feel to it. His limp, which used to only show itself on rainy days, was getting more noticeable.

Still, even in his late sixties, you wouldn't want to bet against the old man in an arm-wrestling contest.

"How's my boy?" he said, giving Derrick a solid thump on the back.

"I'm good, Dad," Derrick replied.

"What brings you here?"

"You're the only dad I got. I figured I owed you a visit."

"How many times I gotta tell you, you can't bullshit a bullshitter. You're here for a job."

"That's classified, Agent Storm. I'm quite sure the CIA wouldn't want its secrets shared with the FBI," Derrick replied.

"Even an old retired hack like me?"

Derrick changed subjects: "What's up with the Buick?"

Carl thumped the side of his '86 Buick Electra, of which he was the original owner. Though he had been a small boy at the time, Derrick could still remember the day his father brought the car home, bursting with pride. He gave his son a long talking-to about the importance of buying American—a lecture that had apparently stuck, given Derrick's Ford fetish—and they took the Electra on a drive that day. Derrick sat in the back, on velvety cloth seats so nappy he could write his name in them. He could still hear his father extolling the car's "pickup," when he mashed the gas pedal and the 3.8-liter V6 sent the car hurtling down a little-used country road.

It had seemed like a luxurious road-eating machine back then. Now it looked like a rolling box, maybe two generations removed from the aircraft carrier–sized Buicks of the sixties and seventies. The last time Derrick had looked at the odometer, it read 57,332—but that was misleading, since it had flipped at least three times.

That Carl had kept it on the road all this time was a testament to his gift for mechanics, his parsimony, and, mostly, his stubbornness.

"The damn blower on the AC only works at one speed," Carl grumbled. "Blows on low the whole time."

Derrick went over to have a look. One of the more unusual features of this particular Buick was that its hood hinged in front and opened away from the windshield, the opposite of nearly every other passenger car that ever rolled off the line in Detroit. It made the car an enormous pain to work on, which only made Carl that much more devoted to it.

"I replaced the fan and the relay and the dang thing still won't run right," Carl added. "I can run electric to it through an outside toggle switch and get it to work. But as soon as I assemble it right, it doesn't run on different speeds. Just low."

"You check the fuses?" Derrick asked.

"What, do I look like I got hit with a moron stick last night?"

"Yeah but I decided to be polite and not mention it."

Carl grunted. Derrick studied the offending unit and the various wires leading from it, marveling at the relative simplicity of the Buick's innards. As Carl had carped many times, modern-day cars were largely regulated by their various computer systems. Unless you had your own computer to run diagnostics on them, they could be virtually impossible for an at-home mechanic to fix. It's why Carl refused to get rid of the Buick: Its problems, while sometimes legion, were at least repairable without digital assistance. Neither man needed to say what pleasure they both got from this.

On the radio, the Orioles had pushed three runs across in the bottom of the seventh to take a 6–5 lead over the Angels.

"It's good to have Markakis back," Carl said. "We would have beat the Yankees last October if we'd had Markakis in the lineup."

The Orioles had long been "we" in the Storm household. With a few exceptions, this had been an act of shared suffering by the Storm men.

"We would have beat the Yankees if Jimmy Johnson had been Jimmy Johnson," Derrick said.

"Didn't realize you still paid that close attention."

"Some things are in the blood, whether you want them there or not, old man."

"Hey, it was only fifteen years between postseason appearances," Carl said, then added in a lower voice: "It better not be another fifteen or I might not make it."

Derrick let the macabre comment pass.

"I see the old Westinghouse still works," he said.

"Yeah. Why? You want to take it apart again?"

Derrick laughed. As a boy, his father had insisted his son know how to take apart and reassemble a radio—and understand the functions of all the parts he saw along the way—as if this were some basic survival skill every young man needed.

"Let's just worry about the car, Dad."

The younger Storm probed the Buick with his eyes first, then his hands. Soon, he zeroed in on a bundle of wires near the windshield-washer fluid reservoir.

"Here's the problem," he said. "Check out the fusible link wire."

Carl frowned, cursed, and grabbed some drugstore glasses off his workbench. Once the glasses were perched on the end of his nose, he shined a flashlight at the offending area. "I'll be damned," he said, looking at a wire that had been Southern fried into a melted mess. "I can't believe I missed that."

"I'm pretty sure that's your culprit," Derrick said.

Carl took a glance at his wristwatch, a Casio that was at least as old as the car. "Auto parts store is closing up. I can tackle this in the morning. Let's get a beer."

Derrick followed his father into the time warp that was his boyhood home. Little had changed about the house in well over thirty years. The house cried out for a woman's touch, but Storm's mother had died in a car accident when he was five. Derrick had only vague memories of her and knew little about her. The sum total of what his father ever said about her was "She was a heck of a woman, your mother." Then he'd make an excuse to leave the room.

Carl went over to the mostly barren refrigerator—current inhabitants: mayonnaise, Kraft American singles, yellowing lettuce, hamburger rolls stale enough to be brittle to the touch—and grabbed two cans of Pabst Blue Ribbon from a half-full twenty-four-pack. In his years away from his father, Derrick had developed a palate for crafted microbrews of varying sorts. He was currently indulging an IPA phase. But in the house of his father, he honored the local custom: an American macrobrew.

They settled into seats in the living room—Carl in his favorite Barcalounger, Derrick on the paisley patterned sofa—and cracked open the beers. This was a kind of unofficial ritual between the Storm boys. Derrick shared most all of his cases with his father. It was partly because he valued his father's insights. It was mostly because Carl Storm was his insurance policy. Jedediah Jones would leave Derrick Storm to rot in that Tibetan prison if it was politically expedient. Carl Storm would never rest until his son came back safely.

And so, as they drank, Derrick told his father about the trail of dead bankers, the certainty of Volkov's nefarious hand at work, and the possibility of Chinese involvement. Carl Storm listened with the practiced ear of a seasoned investigator. Carl had been career FBI, joining the Bureau in an era when it wasn't quite as polished as it had since become. Back then, it was more of a blue collar crime-solving unit. Their suits were cheaper and so were their educations. The Hollywood influence had yet to transform them into self-styled supercops. They were more like regular cops, albeit very good ones. You still didn't want to get Carl Storm going on how J. Edgar Hoover had really gotten a bad rap from the media.

Of all the things Carl had taught Derrick through the years, the ability to think like a detective was chief among them. In many ways, the son's abilities now outstripped the father's. But the old man could still surprise him. It took two beers' worth of time for Derrick to lay out everything.

"It sounds like your spook buddies are too focused on finding a link between the suspects that's either a person or a business deal," Carl said when Derrick had finished. "What if the link is what they did separately? You said Kornblum and Motoshige had their hands in a lot of things, but Sorenson only did those fancy money swaps, is that right?"

Derrick nodded. Carl continued: "Then this is just a theory to kick around until something better comes along, but money-swapping might be your common element. It's the only thing all three shared that we know of for sure."

"Good point," Derrick said.

"Hell yeah, it's a good point. Look, son, I know you think your dad doesn't know his ass from first base, but if I learned nothing else in my years at the Bureau, it's that stuff like this always comes down to one thing: money. You follow the money, you'll find your bad guy."

"So how do I do that in this case?"

"You're asking me? Fer chrissakes, I can barely make change at the grocery store. I'll tell you one thing, though, and that's that I don't like the sound of any of this. How many times I gotta tell you, you can't trust those CIA spooks. They're setting you up for something and you don't even know what. That Clara Strike woman is trouble. Is she involved in this?"

"Not that I know of."

"Yeah, but that goddamn Jedediah Jones is, I'm sure. That man is a snake in the grass."

Derrick didn't need to be reminded. To use a baseball analogy, Derrick was like a pinch hitter being brought in to face a pitcher he had never seen before. The guy might be throwing sliders low and outside. Or his first pitch might be a hundred-mile-per-hour fastball aimed at Derrick's ear.

As Derrick's brain whirred, Carl's eyes involuntary drifted toward the picture of Derrick's mother that still adorned the mantel. She had been a beautiful woman—her son's strong features came straight from her—and now she was frozen in time. The picture, like everything else in the house, grew ever-so-slightly more dated with each passing year.

"I'll be careful," Derrick said, then looked up at the picture. "Hard not to miss her, isn't it?"

"She was a heck of a woman, your mother," Carl Storm said. Then he crushed his beer can between his hands and vaulted himself with surprising agility from the Barcalounger. "Anyhow, if you're staying for dinner, we might want to pick up a pizza or something. I don't really have any food in the house. I'm gonna go wash up."

Derrick listened as the shower in the upstairs master bathroom turned on. In a few hours, he would have to head to the airport and catch a red-eye heading east. He had time for dinner. He consulted a menu, picked up the phone, and ordered a large sausage pie that he knew would be eaten with no mention of the woman who watched over them from her place on the mantel.

CHAPTER 8

WASHINGTON, D.C.

Roughly twenty miles away from the Storm ancestral home, just a short trip down Interstate 66 and across Constitution Avenue, Senator Donald Whitmer (R-Alabama) was pacing around his corner office in the Dirksen Senate Office Building. And he was fuming.

Ordinarily, there was only one thing that would get Donny Whitmer this mad, and that was if the Alabama Crimson Tide football team somehow lost.

Jack Porter had unwittingly stumbled on a second.

"You're wrong," Whitmer roared at Porter. "Goddamnit, that's impossible."

Porter was a pollster. The best. A pro's pro, he had been around for twenty years and had developed statistical methodologies that would be the envy of Gallup, Quinnipiac, and every other public pollster out there—if only they knew them. He had advised the election efforts of sitting presidents—and future presidents—congressmen, senators, pretty much anyone who could afford to pay his rates.

This was the third campaign Porter had worked for the Alabama senator. In the first two his information had been dead-on. Months out, he had identified areas of the candidate's strengths and weaknesses with voters that allowed Whitmer's campaign to tailor its message and target its delivery. In the closing weeks, he told Whitmer exactly where to put his resources. His final polling had always turned out to be accurate within one percentage point of the actual election results.

He was a good man. A smart man. An honorable man. And he was never wrong.

"You're wrong, you're wrong, you're wrong," Senator Whitmer yelled.

"I'm sorry, Senator," Porter said. "But the numbers are what they are."

Thirteen points down. That's what Porter was trying to tell him. But there was just no way he was thirteen points down. He was *Donny Whitmer*, damn it. As chairman of the all-powerful Senate Appropriations Committee, Whitmer was the kind of man who could turn a cabinet member into a fawning sycophant, have a governor crawling on his hands and knees, or make a lobbyist jump through a flaming hoop.

During twenty-four years in Washington, Whitmer had become known as a legislator who could untie the purse strings of government and sprinkle gold on just about anything. He had delivered for his constituency countless times, the undisputed king of the pork barrel project. There were not only bridges to nowhere in some parts of Alabama, there were bridges *from* nowhere, an even more impressive feat. There wasn't a pet project he couldn't get funded, even if it was just relatively small potatoes. Two hundred grand for a children's museum. Four hundred for some small city park. Eight hundred to preserve some historical landmark.

It didn't take much, relatively speaking, to make people feel like they owed you forever. And Donny had been doing it for years. Now silver-haired and seventy, he still considered himself at the peak of his powers. He was listed at number nine in *Washington Magazine*'s "Hundred Most Powerful People in D.C." He hadn't been out of the top twenty in years.

So there was no way, just no goddamn way, that he was thirteen points down—in a *primary* no less—to some Bible-thumpin' Tea Party asshole.

"But that's . . . What in the hee-haw hell is going on down in that state of mine?"

Porter lifted a thick white binder off his lap and turned the pages in chunks until he arrived at the section he needed. "These are your numbers among nondenominational Christians. You're green. He's red."

Porter held up a page in which the red bar stretched conspicuously farther than the green bar.

"Holy Mother of God," Whitmer said.

"Here are the Baptists," Porter said, turning one sheet over to reveal a page that looked identical to the last.

"Oh, sweet Jesus."

"The Methodists look like this," Porter said. The bars were slightly closer in length, but red still easily outdistanced green.

"And here are the Episcopalians," Porter finished, holding up another page that was nothing but bad news for the senator.

"Since when the hell do Episcopalians give a crap about religion?" Whitmer demanded. "Oh, Jesus Christ, what about the atheists?"

"Ah . . . they're all Democrats, sir."

"Okay, okay, I'm sick of talking about the damn Jesus freaks," Whitmer said. "They're going with that Tea Party sumbitch. I get it. Let's talk geography. There's got to be somewhere in the state I'm doing well. Maybe we can build on that."

Porter nodded, turning chunks of pages in his binder until he reached the right place.

"Okay, we've done some county-level work. If you want us to go finer than that, we can, but that's going to add to that estimate I gave you," Porter said.

"County is fine," Whitmer said.

"Okay. You're doing better in the southern part of the state. Mobile and Baldwin Counties still remember all you did after the BP spill."

"Damn right," Whitmer boomed. "And well they should. There's two hundred thousand people in Mobile. Maybe we just got to make sure they get out and vote."

"Well, I said you were doing better there. I didn't say you were winning it. It's pretty much a dead heat."

"Oh," Whitmer said.

"I'd still recommend a strong get-out-the-vote effort there," Porter said.

"Of course."

"Now, those are areas of relative strength. Areas of weakness are, well, here. You can see for yourself. Again, you're the green shades. He's the red shades. Statistical ties are gray."

Porter held up a page with a map of Alabama. There was a green patch in Marengo, the senator's home county. There was some gray along the southern coast. Otherwise, the whole map was awash in varying shades of red. The more rural, the more red. Some areas were practically magenta.

"Oh, Jesus Christ," Whitmer said again. He reached in his drawer and pulled out a flask of vodka. He had a luncheon to attend and didn't want to smell like bourbon.

"Well, it's interesting you should put it that way, because I have to tell you, some of those Christian voters we polled mentioned your tendency toward blaspheming. You might want to curtail . . ."

"Goddamnit, don't tell me how to talk, boy," Whitmer said. "Just tell me what to do about those thirteen goddamned points."

"A scandal would do nicely, sir," Porter said, evenly. "Set him up with a whore, leak pictures to the press."

Whitmer was already shaking his head. "We tried that before we even knew he was this big a threat. Didn't work. The sumbitch has too much Jesus in him. He chastised the woman for trying to seduce a married man, lectured her about the sanctity of marriage, then actually got her to pray with him. Last I heard, she was volunteering in his campaign office and going to his damn church."

Porter absorbed this for a moment. "Well, then there's only one thing that's going to do the trick: money. It's getting late in the game, but it's not too late. If you were to launch a major ad-vertising blitz—from Huntsville to Birmingham to Mobile to every small town in between—you'll be able to take the guy's legs out from under him. But you'll have to go negative, real hard and real fast."

"Yeah," Whitmer said. "Yeah, you know, I like the sound of that. Tell people he's Jewish. Airbrush a yarmulke on him. Better yet, Muslim. Or gay. How much do I need?"

"How much do you have in your war chest?"

"A million two."

"Not enough," Porter said. "You're talking about a double-digit disadvantage. You'll need at least five million to move the needle."

"Jesus," Whitmer said.

Forget vodka. Whitmer went over to the highball glasses he kept in the bookcase along the far wall. He opened up a cabinet, pulled out a bottle of Clyde May's Conecuh Ridge Alabama Style Whiskey, poured himself three fingers, and downed it in one gulp.

"Want some?" he asked.

"No, thank you, Senator."

"You got any *good* news to tell me?"

"No, Senator."

"Then you best be moving on."

As Porter departed, Whitmer paced around his office, unable to believe this turn of events. It was six weeks to go until the pri-mary. Whitmer hadn't even bothered paying for polling before this, because there seemed to be no point—surely, no one was taking this Tea Party asshole seriously.

And now it looked like Whitmer's political life was at stake. Was his constituency really turning on him like this? Was he re-ally going to have to pack up his life in Washington and head back to Alabama in shame and defeat, a four-term senator whipped in a primary by a some small-town deacon? Was he really going to be another in a long line of victims of this Tea Party nonsense?

No. Not Donny Whitmer.

He gripped the Clyde May, practically ripped off the cap, and didn't bother with the formality of a glass this time. He poured a long swallow down his throat.

He just had to think of a way to come up with five million dollars.

His mind soon struck not on an idea but a man. He was a man who owed him a favor. A big favor. A five-million-dollar favor, perhaps.

Whitmer was so excited, he sat down and wrote the man's name down on a legal pad. Lately, he had been getting more forgetful—particularly when he was agitated—and he found that writing things on his legal pad, in neat block letters, helped him keep his thoughts straight, especially when he came back to them later.

He looked down at the name and smiled.

CHAPTER 9

PARIS, France

The reporter could only be described as ruggedly handsome, with dark hair and eyes, a square jaw, and muscles toned in a way that no working journalist's ever had been. He was just hoping no one would notice that part.

In keeping with his cover, his outfit consisted of a well-worn tweed blazer, khaki pants that just barely missed matching, a white shirt with faint stains from a lost battle with a long-ago chili dog, and scuffed oxfords. He kept a spiral-bound reporter's pad in his left pocket and two pens in his right: a primary pen and a backup in case the first one failed. A reporter could never be too careful.

If he bore a striking resemblance to a man who had once been a Venetian gondolier—to say nothing of scores of identities that might or might not have come before it—it was surely a coincidence. From the moment Derrick Storm landed at Charles de Gaulle Airport, his passport and press credentials identified him as Cleveland Detroit of *Soy Trader Weekly*.

He was a serious reporter for a serious soy-related trade publication, one that could not dare blink in its protracted circulation battle with the much-hated *Soybean America*. If any curious party decided to Google him, they would find an elaborate website with a host of articles on the subject of soy, carefully constructed to appear to be the work of a small cadre of fair, balanced soy-knowledgeable journalists—really the handiwork of some of the CIA's more agriculturally savvy interns. The website contained links one could click to contact *Soy Trader Weekly*'s editors, to read about *Soy Trader Weekly*'s history, to advertise in *Soy Trader Weekly*, even to subscribe. The CIA interns were still figuring out what to do about the fourteen people who had already taken them up on their 52-weeks-for-the-price-of-50 offer.

That was not Cleveland Detroit's problem. His sole focus was finding the spy hidden amid all the subministers, undersecretaries, assistant minions, and vice bootlickers who would be traveling with the Chinese Ministry of Finance in support of their boss's big speech. The Chinese finance minister had come to Paris to publicly address the Economic and Financial Affairs Council of the European Union, better known as the Ecofin Council, or just Ecofin. It was considered a highly anticipated appearance from a Chinese agency not noted for its transparency.

The speech was being given at the Hotel de la Dame, a swank Left Bank *auberge* that found subtle ways to remind its visitors that Churchill considered it his favorite Parisian destination and Mitterrand had chosen it as the place where he cheated on his wife for the very first time.

For purposes of this occasion, the entrance to the hotel was blanketed with security, both a Chinese Ministry of State Security detail and local French authorities. None of it was a problem for Cleveland Detroit, whose fake paperwork was scrupulously authentic. He breezed through a document check, a metal detector, and then a pat-down from a Frenchman who was so concerned about finding larger weapons that he did not notice the hidden microphone and button-mounted wireless camera that were feeding sound and footage to Room 419. There, an agent who was part of the CIA's China contingent—and had been put on loan to Jedediah Jones's unit for the evening—had set up shop. If anyone could help Storm sniff out his target, it would be the agent in Room 419.

"I'm in," Storm said when he passed through the last layer of scrutiny.

"Excellent work." A voice in Storm's microscopic earpiece crackled.

"You've got eyes and ears?"

"Affirmative," the agent in Room 419 said.

"I'm going to have a look around. Maintain radio silence unless there's someone I need to know about."

He entered the lobby, which was swarming with people of all nationalities, some important, some merely self-important. As Storm ranged through the crowd, the agent occasionally interrupted with something like "That's He Ranqing, the deputy director of the Budget Department. We think he's legit." Another time it was "You just bumped into Wang Hongwei. Allegedly he does tax policy. He's really counterintelligence. Stay away."

Storm tried to focus on the small number of Chinese women in the crowd, but it wasn't fruitful. The agent in Room 419 identified all of them as being low-level administrative and clerical help. None of them were new to the ministry.

Finally the agent told him, "The speech starts in five minutes. Better get inside."

Heeding his instructions, Storm went into the ballroom, where the entire Parisian foreign press corps had already assembled for the speech. It included the Associated Press, the Agence France-Presse, a half-dozen-or-so American newspapers and magazines, another dozen-or-so publications from around the world, and a smattering of bloggers, Tweeters, and hangers-on, all of whom were shunted into a small roped-in area off to the side of the speaker's podium.

There was no room for Cleveland Detroit in the front row of the press section, so that was exactly where he went. He wedged himself between correspondents from the *Asahi Shimbun* and the *New York Times*, both of whom shot him annoyed glances. Unconcerned about playing nice, Detroit accidentally elbowed the *Times* guy in the ribs often enough that he finally retreated farther back.

Throughout the speech, Storm tried to peer into the clump of

Finance Ministry officials to the side of the podium, to see if there were any women lingering among them, but his line of sight wasn't the best. He saw none.

Then the speech concluded, and a press secretary burst out of the pack of Finance Ministry bureaucrats.

A female press secretary.

She glided up to the podium, her willowy body moving in long, effortless strides. She offered the finance minister a shy smile as she adjusted the microphone to her mouth.

"The finance minister will now take some questions," she said in smooth French, then pointed to one of the journalists. "Yes, Mr. Eli Saslow of the *Washington Post*, go ahead."

Storm watched, captivated, as the woman facilitated the press conference. Her flowing black hair cascaded with casual radiance down the back of her white blouse. Her dark eyes were set off by sculpted, high cheekbones. She switched easily between French, Mandarin, and American-accented English. She moved like raw silk floating on a gentle breeze.

"Who is *she*?" Storm whispered.

"I don't know," the agent upstairs answered. "I've never seen her before, and I've been working the Finance Ministry for months now. She's a new actor. I do believe you may have found your mark."

"Well, then," he said. "It seems like Cleveland Detroit needs to do a little investigative reporting."

AS THE PRESS CONFERENCE ENDED AND THE FINANCE MINISTER made his hasty exit, Storm stayed near the scrum of journalists still forming a semicircle around the podium, comparing notes and thoughts on what they had just heard. They mostly ignored Cleveland Detroit, who wasn't part of their usual gang.

Storm didn't care. His attention was centered on the woman in the white blouse. She was engaged in a series of one-on-one conversations with members of the Fourth Estate, perhaps taking interview requests. Storm waited until she dispatched their queries and appeared to be alone before he moved in.

She had an alluring smile, and Storm allowed his eyes a brief up-and-down of her outfit. The blouse flattered her slender torso. Her skirt was just long enough not to create an international incident if she decided to bend over.

"Excuse me," he said. "I'm with *Soy Trader Weekly*. My name is Cleveland Detroit."

"Ah, yes, Mr. Detroit. I saw your name on the press pass list," she said, then added: "It's very unusual."

"Mom was an Indians fan, Dad was a Tigers fan. Those are American baseball teams."

"Of course," she said. "Anyhow, how can I help you?"

Storm was prepared: "We've heard reports that due to above average rainfall in the Yangtze region, Chinese soybean exports are expected to rise one point seven four percent in the coming quarter. Do you have someone who might be able to comment on that and also talk about the potential impact on the soy futures market?"

"I might be able to connect you with our vice minister of agriculture. He will be able to give you the kind of"—she paused to come up with a polite phrase—"highly detailed information you seem to be seeking."

"That would be most kind of you. And forgive me for getting so excited by the soybean. Economically, it *is* the world's most important bean, you know."

"I . . . I was unaware of that," she said. Their bodies had drifted closer. In her heels, she was just a few inches shorter than he. Storm couldn't help but notice their heights were well matched for dancing. Perhaps they could do a nice tango . . .

Focus, Storm. Or, rather: *Focus, Detroit.*

"I'd be happy to tell you more about the soybean," he said. "Someone in your position ought to be aware about it, since it was your ancestors who first cultivated it some five thousand years ago."

"Really?" she said, like he was telling her someone had discovered a new continent or was revealing the true nature of the atom.

They drifted even closer. He could feel the heat of her body. He had become acutely aware of her eyes and, more specifically, his desire to spend an entire evening swimming in them.

"Yes, it's true. We in the United States are relative newcomers to the plant. We've only been at it for three hundred years or so. And even though we're now the world's largest producer of soy products, we owe a great debt to your country for introducing it to us. Would you like to hear about a Chinese-American I consider the Johnny Appleseed of the soybean? I'd be happy to tell you about it, Miss . . ."

"I'm sorry, I haven't introduced myself," she said, making a business card materialize from he knew not where. She handed it to him. It was done in the Western style, with the first name first. It identified her as "Ling Xi Bang, Press Secretary, Ministry of Finance."

"What an unusual last name," he said. "Is it pronounced 'Zi Bang'?"

"Actually, when Mandarin is Westernized, the 'x' is pronounced like 'sh,'" she said. "So it's 'She Bang.'"

Storm only hoped she did not notice his Adam's apple bob up and down from his gulping. "How . . . how interesting," he said.

"Almost as interesting as the soybean," she answered in a low purr. Their faces were nearly touching.

There was, of course, absolutely nothing interesting about it. And Storm knew that. He had to tread carefully. If she was a spy—as both the agent in Room 419 and Storm's own intuition seemed to indicate—she would be feeling out him just as surely as he was feeling out her. If she knew he was also a spy . . .

But no. She couldn't. Everything about *Soy Trader Weekly*'s Cleveland Detroit—from his press credentials to his website— had been meticulously constructed. There was no way she was onto him. He made his move.

"Ms. Xi Bang, forgive me for being forward, but as a journalist,

I always try to tell the truth. And the truth is, I'd like to take you to dinner."

"Can we have something made from soy?" she asked.

"Tofu?"

"Perfect."

"I find it's excellent when drizzled in soy sauce," he said.

"Do you think we can find a bistro nearby that would serve it to us that way?"

"I happen to know of one. I'll meet you in the lobby in fifteen minutes."

"Make it ten," she said.

She smiled. He winked. She turned. Storm gave the button camera the sight of her shapely legs as she departed.

As soon as she was a safe distance away, Storm's earpiece came to life. "Storm, did you really just seduce a beautiful woman by talking about soybeans?" the agent asked.

"Happens all the time," he replied. "Just your typical story of soy meets girl."

AS STORM PERFORMED ONE LAST SWEEP OF THE LOBBY, THE AGENT in Room 419 told him that Jones's people had confirmed what he already suspected: The name Ling Xi Bang did not appear in any of the Chinese Finance Ministry's materials. She was, apparently, a press secretary who had never written any press releases.

"Is it possible she's just a new employee?" Storm asked.

"Yes," the agent said. "But it's more possible her handlers didn't do a very good job establishing her cover."

"Sounds like she needs a job at *Soy Trader Weekly*."

"Just be careful, Storm."

"Right."

"She can't get the slightest clue of who you are. We lost an operative in Shanghai just last month to this sort of thing. The Chinese don't play nice. The Geneva Convention is a running joke to them."

"Right."

"And, remember, because it's so small, the effective range of the equipment you're wearing is only two thousand feet," the agent said. "If you get in trouble, we'll have people on the ground who can give you backup. But you have to stay in range."

"Right."

"There's a French-Asian fusion place along the Champs Élysées that's close enough," the agent said. "They even have a grilled tofu dish on the menu."

"Sounds perfect," Storm said.

Then he ripped out the earpiece, microphone, and camera and deposited them in the nearest *poubelle*.

For the next minute or two, a passerby would have heard something that sounded like a trash can saying, "Storm . . . Storm, do you copy? . . . Storm, are you there?"

SHE HAD CHANGED INTO A RED DRESS WITH EVEN LESS LEG COVerage than her skirt had offered. The neckline was a style the name of which Storm couldn't quite remember. Did they call that a princess cut? A cupid cut? Whatever. Storm just called it delicious.

As she walked toward him past the concierge desk, every male eye in the room followed her. The Englishmen in the lobby had to do it surreptitiously, so their wives wouldn't notice them gawking. The Americans were slightly more obvious. The Frenchmen didn't bother hiding it at all.

Cleveland Detroit was silently cursing that he had to be Cleveland Detroit. Derrick Storm would have had his Hermès tuxedo newly pressed, his Gucci shoes polished to a high shine, his black Brooks Brothers bow tie crisply knotted.

Then he reminded himself that, no matter what anyone says to the contrary, it's the man that makes the clothes. He rose from the chair he had been holding down and greeted her with a light peck on the cheek. The electricity he felt when his lips brushed her skin was enough to weaken his knees.

"You look incredible," he said.

"Thank you."

"Shall we?" he said, offering her his arm.

She locked arms with him in a way that allowed him to briefly feel her body pressed against his. It left him with a powerful urge to make sure that wasn't the last time he felt that particular sensation. "We shall," she said.

As they strolled arm in arm out of the hotel, down toward the Seine, Storm allowed himself one more admiring glance, then started his subtle interrogation with seemingly harmless questions about her childhood.

It turned out that, unlike most of the employees in the Finance Ministry, she did not have an important father or other family connections. She was from a poor peasant family in rural Qinghai Province. The One-Child Policy was firmly in place at the time of her birth, and many families in her village drowned their infant daughters and waited on sons to arrive. Despite cultural biases against educating girls, she had managed to excel in school. When she recorded the best score in the entire province on the Chinese version of the SAT, she was invited to attend Peking University in Beijing. There, she finished at the top of her class. Her credentials had been so impressive that the Finance Ministry had been willing to overlook her gender.

"Your English is so flawless," he said at one point—and could have added *you must be a spy*. Instead, he gave her an easy out: "You must have studied abroad."

"I spent a semester at USC," she said.

"Ah, the University of Spoiled Children," Storm said. "I went to journalism school there. Which was your favorite pizza: Roma's or Geno's?"

"Roma's," she said quickly. "They had the best crust."

And that's when Derrick Storm knew that everything Ling Xi Bang had said to him was likely a lie. He had fabricated the names of the pizzerias. He was almost surprised she fell for such an easy ruse. She obviously hadn't been well briefed.

No matter. He had found what he came to Paris to look for. That was the first objective. The second was to woo her into trusting acceptance. It was not necessarily that she was going to tell him anything. But if he got close to her, he might overhear a conversation, or sneak a glimpse into her briefcase, or arrange for her to "lose" her phone and secret it off to a CIA tech. There was always a way.

This, he knew, would involve some romance. Perhaps even physical contact. It was hard work, sure, but for the good of national security, Derrick Storm would make the sacrifice.

They found a small café a block in from the Seine. The evening was warm enough that they dined *al fresco*, allowing them to see the spires of the nearby Notre Dame illuminated against the night sky. He ordered a bottle of Domaine Viret and offered a toast to "our two great cultures."

They touched glasses and began a free-ranging discussion. He talked about the chemistry that made glycine, found in abundance in soybeans, the best-tasting of the nonessential amino acids. She told stories from the finance minister's trip to Indonesia, where she attended the ritual sacrifice of a water buffalo. They laughed. They lied. They drank wine in great volumes.

As they spoke, their legs kept brushing. She touched his arm and laughed when he told jokes. Through it all, there was a small part of Storm's brain that remained wary. He knew he was not being as faithful to his cover story as he needed to be. Yes, he kept inserting details about soybean cultivation that he had gleaned from his crash course during the plane ride across the Atlantic. But she was getting too much Derrick Storm, not enough Cleveland Detroit.

He even told her the cupcake story. It was his sixth birthday, toward the end of the school year. He was just finishing up an otherwise wonderful time in full-day kindergarten. Except he had this lingering sense of dread. His teacher, Mrs. Taylor, kept a poster with everyone's birthday on it. All school year long, he had watched as class mothers showed up after lunch on their child's birthday with gorgeous platters of fresh-baked cupcakes. But he didn't have a mom anymore. He had a dad who didn't even know how to turn on an oven. He was sure his birthday was going to pass with no cupcakes. There was a hope, but . . . Mostly, he already could just taste the shame of being the only kid who didn't have cupcakes on his birthday.

The big day came. Lunch came. Lunch went. Sure enough, no cupcakes. He was crushed. Then, just before recess, there was a knock on Mrs. Taylor's door. And there was his old man, with a lopsided grin and the ugliest, sloppiest, most wonderful pile of cupcakes anyone had ever seen. He had not only overfilled the cups, he had put on twice as much frosting as the recipe called for. It made for a delicious mess. Everyone in Mrs. Taylor's kindergarten agreed they were the best cupcakes of the year.

"I can tell you love your father very much," Xi Bang said, patting his hand.

"In his own way, he was the best dad a kid could have," Storm confirmed.

Storm was saved from further sentimentality when a wandering street musician with a violin set up shop nearby. His first song was "The Vienna Waltz," one of Storm's favorites. He couldn't help himself. He swept Xi Bang up in his arms and satisfied his previous suspicion that they were more than suitable as dance partners—to say nothing of their potential ability to partner in other, more aerobic activities.

"This song," he said as he twirled her across the sidewalk. "We'll dance to it at our wedding."

"Will we now?" she said. "Who says I don't get to pick the song?"

"Because this one doesn't need a full symphony. It sounds beautiful when played by a small string quartet. That way, we can keep the ceremony small and intimate. Is that okay?"

"Yes," she said, burying her face in his chest. "Intimate is good."

They danced some more, drank some more. When the check came, he told himself it was time to recover his wits. The walk home, he knew, would be the dangerous part. If she had sniffed out his lies the way he had hers, it would be easy to lead him into a trap. If Storm wasn't careful, Chinese agents could easily kill him, dump his body, and turn Cleveland Detroit into a conundrum for French authorities.

And, sure enough, as they staggered drunkenly home, leaning on each other the whole way, he felt his internal alarm bells ringing as she dragged him into an alley. His body tensed. His eyes cast furiously about. He readied himself to fight. Or flee. Whichever seemed most appropriate.

Then she planted her lips on his and pressed her body tight against him, fairly slamming him into the wall of a brick building. It was around that time that Storm realized that the only people in the alley were two lovers, one American, one Chinese, bathed in Parisian moonlight.

"I've got a suite at the hotel all to myself," she said when they surfaced for air. "Come back with me."

He answered with another long kiss. And so it was that a suite at the Hotel de la Dame became witness to the collision of two great cultures.

THE NEXT THING STORM KNEW, HIS PHONE WAS RINGING. IT WAS morning. The other side of the bed was empty. It took him a moment to remember where he was and, more importantly, who he was.

Then it finally clicked in. He answered the phone with: "Cleveland Detroit."

"Storm, it's me," said the rough-hewn voice of Jedediah Jones.

"Go ahead," Storm said. Wherever Xi Bang was—the bathroom, perhaps?—she was likely out of earshot. But caution was still called for.

"We've got another dead banker missing a whole lot of fingernails," Jones said. "Volkov has struck again."

"Where?"

"London."

"And?"

"You're my nearest boots on the ground. Get over there. Check out the scene. Learn what you can learn about the victim. I'm arranging an escort for you to London."

"E-mail details," he said. "I'm on my way."

"Just make sure you're free of tails when you leave the city."

"Got it," he said, then turned off the phone.

Storm began collecting his clothes, which were strewn in various rooms of the suite. He already had a lie prepared for Xi Bang: He was being called to London for breaking soy-related news and would have to rejoin the Finance Ministry at some later time to finish his story.

He kept expecting he would find Xi Bang somewhere, perhaps reading the paper or sipping coffee. Perhaps there would even be time for a brief but rewarding reconnoitering of any territories that had been left unexplored the previous evening.

But she wasn't in the sitting room. She wasn't on the balcony. She wasn't in the bathroom, either.

As Storm found the last of his clothing, he acknowledged what he should have known the moment he saw the empty bed:

Ling Xi Bang was gone.

CHAPTER 10

NEW YORK, New York

From its burnished walnut lockers to the portraits of its past presidents that hung on the walls, the Trinity Health & Racquet Club smelled like old money.

With good reason. Everyone there had it. Lots of it. On the rare times when the club actually accepted a new member, he—and all but two members were male—had to put up a nonreturnable fifty-thousand-dollar bond in order to gain access to its indoor and outdoor tennis courts, its racquetball courts, its squash courts, its fitness center, and its dining and locker room facilities, which included the best sauna in lower Manhattan. The fifty grand requirement was not because the club particularly needed the cash. Its endowment was now somewhere over thirty million dollars, enough to run the club for nearly three years without collecting a single dollar in dues. It was just to keep out the riffraff.

G. Whitely Cracker V was a legacy here—the third generation of Crackers to belong. His grandfather, Graham W. Cracker III, had been one of the founding members. His portrait hung on the wall just outside the dining room. Whitely's father, G. W. Cracker IV, had served three terms as president. His portrait was near the bar.

It was widely anticipated, even expected, that someday Whitely would take his turn at the helm; and that when his term was over (or his two or three were over), he would also be immortalized in oil-based paint.

In the meantime, Whitely came here for his biweekly tennis match, an event he treated with only slightly less reverance than a priest treated high mass. He always played singles—against a rotating cast of opponents—and one of his secretary's jobs was to make sure at least one of his usual adversaries was available. If the opponent dared be a no-show, Whitely was too nice to say anything to the man's face. But the offender might suddenly find that his locker had been moved—strictly because of some remodeling, of course—so that it was next to a pillar or wedged in a corner.

The match simply was not negotiable for Cracker. Whatever was happening in the markets didn't matter. Whatever was happening in his personal life didn't matter. There were two times each week when Whitely Cracker was simply unavailable to the outside world, and it was the hour and a half—or two hours, if the match went long, into a third set—that he dedicated to this game.

Which is not to say he took the sport itself that seriously. In truth, it was more about having an excuse to get out and run around, to keep himself in fighting shape. Whitely was only a modestly good tennis player. His fitness and court coverage were his best assets. His serve was not particularly imposing. His forehand, while steady, scared no one. His backhand was famously erratic. His net game was such a disaster he only wandered up there when forced by circumstance.

But, ah, he played with passion. He prided himself on being able to routinely beat better players on grit alone. And his secretary understood that she should attempt to schedule him a better player before she turned to the lesser ones. Losing did not bother Whitely Cracker. He would rather lose to a good player than beat a mediocre one.

On this day, Cracker was losing. He was playing Arnold Richardson—of the New Jersey Richardsons—who had played number six singles when he was at Dartmouth. Richardson's strokes were far superior to Whitely's. And even if Whitely could occasionally outlast him during a rally, it wasn't enough for him to mount a serious threat.

Richardson won the first set 6–2 and was up 3–1 in the second when there was a parting of the two sides of the heavy plastic curtain behind the court. From the opening emerged Lee Fulcher, a developer who fancied himself a Trump-in-waiting but was really just a mid-sized player in the outsized game that was Manhattan real estate.

Fulcher always looked like a heart attack waiting to happen, with shirt collars that were just a little too tight—owing to his refusal to admit he was gaining weight—and a face that flushed easily. This occasion was no exception. Even his scalp, exposed by his receding hairline, appeared to be scarlet. He was quite a sight, charging across the court, still fully dressed, from his tasseled loafers right on up to his double Windsor–knotted tie.

"Jesus, Lee," Richardson said, pointing with his racket. "Your shoes. Todd just had these courts resurfaced. You're going to get them all marked up."

Fulcher ignored him as he steamed across the court toward Whitely.

"Seriously, man," Richardson said. "I think there's something in the bylaws about appropriate footwear. If there are scuff marks, you're paying for it."

The words didn't even appear to be hitting Fulcher's ears. He started fuming shortly after he crossed the net.

"Your goddamn secretary wouldn't tell me where you were," Fulcher shouted at Whitely.

Note to self, Whitely thought, *give secretary a raise.*

"But I called the tennis manager and he told me you were down on Court Three," Fulcher said.

Note to self, Whitely thought, *have tennis manager fired.*

"Okay, you found me," Whiteley said, keeping his tone amiable. "What can I do for you, Lee?"

When he reached the service line, Fulcher stopped and declared: "I've got a goddamn margin call on the Mulberry Street project."

Whitely absorbed this news without visible reaction. He brought his wristband to his forehead and blotted perspiration.

Fulcher was still raging: "Can you believe those pricks at First National? It's like we've never even worked together, like they don't even know me. They're treating me like I'm some goddamn first-time home owner who missed his first three months. I'm not some fly-by-night. Goddamnit, I'm Lee Fulcher! Don't they remember 442 Broadway? Or . . . or . . . the West Side condos? They made a killing on that. I mean, goddamnit."

"Relax, Lee. Margin calls happen," Whitely said philosophically. "Can you cover it?"

"Yeah, but I need everything," Fulcher said.

Whitley looked down at the strings on his racket, straightening one row that had gone just slightly askew. Lee Fulcher was by no means Prime Resource Investment Group's largest investor. But he wasn't the smallest, either. Whitely would have to look it up to be sure, but off the top of his head, he knew Fulcher's account was in the forty-million-dollar range.

"Is that going to be a problem?" Fulcher prompted.

"No. No, of course not," Whitely said. "When do you need it?"

"Tomorrow. They just sprung this thing on me. I tried to negotiate, but they said they were pulling the plug unless I could cover it. Can you effing believe that?"

Whitely mopped his forehead again. Teddy Sniff was going to have a conniption. This was going to be a scramble. Whitely wasn't sure what kind of cash they had on hand, but he was certain they didn't have forty million bucks just lying around. He'd have to sell a bunch of positions he had really needed to hang on to. Especially now. He'd be taking a hell of a bath. Another one.

"You'll have it, right?" Fulcher asked.

"Yeah, Lee, of course," Whiteley assured him. "Absolutely. No worries."

Fulcher stared at him for a hard second, like he wasn't sure he could trust what he was hearing.

"Okay," Fulcher said. "Let's say three o'clock. You can wire it to my main account. Your guy has the number."

"Deal," Whitely said.

Fulcher finally began retreating from the court.

"Hey, Fulcher, you might want to check the couches for loose change on your way out," Richardson said, taunting him as he passed by. "Maybe see if someone left a quarter in one of the vending machines."

"Screw you, Arnie."

"And while you're at it, buy some freakin' tennis shoes for next time you come on the court, huh?"

"Hey, Arnie, be nice," Whitely said. "But Lee?"

"Yeah?" the man said, pausing just as he was about to disappear behind the partition.

"Arnie is right about one thing," he said. "Please don't wear those shoes out here again."

THE SUV WAS PARKED HALFWAY DOWN FULTON STREET, A BLOCK from the club. It had windows tinted so dark they were, technically, illegal. The people inside the vehicle were not concerned about the penny-ante fines that might result from such an infraction. Their greater worry was having someone realize that inside that boxy black truck was a trove of surveillance equipment.

"Did you get all that?" the man working the monitoring equipment asked the driver.

"Yeah," the driver said.

Bugging the racket club had been a real pain. The place had twenty-four-hour security and had been able to afford the best. But they knew Cracker went there at least twice a week for roughly two hours a shot. Their stalking of Whitely Cracker was a round-the-clock venture. And that clock couldn't have a four-hour hole in it each week.

The man thrust his shoulders in between the driver and the front passenger seat, so his head was even with the driver's.

"Should we move in? We could take him right now. End this thing," the man said.

"Where? When he comes out of the club? Right there on the curb?"

"Yeah, sure. Why not?"

"No. Not yet," the driver replied. "We've been patient for a reason. We've got to do this right."

"But you heard that. Fulcher just demanded his money. All his money. Do you know how much that is?"

"No. But I'm sure it's not nothing."

"What's going to happen when he realizes Cracker doesn't have it?"

"Who knows?" the driver said. "Maybe our boy is going to be able to come up with it. He's resourceful."

The man retreated to the back of the truck. All the coffee he had been drinking to stay awake was pressing at his bladder. He needed to pee. He shook his head and grabbed the Gatorade bottle he had been using for that purpose.

"It feels like we're just delaying the inevitable," he called as the urine hit the bottle.

"I know," the driver said. "Just be patient. It won't be much longer."

CHAPTER 11

BLOIS, France

Cleveland Detroit had performed the necessary measures to ensure his departure from Paris was unaccompanied by any prying parties. Once he cleared city limits, Derrick Storm pointed himself toward the designated rendezvous point, a manor house that was only seven hundred years old and therefore not considered very interesting by the French.

The house was on the outskirts of Blois (pronounced "blah"), southwest of Paris. Storm was expecting to be met by an escort from French authorities, as Jedediah Jones had promised—some kind of lights-flashing ride through the Channel Tunnel, at which point he'd be turned over to the British, who would speed him on to London in similar fashion. Storm never knew how Jones arranged such things three thousand miles from home, in foreign jurisdictions. But Jones had never let him down.

Until this time. Storm arrived at the manor grounds, passed through the outer walls, and knocked on the front door of the main house. It was answered by a weathered old caretaker. Storm was quite the sure the man was an operative . . . for the French resistance during World War II. But, following orders, he said in French: "Jones sent me."

Usually these three words were enough to make things happen. Instead, the caretaker welcomed him with all the warmth French hospitality is famous for, which is to say he looked at Storm like he was wearing a shirt made of donkey dung.

"*Qu'avez-vous dit?*" he asked. Approximate translation: "Say what, homey?"

Storm had switched to French and started to explain himself when he heard the distant sound of helicopter rotors chopping the air. If Storm knew Jones, that meant his ride had arrived.

"Never mind," Storm said, changing back to English. "Wrong house. My sense of direction must be a little . . . Blois."

Storm chortled at his own joke as he turned to go.

"Oh, you must be the American," the caretaker said in English, grabbing Storm's arm with surprising strength. "Stay right here. I have a few things for you."

Storm stood at the door of the manor house until the man returned with a change of clothes and a rectangular-shaped package, approximately a foot in length and perhaps half that in width. It was wrapped in plain, brown paper.

"Here," he said. "He said you might like this."

"Is this . . . a toy?" Storm said, feeling the gleam forming in his eye.

The caretaker tilted his head, as if Storm had re-donned his donkey dung shirt. By now, the helicopter was coming in for a landing, flattening the grass in a nearby field with its downdraft.

"Never mind," Storm said, peeling away the brown paper to reveal a box. Printed on the side in bold, block letters was the name "ACME."

"It *is* a toy," Storm exclaimed. The ACME thing was a running joke between him and Jones, both fans of classic Road Runner cartoons. Storm went into the box and pulled out what appeared to be a sleeve like the one quarterback Robert Griffin III had popularized in the NFL.

"What . . . what is it?" Storm asked, sliding the sleeve on his arm. At the end near his shoulder, it had two straps that Storm strapped around his torso, keeping the sleeve in place. Over the forearm, there was a nearly flat housing with a small aperture near the wrist.

"It's a kind of grappling hook," the old man said. "The line is as thin as dental floss but stronger than steel. The latest in nano-technology. The line accelerates at ninety-six feet per second squared—"

"That's three times faster than gravity," Storm interjected.

"—and the hook forms as the line pays out. Except it's not really a hook. It's more like a disk. It is only eight centimeters wide, but it will stick to virtually any material or structure, even a flat wall, and be able to hold five hundred pounds."

"Yet it couldn't weigh more than about two pounds itself," Storm said, hearing himself sounding a little too gee-whizzish.

"Again: nanotechnology."

"So *not* Blois," Storm said to himself.

"Just make sure you read the instructions," the caretaker said

"Why would I do that?"

"I was told you would ask that," he said, chuckling. "The answer is: because Jones said so."

Storm went inside and quickly changed into the new clothes, silently thanking Jones for arranging a more Derrick Storm–like outfit, one that actually matched. It also included one of his favorite kind of fashion accessories, the kind that took bullets. The 9mm Beretta wasn't necessarily Storm's gun of choice, but it would beat a good talking-to if he bumped across someone with a bad attitude. He slipped the grappling hook sleeve onto his arm, over his shirt but under his jacket, leaving the small aperture just barely peeking out from the jacket's cuff.

He left without further comment, jogging to the waiting helicopter, a Griffin HAR2 that had the markings of the Royal Air Force. Storm clambered into the main hold. There was a seat with a helmet sitting on it that he assumed was for him. He donned the helmet and strapped himself in.

"You're late," Storm said into the helmet's intercom.

"Sorry, sir," the pilot replied.

"What, did you get caught in queuing on the M-1?" Storm joked. "Or was it that the destination made your navigation sort of . . . Blois."

The pilot did not reply.

Storm tried again: "Or maybe the helicopter is having a . . . Blois day."

The pilot punched a few buttons on the control panel.

"Oh, come on, nothing for that? You have such a . . . Blois sense of humor."

Still no words from the pilot.

"Get it? Because you're going to a city called Blois and . . ."

"You think a joke improves when you have to explain it?" the pilot asked.

"Right. To London, then."

Storm felt the surge of the chopper lifting upward then watched out the small side window as the fields of northern France passed underneath. He turned his attention to the grappling hook, tossing the instructions onto the floor of the chopper. By the time they reached the iconic shores of Normandy, he felt comfortable with the device's operation.

Somewhere over the English Channel, he dozed off.

LONDON, England

It was mid-morning by the time Storm landed near the crime scene. He felt refreshed from the nap and was keen to be able to do his own investigating, not just rely on reports from others. He didn't necessarily think he was smarter than any of the agents who had combed through the other scenes. But he did know Volkov. Maybe there would be something the other agents had overlooked or the significance of which they didn't understand.

The building where the killing had occurred was filled with fashionable condominium lofts in a reclaimed industrial building along the south bank of the Thames, two turns of the river away from Parliament, not far from King's Stairs Gardens.

This was a part of London that had undergone much change since World War II, and its rejuvenation had continued into the twenty-first century, albeit haltingly. Next to the loft, rising forlornly from the earth, there were empty steel girders of what would someday—if the financing could ever again come together—be an office tower to approach the Shard as one of London's tallest buildings. The superstructure had been completed, but construction had since been halted, a reminder that England had not been immune to the economic malaise that had gripped Europe. Storm wondered idly how many millions of dollars of steel had been used in making what was essentially a towering skeleton.

Storm entered the condo building and rode to its top floor, the eighth, which was swarming with officials of all stripes. At the front door, he was handed a pair of latex gloves by a uniformed man, who logged Storm's entry. He walked through the foyer, into a sitting room, then toward where all the action seemed to be taking place: the office, in the northwest corner of the loft.

At least in the Western world, crime scenes always looked the same. There were people in varying kinds of uniform running around, working on their small piece of the action, doing their duty. And then, somewhere, not in uniform, there was the person in charge.

Storm finally found that person in the office. He was tall, bespectacled, and gentle-looking, with long, chestnut-brown hair tied back in a ponytail. He looked less like a Scotland Yard detective and more like someone you might find in a computer science Ph.D. program. The man was staring at something on a clipboard, looking up as Storm approached.

"Hi, I'm . . ."

"Derrick Storm," the man said. "And I'm Nick Walton, Scotland Yard. I've been told to cooperate fully with you. Would you like some tea?"

Okay, so maybe there *were* small differences in crime scenes. "No, thank you," Storm said. "What do we have here?"

Storm gestured toward the corpse still duct-taped to a desk chair. The man had slumped forward slightly against his restraints, his head lolling to the left. The angle gave Storm more of a view than he needed of the missing portion of the back of the man's skull. The man's right hand, which hung at his side, looked like raw meat. Volkov's work, for sure.

"Victim's name is Nigel Wormsley," Walton said. "He was an executive vice president at Queen Royal Bank. I'm told that might be of interest to you."

Storm just nodded.

"Took two bullets right between the eyes from close range," Walton continued. "The shots were close enough that the entrance wounds merged into one hole. But from looking at the edges of the one on the left, it appears to be forty-five-caliber. That's my best guess. As you know, we're not as accustomed to gun violence as you Yanks, so I don't get as much practice on that sort of thing."

Storm let the cheap shot—if, in fact, it was intended as a cheap shot and not merely a statement of fact—pass without comment.

"If you want to have a look, you have to sort of get underneath him and look up," Walton said. "Obviously, it's not as hard to see the exit wound. And I'm sure you noticed that his hand is a bloody mess. Whoever did this is some brutal bastard."

"Any other victims?" Storm asked, braced for the answer.

"No, just Mr. Wormsley," Walton said. "He has a house in the country where his wife and son stay. This has been described to me as his city crash pad."

Storm looked around at the office, with its sleek, modern furnishings. Either Wormsley or his decorator had expensive tastes. The office had large, nearly floor-to-ceiling windows that offered an expansive view of the city.

"Nice crash pad," Storm said.

"Mr. Wormsley was a very wealthy man, as you might imagine," Walton said. "I'm told his bonus alone last year was in the millions of pounds. Not bad, eh?"

"Do you know what kind of work he did at Queen Royal?"

"I don't know. Banker stuff. Does it matter?"

"It might," Storm said. "Do you happen to know if he was involved in currency trading?"

Walton's right eyebrow arched. "Yes, as a matter of fact. He was executive vice president in charge of currency exchange."

Good old Dad. His hunch had been correct. Of course. It was now no coincidence: four bankers, all involved in currency trading, all tortured for some reason. What that reason was remained unclear.

Storm studied the desk without touching anything. It was a large, open surface, mostly devoid of tchotchkes or mementos. There was a good bit of blood, now congealing or congealed, pooled on top. That must have been where Volkov yanked out the man's fingernails. There were a few picture frames and a paperweight on the floor nearby, as if someone had swept them off the desk.

"Anything taken?" Storm asked.

"We won't know until the wife gets here to have a look around. She should be here anytime, and we were hoping to get Mr. Wormsley out of here before she does her walk-through, so if you need to examine him, you might want to do it now."

Storm did not make a move toward the body. There was nothing it could tell him, unless it suddenly started talking.

Storm looked at the walls, spying an original Modigliani that was staring back at him with that distinctive face—sad and warped. It had to be valued in the millions of dollars. Volkov clearly hadn't known the painting's value. It wasn't like him to pass up an opportunity to enhance his payday. Or maybe he just knew it would slow his getaway unnecessarily.

"So that's about all I know for now, at least until the labs come back and tell me more," Walton said. "Is there anything you can tell me?"

Storm decided that there was nothing more for him at the scene, and that therefore he might give Scotland Yard a little parting gift. His gaze drifted out to the London skyline as he spoke.

"Your killer is a Russian national named Gregor Volkov. The ripped-out fingernails are sort of his signature. He is about five-foot-four, powerfully built. He wears an eye patch and has burn scars on his face. My people can provide you a recent picture, but it probably won't do you much good. He more than likely entered the country under a different name and is almost certainly now gone. He is not the type to linger."

"I see, and why does Mr. Volkov wish ill on . . ."

Storm was no longer listening. His eyes stopped on a solitary figure, dressed in black, gripping the side of a column in the unfinished skyscraper next door. It couldn't be a construction worker or anyone with an authorized reason to be there. The site was inoperative. Whoever it was, he was long and lean and, from the looks of things, not afraid of heights. Storm couldn't see the man's feature's because his face was obscured by a camera with a big chunk of a long lens attached to it.

Walton was still talking when Storm interrupted: "Was Mr. Wormsley famous in some way?"

Storm had already looked away, so the photographer wouldn't know he had been spotted.

"No, just rich. Not famous."

"Is there any reason why the paparazzi would be interested in this case?"

"Why do you ask?"

"Look quickly next door, at roughly our height. There's a man with a camera taking pictures. Don't look too long. I don't want him knowing we're aware of him."

Walton did as instructed, then said, "That's not paparazzi, mate."

"How do you know?"

"After Princess Kate's bits showed up in print, we finally cracked down on that sort of thing. Part of the crackdown was making sure the paparazzi didn't tread on private property. The fellow over there is clearly on private property—the angle the pictures are being shot at would make it clear he was close to the same level as us, and it would be impossible to achieve that in a public place around here. If he tried to sell them, he'd be looking at a big fine. So would any media outlet that bought them. He wouldn't be one of the paparazzi. That said, I don't know who he is or what he's doing."

Storm was already on the move. "Well," he said. "Then perhaps I should find out."

STORM RODE THE ELEVATOR BACK DOWN AND CROSSED QUICKLY out into the street. This could be a fool's errand, he knew. For whatever Walton said, it could just be a paparazzo, looking to shoot pictures of a sensational crime scene. Or it could be some kind of weird thrill-seeker who mixed a fascination for gruesome killings with a thing for heights.

Or it could be that the Chinese Ministry of State Security had sent someone to make sure Volkov had done his job right.

Whatever it was, Storm was going to figure it out by having a polite conversation with the man. Or a not-so-polite conversation. That part really depended on how forthcoming the photographer felt like being.

Storm reached the construction site and surveyed the outside. It was surrounded on all sides by a razor-wire fence. It was not insurmountable, but it was just imposing enough to give Storm pause.

How had the photographer gotten in? Storm did a quick lap around the building and found what he was looking for on the far side. Someone who was apparently handy with bolt cutters had clipped away a narrow section of razor wire. Storm took advantage of the gap, vaulting himself over the fence in that spot.

From there, the path was easy to follow. The ground was soft, and the only fresh footprints led directly to the building. A glass skin covered the first three floors—as far as they had gotten before the money ran out—and Storm tracked the footprints through some front doors.

The inside of the building was completely unfinished—just the steel columns leading up toward the sky. In the middle of the structure there was a lift that led to the crane that was still in place, fifty or so stories up, where someday it would perhaps finish the top floors of the building.

Storm went to the lift and pressed a large green button. Nothing happened. He pressed the red button above it. Still nothing. The lift car was just sitting there, idle, inoperable, same as everything else in the building. Obviously, the power had been cut off.

Storm looked up at the photographer. He counted beams. The man was ten floors up, still firing away from behind his telephoto lens. He must have climbed there.

Storm knew he would have to do the same. The only good news was that the photographer was more or less trapped. That there were no quick ways up meant there were also no quick ways down—at least not any ways that wouldn't have a sudden, painful end. Plus, Storm had the persuasive powers of the Beretta to aid his cause.

Storm walked to the nearest column and started working his way upward. The climbing was not especially difficult, at least not for a man of Storm's strength and fitness level. The columns had enough notches that they were easy to scale. Storm gained quickly on the photographer, who was so engrossed in documenting the crime scene that he didn't notice he was about to have company.

As Storm made his silent ascent, he stayed directly below the photographer so the man wouldn't see him. Storm allowed himself occasional glimpses upward. The photographer was dressed in all black, from his boots to his one-piece suit to his ski mask. A classic cat burglar. He was not as tall as Storm thought. His thinness just made him appear so.

Storm was now one floor below, still out of the photographer's line of sight. He paused to consider his next move. He did not want to approach from directly below the man. The man would be able to kick him in the head, which Storm needed like, well, like he needed a kick in the head.

With that in mind, Storm decided he'd have to walk to the next column, about thirty feet away. He could climb that one, get on the same level as the photographer, and pull out his gun. Then he'd have the guy exactly where he wanted him.

Storm looked at the distance, trying to get his mind in the right set. Storm wasn't particularly acrophobic, but he was as aware as any other human being that a fall from ten stories up would probably hurt a little. Really, it was just a trick of psychology. After all, if you placed the beam on the ground and told him—or anyone else with a reasonable sense of balance—to walk those thirty feet, he'd be able to stroll along, even sprint it, without a second thought. Put the same beam ten stories up and it was heart-in-throat, shuffle-inch-by-inch time.

So the trick was to convince himself that the beam was really on the ground. Yes. It was on the ground. What did people always say? Just don't look down. Great advice. It ranked right up there with telling a man who was being chased by a grizzly bear to run a little faster.

Nevertheless, it was all Storm had. He left the safety of the column and, without looking down, began calmly walking.

Ten feet. No problem. Fifteen feet. The wind gusted a little. He didn't let it rattle him. Twenty feet. A bird flew by—below him. He willed himself not to be bothered by it. His sole focus was that next girder.

He was perhaps twenty-five feet in—five feet to safety—when disaster struck. His foot hit something. He couldn't see what, but it felt like a thin piece of metal. Automatically, Storm looked down. It was a T square. Some worker or engineer or someone had left it there, except now it had been kicked free and was hurtling earthward. Storm watched it fall and hit the concrete floor ten stories down with a tremendous clattering.

The photographer's head snapped immediately in the direction of the sound, which naturally drew his eye downward—and directly at Storm.

Storm drew the Beretta. "Freeze," he ordered.

Without a word, the photographer slung the camera around his neck and started climbing the column. Storm had a shot at the man, but not an especially good one. There were beams in the way. Plus, what if he actually hit the guy? You couldn't interrogate a dead man.

Then there was Storm's worry about the gun's recoil knocking him off balance. A 9mm didn't have a lot of kick, but it would give him a little push, and Storm wasn't braced on anything.

As it was, Storm felt his balance starting to go. Looking down at the T square then up at the photographer had disoriented him. The awareness that he was 120 feet in the air, perched on a foot-wide piece of metal, crashed into him.

He lurched to one side, then the other. His stomach did a somersault. He was going to fall. He threw his arms out to try and steady himself, as with a tightrope walker's rod.

It didn't work.

Storm felt himself going over.

In a last-ditch effort at saving himself, he flung himself toward the next column. He caught it with both hands, then pulled himself to it, hugging it as if it were the waiting arms of his mother. He allowed himself a moment to feel safe, then he cursed loudly when he heard something heavy striking the concrete far below.

The Beretta. He had dropped it.

There was no going back for it now. The photographer had gained a full story on him, and was apparently intent on going higher. Why was the man heading up? What was there to gain from that?

There was no point in trying to ponder that strategy. Storm dashed back across the beam—to hell with being ten stories up—and reached out for the column directly below the photographer.

Then Storm started his own climb to the sky.

. . .

STORM WAS GAINING ON HIM. THERE WAS NO QUESTION ABOUT that. The photographer was no slouch as a climber. And he was in nearly as good shape as Storm. But Storm was stronger and faster.

It was just that the progress was slow. By the time they reached the twenty-fifth floor, Storm had cut the photographer's lead in half, down to one level. By the fortieth floor, he was half a level away. Storm could feel the lactic acid building in his muscles and the rawness from where the steel was eating into his fingers, but he was thankful for the pain. It gave him something to concentrate on other than the dizzying heights they were reaching. All of London was growing small beneath them.

By the time they passed the base of the crane, at the fiftieth floor, the photographer was a mere few feet away. It was halfway between the sixty-second and sixty-third floors that Storm was able to reach out and grab the man's ankle with his right hand. The man kicked furiously, but Storm just squeezed harder. Slowly, carefully, Storm started dragging the man toward the sixty-second floor.

"We can do this one of two ways," Storm said between huge gasps of air. "The hard way or the easy way. What's it going to be?"

"Let go," the photographer said. Only it wasn't a man's voice. It was a woman's.

"I can't do that," Storm said. "You and I need to have a conversation about those pictures you were taking. You're going to tell me who you are and why you're photographing that crime scene or I swear to you, I will throw you off this building."

The woman's response was to kick some more. Storm was easing his way down toward the beam, inch by inch, dragging the woman with him. The descent wasn't easy, especially not doing it one-handed while the other hand had to keep taming a flailing limb. But Storm was making progress. Finally, he reached the beam below him and anchored himself to it by wrapping his legs around it. He had leverage now. This would be over with quickly.

He tugged. The woman was resisting with every bit of strength she had left, but she was tired after her long climb. She was almost in his grasp. Just a little longer. She was trying to scramble toward the outside of the column—the more dangerous side. It was a desperate attempt to get farther away from Storm and perhaps shake loose from his clutches.

Then she slipped. She had been bucking so violently against Storm's hold—and her forearms had grown so tired from all the effort—that her fingers failed on her, losing the handhold they had on the column.

She fell, letting loose a high-pitched scream. Storm still had his grip on her ankle and felt his shoulder ripping away from its socket as the full weight of her plummeting body suddenly became his to bear. The only thing that saved him from having her momentum carry both of them down to oblivion was the column itself. He was on the inside part, while she was on the outside.

They stayed there for a second—her dangling upside down, sixty-two stories up, him hanging on with all his strength. Her ski mask had fallen off, and Storm felt himself gasp as he saw her long, black hair cascading downward and recognized the cheekbones that that had been hiding underneath.

It was Ling Xi Bang.

Despite himself—despite all the times he had steeled himself against engaging his emotions during a mission—he still felt the sting of betrayal. Yes, he had been using her in Paris, trying to get close to her to pry secrets out of her, just as she had been using him. But hadn't at least some of what they exchanged been real? The waltzing? The storytelling? The moonlight stroll?

But no. It had all been a lie. It actually disgusted him, to know he had lain with someone who could unleash Volkov on innocent civilians.

"How could you hire a man like Volkov?" Storm shouted.

"No. It wasn't me, I swear."

"Then why were you taking pictures?"

"I'm trying to figure out what's going on with these dead bankers, just like you," she said. "The difference is, we don't have as cozy a relationship with the Brits, so I can't just call up Scotland Yard and get invited to the crime scene."

"You're lying," Storm said.

"No. Please. Think about it: Why would I take pictures if all we wanted was to have these men dead? Because I'm investigating, too."

The pant leg Storm was hanging on to was made of a slippery fabric. His hand was slowly sliding toward her boot. He wasn't going to be able to keep her suspended that way much longer. Shouldn't he just let her fall? She was an enemy operative, after all.

But maybe there were parts of her story that made sense. And maybe, Storm admitted to himself, he wasn't ready for his time with Xi Bang to end with one night in Paris.

Meanwhile, she was trying to arc her body around so she could get a grip on the building and save herself. But there was only so much a human body could bend backward, even one as lithe as Xi Bang's.

"Nonsense," Storm said. "We're on to you, Agent Xi Bang—or whatever your name is. You're engineering some kind of plot to undermine U.S. currency by—"

"It's not us. For the love of God, stop and think about it. Why would we want to destroy your economy? We're your biggest investor. No one owns more American debt than China. If your currency crumbles, all that debt loses its value. We'd go bankrupt right along with you."

He was holding her by the boot now, and nothing more. And the boot wasn't staying put. She was working her foot to try and keep it on, but it was slowly sliding off despite her best effort.

"We're every bit as concerned about these bankers as you are," she continued. "And I can prove it to you."

"How?"

"Come to Iowa with me."

"Iowa? What's in Iowa?" Storm asked.

"There's a man in Ames I want you to meet. You can keep me

in handcuffs the whole trip if you want, I don't care. Talking to this guy will prove to you that I'm on your side. Now, please, help me up."

Storm decided that a Chinese agent wouldn't be able to invent a story involving Ames, Iowa, while hanging upside down from a skyscraper. "Okay," he said, reaching out with the hand on the other side of the column, the one that wasn't holding the boot. "Take my hand."

The boot was nearly off now. Xi Bang tried to reach up and grab Storm's free hand, curling her body into a C-shape. Her fingers were inches away from him being able to grab her and haul her to safety.

Then the boot came off.

Xi Bang screamed. She was free-falling spread-eagle, faceup, like a terrified snow angel.

Storm didn't hesitate. The grappling hook. It was still on his left arm. His right hand flew to the activation button, and he aimed it at Xi Bang's midsection.

The line shot out at ninety-six feet per second squared, three times faster than gravity. Storm watched in fascination as the end of the line formed into a disk, seemingly out of thin air. Then, just as the Frenchman had said it would, it attached itself to Xi Bang's catsuit, and through the miracle of whatever science Jones's people had produced, it held firm.

Storm grunted as the line tightened, slamming him against the column. Xi Bang swung gently fourteen stories down and landed—albeit perpendicularly—against the side of the building. Then she slowly began walking herself upward. Storm could feel the sleeve's straps digging into his side, but they held.

Soon, she had reached the place where Storm was clinging to the column, shimmied around, and collapsed into him, panting from exertion and terror. He enveloped her, feeling their hearts pounding against each other.

"Now," he said, "what were you saying about handcuffs?"

CHAPTER 12

WASHINGTON, D.C.

This was a town that was all about doing favors. Nearly a quarter century hanging around the halls of power had taught Donny Whitmer at least that much. Big favors. Small favors. You did them if you could, because you never knew when you might need to call one in.

Like, say, when you were thirteen points down in a primary against a Tea Party candidate who apparently had every Christian in the state of Alabama ready to pull the lever for him, and you just didn't have time to make the two thousand phone calls that would be necessary to raise the five million bucks you needed to ruin the bastard.

You know. Times like that.

In this case, the favor Donny Whitmer had done seemed straightforward enough. About three weeks earlier, his best donor had called him. There was an appropriations bill coming up for a vote, one of those big, messy, fifteen-thousand-word piles of slop that the Senate needed to pass to avoid yet another threatened government shutdown. The donor wanted a rider placed on the bill. Just a little rider.

It was the kind of thing that Donny Whitmer had specialized in throughout his career. He had learned exactly how to slip them in—you always waited until the last minute—and because he was the chairman of the Senate Appropriations Committee, he never had much problem doing it. It was how he had gotten the entire Alabama section of I-20 repaved, even though it didn't really need it. It was how he'd funded a study of pygmy butterfly larvae at the University of Alabama, which might or might not have found ways to shunt the money to the football team. It was how Donny Whitmer had become Donny Whitmer.

In truth, he didn't really understand the rider this donor wanted. It was an obscure change to Federal Reserve policy, one that placed restrictions—generous ones, but restrictions nevertheless—on the amount of government bonds the Fed could sell each month.

Why the donor was asking for it or how he would benefit was something of a mystery to Donny. But the guy had been so generous over the years, Donny didn't pry. He called the clerk of the Senate and told him he had a little bit of language to insert into the appropriations bill. It was perhaps five hundred words long. The clerk added it without comment or question because, hey, it was the chairman of the Appropriations Committee and this was an appropriations bill.

Donny was ready with a story for anyone who asked. He was going to make all kinds of noise about how the Federal Reserve was constantly overstepping its authority and how the entire Federal Reserve system had gotten out of whack. It was a takeoff on a favored rant among hard-core fiscal conservatives, so no one would think too hard about hearing it coming from Senator Whitmer. They would know he was facing a rugged primary challenge and think he was using this to pander to his base.

Instead, no one asked. That was the magic of sneaking a rider in at the last second: No one even read it. Everyone had haggled themselves to death and was just ready to be done with the whole thing. The President, desperate to avert a shutdown that would tarnish his administration, had signed the bill into law at two minutes before midnight.

Whitmer had mostly forgotten it. He had just stored it away

in his forever-growing bank of favors done. And now, sooner than he ever thought he would need it, it was time to make a with-drawal.

And hope like hell there was five million bucks in the account.

He waited until his staff was gone and he had his spacious of-fice in the Dirksen Senate Office Building to himself before he made the call. He didn't want to risk anyone hearing what might need to happen.

He picked up his office phone, then put it down. Cell phone. That would feel more personal. He stuck the Bluetooth in his ear. He pulled the phone out of his pocket. He dialed.

"Well, hello yourself, young man," Donny said, feigning warmth. Damn caller ID. You didn't even get to say "This is Senator Whitmer" anymore.

"I'm fine, I'm just fine," Donny said. "Thank you for asking. How're you?"

Southern charm. Donny had lots of it.

"Well, that's just great to hear. And how are the wife and kids?"

The personal touch. You had to give it the personal touch.

"Kindergarten? Is he in kindergarten already? My, my, it seems like just yesterday I was getting that birth announcement. How time flies."

He was now strolling around his office. Clyde May was call-ing to him.

"Readin' already? Smart boy, smart boy. He's just a chip off the old block, isn't he?"

Flattery. It gets you everywhere. God, he despised this.

"Well, if that private school of his needs a little something-something, you just give ol' Donny a call, you hear? Turns out the junior senator in your state owes me a favor."

Or at least she would if Donny needed her to. Thank God she wasn't one of those uppity women senators who refused to play ball with the boys.

"That's mighty nice of you to notice. Sissy put me on one of them low-carb diets. I miss her cornbread something awful, but I lost ten pounds since March."

Yes, apparently flattery went both ways.

"Wouldn't that be nice. We'll have to get the NIH to look into that," Donny said, laughing a little too hard at a joke that wasn't even that funny. When you got right down to it, nothing about dieting was funny.

Finally, they were through with the necessary small talk, and Donny heard the donor say the words that could get the conversation rolling: *To what do I owe the pleasure of the call, Senator?*

"Well, I'm glad you asked," Donny said, eager to get on with it. "You may have heard, but it looks like I'm going to be facing a little primary challenge come June."

Little primary challenge. A euphemism if ever there were one. Donny Whitmer was facing a little primary challenge in the same way Sandy was a little rainstorm.

"Mmm hmm, he's one of those Tea Party assholes. Goes on and on about how he'll never raise taxes, he'll cut guv'ment spending, cut this, cut that, won't compromise, won't work with no one on nothing. Now, you know I'm a proud conservative, but we still need to be able to reach across the aisle if we want to get anything done in this town. It ain't enough just to stick your fingers in your ears and say 'no, no, no' all the time. But that's what these fellas want to do."

Donny listened for a moment. This whole thing had to go at the right speed. He felt like he was making good progress.

"Yep, you know the type. And to make it worse, the sumbitch thumps the Bible every chance he gets. Now, I'm as God-fearin' as the next man. And if you want to pray in school, I say go right ahead. But this sumbitch, he's talking like he's gonna get a cross stuck atop the Washington Monument. I don't need to tell you, we can't let these people take over the party. They got this social agenda and—"

The donor interrupted him with enthusiastic agreement. That was good. Donny took over where he'd left off:

"Exactly. A distraction. That's what I always say, too. It's a distraction. I mean, I'm not too fond of these queers marrying each other. But we got bigger problems in this country right now than whether a couple a dykes get to say 'I do.'"

More listening. The guy was ranting a bit now, but ol' Donny was going to let him. Donny strolled over to the putter and golf balls he kept stashed in the corner. He used the head of the putter to position a ball just right, then with a nice smooth stroke rolled it across the carpet toward a coffee table leg. The ball stopped just short of the leg. Damn it. Donny hated short putts.

The guy finally finished, and Donny dove in with "Well, that's what I'm saying exactly. Guys like this, they just have no under-standing of . . . of . . . the *sensitivity* of some of these more complex issues, especially in the financial markets."

And then, without hesitating, without giving the guy a chance to say anything, Donny started putting the hammer down: "It's like that rider I was able to get passed for you a few weeks ago. You remember that?"

Yes, the guy remembered that. Of course he did.

"Well, that's just the kind of thing I'm talking about. You think that Tea Party sumbitch would do that for you?"

Subtle, Donny. Subtle. But at least it redirected the donor into talking about this, ahem, little primary threat.

"Well, it's nothing to be too concerned about, but you never can be too careful," Donny said. "I pay my pollster to worry about these things, and he's doing his job, that's for sure."

His job. Right. Thirteen friggin' points of a job.

"No, no. No one here is panicking. There's no need to panic. It's just these things can get unpredictable at the end. There's an anti-incumbent wave sweeping around, and before you know it, everyone wants to just vote out whoever has been in, never mind that the person who's in has been serving their interests faithfully for many years."

Finally, the sweet-sounding sentence poured out of the man's mouth: *Anything I can do to help?*

"Well, now, I'm glad you asked. I could use a little something extra for some advertising my people say will help."

How much?

"My people say five million dollars would do it," Donny said, and didn't give the man time to object before continuing: "Obviously, we'd set it up as a super PAC. God bless Citizens United. We could give it one of those vague names like 'Voters for Alabama,' or, hell, call it 'Roll Tide for Senate.' "

Actually, that wasn't a half-bad idea. In Alabama, the only thing that could trump the religious vote might be the Crimson Tide vote. Donny sat heavily at his desk, took out a fresh legal pad, and wrote "ROLL TIDE PAC" in block letters on top.

"Point is, my colleagues who have successfully fought off these Tea Party challenges have all had super PACs behind them. So what do you say. We good?"

Donny held his breath. He was ready for a variety of answers, all the way from "yes," to "let me think about it," to an offer to hit up some of his well-heeled buddies on Donny's behalf. Instead, Donny was shocked by the donor's reply.

"What do you mean, you don't have it?" Donny said, hearing himself yelling slightly. "You have it. You always have it."

Donny shoved the Bluetooth deeper in his ear. He was suddenly having trouble hearing the guy.

"Well, now, I know it's a lot. But let's talk about that rider. I mean, how much is that worth to you? To just be able to call up a . . . a sitting U.S. senator who can put whatever bill you want into law? I'd say that's worth five million dollars. Hell, I'd say it's worth a lot more than five million dollars. People pay office buildings full of lobbyists a lot more than that to have not near as much pull."

The guy wasn't disagreeing. But he wasn't offering to come up with the money, either. Donny could tell the guy wasn't sufficiently motivated. It was time to give him the motivation. Donny hadn't known why this donor wanted that rider. But if he knew rich guys—and, Lord, he knew rich guys—they never wanted other rich guys to know what they were up to. It was time to use that as leverage.

"Well, now, let me put it to you another way: What's it worth to you for me to not mention that you were the one who asked me to put the rider in? Is that worth five million? Because, you know, I could just keep on keeping on. Or I could have my press office put out a big ol' press release, saying that the world has *you* to thank for this change to Federal Reserve policy. What would you think about that?"

This, as Donny suspected, got the man's interest. In fact, it changed his whole tone. And his answer.

"Sure, I can give you some time to think about it. But not much time. We'll talk tomorrow?"

Suddenly, they were back to small talk again.

"Well, thank you. And you give my best to your lovely bride, you hear? . . . All right, then. You have a nice night now."

He disconnected the call and let out a long breath. He was shaking slightly. He went over to the Clyde May and took a slug from the bottle.

There were a lot of emotions coursing through him, perhaps none stronger than disbelief. He knew he might try to spin it in his own mind, but he'd only be fooling himself. The fact was he had—for the first time in a long and otherwise distinguished political career—just committed extortion.

CHAPTER 13

AMES, Iowa

The man looked like he had been hiding for at least a decade off the grid in Montana, in a place where he subsisted on squirrel, elk meat, and indigenous berries. His beard covered his entire face and hung to the top of his chest. His straggly hair was at least that long in the back. He had an offensive lineman's body, both in height and girth, which only made the thick, John Lennon–style glasses on the end of his nose that much more incongruous.

"Derrick, I'd like you to meet Dr. Rodney Click, assistant professor of economics here at Iowa State," Ling Xi Bang said. "Is it correct for me to call you a quantitative economist? Do I have that right?"

"'Geek' will also do nicely," Click said, offering Storm a good-natured smile and a handshake.

"I'll just call you Doc, if it's okay," Storm said, pumping his hand.

"I'm sure I've been called worse. Anyhow, come into my office," Click said, turning and calling over his shoulder: "I just can't believe the CIA is interested enough in my theory to pay me another visit."

Storm shot a glance at Xi Bang that seemed to say *Another visit, huh?* It didn't take being a quantitative economist to do the math: Xi Bang had been here before, and had told the guy she was with the CIA. Xi Bang just smiled at Storm demurely. Their trip out to Iowa, which had included a brief stop at a hotel room near Kennedy Airport, had given whole new dimension to the word *layover.*

"You have to understand, most of the time when I do a paper like this, I assume it's just going to be read by other academics," Click continued as he led them into a small rabbit den of an office, with walls lined by packed bookshelves. "The *Journal of Global Economics* isn't going to be confused with a page-turning thriller. It's not like I'm Michael Connelly here."

Click settled himself into his chair, which groaned accordingly. Storm and Xi Bang took chairs on the other side of his desk.

"Trust me when I say I found it riveting," Xi Bang said. "And I'd like you to explain it to my CIA colleague here the same way you did to me."

"Then I guess I'll start in the same place, with a little background," Click said, aiming his attention at Storm. "I don't mean to sound like I'm talking down to you, but how much do you understand about the foreign currency exchange markets?"

"Enough to fill a thimble," Storm admitted.

"Okay, the basics: The foreign exchange market, sometimes called ForEx, or just FX, is the largest and most liquid market in the world. In some ways, it's the most volatile, too. Roughly four trillion dollars' worth of currency is traded every single day. Now, a minority of that volume is what you would think it is: Individuals or corporations that do business in one currency suddenly need to pay for something in another currency. So, say you're vacationing in India. You land in Mumbai and you change dollars for rupees."

"Except I always save some greenbacks for bribes," Storm interjected.

"Of course. In any event, that kind of transaction—which you could argue is what FX was created for—is maybe twenty percent of the market. Eighty percent is banks, hedge funds, and other large financial institutions making speculative trades. That's why there's so much volatility. There are all kinds of complicated ways they can make money on these trades, some of which rely on factors the average investor wouldn't think of. So, for example, there's one kind of trade, a carry trade, that works because of differing interest rates being offered by the central banks of various countries. Other trades are more straightforward: investors betting which way a currency will head based on some intuition or knowledge about that country's economy."

"So it's a lot like the stock market: rich guys gambling with other people's money," Storm said.

"Yes, but there's an important difference," Click said. "The FX is not a regulated exchange. Every deal is essentially done on a handshake, or a virtual handshake. There's no government watching over it, no special clearinghouse, no rules about the size of the trades, no one watching out for insider traders, no safeguards put in place to prevent large swings in the market. The New York Stock Exchange suspends trading if stock prices are dropping too far too fast or if there's some kind of disruption in the markets that everyone needs to stop and digest. Not so with FX. It is open twenty-four hours during business days. If traders choose to bail on a certain currency, its value can—at least in theory—drop to zero, and no one will stop it. It's a marketplace that relies solely on market forces for regulation."

"Sounds like the Wild West," Storm said.

"More than you know," Click said. "Because another key principle is this: All major currencies in the world today are what we call fiat currencies. They're not backed by any gold or silver or other commodities. They have value because the government that issues the currency says it has value, and the marketplace chooses to agree with it because the economy supporting the currency is fundamentally sound."

Storm shook his head. "So it's all based on shared faith."

"Exactly. Especially with the U.S. dollar. A certain percentage of the value of our money comes from the fact that we're considered the one unassailable currency—the too-big-to-fail currency.

If you're an international investor and you have a pile of money sitting somewhere, chances are you're going to have it there in U.S. dollars. But economists have always speculated about what would happen if that stopped being the case.

"Now, bear that in mind when I tell you about October 2, 2008," Click said. "If you think back to what was happening then, the financial world had pretty much gone haywire. Lehman Brothers had failed. Fannie and Freddie were teetering. AIG was about to collapse. Banks were petrified to lend each other money. There were runs on mutual funds. People were selling their entire portfolios and burying the cash in the backyard. It was a wild time, and pretty much every other day brought some news that no one ever thought they'd see. I think that's why what happened on October 2 didn't get much attention. Well, that, and it was over so quickly. The mainstream media didn't even have time to understand it."

"Understand what?" Storm asked. He realized he had scooted to the edge of his chair. Click, likewise, had leaned forward, so that his large body was smothering the edge of his desk.

"For about twelve minutes on October 2, 2008, the U.S. dollar lost roughly fifty percent of its value," Click said, with all due drama.

"But . . . but wouldn't that be impossible?"

"You would think so. You would have thought it was impossible for GM to go bankrupt, but that happened, too. Like I said, it was a wild time."

"So what happened?" Storm asked.

"Well, that's the question I have spent the last four years researching," Click said. "The short version is that one of the most active and largest currency traders in South Korea decided he was done with the U.S. dollar. It wasn't a particularly rational decision on his part. But, mind you, the Koreans were watching everything going on with the U.S. economy with disgust. They saw it as our lack of financial discipline over many years finally coming back to haunt us. So this guy essentially just cashed out and moved all his money into other currencies."

"But . . . I mean, how many dollars are in circulation in the world?" Storm asked. "One person couldn't possibly make that big a difference."

"To answer your question, it depends how you define what 'in circulation' means. For sake of conversation, let's just call it ten trillion. So, no, you wouldn't think one investor, no matter how rich, would matter that much. But it turns out he did what's called a double-back trade. I'm not sure I could explain the mechanism in a way that would make sense to you—no offense. Suffice it to say, it's a trade whose impact on the value of the currency involved is not just double. It's more like quadruple. And it was a huge trade to start with. It ended up triggering a classic negative feedback loop—a trend that started feeding on itself. Most of the trades were being done by computers that had been programmed to make certain moves when a preset value threshold was breached. The major stock markets around the world have checks against that sort of thing getting too far out of control. But, again, FX is an unregulated market. So there was nothing to stop these computers from doing their thing, and for twelve minutes, the value of the U.S. dollar collapsed in a way no one could have ever imagined."

"But you said it only lasted for twelve minutes. Why?" Storm asked.

"Someone at the Fed saw what was happening, and the Fed swooped in and saved it. One of the ways the Fed controls monetary supply is through a big stockpile of government bonds it owns. It quickly sold a whole bunch of them for bargain prices to banks that recognized what a good deal they were getting. The Fed lost a pile of money, but in doing so it took a whole bunch of money out of circulation. From there, simple supply and demand took over. Supply had been constricted. Fewer greenbacks available made them more valuable, the negative feedback loops reversed themselves, and the dollar bounced back to what it had been twelve minutes before. To the media, it looked like one more bailout from Uncle Sam, and one that they couldn't argue with. So it was sort of a nonstory."

"Okay, so . . ." Storm said, then turned to Xi Bang. "I'm sorry, what does this have to do with four dead bankers?"

"Well, I can show you if you like," Click said, hefting himself out from behind his desk. "Come with me."

STORM AND XI BANG FOLLOWED CLICK DOWN A HALLWAY, INTO A stairwell, then down some steps into the basement. Click turned into a room with several towers of servers, most of them at least as tall as he was. He sauntered up to one of them that had a keyboard and monitor built into the middle.

"Sorry to make you walk," Click said. "I could access this from my desktop, but it takes forever to load, and I already have the model running down here."

"I think I can handle the exercise," Storm assured him.

"What you're about to see in operation is the ISSMDM, the Iowa State Sudden Monetary Depreciation Model."

"Everyone in the discipline now calls it 'the Click Theory,'" Xi Bang interjected.

"Yes, well . . . ," Click said, as if all the attention from the enormous world of quantitative economics embarrassed him. He fiddled with the keyboard, then brought up a screen filled with numbers. "Now, bear in mind, this is a computer model of the FX. It's a re-creation of reality, but it's one I've spent four years perfecting. It allows me to predict the impact of a trade within a ninety-nine percent confidence interval."

"Okay, so what am I looking at here?" Storm asked.

Click jabbed a finger at the screen, to a column of numbers expressed to the fifth decimal place. "There's the value of the U.S. dollar relative to a variety of currencies in current market conditions. There's the euro, the Swissie, the Aussie, the loonie, etcetera. I've just put ten up there right now, but obviously I can show you any currency you'd like to see. Here's what happens to the value of the U.S. dollar when you sell a yard of greenbacks for, say, British pounds."

"A yard?"

"Sorry. That's FX slang for a billion."

"The trades are really that large?"

"Some of them, yes," Click said. "You have to recall, a lot of these trades are only making money way out on the margins, and only in very small percentages. So you need to make very large trades in order for it to be worth your time. So, anyhow, here's what happens when I sell a yard of dollars."

Click touched a button. Storm kept his eyes on the numbers.

"But nothing changed," he said.

"Exactly. Nor would we expect it to. With ten trillion in circulation, shifting a billion one direction or another is like trying to move a hurricane with a ceiling fan. Now, here's two yards."

Storm watched as the last number on the screen, the one five spaces over from the decimal point, changed from 7 to 6. "Okay, I see it," Storm said.

"Right. Now here's five yards."

This time, both the last digit and the second-to-last digit moved.

"Got that? Good. Now, here's five yards, executed as a double-back trade," Click said. The third-to-last digit changed, as did the two next to it. "I just affected the value of the U.S. dollar by a tenth of a cent. Still not that big a deal, right? I mean, the value of the dollar can fluctuate more than that on a daily basis and life as we know it goes on just fine."

"Yeah, this doesn't exactly look like financial Armageddon," Storm confirmed.

"Trust me, we're getting closer to Armageddon. Okay. Watch this. Here's ten yards double-backed."

The dollar in Click's model was suddenly worth two cents less. "Still not much, right? But that's because the negative feedback loops haven't swung into action. It takes a little to make that happen. But, in the case of the Korean in 2008, we were talking about a one-hundred-fifty-yard trade—a historically large trade, all in one direction. Nothing like that had ever happened before. And, voilà."

Click pressed a button. The dollar immediately lost seven cents against the British pound. "Now, wait for it . . ." Click said. And, sure enough, Storm and Xi Bang watched a simulated economic disaster unfold: The drop surged to ten cents. Then fourteen cents. Twenty-two cents. Thirty-eight cents.

Click pressed another button and the free fall halted. "I just hit pause. Bear in mind, because this server is so powerful, I'm able to speed up the action so it's happening faster than it would in real life. You just watched about fifteen minutes of simulated action. Now watch what happens when I have my simulated Fed step in to regulate the monetary supply by selling its bonds like it did in 2008."

Click tapped a button, typed a few commands, then stepped back. Sure enough, the dollar quickly regained its lost ground and was soon trading at what appeared to be the same level as before.

"So, basically, no harm, no foul, right?" Click said. "As long as we've got Papa Fed watching our backs, we'll be fine. But watch this. I'm going to execute six trades similar to the Korean trade of 2008, and—this is vital—they're going to happen simultaneously, in six different currencies, all double-backed."

Click's fingers danced across the keyboard for about thirty seconds. Then he said, "Ling, would you like to do the honors? Press this button right here."

Xi Bang slid to the computer keyboard, brushing Storm as she did. He was so engrossed in the demonstration that he nearly— nearly—forgot just how interested he was in seeing to it that their own foreign exchange program continued.

"This one?" she said.

"Yep. Go ahead."

Xi Bang depressed the button and the numbers on the screen jumped at once. The numbers in the column on the left side, representing the U.S. dollar, ticked steadily downward. The column on the right, representing the other currencies, climbed accordingly.

"Now, I'm going to have the Fed intervene, in the same way it did before," Click said.

The numbers on the left side continued their slide. It had no effect. By the time the numbers on the screen finally begin to stabilize, the dollar was a quarter of what it had been.

"What you've just seen would take place in about two hours of real time," Click said. "So we'd be talking about the U.S. dollar losing three quarters of its value in two hours. The instability created in U.S. markets would be almost impossible to fathom. And that's not even counting the ripple effects it would have across the globe. It more than likely would throw the world into a kind of financial Dark Ages that would last . . . well, who knows? Luckily we've never had the chance to find out. Suffice it to say, it would be bad."

"And six traders, spread out across the globe, making large enough trades, could make this happen?" Storm asked.

"Yes," Xi Bang said. "That's a very basic summation of the Click Theory."

"What would happen if it was just four traders?" Storm said.

"It would be enough to trigger the slide, but the Fed could still save it."

"So six is the magic number."

"That's right."

"Is there any way to stop it?" Storm asked.

"Yes, in theory," Click said. "If the Fed sold everything it has—I'm talking everything, including the kitchen sink—it might have an effect. It would be an extraordinary measure on the Fed's part. You literally have to max out the size of the Fed's intervention, and even the model says we'd be looking at a forty-seven percent chance of a correction. Basically, it would be a coin flip as to whether it would work."

"And without the Fed?"

"Armageddon guaranteed," Click said. "Mind you, it's a theoretical model. But the math, once you understand it, is really quite simple."

"Like three plus three equals six?"

"More like any number times zero equals zero."

Storm nodded, then pulled out his phone.

"What are you doing?" Xi Bang asked.

"Following my intuition," Storm said.

STORM STEPPED OUT OF THE SERVER ROOM, CLIMBED BACK UP the steps, then walked outside into the mid-afternoon Iowa sunshine, the kind that made crops grow and Storm squint.

No one would go to all the trouble to engineer a catastrophe unless they had neutralized the Fed's ability to avert it. If Storm was able to find someone who had been tinkering with the Fed—either its personnel or its policy—he would be a lot closer to finding whoever hired Volkov.

And, much as Storm dreaded doing it, he knew he was one phone call away from a man who could probably find out what was happening, a man with his fingers stuck in pies all over Washington. Storm pulled out his satellite phone and pressed each button firmly, deliberately. He had learned this was not the kind of phone call you made lightly.

"What is it, Storm?" Jedediah Jones said, his voice sounding extra gritty, like he had just gulped an additional helping of sand.

Storm inhaled, to give himself one more second to think things through. This was a game he had played with Jones many times, the one where each man decided how much he could afford to show the other—and, more to the point, how much he could get away with holding back. For a man like Jones, information was like an Allen wrench—the more he got, the harder he would turn the screws later. And yet, in this case, there was no avoiding it: Storm would have to give some to get some. Given what he had just heard, there was too much at stake not to engage Jones and his considerable resources.

"I need some of your moles on Capitol Hill to do a little fishing," Storm said.

"Yeah? What kind of fish are they trying to catch?"

"I'm curious if anyone is tinkering with the ability of the Federal Reserve to sell government bonds."

"Really?" Jones said, almost sounding amused, because he knew, too—knew the game had already begun. "And why do you want to know that, Agent Storm? You wondering if now is the right time to invest?"

"Like I said, just curiosity."

"Where are you right now?"

Jones had ways of finding out if he really wanted to know, so Storm didn't bother lying: "Ames, Iowa."

"Ames, Iowa? What's in Ames, Iowa?"

"Mostly corn. But also a major American university."

"Does this have something to do with dead bankers?"

"It might, it might not," said Storm, even if he knew Jones could see through his noncommittal answers. "But probably it does. That's what you've hired me to investigate, after all."

"Yes, I'm aware. Can you give me a little more to go on?"

"Not really. I don't know much myself right now. But maybe you could look into the person at the Fed who does this sort of thing and see if anything has changed about him or her? Maybe it's a different person now? Maybe there's been some kind of procedural change in that department lately? Maybe this person has been compromised in some way?"

"Who might be doing the compromising?" Jones asked.

"Wish I knew," Storm said as he watched some college kids flipping a Frisbee, blissfully unaware of how precarious everything about their way of life had suddenly become.

"So I'm supposed to just nose around the Fed's bond sales department until someone admits they've been taking bribes?" Jones asked. "Any guidance about how I should go about that?"

"Say 'please' a lot," Storm said. "People really like good manners."

"I'll keep that in mind."

"Just trying to be helpful," Storm said, then ended the call.

. . .

WHEN STORM RETURNED TO CLICK'S OFFICE, THE ECONOMIST
handed him a bound copy of the article that had been the basis for
the Click Theory. Storm read it fast, skipping over the equations.
Still, he felt like he was starting to understand it. Having seen the
model in action helped.

"So there's one thing I still don't understand," Storm said, as
much to Xi Bang as to Click. "Say you're the person killing these
bankers. Why? What are you getting out of that? Dr. Click's model
would say you need these bankers alive, acting in concert, not in
a morgue somewhere."

"Well, we've already had some time to think about that and
we have a theory," Xi Bang said. "You have to recall, they were
not just killed. They were tortured first."

"Yeah? So?"

"We believe they were tortured for their MonEx passwords,"
Xi Bang said.

"Translate, please."

"The MonEx Four Thousand is the brand of terminal used by
most major international currency traders," Click said. "Part of
what makes it popular is the speed with which it completes trades,
and that it allows you to access all your accounts through one
interface."

"So if you were looking to pull the so-called Korean trade,
that's what you'd use," Storm said.

"Exactly," Xi Bang said. "So, basically, Volkov is collecting
these passwords for someone else, someone who would know
how to use them to pull off this doomsday scenario."

"Well, then isn't this an easy problem to solve?" Storm said.
"We just call the people who make the MonEx, tell them those accounts have been compromised, and ask for them to be shut down."

Click had started shaking his head midway through Storm's
so-called solution.

"MonEx makes the terminals and licenses the operating system that runs them," Click said. "But for liability reasons, it disavows any control over the accounts created on them or what happens with the accounts. Essentially, MonEx is insulating itself legally from this very sort of thing. It's saying, 'Hey, we just make the tool. What people do with the tool is up to them.' The only person who can terminate an account is the pass code holder. And traders treat their pass codes like something more than gold. They are instructed to share them with absolutely no one. Not their spouses. Not their employers. Not anyone. The idea is that if they should happen to die, the accounts die with them."

"Instead, even though these traders are dead, their accounts live on."

"As far as the MonEx is concerned, they're still alive, yes," Click said.

"But, okay, let's just say Volkov is able to get two more pass codes and is able to feed them to someone who can make the Click Theory a reality? Why would that person want to do that? Who would actually benefit from the dollar plunging in that matter?"

"Anyone could," Click said. "Anyone who has advance knowledge that a market is about to make a dramatic move in one direction can use that knowledge to make an extraordinary profit."

Storm leaned back in his chair, the copy of Click's article resting on his chest as he stared up at the ceiling for a moment.

"And how many people read the *Journal of Global Economics*?" he asked.

"There are maybe a few thousand subscribers spread out across the world," Click said. "Most of those are going to be large university libraries, so there's no telling how many people are actually reading it. There are probably some large, institutional investors that subscribe, maybe a few of the shops on Wall Street. But when you get right down to it, it might be no more than fifteen hundred people, worldwide. Why do you ask?"

"Because," Storm said, "at this point, that's our suspect pool."

CHAPTER 14

NEW YORK, New York.

Time was running short. The ghosts were blinking. There were three of them left, flashing pink-white, pink-white, pink-white. They would soon be deadly again. The window of opportunity was closing fast.

Whitely Cracker waited until the last possible second, until he had all three of the ghosts lined up perfectly. Then he slammed the joystick hard to the right, making Ms. Pac-Man plow through them in quick succession. A jubilant sound escaped the machine. A 400, 600, and 800, packed tightly together, floated toward the air. Victory. Victory. Victory.

Ordinarily, Whitely loved that move. Line 'em up, mow 'em down. The ghosts never knew what hit 'em. Nothing was more satisfying.

Except today, it gave him no satisfaction. And so, even though there were just a few pellets left to gobble before he reached the next screen, he committed video suicide, leaving Ms. Pac-Man to be consumed by the soon-to-be-regenerated ghosts.

Then he left the arcade room. He was still wearing his driving cap and driving gloves, having just made the trip in from Chappaqua. Finally, he took them off and got to work. He had his own ghosts to avoid.

The margin call bothered him, no question. He had played it cool on the tennis court, because no one wants to see their invest-ment manager looking otherwise. But the first thing he had done on returning to the office was take a gander at Lee Fulcher's ac-count. The grand total was $43,509,184.33, and Fulcher wanted everything, right down to those last thirty-three cents. It was just damn inconvenient, to say the least. Whitely was in a moment where he needed more liquidity, not less.

Still, a client was a client. And it was Fulcher's money, after all. Whitely had assigned Teddy Sniff to come up with the cash from whatever holes he could find it in, then done his best to put the whole thing out of his mind.

He settled in front of his MonEx 4000, entered his password, and began making trades—unaware, as ever, about the cameras monitoring him.

Whitely could feel himself growing more serene as he settled in. His brain had been working on what moves to make the entire time he had been playing video games, and he came out swinging. It sometimes surprised Whitely where the trades even came from. At times, it was like they burst unbidden from his subconscious, and he was just following his impulses.

He had just successfully bid on six thousand troy ounces of gold when the instant messenger function on his MonEx filled the top of his screen. It was from another trader in Manhattan.

Thanks for buying that option from me, but why are you just giving me money? You know it's never going to drop that far.

Whitely paused for a second, trying on several possible re-plies. He went with:

What can I say? Consider it corporate welfare.

He went back to his next trade, dumping a few hundred thou-sand shares of a blue chip stock that he had a hunch was going to miss its earnings expectations. Then the IM popped up again, from the same guy:

The great white is up to something.

Having already gone the modest route, Whitely kept with it:

Just trying to make you look good. And I might be willing to do it again. How about Mickey D's at 60?

Having tossed out the bait, he waited to see if the guy would bite. Sure enough, he did.

You're nuts. But sure. How much?

Whitely wrote back quickly.

350?

The man would know he meant 350,000 shares. And he didn't hesitate.

Done. Easiest money I'll make today. I still think you're nuts.

Whitley was considering if he should try to lure the guy into one more supposedly-too-good-to-be-true deal, but he became aware that Theodore Sniff was lurking in his doorway again. Ordinarily, he would have just ignored the accountant. But since he had given Sniff a specific errand, he might as well get it over with.

Whitely looked up. Sniff was wearing a suit that looked like it had been balled up and stuffed in a trash can for several days before he put it on.

"Teddy, did you sleep in that suit or something?" Whitely asked.

"No, I . . . It just came from the cleaners," Sniff said. He was always at a loss to explain his various deficiencies to his boss. Of course, only so much of it was Sniff's fault. It was as much Whitely's incomprehension as anything. Men with perfect hairlines could seldom understand balding.

"Well, tell them to actually press it next time," Whitely said. "Or maybe switch dry cleaners? I'm just trying to look out for you, buddy."

"Thank you."

"By the way, did you get anywhere with that girl from Match dot com?"

"We met for coffee and now she doesn't answer any of my messages," Sniff said. "I winked at her three times, but she just ignored me."

"Well, look on the bright side: It's better than that girl from quote-unquote 'Ridgefield, Connecticut' who turned out to be a Slovenian prostitute," Whitely said. "Anyhow, what's up?"

"It's . . . it's the Fulcher margin call."

"What about it? We ready to deliver? He needs the money by three."

"Yeah, about that . . ." Sniff said, and suddenly he couldn't look at his boss. The carpet in front of him had gotten far more interesting.

"What, Teddy?"

"We don't have it."

"So you keep saying. But how is that even possible?"

"Well, that donation you just made didn't help," Sniff said.

"Still, I . . . I just don't understand: My trades are good. My trades are great. I can count on one hand the ones that go bad in an entire month. I've got to have one of the best win-loss records in the business. How is it *possible* we don't have the money?"

"I'm just telling you what the books are telling me," Sniff said. "The books don't lie."

"Yeah, well . . ." Whitely said, running his hands through his perfect coiffure, actually mussing it slightly.

"So what do we do about Fulcher?"

Whitely stared into the distance. He tented his hands, brought them to his lips, and held them there for ten seconds.

"His margin call is at First National," Whitely said at least. "We know some people there. Call them up and convince them to hold off on the margin call for a week or two. We'll make sure Fulcher knows we did him the favor and tell him to just rest easy, that we'll have the money when the time comes. And by then, we will."

Sniff mumbled something that Whitely couldn't hear. Only the sensitive microphones picked up the words and piped them straight to the eighty-third floor.

And the words were: "I doubt it."

CHAPTER 15

WASHINGTON, D.C.

Donny Whitmer had been up all night.

Normally, that meant drinking booze and chasing tail—the preferred pastimes of powerful men the world over.

But this time was different. Donny Whitmer had discovered, somewhat to his surprise, that even after all those years in Washington, he still had a conscience. And that conscience was in something of a crisis.

It ate at him, what he had done. Threatening his best donor with exposure like that. It was actually making his stomach hurt—to stoop that low after a lifetime of honorable public service. It was so unbecoming of a senator. He tossed and turned in bed until Sissy made him sleep in the guest room.

Somewhere after midnight, the thought occurred to him: In the morning, he'd call the guy and tell him he didn't mean it. It was a bluff. It was said out of anger or out of fear. No, better yet, it was a joke. Ha ha, good one, right, buddy? Because ol' Donny would never do something like that.

The next morning, before Donny even finished his coffee, Jack Porter was back in his office. They had done some more polling. There were more charts and graphs. The Tea Party sumbitch had much better name recognition than anyone had realized, much lower negatives than seemed possible, and what's more, there were fewer undecided than there should have been six weeks out.

In other words, the problem was worse than Donny had thought. Yesterday had been a little dreamlike—nightmare-like— but today the reality was setting in. He might really be done. He found himself ignoring Porter and looking around his office, at the view of the Capitol that he commanded from his corner office, at all the knickknacks and plaques and commendations he had collected over the years, and he just didn't want to pack them up. He wasn't ready to be done.

More than that, the *people of Alabama* couldn't afford to lose him. All those pork barrel projects he shoveled their way meant jobs. And jobs meant everything. This neophyte Tea Party jerk wouldn't have a clue how to work the levers of government to get that sort of thing. The sumbitch would probably sell his political soul trying to back a long-shot Supreme Court pick who had promised to overturn *Roe v. Wade*. How many paving contracts would that provide to the constituents? None. The thought bothered Donny even more than the thought that he wouldn't be able to boss around lobbyists anymore.

Eventually, he had booted Porter from his office, closed his door, and told everyone not to bother him. He needed to think.

Five million dollars. And, really, only one place to get it. All his other top donors had Alabama ties. They would have sniffed out that Donny was in trouble and therefore would know he was desperate and therefore wouldn't give him a dime. The *Birmingham News* had not done any polling yet, but it had written some flattering stories about his challenger and about the grassroots devotion he seemed to be engendering.

Donny had to put more pressure on his best donor. That was his silver bullet. He had threatened exposure of the rider. That was a good start. What if he also . . .

The phone rang.

It was his donor.

The donor who was the senator's last chance to change all that red on Jack Porter's charts to lovely, luscious green.

"Hello there, young man," Donny said.

He listened.

"No, no, you're not interrupting anything. And, besides, it's a pleasure to hear from you. Always a pleasure."

As if Donny hadn't just threatened the man the day before. The man was talking, and Donny realized he was holding his breath. Why couldn't the guy just cut to the chase, say he was giving him the money, and end it there? Or maybe he could just say he wasn't giving him the money and Donny would accept . . . Hang on. Did Donny really just hear that right? Yes. Yes, he did.

"Well, that's mighty generous of you," Whitmer said. " 'The Alabama Future Fund.' That sounds mighty fine."

Donny stood from his desk and strolled to the window to admire the Capitol. Maybe he'd get to keep this view after all.

"Well, of course, we could put another name at the head of the PAC. Whoever you wanted. Doesn't matter to us, as long as . . ."

Donny listened for a moment.

"Yes, yes. The PAC has to list its donors, but . . ."

Donny looked for his putter. He needed to do something with his hands.

"Well, there are things you can do on your end to obscure the origin of the money if that's how you'd like to do it. That's not hard. Or we can do it on our end. I could have my lawyer do that part if you'd like. It's the least I can . . ."

Forget the putter. His hands were shaking too badly. Five million bucks. Alabama was about to get itself a big dose of Donny Whitmer.

"Oh, no. Don't worry. There is not the slightest chance it could be traced back to you. We can even split it up five ways so it looks like it's coming from five different places. You can trust ol' Donny now. You wire that money over and we'll take care of it."

Donny was so excited—and so worried he'd forget the

details—that he turned to the next fresh page on his legal pad. He wrote "ALABAMA FUTURE FUND" and "$5 MILLION" and "SPLIT INTO FIVE LLC'S." Then he wrote "THANK YOU" and the donor's name, and underlined it three times so he'd remembered to write a nice thank-you card. Manners were manners, after all.

"Well, I have to tell you, I really do appreciate this. And you better believe I'll remember next time you need anything. You just call ol' Donny, you hear?"

Right. Maybe it wasn't extortion after all. It was just another favor being done in a town full of favors.

He ended the call, his hands still shaking. It was all being put in play. With the five million in place, Donny's people would be able to make a media buy that would start hitting next week.

Then see what goddamned Jack Porter's charts would look like.

CHAPTER 16

AMES, Iowa

If he had been in Florence, Derrick Storm would have known at least three restaurants that would have been just perfect—two with a view of the Ponte Vecchio and one tucked high in the hills near the Basilica di San Miniato al Monte. At his favorite spot in Jakarta, he wouldn't have needed to look at the menu, just ordered a prawn nasi goreng that would have blown his date's mind. In San Francisco, he had a hideout where the maître d' would have escorted him to his preferred table and opened a bottle of Joseph Phelps Insignia without Storm even having to ask.

In Ames, Iowa, he was stuck driving around aimlessly until he found a Buffalo Wild Wings.

A franchised eatery wedged between a Target and a Pizza Hut was not, perhaps, the first place anyone would think to look for two international operatives in the middle of investigating a plot to cripple the global economy. But after a series of meals that had consisted of whatever the airline put in the box, they were ravenous. And the beer was cold. And there was nothing like a heaping pile of spicy wings to clear the mind, to say nothing of the sinuses.

It had been a productive afternoon and early evening with Dr. Rodney Click. Storm and Xi Bang had rounded out their education on the foreign exchange markets. They had received an introduction into the workings of the MonEx 4000, for what little good that did. They had tried a variety of scenarios on the Iowa State Sudden Monetary Depreciation Model.

Then Storm had put Click to work: Now that they knew the Click Theory was being put into practice, could he use his model to predict which bankers might be targeted? Which bankers would be most likely to have the influence needed to pull off Armageddon?

Click said he'd work on it through the night and get back to them in a day. Or maybe two. If he was lucky. Then he shooed Storm and Xi Bang out. The Buffalo Wild Wings had been their first stop.

"I have to admit," Storm said, after they had both knocked the edge off their hunger, "I always feel a little guilty eating Buffalo wings."

"Why?" Xi Bang asked, wiping sauce from her chin.

"It's just thinking of all those poor buffalos, wandering around the Great Plains without their wings, grounded forever."

"Oh, stop."

"Well, seriously, have you ever *seen* a buffalo with wings?" Storm asked.

She rolled her eyes, swallowed the last quarter of her beer in one gulp, and motioned for the waitress to bring her another.

"Time to catch up, Nurse," she said, nodding at Storm's glass, still half-full.

"How do I know you haven't spiked this with something while my back was turned? Maybe it's rotten with Rohypnol and you're going to take me back to a hotel room and take advantage of me."

"Maybe I am," she said.

Storm's response was to tilt back his beer and drink until it, too, was empty. Xi Bang just laughed. She had left her silk dresses and traffic accident–causing skirts back in Europe and donned attire that was less conspicuous: black slacks, a fitted charcoal turtleneck, heels that were a mere four inches. She was still stunning— there was nothing she could wear, short of a king-sized sheet, to hide that—but at least she wasn't calling as much attention to herself.

Storm was also dressed comfortably: fashionably cut jeans, open-collar shirt, cashmere blazer. He had gotten his share of flirty smiles from the hostess and the waitress—that whole ruggedly handsome thing—but he had ignored them. There had been some waitresses and hostesses in his past, and there would likely be more in the future. But women like Ling Xi Bang—intelligent, worldly, mysterious—were far more interesting to him.

"Okay, so, seriously, when were you on to me?" she asked.

"Well, I was curious from the start," Storm said. "I've been around a lot of media events, but I'm not sure I've ever seen a press secretary as gorgeous as you."

She looked down, blushing.

"But what really did it was when I asked you whether you preferred Roma's or Geno's."

"The pizza places. You made them both up," she said. "I should have known. They threw this backstory at me last-minute, and I just didn't have time to research it like I usually would. I don't usually do a lot of undercover work. I'm mostly an analyst. They only put me in the field this time because one of my areas of expertise is finance."

"So all that poor-little-Ling-from-Qinghai stuff, that was all made up, right?"

"Every word of it," she said.

"You sold it well. I was ready to believe that part."

"Thanks."

"So where did you get your English from? You must have spent some time in America. You have too many American idioms not to have."

"My parents sent me to a boarding school in Virginia," she said. "Not in the D.C. area where you grew up. Way down south, in the tidewater part of the state. Most of what I learned about espionage started with sneaking off after lights out and meeting up with boys behind the field house. That and hiding cigarettes."

"Boarding school, huh? Your parents must have been well off."

She nodded. "My grandfather, my mother's father, was high up in the party," she said. "He used his influence to arrange my mother's marriage to a wealthy businessman from Shanghai. That's where I really grew up. The part about Peking University is true, though. I really did graduate in the top of my class. My father wanted me to go into his business. But I knew that was really code for: *Go into my business for a few years until I marry you off to whichever vice president I want to take over the company when I retire.* I didn't want any part of that."

"So how did you end up with the Ministry of State Security?"

"Who says I'm with the Ministry of State Security?" she said, letting only the slightest smile slip.

Storm affected a German accent: "Ve haff vays of making you talk, Agent Xi Bang."

"My grandfather still had party connections," she continued. "He got me an internship in the Ministry of State Security. That seemed a lot more interesting a path than becoming someone's wife."

"Do you ever think about marriage?" he asked.

"Why, Agent Storm, are you proposing?"

"I thought I already did. We're going to dance to 'The Vienna Waltz' at our wedding, remember?"

Fresh beers arrived on the table. A Widmer Brothers Drifter Pale Ale for her. An Arrogant Bastard Ale for him.

"Okay, so what about you?" he said. "When were you on to me?"

"Cheers again," she said, touching her glass to his.

"Cheers again," Storm said. "And stop stalling. I showed you mine. You show me yours: When did you figure me out?"

"I was suspicious the moment I laid eyes on you," Xi Bang said. "The way the other correspondents looked at you, I could tell you weren't part of the usual herd. Plus, that jacket? Atrocious. The media actually dresses a lot nicer than that these days."

"Well, the correspondents from *Soy Trader Weekly* are noted for their down-to-earth apparel," Storm said.

"Ah, yes, *Soy Trader Weekly*. Nice website, by the way. But that's how we actually made you."

"How? That website was perfect."

"Yeah, too perfect," Xi Bang said. "When our techs tried to hack it, they couldn't. It had CIA encryption on it. You want to tell me *Soy Trader Weekly* has access to that?"

"Amateur mistake," Storm said, making a mental note to tell Jedediah Jones about that flaw.

They dove back into the pile of wings, doing an efficient, if messy, job of shrinking it. Storm, as usual, ate like he had an empty leg. But Xi Bang held her own. And when the waitress came and asked if they wanted seconds, they shared a half second of silent communication before deciding, yeah, that would be fine.

"So you know your reputation precedes you in the Chinese intelligence community," Xi Bang said as they waited for the next round of wings to arrive. "From the stories that circulate, I figured 'Derrick Storm' was actually an amalgam of several different American operatives."

"Nope. Just me. What made you think that?"

"I don't know. I just assumed that all of what I heard couldn't be true. Or that if it was true, it had to be multiple agents' legends rolled into one."

"I guess it depends on what you heard."

"Were you in Morocco a few years ago?" she asked.

Storm just shrugged.

"What about 'The Fear?' Did you really take him out?"

He said nothing. But Xi Bang caught his tell: The corner of his mouth pulled up a fraction of an inch.

"There's also a rumor you once killed an enemy agent with a melon baller."

"People exaggerate," Storm said at last, shaking his head. "It was an ice cream scoop."

She checked to see if he was kidding. He wasn't. She knew better than to ask for details.

"So," he said, switching subjects with the tone of his voice, "it looks like our interests in this current case are aligned."

"Kind of strange for two countries that act like enemies half the time, isn't it?" she said. "But, yes, my people want Volkov stopped as bad as your people."

"If I may ask, what are your orders?"

"Probably the same as yours: If I see Volkov, I shoot to kill," she said. "My country still talks a big game about Communism, but the fact is there are very powerful business interests that have substantial influence on the party. Those interests have made it clear that a strong U.S. dollar is their priority. And therefore my bosses have made it clear this thing with Volkov is my priority. My role is supposed to be more investigative, but if I get a shot . . ."

"I understand," Storm said. "We should work together."

"Work together?"

"We can go back to being enemies later," Storm promised. "I'll even let you tie me up."

"That sounds great, but . . . can we do that?"

"Sure, you just take some rope and . . ."

"No, I mean can we really work together? I mean, I know we've been doing that informally. But I'm not sure if I can formally . . ."

"Formal, informal—doesn't matter," Storm said, dismissing the thought with a backhanded wave. Sure, Jones and his superiors in the high reaches of the CIA would have a fit if they knew Storm was in bed—literally and figuratively—with a Chinese agent. But this wasn't the first time Storm had made an alliance that the CIA wouldn't approve of. Besides, wasn't that why Jones hired him? To do things that Jones and the agency couldn't do themselves? To give them plausible deniability when it all went wrong?

"All your people are going to care about is that the job is done," Storm continued. "Same with my people. We've got to figure out who hired Volkov and stop whoever is behind it. We're going to be a lot more likely to accomplish that working together and sharing information.

"Besides," he added, "I don't want to have to chase you up any more skyscrapers."

"What? Can't a girl play hard to get?"

"I hope not, Agent Xi Bang," he said, grinning. "I sincerely hope not."

THERE WERE FIVE FLIGHTS A DAY OUT OF THE AMES MUNICIPAL Airport, none of which left after dusk. Yes, one phone call to Jedediah Jones would change that. Yes, there were other ways out of Iowa.

But Derrick Storm and Ling Xi Bang told themselves they were stuck, stranded and marooned until morning. And, in any event, they had nowhere to go—at least not until Click's model gave them some answers or, sadly, until Banker No. 5 met his end.

So it was that they ended up at making a short stumble up the street to a Days Inn. They decamped in Room 214, then subjected anyone unfortunate enough to be inhabiting Room 212 or 216 to something that might have sounded like a TV at too high a volume, tuned to Animal Planet.

Then, after a short respite, they did it again.

Later, as they lay naked, the sheets a tumble at the bottom of the bed, Storm let his fingertips follow a meandering path across Xi Bang's rib cage, stomach, and thighs. He was propped on one elbow. She was lying flat, her eyes fixed on some point in the darkness, enjoying his touch.

She broke the stillness by asking, "Was the cupcake story true?"

"Yeah, actually, it was," Storm said. "Every bit of it."

"Do you remember your mother?"

"Not really."

"So it was just you and your dad?"

"Yeah, but it's not like I ever felt I was missing anything," he said. "You can't miss what you never knew in the first place. I have a great dad. That's enough."

"I can't believe he never remarried."

"Forget remarried. He's never even dated," Storm said. "He acts like replacing her in any fashion would be an act of betrayal. I think his general attitude is that she was the love of his lifetime, the one and only, and that to behave otherwise would diminish that somehow."

"I can't decide whether that's romantic or sad."

"Maybe it's a bit of both," Storm said.

"What do you think? Is there one or are there many?"

"I believe that the human capacity to love is not a one-shot deal."

"So that's how it is for you, Storm? Love as a hundred-round magazine? Set the gun on automatic and spray it around?"

"I never said that," Storm said. "Love is like a bullet, though. You know the instant you've been hit. And even if it's just a glancing blow, you're never quite the same. The bullet either buries itself deep inside you, or it takes some piece of you away with it."

He was thinking about Clara Strike when he said it. How many chunks of him had she taken out over the years? And yet how many times did he keep returning to face the firing squad?

"I see you have a lot of scars, Derrick Storm," Xi Bang said, tracing a network of forever-puckered skin on his abdomen. If only she knew how deep some of them went.

"What about you?" he asked. "Ever been in love?"

"I've dated," she said.

"I didn't ask about dated. I asked about love. Real love. The kind of person who's always with you, even if your lives take you in very opposite directions."

"Maybe," she said.

"What does that mean?"

Her response was to close her eyes and hum "The Vienna Waltz." "We should dance some more," she said.

"You can . . . ," Storm began, then was interrupted by his satellite phone ringing.

"You have to take that," she said.

"No. I can ignore it."

"Either you answer it or I will. And then you'll have a lot of questions to answer from whoever is on the other line."

"You're tough, Ling Xi Bang."

"You have no idea."

Storm rolled over, groped around until he found his pants on the floor, and fished the phone out of his pocket. The caller ID came in as restricted. Hello, Langley, Virginia.

"This had better be good," Storm said.

"It is," the pebble-riddled voice of Jedediah Jones informed him.

"Well, talk then," Storm said, shifting so Xi Bang could hear it.

"Is someone else there?" Jones asked. Storm sometimes swore his phone had a camera hidden on it, but he had yet to find it.

"No. Just me."

"That question you asked me about looking for someone at the Federal Reserve who is capable of playing with the Fed's government bond sales?"

"Yeah?"

"Turns out you were on the right track. You just had the wrong institution."

"Oh?"

"Are you familiar with Senator Donald Whitmer of Alabama?"

"Donny Whitmer? Yeah. Sure. What about him?"

"Three weeks ago, he snuck a rider into an appropriations bill that puts limits on the Federal Reserve's ability to sell bonds."

"In other words, he wiped out the last possible buttress to preventing the currency destabilization predicted in the Click Theory."

"Exactly. We have no idea why he's done this or who he might have done it for. But it feels like too big a coincidence to be dis-

missed. Whitmer usually uses his pull to lavish pork on his constituents, not pass obscure-sounding policy changes."

"What's your theory?" Storm asked.

"Well, here's an interesting little fact: The word is that Senator
Whitmer has a big primary battle on his hands and that it isn't going well. Donors have been jumping off his ship like they know
it's sinking. And then suddenly, right when he needed it most,
someone formed a Political Action Committee to support Senator
Whitmer. It's called the 'Alabama Future Fund' and it already has
five million bucks in it."

"Think it's some form of bribery?" Storm asked. "Whitmer
adds the rider in exchange for five million bucks?"

"Either that, or Whitmer called a chip in when he realized he
was in trouble."

"Either way, it's something we need to look at. And hard. Whoever put all that money into that PAC is probably the person who
hired Volkov," Storm said.

"Or maybe it's a group of people, but yes. The only problem is
we don't know who it is."

"Doesn't a PAC have to list its donors?"

"Eventually, yes. But a PAC can choose to report its donors on
a quarterly basis, and the quarter isn't over yet."

"Well, okay, so can't the nerds figure it out?"

"Yes, but it won't get us far. If someone wants to obscure the
source of PAC funding, it's as easy as creating a limited liability
corporation. I'll bet you a case of Scotch that the PAC's donor
will turn out to be an LLC with a post office box in Delaware."

"No bet," Storm said, knowing Jones was right. "So what are
you proposing?"

"I'm going to make myself an appointment with Senator Whitmer and find a subtle way to inquire who his sugar daddy is," Jones
said. "But I have to set it up right, go through channels, talk to
some lawyers. It might take some time."

"We don't have time," Storm said.

"That's the only way, Storm."

"We've got four dead bankers already. Who knows when the fifth and sixth are going to fall? These are men with families. We can't just sacrifice them because you have to be polite. If you don't have the guts to do it, I will. I'll go to Washington and ask him myself."

"Storm, under no circumstance are you to engage the senator, do you understand? That's a direct order."

"Why are you stalling?" Storm barked.

And then Storm answered his own question. Donny Whitmer was the chairman of the Senate Appropriations Committee, a powerful man who controlled the lid of the cookie jar that was government spending. Jones didn't want to risk having his hand slapped away from the cookie jar. This was all about Jones's budget, his preservation of the chunk of bureaucratic turf he had carved out for himself.

"Just stay the hell away from the senator," Jones said. "I'll handle this."

"Fine," Storm said, then ended the call.

"What's going on?" Xi Bang asked.

He filled her in on the half of the conversation she had missed.

"So what's our next move?" Xi Bang asked.

"Jones said I couldn't engage the senator," Storm said. "He didn't say anything about you doing it. And it turns out Senator Whitmer has a certain reputation as being . . . fond of the ladies. Think you can go to Washington and, uhh, talk with Senator Whitmer? Maybe figure out who this donor is?"

Xi Bang rolled her eyes. "Washington and Beijing are supposed to be so different. Capitalists versus Communists. Two-party versus one-party. Americans versus Hans. But underneath it, they're all just a bunch of dirty old men."

"Dirty old men are a universal constant across cultures," Storm confirmed. "So will you do it?"

A knowing grin spread across Ling Xi Bang's face. Then she immediately snapped into character, and a perfect accent from somewhere deep within the American South poured out of her. "Why, shoot, sugar britches, I'd just looove to have a little chat with the senator," she said.

"That's the spirit."

"The only question I have is how I get into his office," she said. "You can't just stroll into those buildings."

"You can when you know the people I do," Storm said. "Just get yourself on the ground in D.C. I'll take care of you from there."

CHAPTER 17

JOHANNESBURG, South Africa

I t was all going wrong. Just awful, dead, horribly wrong.

Volkov had entered the operation a man down as it was. Not that Yuri had been much help when it came time to doing the wet work, but he'd been a warm body who knew how to pull a trigger. He'd had his uses. Nevertheless, Volkov had opted against hiring local help to augment his numbers. He never trusted locals, and besides, five men—five of *his* men, anyway—would be enough to do this job.

Naturally, there were security forces to contend with. Volkov had counted on that—every white person with more than two rands to rub together in South Africa had armed security forces, and a wealthy banker like Jeff Diamant had enough to afford a good one. As a result, Volkov and his men had spent a day doing their usual surveillance, locating the weak points in the ten-acre compound where Diamant resided, assessing security patrol patterns, figuring out where the cameras were located, finding the threats that needed to be disabled, making their plan.

Everyone's role had been quite clear. They would each approach the main house through the trees that surrounded it, each coming from a different direction, quietly deactivating the various security apparatus he met along the way. They would surprise and kill each one of the seven guards who were stationed at various points throughout the compound. They would silently raid the main house and find Diamant and his wife asleep in bed. They would do what they came to do, what they always did.

The plan was perfect. Volkov never moved on a target with anything less.

Then Nicolai, who had been assigned to the south approach, had forgotten to take out the pit bulls that were known to guard that area. It was the first thing he was supposed to do after short-circuiting the electric fence and scaling the compound wall: find the sleeping dogs using his thermal night vision goggles, fix the silencer on his gun, and put two well-aimed bullets in the dogs' heads.

Instead, Nicolai just inexplicably blundered on through, forgetting about the dogs entirely. The brutes woke up, making a bawling racket as they charged. Nicolai was able to kill the first from about five feet, but the second one managed to sink its teeth into Nicolai's thigh. Nicolai beat the dog with the gun butt and finally shot it dead. But by that point, the dogs were no longer his biggest problem. He had not had time to put his silencer on, so if the baying dogs hadn't alerted everyone to his presence, the gun-shots surely had. Nicolai was still trying to pry the dead dog's jaws open and get the thing's teeth out of his thigh when a security guard put a double tap between Nicolai's eyes.

From there, everything was just a mess. An alarm sounded. Floodlights positioned all around the main house instantly flashed on, illuminating the two hundred feet of lawn surrounding the house. Lights also came on inside the guardhouse and the main house. The guards sprang to life. They were surprisingly well coordinated, as if they had trained for this sort of thing and were merely implementing an oft-drilled exercise. They fanned out over the compound, immediately discovering two more of Volkov's men, making their approaches from the southwest and southeast, respectively. A gun battle ensued. Yes, Volkov's men got their shots in, killing one guard and wounding another. But they didn't last long. Just like that, it was five against two. There was only

Volkov, coming in from the northwest, and Viktor, approaching from due east.

Then they found Viktor. He also put up a fight, taking out two more security guards. But he was ultimately outflanked and ended up taking a bullet to the side of his head.

Volkov didn't know any of this yet—or at least he didn't know precisely. He had just heard a lot of gunfire and was aware his men were no longer responding on radio. This was more than enough to tell him his carefully constructed plan was now a pathetic shambles.

Any other man might have at least considered aborting the mission. Not Volkov. He just retreated and reassessed, scrambling up a chunky baobab tree that gave him a view of the entire compound. This was not yet a loss. Just a setback.

He surveyed the scene with his thermal goggles, using their telephoto function to zoom in and out until he located all four of his men's bodies, confirming that he was now alone. He also found the three dead security guards and watched as the wounded one joined the healthy three in withdrawing back to the main house.

Volkov knew that for whatever training they had, they would still be terrified and uncertain. If he waited, they might think the attack had ended and then he'd be able to move on the house and pick them off. Four against one—rather, three and a half against one—was not particularly daunting to a man of Volkov's ability.

That changed quickly when the South African Police Service arrived. They came in force, with five marked cars and three unmarked pulling through the front gate and parking in the broad, circular driveway adjacent to the main house. Volkov counted fourteen cops disembarking from those vehicles. Fourteen cops plus three remaining healthy security guards. Volkov could handle four-to-one. Seventeen-to-one was beyond even him.

Then more forces arrived. Crime scene techs. Other cops, whose purpose he could not immediately identify. Some uniformed. Others not. It was a small army against one man.

All the one man had was the element of surprise. They didn't know he was out there. They would make the assumption that they had either killed all of the invaders, or that any other thugs had run off when the gun battle turned against them.

Sure enough, the cops soon began overtaking the grounds as if they owned the place and had nothing to fear. The bulk of them busied themselves by throwing up lights over the bodies of Volkov's fallen teammates, then hustling and bustling around the corpses, taking photos and collecting shell casings.

But four of them, all uniformed officers, began combing the compound with flashlights, likely looking for other evidence. They spread out—ten acres was a lot of ground to cover—and made the terrible mistake of not working in pairs. Volkov noted their vulnerability, but hadn't decided how to capitalize on it until a meat wagon from the local coroner's office arrived. It was as he watched Nicolai getting carted away that he formulated his new plan.

Volkov waited until one of the officers, a young constable, was directly under his tree. He dropped on him from above. With two hundred twenty pounds landing on top of him at high velocity, the man immediately went down, letting out a muffled grunt as he fell. Not giving him a chance to make another sound, Volkov clamped one hand on the cop's mouth then wrapped his arm around the constable's neck. The young man—really, not much more than a boy—struggled briefly but was soon asphyxiated. He was no match for Volkov's enormous strength.

Once he was sure the constable was dead, Volkov released his grip and began pulling off the man's uniform and then putting it on himself, starting with the hat and working down. It was far from a perfect fit, but Volkov wasn't attending a police fashion show. Mostly, he was relying on the fact that it was dark. He rolled the sleeves of the shirt and used his knife to do a quick, barbaric alteration on the length of the pants. He donned the man's utility belt and his gun. He could feel the weight of the constable's car keys in his front pocket and a wallet in his back one.

Volkov knew he had no time to get rid of the body properly.

He improvised, leaning it up against the trunk of the tree on the opposite side of the house, where it would remain in shadows until morning. Good enough. He began walking through the trees toward the main house.

Now for the nervy part: the two hundred feet of open turf between the wooded parts of the property and the house. Pulling the dead cop's hat low over his face, he passed by teams of crime scene techs and medical examiners, albeit with his face in shadow. They paid him no attention. Volkov entered through the front door without encountering any resistance.

Once inside, he was relieved to discover there was no police presence. The assailants, as far as the investigators knew, had not made it in or near the house. Volkov moved through the rooms with confidence, until he came across one of the security guards, sitting in a chair outside a closed door. Volkov could hear classical music coming from inside. He squared his body to the man.

"Can I help you, mate?" the man asked.

"Yes," Volkov said. "Can you tell me what time it is?"

The moment the man looked toward his watch, Volkov reached down, grabbing the man's chin and the back of his head simultaneously and giving them a violent, counterclockwise twist. For Volkov, it was like unscrewing the cap of a large tube of toothpaste. The man's neck snapped easily. The crunching of vertebrae was the only sound it made. Volkov dragged the man off the chair, hauled him into a nearby closet, and left him there. Volkov was not absolutely certain the man was dead, but it didn't matter: He was unconscious, and if he ever did awaken, it wasn't as if he would be able to crawl out. Volkov would be long gone by then.

He went back to the room the man had been guarding and opened the door. Volkov walked fast, like a man who knew exactly what he was doing and why he was there.

Diamant was sitting at a desk, listening to Rachmaninoff. Volkov couldn't help but silently approve of the choice and almost—almost—felt bad to kill a man of such surpassing good taste. The composer represented all that was great about the culture of Volkov's motherland.

Diamant's gaze lifted as Volkov drew near.

"Mr. Diamant, I'm Officer Gregor Volkov," he said, not bothering to come up with a different name. At least it would help explain the Russian accent.

"What can I do for you, Officer?" Diamant asked. He looked weary, confused. This was to Volkov's advantage. So was Volkov's own obvious disfigurement. He saw Diamant fixate briefly on his eye patch and facial scars, but then Diamant quickly looked away. Like many people, Diamant was too polite to stare.

"We've set up our temporary morgue about a mile down the road," he said. "We've got the first of the assailants down there now. It would help us a lot if you would come down and take a look at him."

"But the inspector already showed me pictures. I told him: I don't know any of them."

"I'm aware of that," Volkov lied smoothly. "But sometimes seeing a body in the flesh can change that. Maybe you'll notice a tattoo that looks familiar."

"Can't . . . can't it wait? I'm not sure I—"

"The inspector says time is important," Volkov said. "Maybe you know the perps, maybe you don't. To be honest, sir, I'm just trying to follow orders. And the inspector said to bring you down to the temporary morgue."

Diamant shook his head but said, "Very well."

The banker obediently followed Volkov out of the main house and into the driveway. This was the last part Volkov worried about—he had car keys in his pocket, but he didn't know which vehicle they belonged to. He slid them out, pressed the unlock button on the key fob, and hoped it made something happen. He didn't want to have to hit the alarm button.

After a brief delay, the lights on one of the patrol cars quickly flashed. Volkov allowed himself a quick, smug smile as he opened the back door for Diamant. Once inside, the man would have no way of escaping. Cop cars were good that way.

"I greatly appreciate your cooperation, sir," Volkov said. "Oh, and I must say, that's a nice manicure you have."

He closed the door. The fifth MonEx code would soon be his. Then he would hire a new team—which was never hard for a man with Volkov's connections—and go after the final name on his list.

In some ways, it was the most important. It was the one in New York, after all.

IT WAS TO THE CONSTERNATION OF THE SOUTH AFRICAN POLICE Service inspector approximately two hours later when someone finally realized that the young constable who had been sent to the northwest corner of the property had not reported back in some time.

The inspector tried to reach the constable on the radio and failed. Then someone noticed his patrol car was missing.

They put out a bulletin for the car, thinking it was a weird act of insubordination on the part of a young officer who had inexplicably bailed on an important crime scene. Didn't he know better?

Then a member of Diamant's security forces went to relieve the man standing guard outside of the banker's office and found only an empty chair. He knocked on the door and got no answer. He went inside the office. Diamant was not there.

Nor was he in the bedroom. Nor the kitchen. Nor, seemingly, anywhere else inside the house or on the grounds.

The private security guard took the news of Diamant's disappearance to the inspector, who was already trying to make sense of his officer going AWOL.

Sometime later, off a little-used road, the rear bumper of a police patrol car was spotted half-sunk in a swamp. Sometime after that, around sunrise, the officer's body was encountered slumped against the tree trunk on Diamant's property. The security guard with the snapped neck was found in the closet within the hour.

And then, the terrible discovery by a child on his way to school: a corpse that had been secured with police handcuffs to a jackalberry tree. The body was missing all the fingernails on its right hand. It was quickly identified as the body of Jeff Diamant of Standard Rand Bank.

It took another hour or so for the authorities to unravel the whole mystery, and another hour or so beyond that for the thing to be put in the Interpol computer. From there, the flags went up. Interpol performed its notification protocol quickly.

Jedediah Jones got the call around 5 A.M. East Coast time, just as he was coming in from his daily run. Jones waited until a slightly more decent hour to call Derrick Storm and tell him the fifth banker was now dead. They had already put out the necessary bulletins for Gregor Volkov, but it was redundant. He was already on every Do Not Fly and Most Wanted list across the world. And yet he had once again disappeared into the mist.

CHAPTER 18

AMES, Iowa

The circles under his puffy eyes were dark enough to stand out under the John Lennon glasses. The coffee cup next to him practically had scorch marks from being refilled so often. There was a slight shake to his mouse hand.

If Rodney Click looked like he had been up all night, it was no accident. He had been.

Derrick Storm had not slept much either, albeit for a different reason. But eventually he got that reason—Ling Xi Bang—on the first flight out of Ames, heading for Des Moines and ultimately Washington, D.C. It was around 9 A.M. when Storm walked into Click's tiny office.

Storm wasn't sure he had ever seen such a large man so close to tears. He was mumbling to himself, making little sense to Storm, whose mathematical education ended with Mrs. Beauregard's twelfth-grade calculus class. Click's speech was spiked with phrases like "inputs are just too variable" and "not enough firm data points" and "can't determine the effective calculability" and a whole lot of other things Storm couldn't even parse. It sounded like a mathematician's brain had been split open and was now randomly spilling nonsense.

Storm went around behind the distraught man, put a hand on his shoulder, and spoke in the calm tone of a first-grade teacher.

"Doctor," Storm said. "Could you maybe tell me what the problem is . . . in English?"

"I just can't . . . I can't get the algorithm to give me anything," Click said. "Or at least not anything that I would consider reliable. Put simply, the ISSMDM is designed to only go one direction. You tell it what trades you've made, where you've made them and by whom, and it predicts the result of that trade on relative currency values. I've spent four years perfecting its function, but I've never once tried to make it go the other way—taking a result and then backtracking to the potential source. I thought yesterday I could do it with a few simple modifications, but now . . ."

And then he launched on a long description of what he had tried to do, the vast majority of which was totally inexplicable. Storm listened—sometimes, he had learned, it was important to make people feel heard, whether you actually understood them or not. He made all the right active listening sounds. When he was sure Click was done, Storm patted the man's shoulder again. He walked around to the other side of the desk, then sat down. An idea was coming to him. He looked at the books lining the walls, out the narrow window to the campus below, then back at the man-mountain of an assistant professor.

"What if we started in a different place?" Storm said. "You're asking your model to do a lot of hard work, but in this case, there's a bad guy who has already done a lot of the work for us. Five-sixths of it, to be exact. We already know who five of the victims are."

"I thought it was just four," Click said.

"There was a fifth last night. A South African named Jeff Diamant."

"Diamant," Click said solemnly. "I actually met him at a conference once. A wonderful man. Not at all like most of the others in his field. No ego on him. Very soft-spoken, actually. That's just . . . that's awful."

The men shared an impromptu moment of silence.

"So, as I was saying, what if we take what we know about the five bankers, put that into the model, and ask it to tell us who has a similar profile? Let's work from what's known as opposed to trying to start from scratch," Storm said, then started ticking off the names on his fingers. "Dieter Kornblum. Joji Motoshige. Wilhelm Sorenson. Nigel Wormsley. And now Jeff Diamant. What do they share? What can we glean about them that will allow us to learn who Unlucky Number Six is before it's too late?"

Click tugged on his long beard. "That sounds nice in theory, but we don't have the data. The only information I have about them is the trades they've made. I'd need a whole lot more. You'd pretty much have to hack the FX mainframe, and good luck with that. If I said that thing is the encryption equivalent of Fort Knox, I'd actually be insulting FX. Fort Knox would be easy compared to that. No one could hack that thing."

A smile spread across Storm's face. "Wanna bet?" he said.

Storm pulled out his phone and put in a call to the cubby. Agent Rodriguez answered.

"Javi, it's Storm. Are the nerds occupied with anything at the moment?"

"Yes, but I can un-occupy them if you say 'pretty please,'" Rodriguez said.

"Make it with sugar on top. I need them to break into the foreign exchange market mainframe and give us some information. Think they can handle that?"

"About as easy as you handle that ugly Ford Taurus you drive."

"Hey, no bashing the finest automotive company in the world. I'll report you to the House Un-American Activities Committee."

"You gotta stop reading those old spy novels, Storm. The Cold War is over, bro. Hang on, let me put you directly in touch with one of the nerds."

The line went silent for a minute or so, then Storm found himself talking with a young woman who made it sound like breaking into the ForEx mainframe was roughly on the same difficulty level as ordering a pizza. Storm half-expected her to ask whether he wanted extra cheese.

She told Storm she'd be back to him shortly—*in a half hour or it's free?* he wondered—then put him on hold. Storm told Click what was going on.

"Are you sure this is legal?" Click asked.

Storm just shrugged. "That's what lawyers worry about. Thankfully, I'm not one of those. Why don't you just tell me what kind of thing you'll be looking for once we get inside?"

Ever the professor, Click started his lecture. Storm felt like he needed a spiral notebook, but he did his best to absorb what he was hearing while he kept his phone at his ear. Fifteen minutes later, the phone came back to life.

"Okay," she said. "I'm in. What do we need?"

"Let's start with Dieter Kornblum," Storm said.

Over the next four hours, they slowly built a profile of each banker, putting in all the information Click thought he needed and some he didn't know he needed until it was suddenly available to him. They fell into a pattern where Click asked questions that Storm relayed to the nerd, who then provided the information to Storm, who dictated it to Click, who put it into his model. The process was painstaking at times. But they made steady progress. Storm was forever amazed at the amount of money that was out there in the world, and he began to understand why bankers could refer to it in terms of game theory: When there was so much of it, it didn't feel real.

Finally, Click announced he had all the data points he felt he needed. Storm thanked the nerd for her patience and service, asked her to stay on standby in case they needed more, then ended the call.

"Okay," Click announced. "And now for the hard work."

The hard work turned out to last several more hours. Storm's role was now reduced to that of gopher: He fetched Click coffee; then he got them both sandwiches; then Click asked him to make a cookie run, which explained to Storm where at least a little of the mountain came from.

In between food runs, Storm placed a few phone calls to contacts in D.C. who would help smooth Ling Xi Bang's path to

Senator Whitmer. They were contacts who assumed Storm was acting at the behest of—or with the implicit cooperation of—Jedediah Jones and the CIA. Storm didn't bother correcting them. Nor did he bother telling them the woman they were helping was actually a Chinese agent. There seemed to be no point in burdening them with details.

It was when Storm came back with coffee for perhaps the fifth time that he found Click beaming at him.

"I've got it," he said. "Now, bear in mind, a model like this deals in probabilities, not certainties. But there has to be a sixth banker, and I've run the model numerous times now, tweaking it in a couple of different ways each time just to make sure I can't shake it. And it keeps giving me the same answer. As you can see, there are other names, but none of them got above a twenty percent probability. According to my model, there is an eighty-seven percent chance that this is your sixth banker."

Click tilted the computer screen in Storm's direction. Storm stared for a moment. It was the final piece of the puzzle, the last bulwark between them and financial apocalypse. Storm pulled out his phone to call Jones, then thought better of it. This was starting to feel like one of those times when the less Jones knew, the better.

Instead, Storm typed a quick note to his insurance policy/father, telling him the latest. He always wanted to feel like he was leaving the old man some bread crumbs to follow.

Then Storm fired up one of his People Finder apps and put it to work. Before long, it gave him the business and residential addresses of the man in question.

Storm looked at the time on his phone. It was 3:06 P.M. Volkov had hit the day before, but in South Africa. It would be at least another day before he could get the needed pieces in place to strike again.

Storm would be able to get there first. But there was no time to waste. Not if he was going to protect the man whose name was at the top of Click's screen: the CEO and chief proprietor of Prime Resource Investment Group, G. Whitely Cracker V.

CHAPTER 19

FAIRFAX, Virginia

Old FBI agents don't die. They just start wearing more comfortable clothes.

At least that's how Carl Storm thought of it.

The moment he got the e-mail from his son, Carl Storm went to work. He now had something domestic he could look into, and that was good. It was hard when Derrick was working on something foreign. Foreign meant CIA, and Carl had about as much trust in the CIA as he did in undercooked hamburger. Plus, Carl had few CIA contacts. Domestic, on the other hand, meant the Bureau. The Bureau would never let him down.

And Carl would never let Derrick down.

And so, just to make sure his son's back was covered, Carl started making inquiries. He began with some of his old cronies, who promised to make some phone calls for him. Those cronies, in turn, called other cronies. The FBI had roughly fourteen thousand agents, but they all got around enough that a person with the right connections was never more than a few phone calls away from someone who knew something about what you were looking for.

It took about two hours before Carl heard from one of those someones.

"Carl Storm!" boomed a voice Carl had not heard in many years. "Jesus, how are you?"

"Tired and sick, and sick and tired. I'd bitch about it, but then I'd be another one of those old farts who sits around and bitches all day."

"I hear you, I hear you. How long you been out now?"

"Six years."

"Do those golden handcuffs fit as nice as they say?"

"It seems like you ought to be finding out pretty soon yourself."

"Yeah. Unless Emma decides to go to graduate school, in which case I'm in for a few more years," the man said. "How's your boy doing?"

"He's good. Not married, so no grandkids on the horizon."

"So he's good-looking *and* smart. Never could figure out how you were involved in making him."

"Takes after his mother," Carl said. "She was a heck of a woman."

"I know. I know," the man said, having heard that from Carl Storm before and wanting to change the subject. "Hey, I was thinking about you the other day. Remember Malibu Marv?"

"Of course." He was one of Carl Storm's old collars.

The guy laughed. "So apparently they let the son of a bitch out after twenty years. He had found Jesus, had given his life to God, was turning over a new leaf—all that shit the parole board loves. He went back to the bank where you popped him all those years ago, set up on the street corner, and started preaching there five days a week. With the donations he got, he set up a storefront church that was doing real well. A few hundred people coming a week. A real success story—until they nailed Marv stealing from the tithes."

"Yeah, that's Marv . . . ," Carl said, chuckling. "At least he'll know his way around at San Quentin."

"Too true, too true. Hey, I still owe you for Tucson. Don't think I've forgotten that."

"No, you don't."

"Yeah, I do. I think I'll always owe you for Tucson. You saved my ass, Carl."

Carl just grunted. This was another thing about old FBI agents: They never forgot. And just as it was important for Carl Storm to establish that the debt had been forgiven, it was just as important for the other man to insist that it had not been. It was still owed. What was about to come was another form of payment.

"Anyhow, I got something on that name you're snooping around about. I might be able to put you in touch with someone who has information about something called 'Operation Wafer.'"

"Operation Wafer. Jesus, the names these guys come up with. What's that?"

"Something being put together by the boys in White Collar in New Jersey. I don't know any of the details, just that it involves embezzlement and the guy you're asking about. I don't have the details, but apparently it's big, and getting bigger all the time. What's that kid of yours up to, anyhow?"

"Beats me," Carl said, only somewhat honestly. "I'm just trying to make sure he doesn't get in any more trouble than he's already in."

"Well, anyhow, you'll get a phone call in a day or two. I'll put you in touch with the guy heading the investigation. Can you sit tight that long?"

"No problem," Carl said. "Thanks for the call."

They hung up. Carl Storm stared at the wall for a second, wishing he wouldn't worry, knowing that was an impossible order.

Fathers worry about their children. No matter how old the child gets.

CHAPTER 20

Somewhere over Decatur, Champaign, or perhaps Columbus

Among the many great things about being Derrick Storm, one was that he had friends with their own airplanes that they didn't mind loaning out on occasion.

Among the many great things about private air travel, one was that no one insisted you turn off your cell phone and all portable electronic devices the moment the plane doors closed.

Among the many great things about satellite phones, one was that they worked at thirty-seven thousand feet.

As his borrowed Gulf Stream IV reached cruising altitude, Storm placed a call to Ling Xi Bang, who had been on the ground in Washington for several hours by that point.

"Good afternoon," he said pleasantly. "How did the meet go?"

Storm had arranged for Xi Bang to rendezvous with one of his sources. After she'd uttered a password, he'd provided her with a Senate staff ID card, a Virginia driver's license, and a credit card. They contained her picture and the name Jenny Chang. He'd also given her a small pouch that included what he called "a pill and a powder," then provided a briefing on what those drugs would accomplish for her.

"Went fine," Xi Bang said. "Nice password, by the way. Are you sure you don't have some kind of legume fetish?"

The password had been "soybean."

"At least it's a healthy obsession," he said.

"Where are you right now?"

Storm leaned out the window. "I don't know. That might be Bloomington, Illinois. Or maybe Bloomington, Indiana. But from this height every city in the Midwest looks the same. There's a reason they call this flyover country, you know. Where are you?"

"In Washington."

"I know that. I mean where are you, specifically?"

"Specifically, I'm sitting on a bench at the northeast corner of the National Mall. I was thinking about going to the Air and Space Museum and seeing if I could seduce one of the male tour guides into giving me your country's aerospace secrets."

"You probably won't even have to sleep with the guy. Just offer him some freeze-dried ice cream and he's yours. You'll learn everything you ever wanted to know about Apollo 11. Just be warned: There's no gas left in the tank, so don't think you can use it to get ahead in the space race."

"Yeah, you know we won that one, right? We Communists put a man up in space while you capitalists were still messing around with sending monkeys up there."

"Yes, but think of how much fun the monkeys had."

She laughed. Storm liked the sound of it.

"So I've got you set up with Senator Whitmer at eight o'clock tonight," Storm said. "His staff should be gone by then. He thinks he's going to have an important, one-on-one, face-to-face meeting with Dianne Feinstein. But at the last second 'Senator Feinstein's office' is going to call and cancel. That's when you'll move in."

"Got it."

"From there, just work your magic. We need to know who wanted that appropriations rider and/or who the mysterious donor behind the Alabama Future Fund is. Although, more than likely, it's the same person."

"Right."

"Good." Storm paused for a second, then said: "Now what are you wearing?"

"Are we really going to play *that* game? Come on. I'm in public."

"No, no, I mean it. What are you wearing? Or, rather, maybe I should say: What is Jenny Chang wearing?"

"Same thing I wore yesterday, unfortunately. You may recall I didn't exactly have time to pack when I left Paris."

Storm flashed back to the last outfit he had seen Xi Bang in. It was lovely, but . . . the pants made her legs something of a well-kept secret. And the turtleneck?

"Yeah, that's not going to work for Jenny Chang. She needs something a little more . . . youthful. Something that announces innocence, a lack of sophistication, and, above all else, availability. You said you're on the northeast corner of the mall? Near the American History Museum?"

"Yeah."

"Okay, start walking north. I know a place."

Xi Bang followed his instructions, which Storm didn't mind admitting he enjoyed. It was like having his very own remote control girl spy. Talk about the most awesome toy ever.

Storm proceeded to guide her from the Mall to a mall. It was a store that specialized in making sixteen-year-old girls look and feel like twenty-five-year-olds, even if the only people they fooled were themselves—and old men who could no longer tell the difference. Which is what made it perfect for what Storm had in mind.

"I'm in," Xi Bang said.

"Okay, first step, the skirt. The skirt is key. I'm thinking pleated. And short. You think you can handle that?"

"Am I going to have to get pom-poms with it, too?"

"Only if they have them on sale. Remember, Uncle Sam is footing the bill for this."

Storm could hear the squeal of wire hangers being moved on racks.

"Okay. Pleated skirt. Got it," she said. "Next?"

"Blouse now. Something simple. With buttons. It *must* have buttons."

"Of course," she said. "Let's see what we've got here. . . . How's white cotton with just a hint of spandex?"

"What kind of cut is it? Fitted? Kind of snug?"

"Yes. And it has cap sleeves."

"Perfect. Do they have shoes there?"

"As a matter of fact, they do."

"Do they have black patent leather shoes?"

"You are *such* a dirty old man."

"Dirty, yes. Not sure I qualify as old yet. But I aspire to it."

"All right. Uhh, yes, I have visuals on a pair of black patent leather shoes. They look like Mary Janes all grown up."

"Brilliant. Acquire them, please," Storm said. He heard Xi Bang ask a sales clerk for size nine.

"While she's looking for those, they do have tights there, yes?" Storm asked.

"Yes. Black, white, or gray?"

"Let's go gray. White is a little too Sunday School."

"I can't believe I'm doing this," Xi Bang said.

"Aww, come on, it's fun. It's like having your own personal long-distance shopper."

"I never knew you were so metrosexual."

"I'm not. Trust me. But I've known guys who are, and I've learned about their tendencies in the process of making fun of them."

Xi Bang was talking to the sales clerk again. The shoes had arrived. Storm listened as Xi Bang confirmed that, yes, they were the right size.

"Okay, I've got shoes, tights, skirt, and blouse. What's next?"

"You have underwear?"

"Same stuff I was wearing yesterday."

Storm's mind immediately went to the black lace bra and matching panties Xi Bang had been wearing. "Yes, that will do nicely, actually. Time to hit the fitting room. I want you to try all this on."

"You're the boss."

"I like the sound of that."

"Don't get used to it. I have to put you down now. Hang on."

Storm peered out the window again. They were over Toledo now. Or perhaps Cleveland. Who could tell the difference, besides Toledoans or Clevelanders?

"All right, I'm back," Xi Bang said.

"How do you look?"

"Like a naughty Catholic schoolgirl who's about to audition for her first porno flick. That's the look you're going for, yes?"

"Naturally. Now please take a picture of yourself and send it to my phone. I need to make sure it's authentic. We can't have you risk blowing your cover again, Agent Xi Bang."

"You're getting off on this, aren't you?"

"A little," he said. "Okay, a lot."

Storm waited for the picture to arrive. Thirty seconds later, his phone displayed an image that might have stirred certain yearnings in him. He might have felt a little ashamed about that, but he was fairly certain any other straight male beyond the age of puberty would have felt the same way.

"Fantastic," Storm said. "Just a few finishing touches. Put your hair in a ponytail."

"You're sick, you know that?"

"Just paying attention to detail. Have you done it?"

"Yes."

"Very good. Now I'm sorry, but you've got to go one button lower on the blouse. He has to be able to get a little glimpse of that bra of yours every now and then. But it has to look sort of like a wardrobe malfunction, like you don't know the button is undone or that you're giving him a little peep show."

"This is so over the top," Xi Bang complained.

"This is America. Wardrobe malfunctions happen here."

"All right. I feel like such a slut."

"Another picture, please."

"Fine. But before you even think about putting these on the Internet, you should remember that with just one phone call, I can arrange for you an absolutely humiliating death. And just to make sure we're on the same page: Yes, it will involve sheep."

"That sounds baaaaaad," Storm bleated.

Xi Bang groaned. The photo of the new, even trampier, Jenny Chang appeared on Storm's phone.

"Got the pic. I do believe I'm looking at the real Jenny Chang. All right. Why don't you pay for this stuff, then let's talk about your backstory."

As Storm crossed the remainder of the eastern quarter of the nation, he and Xi Bang brought Jenny Chang alive, creating her history with the ease of two seasoned liars. Storm loved the banter with her, the mix of serious moments and silly ones, her sense of adventure. It was sort of like talking with Clara Strike, except Storm didn't have the feeling that Xi Bang was hiding a meat cleaver behind her back the whole time. For reasons Storm couldn't quite explain, he trusted her.

His plane was coming in for a landing at Westchester County Airport when it came time to end their call. He had to make contact with G. Whitely Cracker V. She had a job to do as well. He just wished it weren't so. As they said their good-byes, she stopped abruptly and said, "Hey, Storm? It's great working with you. Thanks for your help."

Storm just smiled and said, "Always."

CHAPTER 21

CHAPPAQUA, New York

He had been able to rent a Mustang, which meant that for all the turmoil, there was at least one thing right in Storm's world—the throaty, American-made V8 engine at his command.

It was shortly before eight o'clock by the time the Mustang's GPS told him to depart the main drag, King Street, and point himself toward a WASP playground called Whippoorwill Country Club. Downshifting rather than braking, he made the turn and was just starting to enjoy the twisty, back country roads, when the GPS told him he was 250 yards from arriving. He slowed, looked left, and saw nothing. He looked right and saw a narrow driveway that disappeared into the trees up a hill. He twisted the wheel to the right.

Partway up the driveway, he encountered a gate with a call box next to it. Storm didn't feel like having a conversation with a piece of plastic, so he rolled down his window, popped the facing off the box, and hotwired it. "Open Sesame," he said as the gate swung out of his way.

He continued up the drive until he reached the circular end, which fronted a stone-faced Georgian Colonial that resided just barely on this side of ostentatious. The property that surrounded it felt like at least twelve acres. If Storm had had to put a price on the whole thing, he'd have said seven million. That was tip money to a guy of Cracker's wealth. He must have been one of those rich guys who didn't like to get too flashy with his dough. Or maybe his wife refused to upgrade.

Storm parked the Mustang in front of a detached garage that looked like it had room for at least five vehicles. He gave his own car a longing glance as he left it, then walked up to the front door. He rang. Unsurprisingly, the Cracker residence had one of those doorbells you expected to be answered by a butler.

Instead, the man of the house answered, opening the wooden inner door wide but leaving the outer, half-glass, half-screen door closed. He was still wearing his suit pants and a blue button-down shirt, but he had replaced his suit jacket with a cardigan sweater. Welcome to Mister Rogers' Neighborhood.

"Can I help you?" he asked through the screen, looking somewhere between bewildered and awestruck. With good reason. A big chunk of man had showed up unannounced on his doorstep in the dark of night.

Storm had been having a debate with himself as to how much he should tell Cracker and how much he should leave out. He took a look at him, gauging the man. Maybe it was the blond hair or the cardigan, but Storm's first impression was that he was a lightweight. Then Storm looked again and something told him Cracker was made of stern enough stuff. He could handle the truth. What's more, he would insist on it.

"Mr. Cracker, my name is Derrick Storm. I'm working for the CIA on a case that may involve you. Is there somewhere we can talk about a sensitive matter?"

Cracker just stared at him some more. "But . . . how did you get up the driveway? There's a gate."

"Did you miss the part about the CIA?"

"No, no . . . Of course. I'm sorry. Come in. Come in."

Cracker opened the door for Storm, who entered the house. The moment he did, his eyes began scanning the foyer, the hallway, every corner and crevice. It was part of Storm's training to notice things that were out of place, a reflex that had become nearly as automatic as breathing. In this case, all it took was one glance to notice a few things that made him suspicious that Whitely Cracker's house was not as private as Cracker thought. Once in the living room, Storm confirmed it: His hand swept the underside of the coffee table and quickly located a microchip not much larger than a pen tip.

Cracker was oblivious, still trying to play the role of gracious host: "Can I offer you anything to drink, Mr. . . . I'm sorry. I'm a little out of it. What did you say your name was?"

"Dunkel . . . Elder Steve Dunkel. . . . It is so wonderful of you to invite me into your home so I can tell you all about the Church of Jesus Christ of Latter-day Saints. I'd like to talk about God's plan for you. There are some simple steps you and your family can take to find powerful spiritual protection. Have you ever heard the name Joseph Smith?"

As he spoke, Storm had pulled a piece of paper out of his pocket and was scribbling furiously. Whitely Cracker was in serious trouble. Click's model had given it an 87 percent chance that Whitely was the next target. The Storm model had just upgraded it to 100. When he was done writing, he turned the note to Cracker, so he could read: "KICK ME OUT. THEN WALK OUTSIDE W/ ME."

Cracker, who finally realized what was happening, played his part perfectly.

"I'm sorry, young man, but we already attend a church," he said. "But why don't you leave that magazine with me so I can read it at my leisure. I wish you all the best of luck on your mission. Have a nice night, now."

"Thank you for your time, sir," Storm said as he pushed through the screen door and back outside. Cracker lagged about ten feet behind. Storm kept walking until they were in the middle of the expansive front lawn, but still a distance from the trees that ringed the property.

"I'm sorry, I really didn't get your name."

"Derrick Storm."

"Right, right. And you're with the CIA. I don't suppose there's any way I can confirm that?"

"I could have a tactical team land in your yard and surround your house, if you like," Storm said. "Would that do it?"

Cracker looked hard, to see if Storm was joking. He wasn't. "Okay, so we're going to proceed as if you're CIA," Cracker said.

"That's probably the best course of action. Especially since your house is bugged."

"Is that what you pulled out from under the table?"

"Yes. Your house is rotten with bugs. I didn't see any cameras. But the place is all ears."

Storm had never known Volkov to bother with electronic surveillance this elaborate—he usually just did his reconnaissance the old-fashioned way. What's more, the bug Storm had pulled from the coffee table was not the cheap kind he had gotten familiar with in his private investigator days. It was top-of-the-line. But perhaps the setup of the house, with all those trees and all that land around it, had required it. Or perhaps Volkov was changing, growing more sophisticated.

Cracker was struggling to keep up. "So how did you . . . I mean, you just walk into my house and . . . What? Could you smell them or something?"

"I saw a few things that made me concerned the moment I walked in. I've bugged a few houses in my time. You have to know what to look for. Whoever did it was very good, but they weren't perfect. For example, as I walked in the house, I saw a piece of wallpaper that had been recently peeled back and then reglued. But whoever did it was a little hasty about it and the glue didn't entirely take. I guarantee you'd find a bug tucked in there. There are probably a dozen others on the first floor alone. Under furniture. In light fixtures. All over. They're all small, which means they're not very powerful, which means you have to use a lot of them. They're likely transmitting to a unit that's hidden somewhere in your house. If we went up into your attic, we'd probably find it buried in some insulation. That's where I'd put it anyway. Depending on what they're using, the transmitter could be as small as a fist and yet powerful enough to send the signal anywhere within a mile of here."

"But how is that . . . Who would bug my house?"

"Quite possibly the same person who's trying to kill you," Storm said.

"What?!?" Cracker exploded.

"Mr. Cracker, are there children inside the house?"

"Yes, they're upstairs. Their mother . . . my wife, Melissa . . . she's putting them to bed, but . . ."

"Forgive the bluntness of this question, but I don't have time to be polite: Your wife, can she handle herself? Or is she a trophy?"

"Oh, she's whip smart," Cracker said. "Much smarter than me."

"Then you should bring her outside and tell her to get ready to leave. And, naturally, she should take the kids with her," Storm said.

"Yes, of course, but . . . I'm sorry, could you go back to the part about someone wanting to kill me? I'm still sort of stuck on that."

"Let me put this as plainly as I know how: We have a strong reason to believe your life is in grave danger. A Russian assassin named Gregor Volkov is on his way to your house right now to kill you. But before he kills you, he will torture you for your MonEx Four Thousand password, which he is providing to someone who wants to trigger a worldwide financial catastrophe."

Storm expected to see some demonstrable reaction to this news, but Cracker's face betrayed no emotion.

"I see," he said. "And you expect me to believe this . . . why?"

"Think hard, Mr. Cracker. Have you noticed anything unusual in the last few days? Someone following you, perhaps? I've tangled with Volkov before. He's the best of the best and leaves nothing to chance. He doesn't normally use bugs, but they're evidence of his presence. His normal procedure is to have advance teams in place to perform surveillance anywhere from a day to a week ahead of when he strikes. Maybe you noticed a car behind you on your way to work?"

"No, no, nothing like that. You said the man's name was Vol-Koff?" Cracker said, over-pronouncing the name. "And he's Russian?"

"That's correct. Don't bother trying to place him. You don't know him. Volkov is working for someone else. We just haven't figured out who yet."

"Ah," Cracker said. That was it. Just "Ah."

Storm surmised the man must be in shock. A perfect stranger had waltzed into his life and told him he was about to be murdered. He just wasn't processing it yet.

"This is serious, Mr. Cracker. Volkov is a brutal killer. There are five investment bankers dead already. We have reason to believe you're going to be the sixth."

"And why is that?"

"Are you familiar with the Click Theory?"

Cracker tilted his head, wore a brief look of concentration, then said, "No. What's the Click Theory?"

"A quantitative economist named Rodney Click has recreated the foreign exchange market in an elaborate computer model. He has used it to predict that six currency traders, properly placed in the right institutions across the globe, could trigger a precipitous plunge in the value of the U.S. dollar if they all bailed on the dollar at the same time."

"Interesting," Cracker said. "And why would this Volkov fellow want this to happen?"

"Again, Volkov is just the muscle. He's giving the MonEx codes to someone else. Until we know who that person or group is, it's almost impossible to guess motive—other than that it's someone who wants to cause a major financial calamity."

"And Volkov has killed five people already?"

"That's right."

"How terrible," Cracker said. "But what makes you think I'm going to be number six?"

"Professor Click tweaked his model to predict who the sixth banker might be. It reported there was an eighty-seven percent chance it would be you."

"I see." Cracker spoke as if his mind was churning through its own predictive modeling. "Well, in that case, it's a good thing my company has a security force. My chief of security is a man named Barry. He's excellent. I'll alert him to this threat and see to it he treats it with the utmost seriousness. Thank you, Mr. Storm. Thank you so much for coming out and telling me about this."

"You don't believe me," Storm said, flatly. It wasn't a question. It was a statement.

"No, no. I mean, yes. Of course I believe you. It's just that Barry can watch out for me."

"Barry is really that good, huh?"

"Oh, yes."

"So good that he was fully aware that your house—and probably your car and your office as well—have been bugged."

"You make a fair point," Cracker offered. "So what are you proposing I do?"

Storm had already been pondering his options. Volkov had been in South Africa that morning. It was possible he could be in the New York area by now. And if he had enough of a team in place to bug Cracker's house so thoroughly, it meant he had enough of a team in place to move in. Storm considered having Jones pull some levers and get the Chappaqua Police to park a patrol car outside the Cracker residence as a deterrent, but then he thought better of it. There was nothing one municipal cop was going to be able to do to stop a man like Volkov. Storm would just be putting one more person in harm's way.

Besides, Storm could play defense later. First, he wanted to play some offense.

"First, here's my number," Storm said, handing him a Storm Investigations business card. "If you become fearful for your life, call me. Remember that if you call me from your cell phone, your home phone, your office phone, or from anywhere other than a pay phone in the middle of nowhere, someone is probably going to be listening."

"Okay," Cracker said, accepting the card and programming the number into his phone.

"Now our plan: We're going to flush them out of hiding," Storm said. "See who 'them' really is. Hit them before they hit us."

"How do we do that?"

"Mr. Cracker, how fast do you usually drive?"

"I don't know. Maybe ten or fifteen miles over the speed limit. I'm no speed demon, but if you don't go at least that fast around here, you'll get run over."

"What route do you drive to work?"

Cracker told him, finishing with "Why are you asking all this?"

"Because," Storm said, "I need to borrow your car."

FIFTEEN MINUTES LATER, WEARING WHITELY CRACKER'S DRIVING cap, Derrick Storm settled in the front seat of Cracker's Maserati and rolled out the Cracker front gate. He hunched down to appear a few inches shorter than he was. He was counting on darkness to hide the other dissimilarities between his and Whitely Cracker's appearance.

He had instructed Cracker to head back into the house and tell Melissa that he needed to return to the office. This, of course, had two purposes. It would alert Volkov's team that "Cracker" was about to be on the move; it would also safeguard Cracker and his family, since Volkov's men would think that their target was in the Maserati, not back at his house.

If it meant putting himself in danger, so be it. Better him than a hedge fund manager, a housewife, and two children.

He did not bother sweeping the car for bugs; he just assumed there would be at least one and assumed, further, that someone would be listening. He needed to make everything sound normal. He punched the radio on, ready to suffer with whatever auditory assault came next. Cracker struck Storm as the kind of guy who might listen to some truly awful world music, filled with flutes and bongos and crap like that. Thankfully, Bloomberg Business News filled the car's speakers.

As Storm had suspected, there was no one waiting for him at the end of the driveway. There was no good place to hide there, and besides, there was only one way out of Cracker's neighborhood. They could afford to tuck themselves somewhere out on the main road and wait there. Storm drove the twisty part of the route by himself.

He picked up the tail once he reached King Street. It was a white panel van, likely one stuffed full of monitoring devices in the back. Storm smiled. This would be easy. White panel vans were good for a lot of things. Tailing someone surreptitiously was not one of them. The van would be easy to spot the whole drive.

Storm merged onto the Saw Mill River Parkway, an ancient and thoroughly outmoded roadway that predated the Eisenhower Interstate Highway system. It was cramped and winding, filled with blind curves, and yet some cars bombed down it at eighty-five miles an hour like it was a broad, flat stretch of the Autobahn. Yes, Derrick Storm was an international spy who was regularly hunted by assassins and had narrowly cheated death dozens of times, but the Saw Mill River Parkway? Man, that road was *dangerous*.

About ten minutes into the drive, Storm figured out what his move was going to be. He stripped off his jacket, tied it to the steering wheel, then anchored the other end by rolling up the window on it. He wanted to see if he could get the car to continue at least somewhat straight without his hands on the wheel. Yet it still had to allow him to make a left turn.

He fiddled with the jacket until he was satisfied it would work. Then he decided to wait before springing it and untied it. He wanted to lull the van's occupants into thinking this was just another trip to the office by a guy who worked too much. He needed them to be as unwary as possible. Time was on his side.

They had probably been sitting on the house for days and were likely tired from the stakeout. They'd be sleepier by the end of the ride.

He continued onto the Henry Hudson Parkway—Hudson would have begged his crew to mutiny if he could have seen the road they named after him—and kept a steady speed toward Manhattan. The white panel van stayed comfortably behind him, sometimes as much as a quarter mile back. It was the kind of tail being performed by men who had done this before, knew where they were going, and were not concerned about losing their mark.

Storm passed the George Washington Bridge and stayed with the road as it became the West Side Highway, renamed in 1999 after baseball star Joe DiMaggio—another icon now rolling in his grave. As they went below 42nd Street and started hitting lights, the panel van actually got trapped one light behind, causing Storm some mild consternation. He needed the van tight behind him for his idea to work. He relaxed when it caught up.

Storm made the turn toward the Marlowe Building at Warren Street. There were any number of ways to reach Cracker's office, but that was the route Cracker said he took. Then Storm made the right on Broadway. He signaled well in advance of Liberty Street, his next turn. He rigged Cracker's jacket to the steering wheel as he had before.

Storm took one last glance at the panel van. It was still about a block back, cruising through lights that were all timed to stay green. Perfect.

He made the left on Liberty, just beyond a tall building that housed a Sephora and a Bank of America on its lower floors. The moment the van was out of sight, Storm punched the cruise control, which he had set to a pokey twenty-five miles an hour. He sprung from the driver's seat, leaping out of the passenger side. The car was still accelerating and wasn't going much more than about twenty. Storm landed on his feet then quickly rolled in between a pair of parked cars.

Eight seconds later, the panel van eased past him, having just made the turn itself. Another car, a red Honda, followed it ten seconds later. Up ahead, Storm heard the scraping of metal as the Maserati careened along some parked cars. So much for straight. Storm peeked out in time to see the Maserati plow into a yellow cab waiting at the light on Nassau Street. The panel van slowed to a halt behind it. The Honda stopped behind the panel van.

The cabbie had sprung out of his car and was waving his arms in the air, shouting in some language that even Storm didn't understand. The driver of the red Honda—who couldn't see past the panel van to know what had happened, but could make out that the light was green—honked his horn impatiently.

It was a perfect cover. Storm raced alongside the passenger side of the panel van. He was assuming there were two people in the van, one driving, the other in back with the equipment. His plan was age-old and simple: shoot the driver, make the guy in back take the wheel, and go someplace a little more private, then have a conversation with him.

Storm yanked the passenger door open and had the trigger halfway depressed when he realized the barrel of his gun was pointed at Clara Strike.

CHAPTER 22

WASHINGTON, D.C.

Ling Xi Bang camped out near the Dirksen Senate Office Building, spending the final minutes before her appointment on a park bench, where she could monitor the comings and goings in Senator Donald Whitmer's suite. Mostly, it was just goings. Around twenty minutes to eight, the last of his staffers went home, leaving the senator alone.

At 7:57, she watched Whitmer take a phone call that, she knew, would be coming from Fake Senator Feinstein's office. That was Xi Bang's—or, rather, Jenny Chang's—cue to move in. She reached into her pouch and pulled out the pill she had been provided. It was a CIA standby: benzotripapine, which counteracted the intoxicating effects of alcohol. It was hell on the kidneys, she had been told, so it wasn't wise to take it very often. But Storm said Senator Whitmer was a champion drinker, and she needed to be able to keep pace without getting impaired.

Thus prepared, Jenny Chang breezed by Security, into the building, up the elevator, through the front door of Senator Whitmer's office, through the reception area, and to the outside of the inner sanctum without difficulty.

She tapped on the door.

"What is it?" Whitmer asked. He sounded annoyed. Just like a man who had been asked to stay late and then got stood up at the last minute.

Then schoolgirl Jenny Chang appeared in his doorway, clutching a file.

"Why, hello there, young lady," he said, his voice warming up by about fifty degrees.

"Oh my God, I'm so sorry," she gushed. "I thought this was Senator Sessions's Office. I was just supposed to deliver this to him. Oh my God."

Donny Whitmer laughed. "Darling, I'm afraid you're a little lost. Senator Sessions is the junior senator from Alabama and he's in the Russell Building. I'm Donald Whitmer, the *senior* senator from Alabama. Although I've been told I look five years younger than him."

Donny ran his hand through his silver hair. There was nothing like a schoolgirl to bring out the schoolboy in any man, no matter what his age or station in life.

"I'm so, so sorry to bother you, Senator," she stammered. "I'll just . . ."

And then it happened. In all her fluster, Jenny Chang let the file she was holding flop open, dropping its contents on the floor. She immediately stooped down to pick it up, making sure to give Senator Whitmer a nice view.

"Oh my God, I'm such a klutz!" she moaned.

"Here, here, let me help you," Senator Whitmer said, springing out of his chair with very non-septuagenarian agility, until he was kneeling on the floor next to her. Very, very next to her.

"I've got it. I've got it. Please, I don't want to trouble you."

"Now, now, it's no trouble," he said, warmly. "But now you're going to have to tell me who you are. You can't just walk into my office and throw things around unless I know your name."

"I'm so, so, sorry," she said, standing up and holding her arm out stiffly. "I'm Jenny Chang. I'm an intern for Senator Jordan Shaw of Connecticut. I'm sorry. I'm new."

"I can see that," Donny said, taking her right hand softly in his.

"I just love working for her, though. She's just the best. Don't you just love her?"

Senator Shaw was a Democrat, one of the smartest people in the Senate and yet, in Donny's mind, a total bitch—one of those female Senators who most certainly *didn't* play ball with the boys. He hated her.

"Who doesn't love her?" he cooed. "She's a great public servant. You'll learn a lot from her."

"Oh, I know. I know. I'm just so lucky to have landed this internship. It just sucks that it's over in six months."

"Well, there are always other opportunities on Capitol Hill," Donny said. "I might have an opening coming for an . . . energetic young person. If you're interested."

"Really? Oh my God, that would be so amazing! But don't you have to, I don't know, interview me or something?"

"That's a fine idea," the senator said. "How about now?"

"R-r-really? You mean it?"

"No time like the present. If that's okay with you. Why don't you take a seat?"

"Oh my God, that's great," she said, walking toward one of the chairs in front of the senator's desk.

"Not there," he said quickly. "Feels too . . . undemocratic. Why don't you have a seat over there. We can get comfortable. Get to know each other in a less formal setting."

He gestured toward the couch–love seat combination in the corner. She chose the couch. "You mean like here?" she said.

"That's fine. Just fine. Why don't I pour you a drink? You can't work for an Alabama senator unless you learn how to drink a real Alabama-style whiskey."

"Is that . . . is that allowed?" she asked, going as wide-eyed as she knew how.

"Well, that depends. How old are you?"

"I'm twenty-two, but . . ."

He silently gulped. "Well, then, there's no problem at all."

ONE DRINK LED TO TWO. AND THEN MORE.

Jenny Chang was bubbly and enchanting. She arched her back. She crossed and recrossed her legs. She leaned toward him, then away.

It certainly was having the desired effect. Donny wanted her. Bad. Enough that she was quite sure it wasn't his big brain doing the thinking anymore.

Oh, he was doing an admirable job at being gallant and gentlemanly. He resisted sliding down the couch toward her. He asked thoughtful questions and seemed to be interested in her responses—which was impressive, since even Xi Bang wasn't interested in some of the vapid crap that was pouring out of Jenny Chang's mouth.

He even maintained good eye contact as they spoke. Except, of course, every time she looked away from him, she watched out of the corner of her eye as his gaze traveled downward to her breasts and legs.

Soon, she shifted their conversation toward politics, which Jenny indulged even though it, like, sort of, you know, didn't always make sense to her. She had to make him explain things a lot. And drink more as he did it.

When he was done telling a particularly self-important story about victory in a partisan scuffle, she threw her hands up in the air and declared, "It just seems, like, so hard to get anything done around here. It's like everyone's all 'Oh, I'm a Republican' or 'Oh, I'm a Democrat,' and they just argue all the time. They forget that they're supposed to pass laws and stuff."

"Now, now, darlin', don't lose faith in the process."

"Why shouldn't I? Nobody gets anything done in this city anymore without a gun to their head."

"That's not always true. You can . . . you can still get things done if you . . . if you know how," Donny said smugly, a crooked smile on his face. Clyde May had seen to it he was no longer feeling much pain.

"Yeah? Give me *one* example," she said. "Tell me about one time when you got a bill passed without it turning into World War Four between red and blue."

"Well, okay, okay now . . . So, fuh example, a few weeks ago, a friend . . . friend of mine called me up. Needed a favor. Wanted a little something-something passed. So I got it passed for him. Put it into a propro . . . an appropro . . . ," he stopped and drunkenly spit out the word, "an ah-pro-pre-aye-shuns bill, and it sailed right on through."

"Just like that?"

"Jus' like that."

"That must be a good friend," she said, and scooted toward him in a way that lifted her skirt a little higher. "How does one become such a good friend to such an important senator?"

"Well . . . you have to be gen . . . gen . . . gen'rous."

"Maybe I should call up this friend of yours, and he can give me pointers on how to be generous," she said, stooping slightly so as to unfetter his view. "What's this friend's name?"

Donny couldn't help himself. Even though he knew she was watching, his eyes shot down her blouse, to that black lacy bra he had already taken off a hundred times in his mind.

"Tha's parta what makeshimafriend," he slurred. "I can't tell you."

"Oh, come on. *I'm* your friend, right? So you can tell me. I won't tell anyone."

She slid close to him. He wet his lips.

"Oh, you're my friend, all right," he murmured.

"Why don't you whisper it to me?" she purred. She leaned her ear so it was right next to his mouth. Her hand rested lightly on his thigh.

He was pretty much addled in every way a man can be addled. And yet, somewhere in the deep recesses of his mind, in a place that not even Clyde May could reach, there was a small voice that told him perhaps he shouldn't say.

"Now, now," he said. And then, in a minor victory for self-control, he stood up. "Now, if you'll excuse me for one moment, I do believe I need to use the restroom. You'll be here when I get back . . . We'll . . . We'll toast the great state of . . . of Al-BAMA!"

"That we will," she said.

The moment he left the room, she sighed. This was taking too long. And while the Clyde May wasn't getting her drunk, it still burned her esophagus every time she took a sip. She had also been leered at enough for one night. She was ready to be done with this.

She had done her best to pry the information out of him directly. She had failed. It was time for her chemically aided back-up plan. She removed the small glassine envelope of powder she had been keeping wedged in her shoe, parted its seal, then poured its contents into the senator's glass.

Too much pentobarbital would actually kill ol' Donny. Dosed properly, it would take less than fifteen seconds to put him into a sound slumber for four hours. She swirled the glass's amber contents until the powder dissolved.

When he returned, they toasted Al-bama, despite the fact that it had lost a syllable sometime during the night. Then Xi Bang counted backward from ten. By the time she reached two, Donny Whitmer's chin had hit his chest.

Just to have a little insurance in case she needed to resort to blackmail—and because she thought it would amuse Storm—she went over to the slumbering Senator, posed with him suggestively, and snapped a few photos.

She e-mailed them to Storm, then went to work. She had four hours but didn't feel like testing the limits of the drug's potency. She quickly laid the senator out on the couch, where he would think he had just drifted off. He would have a Hall of Fame hangover in the morning. She gave him a quick kiss on the cheek, because she felt sorry that he should make all that effort and not get anything for it.

Then she began rifling through his files. She started with the ones in his office, trying to be systematic and yet also remaining aware the clock was ticking. The moment she determined a file was not relevant—either to the Alabama Future Fund or the appropriations rider—she moved on to the next.

An hour down, she still had nothing. She had been through all the donor files and had moved on to others. She kept checking for false fronts to the filing cabinets or for unmarked files. But everything was straightforward. And dull. And, worst of all, legal. It was feeling increasingly fruitless.

Two hours in, she was starting to panic. She considered calling Storm, but what was he going to tell her? He wasn't there. He couldn't see what she could see. He'd be guessing even more than she was.

She sat down in the great man's chair, trying to clear her mind, staring at the top of his desk as she did so. That's when she saw a yellow legal pad with "ROLL TIDE PAC" written atop it—and nothing else. Curious, she started leafing through it. The next four pages were either nonsense or irrelevant.

Then, on the sixth page in, she hit gold. The words "ALABAMA FUTURE FUND" were prominent at the top of the page. Underneath was "$5 MILLION" and "SPLIT INTO FIVE LLCs."

And then, underneath that, was what she and Storm had come halfway across the world to find. It was the name of the man who had funded the PAC, the man who had hired Gregor Volkov, the man whose orders were directly responsible for the deaths of five bankers and their families, the man who planned to inflict financial turmoil on the entire world.

It was underlined three times, and it was as plain as the senator's block handwriting:

"THANK YOU WHITELY CRACKER."

CHAPTER 23

NEW YORK, New York

Clara Strike had seemed as surprised to see Derrick Storm as he was to see her, if not more so. After all, he was the one who was supposed to be dead.

But before they could deal with any of that, there was a mess to clean up. There was always a mess to clean up when Clara Strike was around.

He needed to pay off the cabbie. The Maserati needed to be towed—Storm didn't want to know what the repair bill would be; he was just glad that Whitely Cracker didn't seem like the kind of guy who would sweat it too much. And, last but not least, New York's Finest needed to be assuaged.

All the while, Storm was annoyed. Annoyed at being lied to about Strike's involvement in the case. Annoyed that there were obviously some moving pieces Jones had not told him about, as usual. Annoyed that for all his annoyance, he kept stealing glances at Clara and feeling the familiar longings. Her curly brown hair. Her shining brown eyes. The small whiffs he kept getting of her perfume. Damn, did that perfume have a hold on him.

During the four years he had been officially dead, Storm had not seen her once. He hadn't even missed her. Or felt bad about leading her to think he was dead. As far as he was concerned, turnabout was fair play. Clara Strike had died on him once, too—died in his arms, even. She hadn't contacted him, hadn't found some small way to let him know it was all one of Jedediah Jones's tricks. She had let him go to her funeral, let him grieve, let him lose a piece of his soul thinking he had lost the woman he loved. He was younger. More naïve. More vulnerable. He still hurt easily back then.

To her, a faked death was just business—an occupational hazard. To him, it had been emotional torture. When he found out she had been alive that whole time and could have spared him all that suffering with one phone call, he swore he would never forgive her. And he hadn't.

And yet.

Here she was. Again.

And here he was. Again.

And he couldn't help it. He found himself thinking of all they had done together—of the bad times, yes, but of the good times, too. He thought about Jefferson Grout, the man who had unwittingly given them their introduction. Back in his private eye days, Storm had spent four months tracking down Grout, who he thought was merely a two-timing spouse. Grout was actually a CIA operative gone rogue. Working all by himself, Derrick Storm of Storm Investigations had succeeded in doing what the combined resources of the CIA had failed at doing for a year. Strike recruited him into what she called "the company" the next day. There had been a whole lot of victories since then—many more W's than L's, truth be told.

So when the cabbie, the Maserati, and the panel van were all gone, and Strike asked Storm to grab a drink, it was something of a reflex to say yes.

"I'm sorry I keep staring at you," she said as they settled into a corner booth at a cozy martini bar in the East Village. "It's like I'm looking at a ghost. I can't believe . . ."

"I know the feeling," Storm cut her off.

"I almost want to ask you how long you've been alive again. I keep forgetting you've been . . ."

"Alive this whole time," Storm said.

"Yeah, it's just . . . I mean," she began, but she was cut off again, this time by a waiter coming to get their order. It gave Storm the opportunity he needed to shift the conversation away from his apparent resurrection.

"I was told you weren't working this case," he said.

"I was told *you* weren't working this case," she echoed.

"You expect me to believe that?"

She shrugged. "I guess Prince Hashem is worth every effort from the United States government."

"Wait, who?"

"Prince Hashem," Strike said. "Don't play dumb, Storm. It doesn't suit you."

"I'm serious. Who is Prince Hashem?"

Strike paused, studying him. Storm sometimes felt like she could read the fine print on the inside of his skull casing. "You're not messing with me right now? You're really not working this case?"

"It depends," Storm said, feeling that sense of bewilderment that only Clara Strike could engender in him. "What case are you talking about?"

"You first."

"No, you first," Storm said. "Let's start with this: Those bugs I found at Cracker's place. I should have known the moment I saw them. Those were yours, not Volkov's."

"*Volkov?* As in Gregor Volkov? What the hell does he have to do with this? He's dead."

Now it was Storm's turn to study her. He couldn't pretend to know all her tells, but he could detect no guile in her. "Okay, what the hell is going on?" Storm said. "You're really not in on this?"

"I think when we say 'this' we're talking about two different things," Strike said. "Simply to mitigate the confusion: Yes, we've had heavy surveillance on Whitely Cracker for two months now."

"Two months? But that appropriations rider wasn't even passed until three weeks ago. That was the trigger for the whole thing."

"Yeah, I have absolutely no idea what you're talking about right now."

He could see she was telling the truth. "So why have you been watching Cracker?"

"Because of Prince Hashem," she said.

It was again Storm's turn to wear a blank look. He shook his head to emphasize his ignorance.

Strike lectured: "Prince Hashem. Crown prince of Jordan. Next in line to the throne of one of the most strategically important countries in the Middle East. A man the United States of America seriously cannot afford to piss off if it wants to continue happy relations with Jordan. Any of this ringing any bells?"

"Not one."

Strike sighed, then laid it out for Storm: "Prince Hashem is one of Whitely Cracker's biggest investors. He's got seven hundred million dollars plowed into Prime Resource Investment Group. Even for the prince of Jordan, that's real money. Most of his fortune, actually. Surely by now you've figured out that Prime Resource Investment Group is in serious danger of going bankrupt."

"Actually, that's news to me. Whitely Cracker didn't get on my radar screen until earlier today," he said. What he didn't add was that he hadn't wanted to breathe a word about Cracker to Jones, and therefore Storm hadn't asked the nerds to do the usual financial workup that would have revealed Cracker's apparent distress.

"Yeah, well, trust me. Whitely has it bad. We're talking Bernie Madoff stuff here. He is in a huge, huge hole. Like billions. With a capital 'B.' He keeps borrowing, and of course everyone gives it to him because he's Whitely Cracker. But it's only getting him deeper in trouble. We're trying to figure out a way to move in and save the prince's money, but of course the CIA can't make a move against an American citizen. We have to wait for him to do something illegal and then send in the appropriate domestic authority. Unfortunately for us, losing billions of dollars isn't illegal. So all we can do is watch and wait and hope."

"And then you swoop in, save the day, and make sure Prince Hashem knows Uncle Sam had his back the whole way, gently reminding him that Iran or Hamas wouldn't be able to do the same."

"Yeah, that's about the size of it," Strike said. "Now, what does Volkov have to do with this?"

Storm told her as much as he dared without over-sharing, reminding himself she still worked for Jones. Storm trusted Clara Strike more than he did Jedediah Jones, but that was like saying he trusted a three-card monte dealer more than a snake-oil salesman. Still, he gave her a basic outline of the Click Theory and how Cracker played into it. He could tell from her reactions that it was genuinely news to her. For once, it seemed Clara Strike wasn't playing a shell game on him.

"If it helps you, we haven't seen any sign of Volkov or his men," she said. "And, believe me, we've been watching. You know Volkov's patterns better than anyone. He's a look-before-you-leap type. He'd never go after Cracker without having done his homework. So I'd say he hasn't gotten here yet."

"More likely, Click's model is just wrong," Storm said. "The sixth banker isn't Cracker. You still have people on his house?"

Strike nodded.

"Good. If Volkov does come slinking around, we'll know. But I'm starting to think that I need to ask Dr. Click to go back to the drawing board. It doesn't look like Cracker will be victim number six."

Storm felt some sense of ease knowing Cracker and his family were safe. But, at the same time, it meant there was some other banker—perhaps with some other spouse and some other children—who was still in danger. And Storm didn't have any idea who it was. The powerlessness was frustrating.

"Well, I'm glad fate has thrown us together again," Strike said when he was through. "It really is great to see you, Storm. I thought you were . . . I mean, it's Jones, so who the hell knows? But there were moments when I really thought you were dead. I'd go back and forth. Sometimes I'd think, *Nah, he couldn't be dead. It'd take a nuclear weapon to kill that son of a bitch.* But then other times I'd think back on the times I almost lost you and think, well, maybe they got you this time. . . ."

"Yeah, well . . . ," Storm said quietly. "Sorry I didn't reach out."

"I'd have done the same thing."

Storm couldn't resist the jab: "You did do the same thing."

"I know, but . . . I mean, really, are you fishing for an apology or something? You know how the game is played. I don't like it any more than you do sometimes. But I also accept it's a part of this world we have chosen to live in. Or maybe it's part of the world that has chosen us. To a certain extent, it doesn't matter. You can gripe and pout all you want, but you and I both know we wouldn't walk away even if we had the chance to. This is who we are."

"Yeah" was all Storm said. Sometimes, it was best not to give Clara Strike any more than that.

She had placed her hand over his. The lighting was low. The martinis were finally taking the edge off the adrenaline rush that Storm had been living on.

"You remember when we found this place?" Strike asked.

"Of course. It was after Marco Juarez," Storm said, feeling the warmth of the memory. Juarez was a Panamanian drug lord. Emphasis on the "was." Storm and Strike had celebrated Juarez's death in Manhattan, reveling in their unlikely survival with a week of sex, food, and booze, in roughly that order. Rinse, repeat. Rinse, repeat. Storm would never say it out loud, but if he had to live just one week of his life over and over again in a loop, that would be the one.

"I thought I'd lost you that time, too," she said.

"Oh that? That was just a flesh wound."

She interlaced her fingers in his. Her eyes were somehow

moist and blazing at the same time. "I've missed you so much," she said. "Sometimes I think about, you know, us, and . . ."

She stopped herself. Storm had turned his head in the other direction.

"I'm not sure I can talk about this," he said.

"Right now?" she asked. "Or forever?"

"I don't know."

Suddenly, she was the one turning her head in the other direction. She stood and dabbed at her face with a Kleenex. Her last words before leaving the bar were:

"Well, just be careful. Right now has a nasty way of turning into forever while you're not watching."

As he watched her walk out the door, he couldn't help but wonder whether the tears had been real.

STORM SETTLED THE CHECK AND DEPARTED. NOTHING ABOUT drinking a martini with Clara Strike had felt right anyway. There were doors he couldn't afford to open, and that was one of them. Certainly not now. Maybe it was because of his feelings for Ling Xi Bang. Maybe it was because there was a man he didn't know whose life he felt he had to save.

Storm dove into an all-night deli, grabbed a black coffee to help clear away the martini fuzz, and typed a quick e-mail to Rodney Click. He told him that Whitely Cracker was an apparent dead end and asked if he had any other leads.

Storm had just hit the send button when his phone rang.

"Storm Investigations."

"Derrick, it's Ling. Can you talk?"

"Go ahead," he said, already enjoying the sound of her voice.

"I've just gotten myself clear of Senator Whitmer's office. The donor is a man named Whitely Cracker."

"What?" Storm said, and not because he had a hard time hearing.

"I got Whitmer drunk and managed to steer the conversation around to the appropriations rider. He admitted he did it at the behest of what he called 'a very generous friend.' I couldn't get him to say who the friend was, but then later, when he was passed out, I found a pad on Whitmer's desk that more or less laid it out. The five million is going to be split into five LLCs, but it looks like all the money is coming from this Cracker fellow. Do you know him or something?"

"Yeah, I was just at his house, as a matter of fact," Storm said. "Rodney Click's model predicted Cracker would be the sixth banker. I guess the model got a little confused. It thought we were looking for a victim and instead it found our perpetrator."

Storm seethed as he thought back to his interaction with Cracker. The banker had let Storm into his house like he was the pigeon, not the hawk. He had pretended nothing in the world was amiss and had acted so guileless when Storm brought up the name Volkov, even asking him how to pronounce it and double-checking that it was Russian. All the while, the man was in Cracker's employ.

Storm was angry at himself first—he had the end of his mission an arm's length away and hadn't realized it. Then his anger turned to Cracker, the man who had inflicted such misery on so many, and intended to cause even more widespread suffering, without any apparent regard for who he hurt. All in the name of the unholy dollar.

Then Storm calmed himself. Anger served no purpose here. And, besides, he could turn his own mistake into an advantage. He could let Cracker continue to believe he was under Storm's protection. That way Cracker wouldn't know that Storm was really coming for him.

And there was no doubt: Storm was coming. By himself. There was no going to Jedediah Jones with this. All he had was the say-so of one Chinese agent—a person he wasn't even cleared to work with. Jones would howl all day long and half the night at the breach of security. And yet Storm didn't doubt her for a moment. He loved the irony: The only person in the whole scenario he could trust was an enemy agent.

Storm was so distracted he crossed Ninth Street without

looking. A Nissan Maxima blared its horn at him. Storm waved apologetically.

"Are you okay?" Xi Bang asked. "What are you doing?"

"Just playing in traffic," he said. "And thinking."

"Yeah, what are you thinking?"

"I'm thinking you and I need to pay a visit to Whitely Cracker tomorrow morning," Storm said.

"And?"

"We confront him with what we know, get him to confess. If he doesn't confess, we take him in anyway and hold him until we can prove this thing to everyone's satisfaction. At least that gets him out of circulation and away from MonEx machines. Can you get yourself to New York? There's a shuttle that leaves Reagan National at six A.M. that will get put you into LaGuardia by seven. I can pick you up there."

"Why, Agent Storm, are you asking me on a date?"

"No. I'm asking Jenny Chang. She's a total hottie. I've seen pictures of her on the Internet, you know."

STORM WAS ON FOOT, HEADED FOR ONE OF HIS FAVORITE HOTELS— the W in Union Square—when his phone blurped at him, telling him he had a new e-mail.

It was from Click, who had not yet managed to unglue himself from his computer keyboard. The professor had spent the day tweaking his model. There were two long, chunky paragraphs detailing how he had altered some of his assumptions and changed a few of the variables. The computer still considered Cracker its top choice for Volkov's brutality, but once you told the computer that Cracker was not an option, it came up with a different candidate.

The man's name was Timothy Demming. He was chief currency trader at NationBank. Click's updated model pegged the likelihood of the next victim being Demming at 73 percent.

"I met him at a conference and he's a typical investment banking jerk," Click wrote. "But there's no question he would be able to order a trade of the magnitude we've discussed. Anecdotally, I'd say he's a strong possibility."

Storm didn't hesitate. He loaded his People Finder app, which told him Demming lived a short distance away, in the financial district. Storm grabbed the first southbound cab he could and only felt a bit ridiculous when he told the driver to step on it.

Second Avenue blurred by outside the window, then Houston Street. New York was the city that never slept, for sure, but it was now after midnight, meaning that those who weren't sleeping at least had the good sense to be doing something other than clogging the streets.

On the short ride, Storm Googled Demming. He was a star at NationBank, all right. There were blog pieces about him with pictures. He was handsome, no question, but in a sort of sleazy way. He looked like someone who would shatter a child's piggy bank just to get himself one more nickel.

Storm arrived at Demming's address to find an upscale co-op, one of those lower West Side high-rises that had started springing up like mushrooms after rain sometime during the nineties. Demming lived on the top floor. Storm paid and tipped the driver and walked through the building's revolving doors.

"Could you please ring Mr. Demming in fifty-two J?" Storm asked the man at the front desk, a paunchy, middle-aged gentleman in a gold-braided uniform with "CLARK LASTER" written in bold letters on a discreet name tag.

"Isn't it a little late for that?" said the man.

"Yes, but it's an emergency."

Laster sighed and made a big show of opening a large book in front of him. "I'm sorry. But Mr. Demming has left instructions not to be disturbed after ten P.M. It says so right here."

Laster turned the book around so Storm could read it. Storm leaned in as if he intended to inspect the document like it was the

Dead Sea Scrolls. Instead, he reached over the desk with his right hand and clamped down at the base of Laster's neck, right over the collarbone.

The man tried to recoil, but Storm held firm. "Oww! Hey, what are you . . ."

The end of the sentence did not escape Laster's mouth. The man was already unconscious.

"Sorry, friend, but I don't have time to do things by the book," Storm said.

Storm hailed an elevator, which took him to the fifty-second floor. It was quiet and hotel-like. Storm walked quickly to Unit J, all the way at the end of the hallway, and rang the buzzer. There was no answer. He rang again. Still no answer.

Demming was likely out. Wall Street types were known to entertain clients until the small hours. Storm decided the most advisable place to wait for Demming was inside his apartment.

He stepped back and looked at the door. It was reinforced steel, the kind that would be very noisy upon breaking. But the lock was operated by an old-fashioned, analog keypad. It took Storm exactly twenty-eight seconds to get it open. There were advantages to growing up with a dad who worked for a time in the FBI's bank robbery unit. Learning how to crack safes was one of them.

Feeling smug, Storm opened the door and walked over the threshold straight into a bloodbath.

It was everywhere. On the walls. On the floor. On the couch. Even on the artwork. It almost looked like it had been coming out of a hose.

Even though he knew he was too late—a step behind Volkov, once again—Storm drew his gun. He entered cautiously, making sure not to step on any of the blood spatters but also keeping his eyes up, in case Volkov and his men were somehow still in the apartment.

They weren't. Demming was. His body was behind the couch. What appeared to be a very large pair of dirty women's underwear had been stuffed into his mouth and tied there by panty-hose. A tuft of pink frill escaped from one side of the gag.

He was shirtless, revealing a series of bruises that made it obvious he had been badly beaten before his death. Ribs that had suffered compound fractures broke through the skin in several places. There were cigarette burns up and down both his arms. His nipples had singe marks above and below them, suggesting that diodes had been connected to them and current had been run through his body. And, of course, the fingernails on his right hand were missing.

The torture had been extensive. Demming had obviously suffered greatly before his death, much more so than the other victims. Someone had wanted Demming to feel pain. Lots of it.

Still, none of that was directly related to his death, the cause of which was quite clear: His throat had been slashed so viciously he had practically been decapitated. That explained all the blood.

Storm reached down and touched Demming's exposed shoulder. The body was cold. So was any trail that might lead Storm from this apartment to wherever Volkov was now holed up.

Storm quickly swept through the remainder of the residence. He did this knowing there would likely be nothing left behind of any use. There hadn't been at any of the other scenes. But he had to check.

Storm worked methodically, going room by room, willing himself to stay focused. Still, his mind wandered: Volkov now had all six MonEx codes. If he knew what to do with them—or had given them to someone who did—a financial tsunami could be heading for Wall Street at any moment. After all, ForEx didn't close on business days. It was like knowing a huge landslide was coming and having no idea how to escape the base of the hill.

The apartment was, as Storm suspected, devoid of anything useful. He was preparing to make his exit when a pair of uniformed police officers entered the front door.

The first thing Storm said was "Before you overreact, I'm with the CIA and I didn't do this."

The lead cop took one look at all the blood, took one look at Storm, then drew his weapon, and aimed it at Storm's chest.

"NYPD," the cop shouted. "Let's see those hands."

STORM ALLOWED HIMSELF TO BE HANDCUFFED, EVEN AS HE TRIED to explain to the officer that this was all just a big misunderstanding. Like the cop hadn't heard that one before.

He was made to lie facedown in the hallway as backup was radioed in. Soon, what felt like half the officers in the New York Police Department's Twentieth Precinct poured into Demming's apartment.

As the next hour unfolded, Storm was allowed to shift to a sitting position, then shunted into the kitchen. Identifying himself as CIA had saved him a ride in a squad car and a trip to the Twentieth Precinct lockup, but it hadn't exactly endeared him to anyone in a uniform.

From his place in the kitchen, he could hear the cops' chatter. Clark Laster had awakened from his sleep hold–induced slumber no worse for wear but substantially pissed off. Laster called the police, who were sharp enough to assume that the man who had asked for Demming's apartment had likely proceeded to . . . Demming's apartment.

The early talk had Storm doing twenty-five to life at Attica, CIA or no CIA. Then the medical examiner, an attractive black woman, arrived and ruined the cops' fun: time of death had been several hours before, meaning this burly stranger who only just showed up had not likely been involved.

Then the medical examiner made things interesting. Demming was actually a hermaphrodite. He appeared to be male, but had both male and female sex organs. Sure enough, the plainclothes detectives going through the apartment found both men's and women's clothing, even though it was clear the apartment only had one inhabitant. This led to the theory that Demming liked be a man during the day, when it was convenient to be a member of the Wall Street boys' club, but sometimes indulged his feminine side at night. It certainly explained the rather large pair of panties in his mouth and the hose that had been used to secure it there.

Storm was a mere spectator to their speculation. It wasn't until an hour later that a woman flashing a detective's badge approached him in the kitchen. She had dark hair, dark eyes, and was easily the most beautiful detective Storm had ever seen.

"Hello, Mr. Storm," she said. "My name is Nikki Heat. I'm with the NYPD."

"Hello, Nikki Heat," Storm said amiably. "Didn't I read about you in a magazine somewhere?"

"Yes. But if you like your head unsmacked, I suggest you don't remind me."

"Consider me advised," Storm said, then jerked his head at a man who had appeared behind Heat, just out of earshot. "Who's that?"

"This is Jameson Rook. He's . . . he's none of your concern."

"Jameson Rook, the magazine writer?"

"Yes," she said, like this annoyed her.

"I never knew he was so handsome," Storm said.

"You really *do* want to be smacked," Heat said.

Storm shrugged as Rook approached. "Excuse me, Detective Heat, but who is this?"

"This is our suspect," she said.

Rook apprised Storm for a moment. "Not possible. He's too good-looking to be a suspect."

Heat threw her hands up in the air. "Before you ladies go off and get a room together, do you mind if I ask him some questions?"

"Sorry, go ahead," Rook said.

Heat turned to Storm: "Can you please explain to me what you were doing in this apartment with Mr. Demming's corpse?"

"To your satisfaction?" Storm said. "I very seriously doubt it. But I can tell you who the killer is."

"Great," Heat said sarcastically. "Can you also tell me where he is, get a warrant for his arrest, and then collar him so I can go home and get some sleep?"

Storm sighed. "That," he said, "is where things get a lot more difficult."

CHAPTER 24

QUEENS, New York

The Delta Airlines terminal at LaGuardia Airport had been under construction so long, Storm swore they could have rebuilt it at least three times already. Yet the scaffolding remained, a temporary fixture that had somehow become permanent.

Storm arrived there at 6:45 A.M., looking wrinkled and feeling worse. It had been a long night with the NYPD, who were eventually convinced to let Storm go his own way. It helped that a CIA station agent had vouched for Storm. Naturally, that added a complication for Storm: The station agent would fill out a report that would reach Jedediah Jones's desk in twenty-four hours or less, which would prompt questions from Jones. But Storm would just have to finesse that.

The final stumbling block had been Laster, the front desk man, who wanted Storm brought up on assault and battery charges; he also hinted at a civil suit, where his pain and suffering would be compensated with tens, if not hundreds, of thousands of dollars. Then Jameson Rook promised that in exchange for letting it drop, he would wrangle the guy an invite to a Fashion Week party that would be crawling with gorgeous models. That turned out to be enough to ease the man's pain and end his suffering.

Storm had thanked Rook for the assist. The two complimented

each other's rugged good looks one last time, prompting Heat to say something about vomiting in her own mouth. Then Storm went off to grab a few quick hours of sleep at the W, ruing the tragic underuse of the Heavenly Bed the whole time.

He had taken a cab out to the airport, having it stop in the garage where he kept his Mustang Shelby GT500—and, more importantly, some spare weapons. He thought about having the cab leave him there, but then opted against it. Counting the rental car he had driven out to Cracker's house, he already had one Mustang out of place that he'd need to deal with later. He didn't want to have to leave another one scattered somewhere else. He completed the trip to LaGuardia in the taxi.

Now he was waiting in the arrivals area, expecting to see a glimpse of something even more heavenly—Ling Xi Bang—when his satellite phone rang. He recognized the country code of the incoming call, which originated in Romania. That could only mean one person.

"Sister Rose," he said. "You've changed your mind about my proposal."

"Oh, Derrick Storm," Sister Rose McAvoy's brogue poured through the phone. "I only wish the purpose of my call was so happy."

"What's the matter?" Storm asked.

"I don't mean to be troubling you. And if you're busy saving the world, you just tell this little old nun to get on her way and go."

"You know I always have time for you, Sister Rose."

"You're a blessing, Derrick Storm, a real blessing," she said. "But I'm afraid what we need right now is not a blessing, but a miracle."

"What's going on?"

"The diocese has decided to shut down the orphanage."

Storm's mind immediately flashed to the Orphanage of the Holy Name, that small bright spot amid all the grimness of Bacau. He saw the eyes of the children whose lives were saved by it. In particular, he remembered a little girl, Katya Beckescu, clutching a tattered teddy bear and chasing butterflies. Storm's heart was immediately transported thousands of miles away.

"But why on earth would they do that?" Storm asked. "I can't pretend to know much about God's work, but if you're not doing it, who is?"

"It's not about that, Derrick. It's about money. The abbey that houses Holy Name is too valuable. The diocese is fast going bankrupt, and it's figured out it can get seventeen million leu by selling the abbey and the grounds surrounding it. That's the equivalent of five million of your dollars. The bishop says selling the abbey can save the diocese, and it's better to keep the entire diocese going than just one orphanage."

"But . . . Okay, can't they just move you somewhere else?"

"There's nowhere else for us to go—at least not that will fit all of us. The abbey is the only place big enough. That's part of what makes it so valuable. What's more . . ."

Whatever she said next was cut short by a stifled sob. Storm pressed the phone closer to his ear. "What is it, Sister Rose?"

"The bishop says that once they sell the abbey, it's time for me to retire," she said, and Storm could practically hear the tears streaming down her face. "They're putting me out to pasture, Derrick Storm. Just like a nag that's no use to anyone anymore. I'll become one of those old crones doddering around the nuns' retirement home, bumping into walls and dribbling porridge out of my mouth. Oh, I know I shouldn't fight it if this is God's plan for me. Lord knows I'm old enough, but the children . . . Who's going to take care of these children?"

"You are, Sister Rose. There's got to be some way to talk the bishop out of this absurdity."

Her voice grew hushed. "I'm afraid there's no talking involved. May God strike me down for talking about one of His servants in this way, but I've seen a lot of bishops come and go in my time, and this one, he's mean as an old donkey. Stubborn as one, too. The only thing he'll respond to is money."

"So you need five million dollars," Storm said. If she had said one million, he could have cut a check right there. But five million was more than he could afford to part with.

"I'm so sorry to bother you with this, Derrick, I just didn't know where else to turn. I have my little network of generous souls like you who can give us enough money to keep bread in the children's mouths. But five million dollars? I don't have any idea where to get that kind of money. But I know you're a man who . . . who knows how to make improbable things happen. And I just thought . . ."

"Say no more. I'll handle it."

"But Derrick, how will you . . ."

"Don't worry about it," Storm said as he caught a glimpse of Xi Bang coming through the security area. "I'll take care of the money, Sister Rose. You just worry about taking care of those children, you hear?"

"God bless you, Derrick Storm. I'll be saying a prayer for you tonight, as I do every night."

And I'm sure I'll need it, Storm thought. "You're always telling me God listens to our prayers," he said. "Maybe you should say one for yourself, too."

"Believe me, I'll be doing that now, too."

"You take care, Sister Rose. We'll talk soon."

He ended the call just as Xi Bang slid up to him and planted an enthusiastic kiss on his lips. She was still dressed in the same outfit, much to the delight of several of the business travelers who had joined her on the 6 A.M. shuttle.

"I have a little present for you," she said.

"I thought this was my present," Storm said, eyeing the outfit.

"No, it gets better," she said, producing a plastic bag from behind her back and ceremoniously presenting it to him. It was festooned with the logo of a novelty shop Storm knew to inhabit Reagan National Airport.

Storm opened the bag. Inside were a pair of SuperSpy Espio-Talk Wristwatch Communicators from Cloak and Dagger Enterprises. "Trade Secret Messages Like Real Spies!" read the package.

"Variable Frequency Dial Allows Multi-Channel Communication! Effective Range 3,000 Feet!"

"I just thought that in the spirit of international cooperation, we ought to get on the same frequency," she said. "This way, we can always be in touch."

Storm tore open the packaging and strapped the watch on his left wrist. He admired it for a moment and said, "It's the best toy I've ever gotten."

CHAPTER 25

NEW YORK, New York

The elevator at Marlowe Tower rocketed its occupants skyward, moving them quickly toward Prime Resource Investment Group's six-thousand-square-foot playground on the eighty-seventh floor.

"I mean, did no one seriously think about that? P-R-I-G. Their company name spells 'prig,'" Xi Bang was saying. "I'm not even a native English speaker and I noticed it."

"Maybe it's intentional," Storm suggested.

"Intentionally what, though? Intentionally elitist?"

"You're not going to launch into a rant about capitalism now, are you?" Storm asked.

And, no, she wasn't. Not after the brief stop she and Storm had made on their way to Whitely Cracker's office. Storm was one of those special customers that Barneys allowed to have private shopping hours, and they had taken full advantage of it. They tore through the store like impulsive children, chattering on their EspioTalk Wristwatch Communicators. Xi Bang had come away with a cutout black dress by Balenciaga, a simple yet stunning piece that had allowed her to gleefully throw her schoolgirl outfit in the trash. She paired it with a Delvaux purse that was just the right size for the sleek 9mm Taurus PT709 that had come from Storm's Mustang.

Storm went with an Andrea Campagna chalk-stripe suit that would allow him to blend with the locals. Fortunately, it was cut broadly enough to cover both his thick chest and the shoulder holster for one of his favorite guns, a Smith & Wesson Model 629 Stealth Hunter, a modernized, slightly more surreptitious version of Dirty Harry's gun that, just like the revolver made famous by Clint Eastwood, used .44 Magnum cartridges.

Their tack with Cracker, which they had discussed while making the remainder of their trip in, was quite straightforward: bluff their way into his office and then confront him. If they got a confession, great. If not, they would just take him into custody, either voluntarily or by force. They'd worry about the legality of it all later.

Once off the elevator, they entered through the opaque glass doors of Prime Resource Investment Group and came face-to-face with an officious receptionist. She knew full well these two well-dressed strangers did not have an appointment. Storm wasn't worried. Thanks to Clara Strike, he knew just the right thing to say.

"Hello," Storm said, then immediately affected an imperious air and a Middle Eastern accent. "I am Mustafa Mattar and this is my assistant, Fatima al-Fayez. We are emissaries from His Royal Highness, Crown Prince Hashem, and we demand to have an audience with this so-called Whitely Cracker at once or we will be forced to withdraw all of the money from our account."

That neither Storm nor Xi Bang looked remotely Arab was not, at least immediately, top on the list of the secretary's concerns. That approximately three-quarters of a billion dollars of her boss's fund was threatening to walk out the door earned more of her attention.

"Yes, yes, of course, Mr. Mattar. Mr. Cracker is . . ."

"Why am I still waiting?" Storm asked, chin held high. "The prince has dispatched me here with a royal order. It is Jordanian custom and law that any emissary of the prince must be treated as if he is the prince himself. Do I make myself clear?"

"Yes, but Mr. Cracker stepped out for just a minute. If you could please have a se—"

"I will not have a seat. And I will not wait. I demand to know where he is this very moment."

"I'm sorry, but if you will have a seat I can call him. He just ran to the deli across the street. I can call him and he'll be back here . . ."

"The deli across the street?" Storm said. "Very well. Miss al-Fayez? We will now depart."

Storm barged back through the glass doors, with Xi Bang close on his heels.

"Nice job there, Mustafa," Xi Bang said, as soon as it closed. "To the deli?"

"To the deli," Storm confirmed.

They rode back down in silence, holding hands as they did so. It wasn't exactly in keeping with two professional members of a prince's envoy, but Storm was fairly confident he wouldn't need that cover again. They reached the street level, pushed through Marlowe Tower's polished brass revolving doors, and were making their way across the street to a deli that had, appropriately, been named "DELI."

Then Storm spied two men sitting in the window.

They were having an intense conversation. One had ash-blond hair and a silver-spoon air about him. The other had an eye patch and a badly scarred face.

Storm's grip on Xi Bang's hand turned vise-like.

"What is it?" she said.

"It's Cracker," he replied. "And he's sitting with Gregor Volkov."

Storm let go of Xi Bang. His hand reached for the Dirty Harry Smith & Wesson.

"Wait," Xi Bang said, grabbing his arm. "Don't just charge in like an idiot. Let's come up with a plan first."

"No," he said, shaking off her grasp. "I've had Volkov slip away from me too many times."

And the part Storm didn't need to say was *It won't happen again*. This time, Volkov wasn't merely going to escape with burns. This time, there would be no second or third or fourth act. This time, Storm was going to keep putting bullets in Volkov's head until the man was down and would never again rise.

In some ways, the whole scene was surreal to Storm. He had chased Volkov across the continents and throughout the years, and now here he was, right in front of him, sitting in a street-side deli, like any common New Yorker, hiding in plain sight. The people ordering their bagels and grabbing their coffees on the way to the office had no idea that of the two men sitting in their midst, one was an international terrorist and the other was plotting a financial catastrophe that would make the Great Recession look like a little tiny cub of a bear market.

Storm raised his gun and took aim.

"Derrick, for God's sake, wait . . . ," Xi Bang yelled after him.

But Storm was already striding across the street with the gun drawn, heedless of the traffic. His eyes and gun barrel were trained on Volkov. The moment he was sure he had a clear shot, he was going to take it. The .44 Magnum cartridge had the power to punch a bullet through the window and still have plenty enough oomph to finish the job.

A propane truck swerved out of Storm's way, laying on its horn.

GREGOR VOLKOV LOVED THIS PART. JUST LOVED IT.

Whitely Cracker, king of the pig American capitalists, had called him in—no, *ordered* him in—like he was some kind of domestic servant, thinking that Volkov would gratefully and happily accept his six-million-dollar payment in exchange for the six MonEx codes.

Because, after all, who was Gregor Volkov to Whitely Cracker? Just some mouth-breathing muscle-head who was not civilized enough to attend the same operas; some two-bit thug who Cracker didn't even want in his office, thus necessitating their meeting in a deli; some dumb Russian who would nibble on scraps even as Cracker feasted from the table above him.

Little did he know.

Little could he guess.

So Volkov was laying it out for him. Everything had changed. Volkov was now the master, and Cracker the servant. They would do with the MonEx codes what Volkov wanted—when and how Volkov said it would be done.

Volkov was enjoying himself so much, he even explained the why of it all. He had been in touch with several powerful Russian oligarchs, who had eagerly agreed to use a part of their windfall from the fulfillment of Click Theory to fund General Volkov's coup against the den of thieves currently ruling over Moscow, crooks whose rampant corruption sapped Mother Russia of her strength. Forget the losses of the Cold War, the absurdity of the Soviet Union, and the joke that was the government that had ruled ever since. At the expense of all the other world economies, Russia would rise again, without her weakling dependents, without the crooks, and with Volkov as its militarily backed dictator.

And, yes, Cracker would play his part. It wasn't just because of the Ruger that Volkov had hidden beneath a napkin under the table as they spoke. It was because Volkov would charge a much higher price for disobedience, one he would extract not from Cracker—at least not at first—but from his family. His lovely wife. His beautiful boy. His perfect girl.

Volkov was just getting to this part when the hairs on the back of his neck suddenly stood up. He hadn't stayed alive in this world as long as he had without developing certain instincts, and one of them was a near 360-degree awareness of his surroundings.

And so he noticed things. He noticed movement. He noticed strange shapes. He noticed when a horn was blown, and that it was not just the *tap-tap* kind of horn a motorist sounded when he wanted to gain someone's attention; it was the angry, heavy horn of a driver who wanted to send a scolding message.

All of these things had come together on the edge of Volkov's consciousness, jolted him out of his conversation with Cracker, and caused him to look out at the street, where he saw Storm charging.

The Russian paused for exactly half a second, calmly weighing his options. Then he removed the Ruger from under the napkin and fired two perfectly aimed shots.

But not at Storm.

At the propane truck.

THE RESULTING EXPLOSION SENT A FIREBALL MUSHROOMING UP through the canyon of skyscrapers that surrounded the lower Manhattan street. The force of the blast at first depressed the truck, then raised it in the air for a split second before sending it hurtling on its side into the storefronts across the street. At least thirty cars were lifted off their tires and scattered about like children's toys, some on their sides, some on their roofs. A motorcycle got high enough to come to rest on top of the stoplights behind it.

Bodies were likewise strewn about. Storm, Xi Bang, and dozens of other pedestrians were thrown flat or into buildings. Drivers of cars were crushed inside their vehicles. Miraculously, the truck driver was blown clear of the cab and wound up with nonfatal injuries. Others were not so lucky.

The percussiveness of the blast had shattered every window on the block from the tenth story down, sending down a rain of glass shards that forced Storm to keep his head low.

By the time he was able to look up, Volkov and Cracker were gone. Xi Bang was already scrambling up as Storm got to his feet. He had a quick decision to make: go after Volkov or go after Cracker. He couldn't chase both.

Cracker was a man with roots only in New York, a man with no training in how to disappear and no real place to hide. Volkov, on the other hand, was a phantom with a long history of being able to dance between raindrops without ever getting wet. Really, it was no decision: Storm had to chase the phantom.

"Cover the front," Storm shouted over the cacophony of car alarms. "I'm going around back to get Volkov."

"Storm, *wait*," Xi Bang shouted. But she might as well have been telling rain not to fall.

Storm dashed into the alley to the left side of the deli, his revolver still firmly in his right hand. The explosion had given him at least one advantage: Anyone or anything that might have been in his way had been blown clear. He made a right around the corner of the building. The back door was still open, swinging on its hinge as if someone had barreled through it at high speed.

The alley was L-shaped, and a dead end. There was no sign of Volkov. There were also no other doors on the street level of the alley. Where could he . . .

Then Storm looked up, just as Volkov scrambled to the top of the fire escape of a five-story brick building. Storm squeezed off a shot, but Volkov had already disappeared over the edge.

Storm instantly assessed the situation. Beyond the brick building, there was a skyscraper the lower levels of which were an open-sided parking garage. Volkov might be bold enough—or desperate enough—to make the leap across the alley separating the two structures and clamber through one of the openings. It would be his only way out.

If Storm tried to run out of the alley and around, he'd be too late. If only he could alert Xi Bang that Volkov would be coming out of the parking garage, she could intercept him.

Then Storm looked down at the small chunk of plastic strapped to his left arm. He felt slightly ridiculous doing it, but he pressed the talk button on his EspioTalk Wristwatch Communicator.

"He's hit the roof of the building just south of the deli," Storm said as he raced toward the fire escape. "He's going to jump to the parking garage on the building next door. Can you . . . ?"

"I'm on it," Xi Bang's voice crackled.

"I'll be adding pressure from behind," Storm said, leaping up and grabbing the bottom of the fire escape.

He pulled himself up onto the ancient iron structure, then

galloped up the steps three at a time, hoping that he might have a shot when he reached the roof. He reached the top just in time to see Volkov slithering over one of the concrete half walls of the parking deck.

Storm didn't take the time to measure the alley to see if he could handle the jump. He just stuffed the gun back in its holster and hurtled himself forward. The roof was perhaps twenty-five yards wide, enough to allow Storm to reach full speed—or at least as fast as he could go in what his father would deride as "faggy Italian shoes." At the edge of the building he leaped.

The gap was wider than he thought. And for one sickening moment, he thought he might not have enough momentum to carry him to the other side.

He made it by an arm's length, slamming into the concrete hard enough to knock the wind out of him. Ignoring the pain, he rolled over the wall and hunched down long enough to pull his gun back out. He stood and aimed it at the nearest human target. But it wasn't Volkov. It was a distraught-looking middle-aged man.

"Don't shoot! Don't shoot!" he yelled, holding his hands in the air.

"Where did he go?" Storm demanded.

"I don't know. He stole my car!" the man said.

"What do you drive?"

"A Toyota Camry."

"Color?"

"It's silver. Are you with the . . ."

But Storm was already running past him. He pressed the talk button on his toy wristwatch. "Silver Toyota Camry, coming out any second now."

"I'll be there," he heard in return.

Several stories below, Storm could hear the shrieking of tires as Volkov took the tight turns of the parking garage at high speed. Storm sprinted toward the stairs in the center of the garage. Volkov was now motor-propelled, but he would have to wind his way down. At least Storm could go straight down.

As he reached the second-to-last story, he heard shots ring out. They sounded like they were coming from a 9mm. He could only hope they were finding their mark. Screams now joined with the bleeping of car alarms to create a soundtrack fit for a disaster movie.

Storm reached the first floor and ran toward the street. When he got there, Xi Bang was approaching the left rear of the Camry slowly, in a low crouch, still clutching her gun, her shoes crunching on a layer of broken glass. The street was strewn with the detritus of the explosion. Several fires had been ignited and the wailing of approaching fire trucks bounced off the concrete canyons. The acrid smell of smoke filled the air. Wounded pedestrians moaned, cowering in whatever shelter they could find.

Xi Bang ignored it all. Her entire focus was on the Camry, stopped dead in the middle of the street. It had stalled out at an odd angle. Its left front tire had been shredded. It had three bullet holes in its side and its windows had been shot out.

Storm brought his gun up, ready to pull the trigger if he saw any sign of movement coming from the inert car. He circled around so he was advancing on the left front of the car.

"Did you hit him?" Storm called, closing in quickly.

"I think so," Xi Bang said. "I don't know how I could have missed."

"This is Volkov we're talking about. It's like trying to shoot a shadow."

They reached the car simultaneously. It was empty. There was no sign of blood. The passenger side door was open.

"Where the hell did he go?" Xi Bang demanded.

"How should I know? I was in the garage."

On the other side of the car, they got their answer. A subway grate had been moved aside.

"He's gone underground," Storm said, spying the Wall Street subway stop three blocks away. "This is the two-three line. If he tries to go east, he'd have to go under the entire East River before he got to another stop. He'll go north, toward midtown."

Storm holstered his gun. He pointed toward the subway stop in the distance and said, "That means he'll try to resurface there. You come from above. I'll come from below. We'll squeeze him till he pops."

THE SHAFT THAT LED INTO THE GROUND HAD A LADDER ON ITS side, and Storm clambered down into the darkness as fast as he could without losing his grip. The subway was not as deep under Wall Street as it was in some parts of the system. But it was far enough down that a fall would likely be deadly.

Somewhere below him, a train was coming. Storm could feel the warm air rushing up the shaft toward him as he continued down, one rung at a time.

Finally, he reached the end of the shaft, some sixty feet down. There was still a faint light coming from the street. The tunnel itself was not lit. Storm peered down. In the dimness, he could only barely make out the track, perhaps fifteen feet below. He saw that the ladder continued down the side of the tunnel. So he could keep descending the slow way. Or he could just make the drop.

He chose the drop. He pulled his gun, then let go of the ladder.

Storm hit the ground and rolled, as he had been trained to do. He immediately swung his weapon up, ready to fire at anything larger than a rat, at any small glint of light, at anything that so much as trickled. But he had the tunnel to himself. Behind him was only blackness. Ahead, there was a faint light as the tunnel bent around to the right.

Storm started running along the tracks toward the light. If Volkov was lying in wait for him around the next turn, so be it. Thanks to his suit, he was a mostly black target against a mostly black background. He'd take his chances with being ambushed.

More than likely, he knew, Volkov was trying to scramble away like the cockroach he was. Storm quickened his pace, keeping his knees high so he'd be less likely to stumble.

He rounded the next corner. Still no Volkov.

But there was something else. The number 2 train was coming from behind him.

Storm was unconcerned. He had noted that the tunnel had cut-outs, places where workers could dive in and wait out the passing of a train. He passed by one, confident he'd be able to reach the next in time, wanting to gain as much ground on Volkov as possible.

The train was bearing down on him. He had veered over to the right side of the track. He saw a cutout on the left side but was already past it before he could react. He could feel the rush of air from the train getting closer. There was still no cutout on the right.

He was already sprinting, but he willed himself to go faster. Storm had once been timed in the 100-meter dash at 10.2 seconds, just off world-class pace. But it still wasn't a match for a hard-charging subway train.

The train's lights illuminated Storm from behind, casting a shadow in front of him that was growing shorter in a hurry. The engineer must have spotted Storm, because the train's horn blared. Storm pumped his arms and legs. He could imagine few more ig-nominious endings: steamrolled by the number 2.

At the last nanosecond, a cutout emerged on the right side. He flattened himself into it, digging his feet into the gravel along the tracks to avoid being sucked inward. The engine ripped past with inches to spare, its passengers unaware of the man panting just off their starboard side.

The moment the train passed, Storm resumed his dash. He heard the train slowing as it approached the station, applying its brakes with a squeal. Then another sound overwhelmed it.

Pop. Pop. Pop.

Gunfire. The large-caliber kind.

Storm willed himself to go faster. There were screams coming from the subway platform. Then more gunfire. Storm lost count of the number of shots. He prayed some of the reverberations were Ling Xi Bang answering. And hitting. But he wasn't hearing her gun.

He reached the back of the train, which had stopped at the

station. There was no room on either side for him to vault up to the platform. Storm swore but did not break stride. He leaped up onto the last car and opened the back door.

Inside the subway car, there were riders lying on the floor, huddled under the benches. Seeing a man with a gun made them only shrink back further. There was no blood that he could see. No one here had been hit. Storm passed quickly through the car's open side doors, gun raised.

Out on the platform, it was bedlam. The gunfire had stopped, but the screaming had not. There were commuters splayed in every direction, hiding behind every bench, sign, and bit of shelter they could find. Some of them were groaning and clutching at parts of their bodies. At least three were prone and either dead or dying.

Storm's eyes were just starting to make sense of it when Volkov tackled him from the side.

Storm's legs automatically braced against the hit. Volkov had tried to take him too high. Storm dipped slightly, then straightened, sending Volkov flying to the side. Storm whirled, ready to put a bullet in his attacker and end this thing.

Then he saw it wasn't Volkov. It was some bald, middle-aged white man in a suit, trying to play hero. The man flinched even as Storm lowered his gun.

"Stay down, damn it," Storm snarled. "And get off me. I'm the good guy."

Storm advanced farther onto the platform, bringing Dirty Harry back up and swiveling it across a landscape of bleeding, dying, and dead New Yorkers. There were more than a dozen of them, in varying states of distress.

Then he saw one who looked achingly familiar.

It was Ling Xi Bang. She was down on one knee, clutching her stomach, trying to raise herself. Storm rushed to her side.

"Are you hit?" Storm asked. But he already knew the answer. He could see the slick stain of wetness on her black dress.

"It's nothing," she said through gritted teeth.

"Lie down. Don't fight it."

"Just help me stand," she said. "He went up the steps. We can still catch him."

Storm had been around enough gunshot wounds to know Xi Bang's was serious. He had been shot in the gut himself. The pain was like nothing he could describe. He could see the agony on Xi Bang's face.

"Actually, forget about me. I'll only slow you down. Just get Volkov," she said, still struggling to get her other leg under her. She attempted to push him away, but there was no strength in her.

Storm knew that if he abandoned Xi Bang and gave chase there was a chance he could catch up to Volkov. The bastard had perhaps a minute lead, but he was on an island with only so many means of escape. Storm could hunt him down, then put him down.

That's when he saw that Xi Bang's leg had been hit, too. It was why she couldn't get back on her feet. There was a pool of red underneath her, and it was spreading fast.

"You're losing too much blood," Storm said, keeping his tone measured, trying to keep the panic out of his voice. "We need to stop the bleeding."

"Just leave me."

"That's not going to happen," Storm said. He had already put one arm around her shoulder. He slid his other arm under her legs, cradled her for a moment, then gently laid her flat.

Moving quickly, he removed his jacket, then his shirt, tearing off a strip with one powerful jerk. He located the wound on Xi Bang's leg. It was just above the knee, on the inner part of the thigh. That explained all the blood. The femoral artery ran along that side. The bullet must have hit it. Storm tied a tourniquet midway up the thigh, tying it as tight as his considerable strength would allow.

"I couldn't take the shot," she was saying, half in a whisper, half in a moan. "There was a woman behind him. She had a child. I would have hit . . ."

"Shhh," he said. "I know."

"He grabbed this old lady and—" She interrupted the sentence with a small howl of pain. "He was using her as a shield."

Storm tore off another strip of his shirt, then folded the remainder into a makeshift pad. He secured the pad with the strip. It was the best he could do until professionals arrived.

Then he moved on to the stomach wound. The bullet had left a neat hole in the dress. He needed to assess what was underneath. Working as gingerly as he could, he began tearing the dress from the hem up.

"Hey," she said, weakly. "Stop being fresh."

"Some guys will do anything for a little peep show," he said.

When he finally reached her abdomen, he was glad that she was looking up at the ceiling and not at his face. Otherwise, she would have seen the grim expression that came over him. Her stomach was bad. Worse than he'd thought. The bullet had torn into her and expanded on impact. The wound was a gaping hole that revealed her shredded insides. Storm could barely even identify the organs whose mangled remains he was seeing. Even if she were on the operating table in the most state-of-the-art hospital room in the world, with a team of the best surgeons ready to dive in, Storm wasn't sure if she could be saved.

On the floor of the Wall Street subway stop, it was hopeless. The only question was how many minutes of suffering she had left. Maybe ten. If she was unlucky.

"I'm cold," she said.

"I know," Storm said, grabbing his suit jacket and wrapping it around her as a blanket.

He slid his right arm underneath her, cradling her in his arms. All he could do now was try to make her feel comfortable.

"Is this what dying feels like?" she asked.

"Shhh . . . ," he said. "Just relax. You're not going to die."

It was a lie. He knew it. He sensed she did, too.

"I love you," she said.

"I know. I love you, too."

Even though he said it mainly to comfort her, it was not without feeling. Somewhere, in the back of his heart, in the part that had resisted hardening through all the missions and all the years, he knew that it might even be true.

"I'm sorry," she said.

"Shh."

Storm could hear the beating of helicopter rotors coming from the street. Was it a Medevac landing? No. Not possible. Helicopters weren't permitted in this part of New York City. Besides, there were enough hospitals within a short ambulance ride that Medevacs were unnecessary. Why would a helicopter be landing on the streets of Manhattan? Storm pondered it for a brief moment, until he became aware that Xi Bang was talking.

"You're going to get him, right?" she was saying. "You're going to get Volkov."

"Yes, honey. Of course."

"Promise me."

"I promise."

"I'm so sorry," she said again, more weakly. Her body was starting to convulse. The wound on her leg had already soaked Storm's makeshift field dressing. It was now a race to see which would kill her first: blood loss or multiple organ failure.

"That night in Paris," he said. "Dancing in the street with you. I was serious when I said we would dance to that song at our wedding."

"Mmm . . ." was all she could say.

But he could see that it had brought a smile to her face. And so, as the last embers of life flickered out of Ling Xi Bang, Derrick Storm held her tightly in his arms and sang her "The Vienna Waltz."

It had been their first dance. And now it would be their last.

CHAPTER 26

LANGLEY, Virginia

Jedediah Jones would have been pulling his hair out, if only he had any to pull.

As it was, he looked like a cross between a stressed-out CFO and an irate customer service representative. He was talking on a wireless telephone headset—an ergonomics expert at the CIA said it was better for his neck—at a volume that was seriously threatening nearby eardrums.

As he ranted, he paced around the cubby, pounding on any table that didn't hold a quarter-million-dollar piece of spy equipment. The nerds were keeping their attention buried in their computer terminals. Eye contact might provoke him further.

"Eighteen dead," he shouted. "Eighty-seven wounded. A hundred seventy people hospitalized. I don't even want to know how many millions in damage. Do you have any regard for private property at all?"

The man on the other end of the line said nothing. Derrick Storm had watched Ling Xi Bang's body get loaded into a New York City medical examiner's truck a mere half hour before. He was not in the mood to answer rhetorical questions.

"On top of that, I've got a propane company saying one of our agents blew up their truck. Do you want to explain to me why that was tactically necessary?"

Still nothing from Storm. Rodriguez and Bryan kept trying to dodge Jones as he rampaged around. Occasionally, they would hand him a piece of paper that he would look at then throw on the floor—which was already littered with things he had spiked.

"I've got the NY goddamn PD saying it's going to send me a bill for a crane to get a motorcycle out of a traffic light," he continued. "A crane! How did a motorcycle get in a goddamn traffic light?"

Jones stooped down and picked up something he had previously discarded.

"Then I've got the NYPD asking me why I brought a helicopter into restricted airspace so close to the Freedom Tower. I would have told them I didn't know, except I was worried that would make me sound like even more of an idiot than I already did."

The helicopter. Storm finally figured it out: That must have been how Volkov made his exit.

"A carjacking . . . a firefight in the streets of Manhattan . . . a subway platform full of shot-up civilians . . . all this and Volkov got away? Storm, what the hell happened this morning?"

Storm was sitting on a bench in a park in lower Manhattan. He was still wearing a good portion of the fluid that Xi Bang had bled out on him. It had started to dry and congeal, making his pants rigid. His hands and face were a mess of blood smears; some of it was hers, some his, from the glass cuts he had suffered. To anyone passing by, he must have looked like a deranged killer. It had not occurred to him to let any of this bother him yet. At the moment Jones had called, Storm had been looking at a tree, wondering how it was that the tree—a stupid, nonsentient piece of greenery—was allowed to still be alive and photosynthesizing while Ling Xi Bang was dead.

"Storm, are you going to say anything?" Jones demanded.

"Mistakes were made," he said, quietly.

"You bet your ass mistakes were made. And the first mistake was hiring you. Do you have any explanation for this incompetence?"

"No." At least none that he felt like giving Jones.

"And, I'm sorry, what the hell were you doing in New York City anyway? I thought you were in Iowa."

"There was a change of plans."

"And when were you going to inform me of this change of plans?"

"There wasn't time."

"I see. And when were you going to inform me of . . . Get me that surveillance camera footage again." Jones interrupted himself to bark at one of the nerds, who complied with his request. "I've got some footage here that makes it look like you're in cahoots with a Chinese agent, the Asian woman you intercepted in Paris. You want to tell me what the hell is going on with that?"

"No."

"You know that's not our deal. If you need help, you come to me. I've got all the manpower we need. I can't have you triangulating in outside help, especially the Chinese, fer chrissakes. Are you still working with her?"

Storm was only barely paying attention to his boss. The moment he mentioned the "Asian woman," Storm's thoughts went to that moment when he spied Volkov inside the deli. That's where it all went wrong, and there was no doubt about whose fault it was. She had asked him to wait before charging in. She had told him they should make a plan. *Don't just charge in like an idiot . . . Derrick, for God's sake, wait . . .* How long would it have taken for two smart agents to come up with a workable plan? Three minutes? Two?

Instead, her blood was on his hands literally and figuratively: first, because he hadn't listened to her very sensible commands, and then because he had placed her directly in the path of a wild sociopath. She had told him she didn't often do fieldwork. She didn't have the training to take on a beast like Volkov. He never should have made her do it.

"Damn it, answer me: Are you still working with her?"

"It's a moot point," Storm said.

"I don't even want to know what that means. I probably don't want to know anything about what happened this morning. But I do have to ask about another report I got, something about you traipsing through a homicide scene? According to one of our station agents, there's an NYPD detective named Nikki Heat who thinks you'd make a great suspect if only she could figure out how to make you one. Maybe I should just turn you over to her?"

Storm had no reply. He was absentmindedly opening and closing his left hand. He had jammed one of the fingers when he made the leap into the parking garage. He was working it to make sure it wasn't broken. His ribs were also starting to stiffen up from when he slammed into the concrete. It didn't matter. The physical pain was a distant tickle compared to what he was feeling emotionally.

"Actually, you want to know what's a moot point? You and this case," Jones continued. "As of this moment, you're fired. Go back to snorkeling or knitting or whatever the hell it was you did while you were dead. You're officially dead again."

"What's going to happen to Whitely Cracker?" Storm asked.

"That's none of your concern."

Storm sat up, actually engaging in the conversation for the first time. "How can you say it's none of my concern? I've developed rock-solid intelligence that Whitely Cracker has masterminded a plot to engineer a financial catastrophe. First, he bribed a senator to implement a change to Federal Reserve policy, then he unleashed Volkov on six innocent men and their fam—"

And then Storm stopped himself. The moment he said the name "Whitely Cracker," Jones should have asked what Whitely Cracker had to do with this. He should have fussed and fumed and acted like Storm was tossing in a random name from some other part of the universe. Storm hadn't told Jones about Cracker being the money behind Donny Whitmer's new PAC; nor had Storm told Jones he saw Cracker and Volkov sitting together in the deli. Jones shouldn't have known the two were connected.

But he did. Of course he did. Clara Strike had been performing blanket, round-the-clock surveillance on Cracker for two months. She would have told Jones what she saw and heard. Maybe Strike hadn't put together the bigger picture of what was going on—she wouldn't have had the context to know the significance of much of it—but Jones had all the information about what was happening.

And he didn't care. Sure, he wanted to know more about what Cracker was up to. That's why he hired Storm in the first place. Maybe he wanted to use it as leverage against Cracker. Maybe he wanted to have dirt on Donny Whitmer, the powerful Senate Appropriations Committee chairman. Maybe he had some other agenda that Storm couldn't even fathom yet, because there were other pieces at play.

But punishing the guilty? Righting the wrong? The morality of it all? That was never Jones's concern. Not then. Not ever—unless it served some other purpose of his. That people were killed, lives were ruined, and hearts were broken? That was all collateral damage to Jones, an unfortunate but necessary by-product of a larger war.

"So you're saying Whitely Cracker will not face any criminal charges for ordering the deaths of six men and the slaughter of their families," Storm said.

"I'm not saying that," Jones said. "I'm saying we're going to deal with him my way. Not yours."

"Do you have him in custody?"

"No." Jones still fumed. "He's in the wind. But right now that is the least of your worries. The only thing that matters right now is that you have been compromised and therefore this is over for you. Drop it. Now."

"Fine," Storm said, calmly. "There's a little dive shop in the Caymans that I've been hoping to visit."

"Storm," Jones said, ominously. "I'm serious. You are off this case. You are finished. I'm not protecting you anymore. I'm not covering for you. You get yourself in trouble, you're completely on your own, you understand? As of this moment, you are a private citizen acting on his own. I'll pay you for your work through nine A.M. this morning and reimburse you for your expenses. But that's it. You're done. Do you hear me? Storm? Storm, answer me."

But Jones was talking to himself. Storm had already ended the call. He had work to do. A maniac needed to be stopped. Justice needed to be served.

Besides, he had made a promise to a dying friend that he did not plan on breaking.

CHAPTER 27

SLOATSBURG, New York

Whitely Cracker had never really been cut in his entire life. Shaving nicks, yes. Paper cuts, sure. And he had once gouged himself with a cheese knife while cutting some particularly stubborn Manchego.

But a full-on laceration? One that was deep and painful and real? One that required stitches? It had never happened.

Now he had a face full of them. The bullet from Volkov's gun had shattered the window they were sitting in front of. Then the force of the propane truck explosion had sent them hurtling into him at high velocity, like hundreds of tiny knives. He counted himself blessed that none had hit his eyes.

The only reason he had not immediately gone to the hospital to seek treatment was that he was running for his life.

The moment he was sure it was safe to come out from the table he had been hiding under, he had scrambled to the garage where he kept his car. The valet had stared at him hard, even asking him in Spanish whether he needed *el doctor*. But Whitely had scrambled into his Jaguar as if nothing were unusual, tipping the man double as if to say, *Don't ask any more questions, okay?* He was just another hedge fund manager with a face full of blood.

Once he got into his car, he drove without thinking. He didn't know where he was driving or why, just that the more miles he put between himself and that nutcase Gregor Volkov the better.

He couldn't go to his office for obvious reasons: Volkov would be looking there. Home was . . . Oh, Jesus, home. He pulled out his phone, called his wife, told her not to panic, then basically instructed her to get herself and the kids as far away from Chappaqua as possible.

Then he drove. He went north, merging on the Deegan Expressway and following it until it became the New York State Thruway and took him into the rolling countryside that Manhattanites merged into one monolithic landscape that they referred to as "upstate."

He made sure—very sure—he wasn't being followed, invoking all the countermeasures he had seen in every spy flick he had ever watched: speeding up, then slowing down; pulling to the side of the road just after blind curves; taking exits, passing through gas stations, then immediately getting back on the Interstate.

When he was sure he was alone, he pulled in at a travel plaza off the New York State Thruway. Now he was sitting in front of a Dunkin' Donuts, sipping coffee, being nervously eyed by an Indian woman in a sari who was trying to stop her two children from staring at him. He needed a plan. And he needed help. He knew that.

But what plan would work? He had no experience at being on the run. Nor did he have any background in having his life threatened.

And who would help him? Barry, his chief of security at Prime Resource Investment Group, was a retired cop but, obviously, something of a moron. The man had allowed Whitely's house, car, and office—and who knows what else—to have the bejesus bugged out of them and had been completely unaware the whole time.

He thought about calling Teddy Sniff, his trusted accountant. But what would Teddy do? Order an audit on Volkov? Make him reconcile his accounts? Teddy would be every bit as unfamiliar with this new terrain as Whitely.

The coffee had run out. He went to get a refill, wondering as he used his black American Express card whether Volkov would somehow have a way of tracing it, and whether therefore this would be the most deadly cup of coffee he ever drank. He was in the midst of pouring his second pack of sugar into the brew when suddenly the idea hit him:

That guy from the CIA. What was his name? Cloud? No, that wasn't right. Rain? No, that was the dumbest name for an action hero Whitely had ever heard of.

Storm. That was it. Derrick Storm. The CIA had to help him, right? He was a taxpayer. And even if he was a taxpayer who paid an effective rate below 15 percent, he was still an American citizen. Storm would be obligated, wouldn't he?

Whitely pulled out his phone, found the name on his contact list, and was about to hit send when he remembered what Storm had instructed him: No calls from his cell phone. Someone would be listening.

Storm said he should find "a pay phone in the middle of nowhere." Upstate New York surely qualified as nowhere. So Whitely started wandering around the rest area, looking for a pay phone, praying they even still existed. Who used pay phones anymore? Whitely hadn't touched one in well over a decade. When he found a small bank of them, he realized he no longer had any idea how to make one work. He no longer had a calling card—that was so quaint, so nineties. He actually needed . . . change? That was also antiquated. Whitely had gone cashless years earlier.

It took finding an ATM machine, pulling out cash, buying a donut, and asking for change in quarters before he had some.

Finally, he was ready. He dropped in four quarters and dialed.

"Storm Investigations," he heard.

"Mr. Storm, thank God. This is Whitely Cracker."

There was a pause, followed by a terse "Yes. And?"

"You said if I became fearful for my life I should call you. Well, I'm fearful for my life."

Another pause. "And why is that?"

"I know this is going to sound crazy. But there's a . . . Jeez, I don't even know what to call him. I guess you would call him a . . . a hired thug. He's Russian, and . . ."

"Gregor Volkov," Storm said, just to speed the conversation along.

"You know about him?"

"Yes."

"Well, then you probably know I . . ."

He faltered.

"I . . ." He tried again.

"I've made a . . . Oh, God, what have I done?"

The weight of it finally hit him. The damage he had caused. The lives that had been shattered. The lives that were now in jeopardy. It had started as a kind of play on his part—just one big investment gambit, nothing more—and it had gone so incredibly wrong.

It was all crashing down on him, all at once. And that was when Graham Whitely Cracker V—mover of billions, master of the universe, scion of the Cracker fortune—started crying.

It was not a small cry. His face had crumpled. His shoulders heaved. He was making this noise that sounded more animal than human, and he knew he must have looked both terrifying and stupid, but he couldn't stop himself. He just leaked tears and snot all over that pay-phone handset and blubbered nonsensical snippets of sentences.

Storm let him carry on. He didn't feel the least shred of pity for Cracker. Storm was more ready to kill Cracker than he was to comfort him. It was all he could do not to hang up the phone at this feeble exhibition, which was as much self-pity as anything.

When he could listen to it no more, Storm finally said, "Mr. Cracker, get ahold of yourself."

Cracker bawled some more, apologizing all the while, but finally started saying things Storm could actually parse.

"Volkov . . . Volkov turned on me. . . . He's told me he's going to kill my family if I don't cooperate. . . . Oh, God . . ."

"Cooperate with what, Mr. Cracker?"

"The MonEx codes. I . . . I . . . I paid him to steal MonEx

codes from a bunch of bankers around the world. And I might have . . . I told him about Click Theory. I can't believe I was so stupid, but he was . . . I mean, he was just this muscle-for-hire, you know? I never thought he would have any plans of his own beyond . . . He was just supposed to give the codes to me, accept his payment, and that was that. But now he wants to use them for his own purpose. He doesn't know how to work the MonEx, and even if he found someone who did, he wouldn't know how exactly to perform the trades you would need to make Click Theory happen. There's probably only a handful of us in the world who truly understand what would need to be done. And with the threats against my family . . . I have no choice."

"What exactly does he hope to gain from this?"

"A planned catastrophe, just like me, but with a different ending," Whitely said. "He was rambling on about returning Russia to her full glory. 'America will sink. Russia will rise.' All that stuff. He's aligned some Russian oligarchs to take advantage of the instability brought on by a triggering of Click Theory. In return, those oligarchs are apparently going to support him in some kind of coup. . . ."

"Making a financially reinvigorated Russia a military dictatorship with General Volkov at the head of it," Storm completed.

"Yeah, that's about the size of it."

Storm considered the ramifications of having a man with Volkov's ruthlessness and ambition with his finger on the trigger of Russia's depleted-but-still-formidable nuclear arsenal. It was not a thought he wanted to entertain further.

"Mr. Cracker, where are you right now?"

"I'm . . . at a rest stop off the New York State Thruway. . . . Just past Exit Fifteen-A."

"First thing I want you to do is call your wife and tell her . . ."

"It's already taken care of," Cracker assured him. "She'll be out of the house in no time."

"Okay, then the next thing you need to do is sit tight and wait for me. I'll be there in under an hour."

Storm knew that as long as Volkov needed him, Whitely Cracker still had his uses.

As bait.

NEW YORK, New York

First problem to deal with: Storm needed a change of clothes. Fortunately, the city of New York was full of establishments that sold those. Storm was soon reoutfitted, in a charcoal corduroy jacket, a snug-fitting black T-shirt, gray cargo pants, and—his father would have been proud—black rubber-soled shoes.

Second problem to deal with: Storm needed a car. Fortunately, the city of New York was full of people who didn't own one of those and therefore needed to rent one. He let his phone lead him to the nearest rental place, and he was soon driving the only Ford they had. A Fusion. Not the sexiest car for an international super-spy, but at least it had a V6 engine.

The third problem to deal with was the most vexing of all: Storm needed the nerds. And, unfortunately, those nerds were not in the city of New York. They were in a cubby deep underneath and/or beside and/or on top of CIA headquarters. And given that he had just been terminated, Storm couldn't just call them.

Unless . . .

Unless he could get a certain someone to answer his cell phone.

One ring. Two rings.

"What do you want?" Agent Kevin Bryan demanded in a fierce whisper.

"Kev. Kev, bro, it's me, Storm."

"Yeah, I know," Bryan whispered. "But I'm sorry, we can't have a conversation right now. I don't talk to dead people."

"I know, I know. But I need a favor."

"Forget it. The way Jones is stomping around here? He'll bust me back to the translating unit if he learns I helped you. You're too hot to touch right now."

"You don't have a choice. You owe me."

"From what? I do n— Oh, wait, because of that twenty bucks you gave Javi? Forget it."

"A debt is a debt," Storm said.

"That debt is not equal to anything you'd ask me to do right now."

"Fine," Storm said. "I'm calling in Bahrain."

Bryan paused. Even in the slippery world of the CIA, there was a code of honor between fellow foot soldiers that would not allow Bryan to back out now, and they both knew it.

"Aww, man, you're unbelievable," Bryan said. "Fine. What do you need?"

"First of all, you can't tell Jones about any of this."

"Believe me, that's no problem. Jones would fire me on the spot if he knew I was even talking to you."

"Good. I actually need something from the nerds. There was an unauthorized helicopter that flew into Manhattan airspace earlier this morning. . . ."

"Yeah, I sort of heard about that," Bryan interrupted. "You are of course aware of what direction shit flows, and I can assure you I've been one of the unfortunate victims downstream of a flood of it."

"Yeah, sorry about that. Anyhow, have the nerds hack into the FAA's computers. The FAA has a flight history database that tracks all authorized *and* unauthorized air travel. I need to know where that helicopter went."

"Hang on," Bryan said, putting his phone down. Storm could hear Jones, still fulminating somewhere in the background.

A few minutes later, Bryan returned: "Okay, I got it. The helicopter took off from and landed at what appears to be the rooftop of an abandoned factory in Bayonne. I'll send GPS coordinates to your phone."

Storm chuckled grimly.

"What?" Bryan asked.

"First Paris, now Bayonne."

"Why is that funny?"

"I've just always thought of Bayonne as the Paris of New Jersey."

CHAPTER 28

FAIRFAX, Virginia

C arl Storm had finally fixed the Buick. The AC blower now ran on low, medium, and high, just as it had when he drove it out of the showroom all those years ago. It had been a problem with the fusible link wire all along. Derrick had been right.

Now Carl was wishing something else would go wrong with the thing, if only because it would give him something to think about other than his son and the trouble he was surely in.

The fact was, Carl Storm didn't have a lot of hobbies. He wasn't one of those old guys who golfed. He did yard work, but he didn't take pleasure in fussing with his garden for hours on end. He worked on his car, but only when it was broken.

About the only thing that could take his mind off things was reading. He was well ensconced in his Barcalounger, in the midst of rereading the collected works of Stephen J. Cannell, God rest his soul, when his home phone rang.

"Hello?"

"Mr. Storm," a crisp voice on the other end of the phone said. "My name is Scott Colston. We don't know each other. But I've been told that because of something that happened many years ago in Tuscon, I'm to call you and brief you on my current investigation.

And I'm to trust that you'll handle that information with due care."

Carl Storm sat up in the Barcalounger and grabbed a pen and pad from the end table at his side.

"You're the guy with White Collar, then? This is in regard to Operation Wafer?"

"That's right," Colston said.

"Tell me about it."

Colston started talking. Carl's pen waved furiously, trying to keep up with the flow of information. There was a time when he would have trusted his memory, when he had this spongy spot in his brain that sucked up the details of a new investigation almost automatically. But he had been out of the game too long. The sponge wasn't as absorbent as it used to be.

Besides, this wasn't his ass on the line. It was Derrick's. And that was a lot more important.

As Colston spoke, Carl peppered him with questions. *How did you first get onto this again? When did this activity start? How much did you say has been siphoned off again? Where is he hiding it?*

He didn't know which parts would end up being important and which were superfluous. He wanted to make sure he didn't miss any details that Derrick needed.

When the man was done, Carl thanked him.

Then he called Derrick.

"Son," he said. "I need to tell you about a little something called Operation Wafer."

The call took Derrick all the way from the city to that rest stop upstate. It took that long for Carl to go through his notes and explain everything to him. But it was time well spent.

By the time Derrick left his car, the outlines of his plan—sort of like the first plinkings of what would soon be a thunderous symphony—were beginning to fall into place. At the very least, Storm had figured out how he was going to deal with Whitely Cracker.

CHAPTER 29

SLOATSBURG, New York

n his line of work, Derrick Storm often saw people on the worst day of their life. But there was something extra pathetic about seeing Whitely Cracker on the worst day of his. Maybe it's because he was so wealthy, so accomplished, had been so protected from the time he was in his crib: When the super-rich fall, they do so from a far greater height; and when they hit bottom, they've landed in a place the existence of which they've barely ever imagined.

As he entered the New York State Thruway's Sloatsburg Travel Plaza, Storm saw Whitely Cracker sitting at a table by himself, hunched over a donut, looking scared and bloody and small.

As well he should have been. He was being hunted by a madman who would not hesitate to slaughter him and his family. His net worth was currently somewhere in the negative billions. And when news of his ruin leaked out and his clients realized their investments had vanished, his once-good name would go down alongside Bernie Madoff's, Michael Milken's, and the names of all the Wall Street swindlers who had come before. His son, Whit the VI, would be the last of the Graham Whitely Cracker line. The little boy would probably change his name just to distance himself from the shame of it.

The man nibbling on that donut had aged twenty years since

Storm had seen him the night before. Storm recognized, in some important way, that Cracker had utterly capitulated to whatever was going to come next.

"Oh, thank God you're here," he said when he saw Storm approaching. "Thank you so much for coming."

It was not the usual you're-probably-wondering-why-I've-gathered-you-here-today tone that Whitely Cracker ordinarily used. It was humble. Sincere.

"I know I don't deserve your help," he added.

"Yes, that's true," Storm said. "And just so we're clear, Mr. Cracker, I'm not here as some personal favor to you and I'm not here because I like you. I'm frankly disgusted by you. Your actions and decisions have resulted in the deaths of dozens of innocent people all over the world. I believe you ought to spend the rest of your life in prison for what you've done. I don't know what the U.S. government will have to say about it. But if I find the opportunity to voice my opinion, I will."

He was thinking of all Volkov's victims when he said it, but Ling Xi Bang most of all. No, Cracker hadn't pulled the trigger on the bullet that severed her femoral artery, nor had he deposited that slug in her gut. Volkov had done that. And Storm recognized that he himself bore responsibility for her death as well. But the fact was, if Whitely Cracker had never come into Storm's life, Ling Xi Bang would still be alive. Storm would always despise him for it. The only reason Storm wasn't consumed with finding a way to make sure Cracker was properly punished was that stopping Volkov mattered more.

"I understand," Whitely said, evenly. "But I want you to know, it wasn't supposed to—"

"I don't have time for your excuses," Storm cut him off. "We have to go. Come on."

Storm turned his back and began taking long strides toward the exit. Cracker left his donut half-eaten and scrambled after him.

"I'm not trying to make excuses. Believe me, I'm not. But I want you to understand what happened. I'm not expecting your forgiveness or . . . or your sympathy . . . or anything. But I would like you to at least know the truth as I see it."

Storm pushed through the double doors into the parking lot, where he spied Cracker's Jaguar.

"We're taking your car," Storm said, without looking back. "And I'm driving."

Storm had first seen the Jaguar in Cracker's garage when he had taken the Maserati. The Jaguar's V12 engine might come in handy. Plus, Jaguar was, technically, a Ford product.

"Yeah, yeah, fine," Cracker said. "Anyhow, as I was saying, I . . . Look, I know you don't want to hear this, but, in all seriousness, no one was supposed to get hurt. Volkov was pitched to me as a mercenary who was an expert in surveillance. He was supposed to spy on these people, steal their codes, and give them to me. Killing was never something we discussed."

They had reached the Jaguar.

"You seriously expect me to believe that?" Storm said. "You hire a man like Volkov for one reason, and that's to kill people. It's what he does. And he does it efficiently and without remorse. I find it hard to believe that a man who does research for a living wouldn't have been able to learn just a little about who Volkov is. Keys."

"What?"

"Give me the keys."

"Oh, yeah. Sorry," Whitely said, fishing them from his pocket and tossing them to Storm. "Look, I know what you're saying, and I know how this must sound, but I'm telling you the truth. You have to remember, I do research on companies, not criminals. There was never any mention of bloodshed when Volkov and I first talked. I was even paying him extra because he said the way I wanted the job done made it harder. But it was also an important part of my plan. No one was supposed to be aware this was happening. I wanted this done quietly, without attracting any attention at all—not from the finance community, not from law enforcement, not from anyone. Then the next thing I knew, he was leaving bodies all over the place and I couldn't control him."

Storm had settled into the driver's side, scooted the seat back, and fired up the engine. Much as he hated to admit it, Cracker's version of the story actually sounded plausible. And, much as he hated to engage Cracker in conversation, his curiosity was getting the better of him.

"But why, Cracker? Why? Why even kick a plan like this into action? I'm pretty sure I know, but I need to hear it from you."

"Because I'm broke," Cracker said.

"So I've heard. How is that possible?"

"I don't know. I really don't. I thought my trades were all good. Most of them anyway. I'm not saying every deal I did ended up being a win. No one in this business has a perfect batting average. But I was winning at least eight times out of ten. Or I thought I was. But I guess . . . Look, I know this sounds ridiculous, but I've always been very process-oriented. I'm all about drilling down very deep, paying attention to the details of each trade, and then letting other people deal with the big picture. I never really paid attention much to the bottom line. And the next thing I knew, my accountant was coming to me, telling me I was broke."

"Your accountant. As in Theodore Sniff?" Storm said, merging into the southbound traffic and accelerating until they were well over the speed limit.

"Oh, you know Teddy, too? Yeah, him. Good guy. Wrinkled suits."

"As you were saying, he tells you you're broke."

"Yeah, broke. And I'm not just talking rich guy broke, where I'm down to that last hundred million that I swore I'd never touch. Apparently, I went through that a while ago. I'm talking billions in the hole. Billions. I could fool people for a while because my name is Graham Whitely Cracker the Fifth, but you can't stall them forever. It was all about to come crashing in on me."

"So you call up your buddy, Senator Whitmer."

"Wow, you've really done your homework. Watch out for that truck."

Storm had wedged the Jaguar into a tight spot between an

eighteen-wheeler and a minivan so he could scoot around a slow-moving Mitsubishi that had taken up permanent residence in the passing lane—a development that made Storm briefly wish the Jaguar had front-mounted rocket launchers.

"Anyhow, yeah, I had read Rodney Click's paper. A bunch of us who are active on the Foreign Exchange Market did. We had even talked about it, in that way you talk about, I don't know, Big Foot or the Loch Ness Monster. Everyone else sort of laughed it off. But I was toying with it in my mind. And, all the while, I was getting more and more desperate each time I talked to Teddy Sniff. Click Theory was looking like my only way out. Then I called up good ol' Donny Whitmer and asked him for a favor and he said sure. Next thing I knew, Click Theory had gone from the Loch Ness Monster to this little goldfish swimming around in a bowl. It was right there for me. All I had to do was reach in and grab it."

"Because you knew you could make a killing if you could dictate when Click Theory was going to come down," Storm said as he settled into some clear road and accelerated.

"That's right. I knew U.S. stocks would go in the dumper while precious metals and anything not connected to the dollar would go out of sight. So it was really pretty simple. I was selling short on everything I could, stockpiling gold and silver and non-U.S. currency, and waiting to make my fortune back."

"And to hell with everyone else," Storm said.

"No, that's the best part," Cracker said. "Rodney Click is a really smart guy, but he has a more theoretical understanding of things. He doesn't fully grasp the way the ForEx works in practice. He overlooked certain corrective mechanisms that would have kicked in when savvy traders looked at the new landscape. If you understand those measures *and* you still have those six traders' MonEx codes? You could wait a week and then completely reverse the effects of Click Theory. I would have made a mess, yes. But it would have been just a temporary mess. I would have cleaned everything up again. It would have all been over in a week, and at the end of it, I would have been whole again."

"At the expense of the people you swindled."

"Believe me, the people I was trading with can handle a few losses," Cracker said. "Look, I know . . . I know what I did wasn't exactly going to win me any Man of the Year votes, but I . . . I do a lot of good with my money, too. I give a lot of it to charity. I try to help the—"

"Save it," Storm said.

"Okay, okay, I know, but I—"

"Shut up."

"Yes, sir."

"Listen, Cracker, if we both get out of this alive—and that is still a big if—there's going to come a time when I'm going to ask you to do certain things. Correction, I'm going to *tell* you to do certain things. You will do them without second thought, you will do them anonymously, and you will do them without hope of recognition or reward. Are we clear?"

"Crystal."

"Good."

They drove in silence for a minute or two.

"Can I ask something?" Cracker said.

"Yes. One thing."

"Where are we going?"

"To see an FBI agent."

"The FBI? Why the FBI?"

"Sorry," Storm said. "You're already out of questions."

CHAPTER 30

EAST RUTHERFORD, New Jersey

The East Rutherford Field Office of the FBI is one of the less advertised posts of America's mightiest law enforcement agency. It can be found alongside Route 17, a clogged commercial byway, tucked in among the big box stores, chain restaurants, and gas stations. It is housed in an unmarked office building that resembles a Tic Tac, because it's long and white and some 1970s-era architect thought rounding the edges at each end would make his creation look distinctive.

And if you are a Wall Street trader, it is the last place you ever want to find yourself.

The East Rutherford Field Office is the home to the famous—or infamous, depending on your point of view—WCCU. The White Collar Crimes Unit. Often working in concert with the Securities and Exchange Commission, the unit employs some of the smartest agents the FBI has, which is important because they go after some of the most sophisticated crooks in America. Most of the agents who land in the WCCU are there because they have MBAs or other advanced degrees; and most, in truth, have a chip on their shoulder.

That, it turns out, is just as important as whatever formal training they bring to bear. The people they deal with seldom recognize they've acted unlawfully and rarely view themselves as criminals. The thief who steals money from a bank understands he is doing something wrong. The thief who illegally leverages a pension fund thinks he's just pushing around paper.

As such, when you catch a white collar crook, there's a certain amount of indignant, I'm-just-doing-whatever-everyone-else-does rationalizing to suffer through. And, to be fair, they're actually right. They *are* just doing what many of their peers do but haven't gotten caught at. The haphazard nature of it is easier to reconcile if you bring a certain attitude—and a certain moral rectitude—to the job.

Storm was coming to this place improvising to a certain extent. He had not yet made contact with the FBI—only his father had—and he did not know how cooperative or forthcoming the fibbies would be with someone who wasn't of their number.

But he hoped they played nice with him. In order for the plan he was currently formulating to work, Storm needed—unfortunately—a rehabilitated Whitely Cracker, one who was financially solvent.

If nothing else, Storm could enjoy the irony of it: He was taking a trader to a place that would feel like prison as a first step to getting him out of it.

He pulled the Jaguar off the busy road and into the parking lot as Whitely stared at the building in stunned awe.

"I've heard about this place," Whitely said.

"Oh?"

"You know how Boy Scouts sit around the campfire and tell ghost stories? This is the kind of ghost story they tell at my tennis club. About people who got taken here. They call this building 'the Poison Pill,' because that's what it looks like and that's what you want to have handy if you're ever asked to go there for questioning. For people in my world, this is like the principal's office, the dentist's chair, and Pa's woodshed—all rolled into one and then made a million times worse."

Storm let the comment pass. He wasn't in the mood for gallows humor from this man. Death wasn't funny to Storm. It was a dull ache in the empty spot once filled by Ling Xi Bang.

Storm parked and got out of the car. With misgiving, he took the Dirty Harry gun out of his shoulder holster, knowing it wouldn't make it past the metal detector. He tossed it in the Jaguar's trunk, away from any skel who might wander through the parking lot and take a shine to it.

They entered the building, crossing the FBI seal on their way to a metal detector, a thorough wanding, and a briefly invigorating pat down.

Once they were through the outer layer of security, an agent asked if they had an appointment.

Storm didn't. But he said, "I'm here to see Scott Colston."

The agent frowned. "I'm afraid Agent Colston is out."

"We'll wait," Storm said.

The man pointed them toward a stiff-backed wooden bench in the lobby. There were no pillows on it. The FBI did not particularly care whether its visitors were comfortable.

About five minutes into their wait, a phalanx of agents burst in through the front doors. Two of them held the double doors extra wide for a burly, goateed agent who was escorting a short, fat, balding man in a wrinkled suit.

A wrinkled suit and handcuffs.

If Whitey Cracker's jaw hadn't been hinged, it would have fallen to the floor. The look on his face was pure confusion, as if he was seeing someone incredibly familiar to him, but in the completely wrong place.

"Teddy?" Whitely said loudly, as Theodore Sniff and his escorts were waved through security. "Teddy, what are you . . . what are you doing here?"

The agents were stone-faced. The burly guy was gently prodding Sniff forward. The accountant was doing anything he could to avoid making eye contact with his boss.

"Teddy, what's going on?" Whitely asked.

Sniff's attention was now firmly fixed on the floor in front of him. They were passing by Storm and Cracker on their way to the elevator. But Whitely was finally starting to put things together: No moneyman was brought into the Poison Pill wearing handcuffs so he could get a good citizenship commendation.

"Teddy, what have you done?"

Still nothing from Sniff. Whitely walked toward the burly guy. "Excuse me, sir. My name is Whitely Cracker and this . . . this is my accountant. Can you please tell me why he's being brought here?"

The man turned to Cracker, sized him up for a moment, opened his mouth, closed it as if he'd thought better of it, then ultimately decided there was no harm.

"Embezzlement," he said.

"Embezzlement? But . . . but who is he embezzling from?"

The man looked at Cracker like he was a prize idiot. "Well, from you, of course."

Cracker's jaw was now through the floor, the subfloor, the basement, the bedrock, and drilling its way to the Earth's core. The worst day of his life had somehow gotten worse: he was not only broke and hunted, he had been betrayed by one of his closest associates.

Another man might have been angry to learn this. That was not Whitely Cracker's nature. He was mostly just bewildered.

"But Teddy . . . Teddy, how could you? After all we've done together? I've . . . I've treated you like family. I've given you extra bonuses, extra vacations. You're my baby girl's godfather, for goodness' sakes. We started out together. . . ."

The elevator had arrived. Sniff and his escorts were getting on board.

"I'd appreciate if you gentlemen could wait here," the burly man said. "It's actually quite helpful to have you here. We're just not quite ready for you yet."

Whitely was only dimly hearing the man. He was busy

beseeching some reaction—any reaction—out of the man who until moments ago had been his trusted right hand.

"Just . . . talk to me, Teddy. I don't . . . I don't understand. How could you do this to me, Teddy? What did I ever do to you, Teddy?"

Finally, Sniff turned to his boss, brought his chin up, and said in a deadly serious voice: "Don't call me Teddy. I hate that name. I've always hated that name. My name is Theodore. Understand, motherfucker?"

AFTER THE ELEVATOR DOORS CLOSED, STORM AND CRACKER WERE shunted over to the bench. It suited Storm well. He needed time to think anyway, to fill in with meat and skin the skeleton of the plan he had made.

Cracker mostly paced. He had a lot to think about, too.

"So," he said at one point, "all those bugs in my house. Was that all the FBI?"

"Actually, that was the CIA," Storm said. "They . . . they were looking to protect the assets of one of your more strategically important foreign clients."

"Ah, yes. Prince Hashem."

"You got it."

They lapsed back into contemplation. About a half hour later, an agent came down and said Agent Colston—the burly guy with the goatee, apparently—was grateful for their patience, but he needed a little more time to interrogate the defendant.

Sniff wasn't the suspect anymore. He was now the defendant.

An hour later, Storm received a text message from Kevin Bryan's cell phone. "A truck has departed Volkov's Bayonne location. Will advise of further movement. You safe?"

Storm thought about his current location and texted back: "Couldn't be safer."

The reply: "Good. Stay that way."

Storm hadn't expected Volkov to remain in Bayonne. He was a predator. Predators stay on the move. It's a fact in the animal kingdom that carnivores tend to have much larger home ranges than herbivores. The equivalent could be said about the human world. Storm was just trying to think about how to use that fact against Volkov.

He wished he could somehow harness the Bureau's considerable muscle, but he knew too much about how they operated. They had laws to follow, jurisdiction to respect, procedure to which they adhered. Most of all, this wasn't their investigation. They had no evidence that would justify action against Volkov. The say-so of one private investigator wouldn't begin to do the trick.

He was back to thinking about what he would be able to accomplish on his own, when an agent came back downstairs, invited them into the elevator, and led them to a conference room on the second floor.

There, Agent Colston received them.

"Thank you for staying, Mr. Cracker," Colston said, then turned to Storm. "I don't believe we've met."

"Derrick Storm."

A smile crept across Colston's face for a brief moment before he tamped it down. "What a coincidence. I was just chatting with a man named Carl Storm earlier this morning. Is he a relative, perhaps?"

"Perhaps," Storm said.

"And what is your interest in this matter?"

"I'm a private investigator," Storm said, presenting his Storm Investigations business card. "Mr. Cracker has me on retainer."

"Fair enough," Colston said. He pivoted his attention away from Storm. "Mr. Cracker, I have to say, it's a little unusual to have the victim of a crime waiting in our lobby when I come in with the man we're accusing of defrauding him. But I suppose it's also convenient."

"Saves you a trip to Manhattan," Cracker said amiably.

"Well, yes." Colston paused, folded his hands, unfolded them.

"I guess we should start at the beginning. I'll spare you some of the details, but I can give you a rough outline of our investigation. We got a tip that there were some financial irregularities at Prime Resource Investment Group that were worth investigating."

"A tip? From whom?"

Colston again wrestled with how much to say. But, ultimately, Cracker would probably learn it anyway.

"Actually, it was your wife."

"Melissa?" Cracker said, as if he had more than one wife and her identity needed to be clarified.

"That's right."

"But how did she . . ." he started, then he shook his head. "And to think people don't believe me when I say she's smarter than me."

"Anyhow, we got some warrants, and sure enough, we were able to find that there had been a steady drip of money out of your accounts, going back years. Like a lot of embezzlers, Mr. Sniff started out small, then got more bold as time went along and he didn't get caught. Eventually, he figured out that you just weren't minding the store at all, and the drip became more like a torrent. He was very sophisticated about how he did it, and it took us a while to unravel it all. But, essentially, he was robbing you blind. He has buried billions in offshore accounts, both in the Caribbean and Switzerland."

"I knew it!" Cracker said.

Colston and Storm looked at him incredulously.

"Well, okay, obviously, I didn't know it. But I just . . . It's like I was telling Mr. Storm before. I knew my trades were mostly good. It just didn't make any sense that I was out of money. Like, a few weeks ago, I had converted some grain futures into . . ."

"Mr. Cracker, if you don't mind, I have a lot of work to do here," Colston said.

"Sorry, sorry. Continue."

"Anyhow, he maintained fake books for you, for a while, anyway. Then he figured out it was actually more fun—for him—if you thought you were broke. It would not only stress you out, it would make you borrow money to try and make up what you had lost, thus putting you in an even deeper hole when he eventually pulled the plug. He wanted you humiliated as much as possible. He maintained fake account ledgers for your clients and the SEC, of course. So it took us a while to untangle it all. Eventually, we were able to establish what he was doing and how he was doing it. But it was more on the level of being able to observe general patterns secondhand. We still had to catch him in the act. So we convinced Lee Fulcher to pretend that he had a margin call and ask for all his money."

"That was fake?"

"That was a trap," Colston said. "Mr. Sniff had grown incredibly greedy. Again, he wanted to put you in the deepest hole possible. We knew that if there was a sudden demand for forty-three million dollars, it would put him into action."

"Because it would make him have to come up with the money?"

"No, actually, the opposite: because it would make him steal the last little bit he could. He knew the margin call would be the thing that pushed you over the edge. This was his last withdrawal before you got closed out for good. Lucky for you, we were watching. He made his move right before the end of business yesterday. We made sure we had it fully documented, then picked him up earlier today."

A look of utter amazement had washed over Cracker. "Unbelievable," he said. "So what happens now?"

"Well, we've been having, ah, discussions with Mr. Sniff for the last few hours," Colston said. "We showed him some of our evidence and presented him with two scenarios. One is where he decides to fight us. He has no assets with which to do so, because we've gotten a judge to freeze all his accounts. But he goes down swinging anyway. We pile on the charges, insist on consecutive sentences rather than concurrent ones, and send him to the nastiest hole of a prison we can find, where he is more than likely raped and beaten by his fellow inmates until he either dies of old age or sheer exhaustion. Or . . ."

Colston allowed himself another small smile before he continued: "Or he cooperates, admits wrongdoing, returns the money he stole from you and your clients, and serves ten years in a minimum security prison for white collar felons. It may be too generous an offer, but it's one that saves us a lot of time and resources that are better spent catching other crooks. And it makes you financially whole a lot faster than if the thing had to drag through the courts."

"And?" Cracker asked, leaning forward.

"He's waiting to sign the plea bargain documents as we speak," Colston said. "The good news for you is that he hadn't spent any of the money he stole. Actually, he had done quite a fine job investing it. I think you'll end up liking the return he got for you."

His fortune restored, Cracker was beaming, enough that Storm was quite sure he had—at least momentarily—forgotten that he still had a sociopathic Russian on his tail.

But after he received assurances that he would get updates from Colston and left the building, it didn't take long for him to remember. He and Storm had made a right turn out of the Poison Pill's parking lot, pulling onto Route 17's three lanes of southbound traffic.

They were no more than a half mile down the road when the bullets started flying.

THREE SLUGS SLAMMED INTO THE BACK OF THE JAGUAR, MAKING three nickel-sized holes in the bumper.

Cracker promptly dove into the well of the passenger seat. "Someone's shooting at us!" he yelped. "Why is someone shooting at us?"

Storm's only reaction was to press the accelerator and look in the rearview mirror for the source of the gunfire. It was a white

Lincoln Mark LT pickup truck. There was a driver and a passenger, neither of whom Storm could make out, thanks to afternoon sun glare. The man shooting at them was standing on the flatbed, braced against the top of the cab. He had an AR-15, the semiautomatic, civilian version of the military M-16.

Storm's first thought was that it was a strange choice. The AR-15 had its uses, and there were reasons it had been the standard-issue rifle of the U.S. Army for more than four decades—it was light, accurate, easy to carry, simple in its design, and cheap to mass-produce. But it was more of a peashooter in a scenario where an elephant gun would have been a better choice. On the back of a pickup truck, Volkov could have mounted a .50-caliber M2 Browning that would have needed about thirty seconds to turn the Jaguar into a shredded heap of scrap. The AR-15's .223-caliber round just didn't pack the same punch.

Then Storm figured it out: the tires. They were trying to shoot the tires, disable the Jaguar, then kidnap Cracker. They couldn't risk killing him. He was their key to unlocking the power of those MonEx codes.

That, Storm knew, was their vulnerability. He relished the idea of getting into a shoot-out with people who would be afraid to shoot back.

More gunshots rang out, but this time they missed low, ricocheting off the pavement. Cars began swerving off the road to get out of the Lincoln's way. New Jersey drivers were a hardy breed, made tough by long exposure to aggressive driving, but gunfire was a bit much even for them.

Storm's plan was simple: find a place to pull over where no one would get hit in the cross fire, take out Dirty Harry, and take his time picking off the three assailants. He reached into his jacket for his gun then swore loudly.

"What is it?" Cracker asked.

"I left my gun in the trunk," he said.

There could be no stopping now. And that would soon be a

problem. This section of Route 17 had lights. Lots of them. So far they had been green. But that wouldn't last.

"Get your sorry ass in that seat and put your seat belt on," Storm ordered.

"But they're shooting."

"Not at you."

"What do you . . ."

"Seat belt. Now," Storm said, jerking the wheel hard to the left to swerve around a Honda, sending Cracker sprawling into the passenger-side door. When he recovered, he complied with Storm's command.

"What are you going to do?" Cracker asked, his voice cracking with panic. "Do you . . . do you have a plan?"

"Yes. My plan is for you to shut up."

Storm began weaving through and around his fellow travelers, slaloming from one lane to the next, leaving a lot of rubber on the blacktop but making sure his tires were never exposed to a clear shot from the gunman. The Jaguar was faster than the Lincoln, but in this traffic, that advantage was mitigated. He needed a clearer, light-free stretch of roadway if he was going to have a chance of outrunning their pursuers.

Then his GPS showed that, as if sent by the gods, a large divided highway was approaching. It was labeled Route 3. Storm allowed himself half a smile. Route 3 led rather quickly to the New Jersey Turnpike. There was only one light between him and more than a hundred miles of uninterrupted highway.

Then the light turned red.

THIS BEING NEW JERSEY, A FEW CARS RAN THE LIGHT. BUT OTHER-wise, the vehicles in front of Storm were dutifully coming to a halt. He tugged the wheel right, steering the Jaguar into the break-down lane, laying off the accelerator but not daring to brake. He couldn't give the thug in the flatbed of the Lincoln a closer shot.

The traffic from the cross street was now easing through the intersection in one continuous line, feeding in from both sides, leaving only a few scant feet between each car.

"Your secretary told me you have a classic video arcade," Storm said as he measured the maneuver he was about to attempt. "You ever play Frogger?"

"No? Why?"

"You're about to," Storm said.

He tapped the brake for a half second as he eyed the westbound lane, then shifted his view to the eastbound lane. More shots were coming from the Lincoln, but they were wild. An Exxon sign beside them shattered. Some flower planters exploded. Storm only prayed the drivers milling about as their gas was pumped didn't get hit by a bouncing bullet.

The Lincoln was closing in. And fast. If he stayed on the brake much longer, he was going to be rear-ended, probably pushing him into another car in the process. He'd be at a dead stop. If that happened, he might as well fasten Cracker into the Lincoln, then shoot himself—it would save everyone some time.

Then he saw an opening, albeit not much of one. Maybe it was enough. Maybe it wasn't. But the moment for further deliberation had passed. Two bullets plowed into the Jaguar's trunk. If the shooter adjusted his aim just a foot lower, Storm would lose any choice he had in the matter. It was time to act. He jammed the accelerator to the floor. The Jaguar leaped forward.

"Brace yourself," Storm called out.

Horns blared. Cracker screwed his eyes shut. Storm gripped the steering wheel as if it were his hold on life itself. He had aimed for a clearing in the westbound lane—the first lane of cars they had to negotiate—but there was no such gap in the eastbound lane. He was heading straight for the passenger-side door of a Subaru. He could see the driver's eyes grow wide and her mouth drop to unleash a scream as she realized she was about to be speared by what appeared to be a runaway car. But Storm couldn't adjust course without clipping another eastbound car. A collision was imminent.

Then at the last second, he nudged the wheel to the right. He squeezed past with inches to spare. Storm let out a rebel yell as they charged toward Route 3, now totally unimpeded.

Behind him, he could hear the crunching of metal as the Lincoln T-boned the Subaru.

Storm only hoped that, because neither car was going too fast, the drivers would be okay. He was not a deeply religious man, but he uttered a quick prayer.

STORM KEPT THE GAS PEDAL TO THE FLOOR UNTIL THEY REACHED the left-hand exit that led to the highway. As they wound around the ramp onto the highway, he eased up on the speed, relaxing his grip on the steering wheel.

Cracker looked like he was going to faint. He started doing some strange breathing exercise. Storm was about to tell him to stop—it was annoying—but then decided to let the man huff and puff. It was better than having to hear him talk.

Storm kept one eye on the road, one eye on his rearview mirror. As soon as they straightened out and reached the merge, he accelerated. A welcome sign told him the exit for the New Jersey Turnpike was a mere three-quarters of a mile on the right.

"So was that . . . was that Volkov?" Cracker asked.

"You got anyone else in your life who might have reason to shoot at you?"

"If I had gone bankrupt? Yeah, a horde. But not now. He's the only one."

"Well, there you go."

"So what are we going to . . ."

"Shit," Storm said.

"What is it?"

The pickup had reappeared in his rearview mirror. Its front grille plate was bashed in and its front bumper was missing, but it was otherwise intact. Its engine must have had enough torque to power it through the wreckage.

The only blessing was that it appeared the shooter had been thrown from the . . .

Never mind. He was reestablishing his position, with his arms draped over the top of the cab. He must have seen the accident coming and saved himself by hunkering down in the flatbed.

"What's going on? Tell me," Cracker said.

"Your friends are back."

He was able to join the southbound lanes of the New Jersey Turnpike without sustaining any more fire from the Lincoln, but by now it was late afternoon. No one was going anywhere at much more than the speed limit. Storm could use the breakdown lanes to pass, but he didn't dare use them to travel: They were a minefield of shredded truck tires and other debris. He'd be too likely to blow a tire.

In those conditions, he couldn't open up any ground on the Lincoln. If anything, the driver of the pickup was taking more chances in his passes, not caring if he clipped the occasional car's bumper, and therefore was gaining slightly on them. The guy with the AR-15 was taking potshots. Even if he was too far away to be able to reliably hit a fast-moving, weaving target, it was tempting fate to let him keep blasting away. Eventually, one of those bullets was going to find its target. Storm was just grateful none of the other cars had been hit. In truth, not many of them seemed to even notice the gunfire. An AR-15 muzzle blast was easily mistaken for a backfiring muffler.

Storm's brow furrowed. Running away was frustrating him, and not just because it wasn't working. He wanted to feel like he was doing something proactive to improve his situation. His current course of action was too passive. Storm hated passive.

"What do you have in this car?" he asked.

"What do you mean, like weapons?"

"That would be a good start."

"Well, I've got a mini Swiss Army Knife on my key chain."

"A two-inch stainless steel blade and a nail file. They might as well surrender to us now. Anything else?"

"Nothing. I'm a hedge fund manager, not a soldier of fortune."

Storm sighed. This was the problem with amateurs. You had to spell out everything for them. "No, I mean, what else do you have in this car? I want you to list every single item in this car that isn't bolted down."

"Uh, okay, let's see," Cracker said, turning around to catalogue the contents of his backseat. "I've got my tennis bag . . . a six-pack of Poland Spring water . . . a CD case . . . a bottle of Macallan I was going to give to a buddy of mine at the club . . . my daughter's car seat . . . a cigar case and . . . That's it. Except for what's in the glove compartment."

Storm felt like he was rescuing a six-year-old. "And what's in the glove compartment, Whitely?"

"Uhh, let's see . . . Some napkins . . . aspirin . . . a tire gauge . . . my insurance and registration . . . and, oh, that's where I put my sunglasses!"

"I'm thrilled for you. Anything else?"

"Nope. That's it. Sorry, there's not anything useful. Like I said, I'm not . . ."

"Actually, that'll do just fine," Storm said. "Get the tennis bag up here and hand me your racket."

Cracker fished out a Head YouTek IG Speed MP. It was made of carbon fiber–reinforced polymer. There were two more identical to it in the bag.

"That's the racket Novak Djokovic uses," Cracker said enthusiastically.

"I'm sure he'd be very proud," Storm replied, rolling down the window and allowing air to rush into the car.

Storm looked at the Lincoln in his rearview mirror, still keeping pace a few cars behind him, weaving in and out of traffic like he was. Storm maneuvered until he had a length of open pavement behind him and drifted into the right breakdown lane.

Then he jammed the brakes, pulled the wheel hard left, and executed a perfect one-eighty into the left breakdown lane—directly into the oncoming traffic.

. . .

A CHORUS OF CAR HORNS BLARED AT STORM, AS DID A SMALL army of one-fingered Jersey salutes, but Storm ignored them and focused on what he was about to attempt.

A little known fact about Derrick Storm—one he seldom bothered to share, because it seldom seemed relevant—was that he was ambidextrous. He could throw with his left arm and his right. The right tended to be more powerful. But the left was, for whatever reason, more accurate. He was relying on that as he got the Jaguar straightened out and pounded the gas pedal.

Gripping the racket, he put his left arm out the window. He waited until the onrushing Lincoln was nearly on them, then hurled the racket, boomerang-style, at the gunman.

At the moment Storm released his improvised projectile, the Jaguar had gone from a dead stop to perhaps twenty miles an hour. The Lincoln was only just starting to slow in response to Storm's move and was still traveling fifty. Counting the fifty miles an hour Storm was able to generate throwing from a seated position, the racket was coming at the gunman at an effective speed of a hundred and twenty miles an hour.

It struck him square in the forehead, knocking him unconscious and sending him careening backward, out of the flatbed and under the tires of an eighteen-wheeler. The truck didn't have a chance to react before flattening the unexpected pedestrian.

"I guess that's one down," Cracker said.

"More like fifteen-love," Storm said.

As they sped past the still-confused occupants of the pickup, Storm spied a break in the concrete Jersey barriers that separated the northbound and southbound sides of the Turnpike. It was an official-use-only U-turn, and Storm decided to officially use it. It seemed prudent to join the travel lanes of the direction he was currently pointed. He allowed himself to creep through the gap, then exhorted the Jag's V12 forward, quickly joining the northbound left lane.

He knew better than to think that simple move would lose Volkov's pickup. Sure enough, as Storm looked back, it was in the midst of pulling its own U-turn. It was not as adroit as the Jaguar, and Storm watched it clip the front bumper of a Chevy Cavalier then slam into the Jersey barrier, gouging its side panel but then speeding forward through the same U-turn that Storm had used.

The Jaguar had gained some ground, but the northbound lanes were not flowing any more smoothly than the southbound lanes had been. The pickup was four cars back, matching the Jaguar's passes car for car. But at least, Storm thought, they weren't being shot at anymore.

Then gunshots rang out again. Storm guessed, from the sound of them, it was either a .38 or a .357. Enough to shred a tire, for sure. Some cars were swerving out of the Lincoln's way into the breakdown lane. Others honked. Others seemed oblivious—a man in the car next to the Jaguar was talking on his cell phone as if he was out for a Sunday drive.

Storm looked in his rearview window and saw a man with half his body leaned out the truck's passenger-side window. It wasn't Volkov. He must have been driving.

So it turned out getting rid of the gunman in the back of the truck had only improved their circumstances marginally. A shooter who had to lean out a car and use a handgun would be more errant than one planted on his feet using a rifle. So the probability of being hit by any one bullet had lowered. But each bullet still carried with it that possibility.

"Okay, I want you to listen to me very carefully, and follow each one of my instructions exactly," Storm said. "And I don't have time for you to question me. Can you do that?"

"I . . . yes, I . . . Yes."

"Very good. Okay, first step. Take the Swiss Army Knife off the key chain."

"What? We're going to challenge them to a knife fight?"

"What did I just say about questions?"

"Sorry," Cracker said, and worked the knife away off the key chain as Storm deftly picked his way through traffic.

"Now I felt some shirts in your tennis bag. Are those made of some kind of blended fabric? Something that wicks away moisture?"

"Yes."

"Excellent. Cut one of them into six long strips."

"Okay," Cracker said and went to work with the knife on the shirts. Storm heard the ripping of fabric. More bullets were coming from the Lincoln. One shattered the right side-view mirror, evoking a yelp from Cracker. But, to his credit, he kept at his work.

"What next?" he said when he was through.

"Take those Poland Spring bottles and empty them."

"Where?"

"I don't care. On the floor."

Cracker did as he was told. "Now?"

"Pour the Macallan in equal portions into all six bottles. And try not to spill any. We need those bottles as full as possible."

Cracker apportioned the Scotch equally, filling each of the bottles roughly a third of the way. "Okay. Next?"

"Stuff those shirt strips in the bottles. Get as much of the fabric into the booze as you can, but leave some of the shirt sticking out the top."

"Uh-huh," Cracker said and applied himself to his task. He was apparently struggling with it: "The mouths of these bottles aren't very big. I'm having a tough time getting them in there. Should I cut narrower strips?"

"No. We actually need a nice tight fit. Tight enough that it won't spill if held upside down."

"All right."

Cracker worked diligently for two minutes, during which time Storm managed to keep the Jaguar shielded from gunfire.

"Done," Cracker said.

"Great. Leave the bottles upright so that they lean against the back of the seat," Storm said, then jerked his thumb toward the rear of the car. "Then go back there and unbuckle your daughter's car seat."

"Uh, all right."

Storm allowed himself to feel optimistic for a moment. He was confident he would soon be rid of the Lincoln.

But the moment didn't last. The Turnpike bent to the left, and Storm needed to make a decision: Going into the left breakdown lane would allow him to pass several more cars and reach an opening that would give him the opportunity to put some significant space between him and the Lincoln; but doing so would also give the shooter a more direct line of fire to the Jaguar's tires for a few seconds.

Storm decided to risk it. He gunned the engine and burst into the left breakdown lane.

It turned out to be the wrong decision. The moment his tires were exposed, a burst of fire came from the pickup.

And the left rear tire exploded.

THE JAGUAR SKIDDED AND SWERVED TO THE LEFT, SCRAPING CON-crete. Storm fought the steering wheel to keep them from losing control altogether, engaging his triceps and biceps in the battle. There were still pieces of tire clinging stubbornly onto the rim, but they were little help. It was all he could do to wedge the Jaguar back into the left lane.

"What's going on?" Cracker called out from the backseat.

"We lost a tire," Storm said. "It's not your problem. Just concentrate on what you're doing."

"Okay. I've got it loose."

Storm was thankful the Jaguar was front wheel drive. The car hadn't lost its power. Just its handling.

It made threading his way through and around the slower traffic an impossibility. Merely keeping the car in its lane had become a struggle. Storm was now limited to moving at the speed of the other traffic.

The Lincoln had taken advantage of this disability and had closed to within two cars. It would soon be directly behind them, or next to them, or wherever Volkov wanted it to be.

"Hand the seat up to me," Storm said.

The car seat was a dense, unwieldy hunk of padding, composite plastic, and metal. It weighed in at roughly thirty pounds, and was bottom heavy, since that's where the metal parts that anchored it to the car lived. Cracker struggled to get it through the narrow opening between the two front seats and into Storm's lap.

"Terrific. While you're back there, get that cigar case. There's a lighter in there, yes?"

"Yeah, of course. It's actually more like a small blowtorch."

"Perfect. Put it behind my back in this seat. I'm going to need to grab it quickly when I turn around."

As Cracker completed that task, Storm rolled down his window and punched on the cruise control at fifty. A small gap opened up ahead of him, but that was fine: He wouldn't have to worry about ramming the car ahead of him while he attempted the stunt he had been planning.

There was now only one car—a green Toyota—between the Jaguar and the Lincoln.

"I'm going to need you to come up here and grab the steering wheel," Storm said. "Keep us straight as best you can. It's going to battle you and try to tug you to the left. But if you get to the side of the wheel, left becomes up and right becomes down. You can use gravity to keep it down. Does that make sense to you?"

"Yeah, got it."

Cracker got himself in position, then put both hands on the wheel. The Lincoln pulled into the left breakdown lane to pass the one car that had separated it from the Jaguar. It was the move Storm had been waiting for.

"I'm letting go now," he said.

The wheel tugged left, but Cracker had all the leverage he needed to hold it in place. Storm grabbed the car seat, twisted his body so he was facing backward, then perched himself on the side of the door, so that both the seat and his torso were outside of the Jaguar.

With both hands, he heaved the car seat at the windshield of the Lincoln, putting as much strength as he could muster into the throw.

It hit the windshield dead center, creating a huge crater. The Lincoln swerved violently, rocking on its suspension, and Storm briefly hoped it might spin out. Instead, it righted itself by side-swiping the green Toyota, which sparked a chain-reaction accident behind it—but did not, unfortunately, slow the Lincoln.

Storm focused on the pickup truck, assessing the damage he had caused. The force of those thirty pounds hurtling backward had not broken the entire windshield, as Storm had hoped—the shatterproof glass did its job and held—but it did punch a car seat–sized hole in the middle. That would have to do.

Storm retreated back into the Jaguar, which was being held steady—or at least somewhat steady—by a very determined Whitely Cracker. Storm seized the cigar lighter and the first Poland Spring bottle and lit the piece of shirt sticking out the top. He hoped Volkov appreciated this tribute to Vyacheslav Molotov, the Russian foreign minister who introduced the world to the crude, homemade bomb that still bore his name.

Storm waited until he was sure the wick was lit, then leaned back out of the car and tossed his creation toward the hole in the Lincoln's windshield.

Unfortunately for him, because he was on the left side of the car and facing backward, he was using his less-accurate right arm. He missed. The bottle bounced harmlessly off the top of the Lincoln's cab and did not ignite until it hit the pavement, well behind the pickup.

There was no more gunfire coming from the Lincoln. Perhaps the car seat had injured or killed the passenger as it hurtled through the pickup. Or maybe he was just reloading.

Storm lit the next wick, then tossed. It missed wide right.

Attempt number three splattered into the grille plate and burst into a fireball, but it was like hitting a charging rhino with a BB gun. The Lincoln was not affected.

Attempt number four hit the windshield in front of the driver but bounced the wrong way and, more to the point, did not go off until it struck blacktop.

Storm had two more chances. Worse, there was once again sniping coming from the Lincoln. The shooter was leaning out his window and squeezing off rounds in steady succession. The first six missed. The seventh struck the Jaguar's right rear tire just as Storm got the next shirt lit.

Storm was thankful he was inside the car when it happened. The wild lurching of the Jaguar might have thrown him had he been trying to hang on outside.

As it was, he was tossed against the side of the vehicle, taking a chunk out of his forehead. It was not a serious wound, but it was a bleeder. Storm cursed as blood poured into his eyes.

"Oh my God, are you hit?" Cracker said.

"Just drive," Storm growled.

The Jaguar was now on its rims on both sides in back, pouring a steady stream of sparks behind it. The engine was working double to maintain the speed requested of it by the cruise control, its twelve cylinders firing furiously.

Storm looked down at the second-to-last Molotov.

"Come on, Derrick," he urged. "Let's do this."

He twisted himself out of the car, exposing more of himself so he could get his left arm free. He focused on the hole in the windshield, except it wasn't a windshield anymore. It was a catcher's glove. And he wasn't a grown man anymore. He was a twelve-year-old pitcher, in his backyard, standing on the makeshift pitchers' mound his father had created for him.

"Keep your eyes on the mitt," his father always told him when he was struggling with his control. "Don't aim. Just throw."

The old man had kept him on target in so many aspects of his life.

This would just have to be one more.

He whipped his left arm, following through as best he could with the throw.

The bottle traced a straight line toward the pickup truck, spiraling gently as it sailed in the air. Throwing a two-inch-diameter bottle through a hole no more than two feet wide from out the window of a fishtailing car traveling at fifty miles an hour was, Storm knew, a nearly impossible task.

But impossible is what Derrick Storm did for a living.

The bottle passed through the hole. The interior of the pickup's cab was suddenly engulfed in flame.

The Lincoln veered suddenly to the right, clipping a car in the right lane then going into a spin. Midway through the spin, it lost its grip on the pavement and rolled.

It rolled once, tossing the erstwhile gunman from out his open window into a stream of oncoming traffic.

It rolled twice, caving in the roof of the cab.

It was when it rolled a third time that the combination of several factors involved—the growing conflagration inside the cab, the rupturing of the gas tank, the twisting of metal—came together to create an enormous explosion.

Storm did not bother to watch the rest. He settled back in the Jaguar, grabbed control of the steering wheel, and went back to the battle of keeping them on the road.

"Is that . . . is that it?" Cracker asked, his face having lost all its color.

"One more thing," Storm said. "Hand me the last bottle."

Storm braced the wheel with his leg as Cracker gave him the bottle. Storm yanked out the cloth, tilted it back, and let the Macallan slide down his throat.

CHAPTER 31

HACKENSACK, New Jersey

They came to a stop at a combination gas station/used car lot just off the Turnpike, a seedy place that had seen everything—except a bullet-riddled Jaguar XJL limping into the parking lot on its rims.

"I'm still confused about one thing," Cracker said as they climbed out. "How did he find us? I mean, you told me all those bugs were CIA . . . so it's not like he could listen to us in my car."

Storm thought it over as he pried open the trunk of the wasted Jaguar. He retrieved the Dirty Harry gun, putting it back in his shoulder holster. Its weight felt good. He checked the revolver. It was full.

"When you were with Volkov this morning, did he touch you at some point? Bump into you? Hug you? Grab you?"

Cracker thought it over. "No, I mean we shook hands, but . . . The only other time we had contact is when he asked to borrow my phone. But I don't think we . . ."

"Let me see your phone," Storm interrupted.

He turned the phone over and located a small piece of black tape that blended nicely with the back of the phone. Storm peeled away the tape to reveal a tiny microchip.

"He put a tracking device on it," Storm said, showing Cracker the chip. "He collected his men and waited until we stayed put for a while. Then he moved in. I'm sure we gave him pause when he realized we were at an FBI office. But he knew time was on his side."

Storm tossed the tape and microchip into a nearby Dumpster and was about to hand Cracker his phone when it rang.

Storm took a glance at the screen. The caller appeared as "GREGOR VOLKOV."

Storm stared at it. "Don't you ever die?" he asked, rhetorically. How could it be that Volkov had survived that accident, unless . . . Of course. He hadn't been in the Lincoln. Storm realized he had never actually laid eyes on the man driving. Whoever it was, it hadn't been Gregor Volkov.

It rang again. Storm answered the call with "What do you want?"

"Derrick Storm?"

"Yes."

"I can't believe it, it is Derrick Storm!" Volkov boomed in Russian-tinted English. "How delightful to hear your voice. I was very surprised to see you in Manhattan this morning. I had been under the impression you were dead. It was a very pleasant impression."

"Yeah, well, the feeling is mutual."

"You must be referring to that little scrape in Mogadishu," he said, laughing.

"Actually, I was referring to the pickup truck that I just saw burst into flames on the New Jersey Turnpike."

"Oh, is that what happened?" Volkov said, as if it were nothing more than the answer to a riddle he'd only casually considered. "I wondered why we lost communication. Too bad. Too bad. They were good men. But apparently not good enough. I should have known they were no match for Derrick Storm."

"I'm assuming you didn't call to praise me, so let's cut to the chase: Whitely Cracker isn't coming with you. He's not going to make those trades for you. He's with me and he's staying with me. So you can either drop it and slither back to whatever hole you hide in, or you can die. It's up to you."

"Tut-tut, Derrick Storm. Do you really think a man as prepared as myself didn't have a backup plan? I certainly hoped the gentlemen in the pickup truck would persuade Mr. Cracker to join me. But I got myself a little . . . insurance."

Through gritted teeth, Cracker said, "What are you talking about?"

"Would you be so kind as to put me on speakerphone? I'd like you both to hear something."

Storm turned to Cracker. "Put it on speaker."

Cracker touched a button. Storm said, "Okay. We're listening."

Volkov spoke to a person in the room with him. "Go ahead, my dear," he said. "Beg for your life."

The sound of Mrs. G. Whitely Cracker V filled the air: "Whitely, honey? I love you. I'm so sorry . . . that I . . ."

"Melissa! Oh my God, what are they—"

"That's enough." Volkov cut them off. "Isn't it fortunate for me that my men were able to grab her just before she hopped away like the little bunny she is. They tell me she almost made it out, too. Would you like to hear from your darling children, Mr. Cracker, or can you trust that if I've got your wife, I've got them as well?"

"What do you want, Volkov?" Cracker said, trying to sound brave. "You want money? I've got all the money you need. I'll give you ten million for each of them, wired to any account anywhere in the world, no questions, no strings. Make it twenty million. Half now and half when—"

"Keep your money, Mr. Cracker. You must not have been listening to me this morning. Why would I want your money when I can have power? Ultimate power. For myself and my country. I assure you, there is not enough money in the world to make me give up that dream. Not even in your bank account."

Storm looked at Cracker's face. His expression was shocked

and overwhelmed and utterly desperate. Without a single word spoken, it informed Storm that trying to talk sense into this man wouldn't work. So, yes, Storm could tell him that there was no point in negotiating with terrorists. Storm could tell him that they needed to take control of this situation, to strike before being stricken, to trust that Volkov was ultimately a pragmatist who wouldn't kill the Cracker family while he still needed them for leverage. Storm could tell Cracker if he acquiesced and did what Volkov wanted, he and his family would be dead the moment Volkov no longer found them useful.

But Storm knew Cracker was beyond listening. Cracker had clearly made his mistakes—his recent actions, in particular, made him anything but the tower of virtuousness the world took him to be. Still, at his core, he was a decent man who would do anything to save his wife and children.

Even if doing it would actually result in them all being killed.

"Okay," Storm said. "So you're holding the cards. How's this going to go?"

"Mr. Cracker will present himself to me at the international departures entrance to Terminal B at Newark Airport in two hours," Volkov said. "Since I know where your mind is going at this moment, let me start by saying that if we find Mr. Cracker suddenly placed on the No-Fly List or if there is anything else done to impede his progress out of the country, the consequences for his family will be severe."

"I under—" Cracker started, but Volkov shouted him down.

"I'm not finished. Mr. Cracker will be carrying his passport, but he will have no other luggage. He will come alone. I have trained my men to know what your CIA agents look like and what their tricks are. If I or my men get even the slightest inkling Mr. Cracker is not alone or that you have organized some kind of resistance, trust that I will mail him back his family in pieces."

"Okay, we got it," Storm said before Cracker could respond. "But we can't make that happen in two hours. Your men destroyed our car. His passport is at his house in Chappaqua. We can't get a new car, get up to Chappaqua, and then get down to Newark Airport in two hours. Make it four hours."

In four hours, Storm could prevail on Jedediah Jones to get a team in place. It would be a team that, whatever Volkov thought, no thugs would be able to sniff out, no matter what Volkov told them to look for.

But in two hours? It would be nearly impossible to coordinate all those moving parts and not have them looking like the Keystone Cops. Someone would screw up.

And Volkov knew it.

"You're a resourceful man, Storm. You can make it happen," Volkov said. "I will see you in two hours, Mr. Cracker. Or I'll enjoy raping your pretty wife while your children are hacked to bits."

THE NEXT UTTERANCE OUT OF CRACKER'S MOUTH WAS A PANICKED what-will-we-do-now-how-are-we-going-to-handle-this-what-will-happen-to-us torrent that made even less sense as it went along. Storm waited it out.

When he was quite confident it was done, Storm said, "Give me your wallet."

"Why do . . . why do you need my wallet?"

"Let's have a return to the no-questions policy, please. Just hand me your wallet."

Cracker reached into his back pocket and pulled out a slender, expensive-looking leather billfold. The only cash in it was a single hundred-dollar bill. Storm picked through the credit cards until he arrived at the black American Express card. He walked toward the used car portion of the gas station, entering a glass door that had a jagged crack running along its lower portion and bells tied to its handle.

Cracker tagged along but, in keeping with the recently reinstated policy, said nothing. The jangling of the door brought a tired-looking black man from a back room.

"Can I help you?"

"Yes, do you know what this is?" Storm asked, holding out the credit card. The man squinted at it for a brief moment, and Storm continued. "Actually, let me just save you the time. It's an American Express Centurion Card, sometimes referred to as the American Express Black Card, for obvious reasons. It is the rarest credit card in the world, and it is only issued to individuals with a net worth of at least twenty million dollars. There is a rumor that it has no limit, but that's actually not true. The last time I checked, the limit was about six million. Point is, it's a lot.

"This is Mr. Whitely Cracker," Storm continued. "As you can see from the lettering on the front, he is the holder of this card. He would like to buy two of your fine used automobiles, and he would like to do it very, very quickly. Can you help us with this transaction, or do we have to take our black card elsewhere?"

The man's eyes had come to life. He didn't need the Cliffs-Notes version of what Storm had just laid out. He was about to sell two cars—probably two more than he had sold in the two weeks leading up to this. "No," he said. "I think I can help you."

"Great. What's the most expensive car you have?"

"I got an oh-four BMW five series," he said. "It's under forty thousand miles. I got it for sale at twenty-one. It's just out there if you want to have a look."

"No need. He'll take it. And please charge him double. What else?"

"I got an oh-five Cadillac STS. It's got a little bit of a—"

"No good. Do you have any Fords?"

"I got a two-year-old Fiesta, low miles, for thirteen five."

"He'll take it. Please charge him triple."

"Uh . . . okay," the guy said and was already banging the numeric pad of an ancient desk calculator. "With tax, that comes to ninety-two thousand, three hundred and—"

"Make it an even hundred thousand," Storm said, handing him the card. "I dislike haggling. But we're going to drive them out of here in the next three minutes."

"You're the boss."

"Do they have gas in them?" Storm asked, handing him the card.

"Yes, sir. Full tanks. I'm going to need his signature on some—"

"Forge it. Just get us the keys as quickly as possible."

"Give me two minutes," he said, shuffling with a little more alacrity toward a computer in the back room.

Cracker waited until the man was out of the room, then said, "Can I ask a question now?"

"Make it quick."

"Why two cars?"

"Sorry to tell you this, mate, but we've got to split up the band. You're going to get your passport and get yourself to Newark Airport, like the man said. I suggest you drive quite quickly if you're going to make it in time. Just make sure you keep your cell phone on in case I need to contact you."

"And where are you going?"

"Bayonne."

"Bayonne? As in New Jersey?"

"Yes," Storm said. "I hear it's lovely this time of year."

CHAPTER 32

BAYONNE, New Jersey

Storm's plan started with one basic, unassailable assumption.

Volkov was lying.

This was based on experience, intuition, and homespun common sense. It's like Carl Storm always said: If a man like Volkov said there was a rat on the moon, don't bring cheese.

So it was that Derrick Storm assumed that the meeting at the international terminal, the passport, the stern warnings about not utilizing the No-Fly List—it was all a ruse to make him think that Cracker was going to be smuggled out of the country to join his family in some foreign locale, where the awful deed would be done.

That, of course, meant that Cracker was unlikely to make it out of New Jersey; that his family was likely there already, holed up in the abandoned factory that Volkov believed no one knew about; that Volkov had probably set up the MonEx 4000 there and had it ready to roll.

As Storm pulled away from the used car lot, he had texted Agent Kevin Bryan: "Volkov Bayonne location still occupied?"

Shortly into his drive, Storm got the reply: "Affirmative. Infrared shows fourteen life forms in building. Helicopter now gone. Must have been a renter."

Storm yearned to have the full support of Jedediah Jones and the nerds—not just furtive texting with one agent—but had roughed it without Jones's resources before. He could do it again. Besides, he knew what involving Jones would look like. With two phone calls, Jones could get everything from the Green Berets to Navy Seal Team 6 dropping in on the building from all sides. It would make for dozens of chances for things to get screwed up. At least working alone, Storm thought wryly, there would only be one chance.

He got off Exit 14A of the New Jersey Turnpike Extension, letting the GPS in his phone guide him through a warren of streets with numeric names in an industrial part of town. Gentrification had come to many previously rusty parts of New Jersey, with the proximity to Manhattan driving a real estate boom that transformed places like Hoboken and Jersey City with condos and office buildings.

Gentrification had not yet found Bayonne. As it had been throughout its history, it was still a manufacturing center; unfortunately it was a manufacturing center for stuff America didn't make anymore. So it was that many of the buildings Storm passed were either boarded up or underutilized. And, as night fell and darkness began making serious headway, what little humanity that did make use of them had gone home.

Storm finally arrived at his target location and peered at it through the gloaming. It was a two-block-long, four-story, graffiticovered brick behemoth, riddled with grime-painted windows that tended to be more broken than whole. Some long-ago owner had done the responsible thing and had the building surrounded by a chain-link fence, to keep out squatters and vagrants. But it had not been maintained. The chain link now offered only a patchwork defense against anyone who cared to inspect the building. Whole sections of it were damaged or missing.

Tufts of weeds, some of them several feet tall, had taken over the parking lot—or at least the parts of it that weren't covered by illegally dumped piles of debris. Storm didn't see any vehicles, but they were probably stashed around back, lest a passing police patrol car notice them and decide to inspect further.

Storm maintained a steady speed as he passed the building for the first time. He didn't dare pass it a second time. A Ford Fiesta driving along a street in Bayonne would not attract the attention of anyone inside the factory. But a car of any make or model driving by for a second time might cause someone to take notice. He turned down the next street and pulled to the side of the road as soon as he was sure he was out of sight.

He glanced at his watch. It had been only a half hour since Volkov issued his edict. Storm thought about the fourteen life forms inside the building. Three of them were likely Cracker's family. That left Volkov and ten hired guns. Storm assumed that, at some point, roughly half of them would depart for Newark Airport, leaving the other half to watch over the prisoners.

That's when he would make his move. It improved his odds— five- or six-to-one felt a lot more manageable than eleven-to-one. Especially when Dirty Harry only had six rounds in him.

He would rid the world of Volkov, save Cracker's family, then call Cracker and divert him from Newark Airport before Volkov's goons grabbed him. Simple.

He was about to get out of the Fiesta when he saw a woman walking along the street. She was alone, which seemed strange in this part of town—and at this time of the evening—and Storm watched her, because he was trained to watch anything unusual. With a distant streetlight behind her casting a shadow in front of her, he could only make out her silhouette. She was walking with the determined strides of a woman who knew exactly where she was going.

And it turned out where she was going was the right side of Storm's car. Before Storm could do anything to stop it, she yanked the door handle and sat down next to him in the passenger seat.

"Nice ride, Storm," Clara Strike said. "Very manly. Do you still like the color when you're PMSing?"

Storm looked over at Strike. She was wearing a skintight top that left little question about how well her physique had held up over the last four years. And there was that perfume, knocking him senseless, as usual.

Storm smiled. Much as Clara Strike could complicate his life, he was glad to see her. Plus, it improved his odds immensely.

"It's a bit underpowered, I grant you. Not the Ford Motor Company's finest effort," he said. "But it's growing on me. I've decided to name her Becky."

"If this gets out in the intelligence community, you know your reputation as America's greatest operative is ruined. Storm gallops to the rescue in a Ford Fiesta? It doesn't play."

"I was in a bit of time crunch. It was the best I could do," Storm said, then changed the subject. "How did you find me?"

"Kevin told me where you were. He thought you sounded like you needed some help. We lost our tail on Cracker after that explosion, and he hadn't resurfaced at any of the usual locations. So I had been looking for something to do anyway. I actually sort of thought he might be with you. Or, excuse me, with Elder Steve Dunkel of the Church of Jesus Christ of Latter-Day Saints"

"He was. I sent him on an errand. Though you probably don't need to bother following him anymore."

"Why not?"

"Prince Hashem's fortune is no longer in danger. Prime Resource Investment Group's financial situation has improved rather dramatically in the last twenty-four hours or so."

"Oh?"

"Turns out Cracker wasn't broke after all. His accountant had been stealing from him."

"Who? Teddy?"

"I wouldn't call him that," Storm said. "Apparently, he doesn't like it very much."

"Huh. Who knew?"

"Certainly not our pal Whitely." Storm paused for a moment, watching as the last shred of twilight disappeared, giving way to a moonless darkness.

"That's a nice little chunk you got out of your forehead," she said, gingerly touching near the gouge. "You okay?"

"It's nothing. Does Jones know you're here?"

She didn't answer. Storm took it for a yes.

"Maybe you should leave," he said.

"He doesn't know," she said.

"Are you lying to me right now?"

"It doesn't matter what I answer, does it? You're not going to believe me anyway. All that matters is that I'm reinforcements, and as far as I can tell you're not in a position to turn down help."

"Jones is a—"

"Look, forget about Jones," Strike said. "Yes, I'm sure he has his agenda. Is this a big shock to you? He always does and always will. Just focus on the here and now. I'm here. You're here. I'm know you're not just visiting Bayonne for the scenery. Kevin told me Volkov is here. Let's make a plan and take him out."

He knew that for the sake of three innocent people whose lives were now in danger—to say nothing of the untold millions more who would be imperiled if Volkov was to ascend to power—Storm had to get over whatever injustices Jones might be planning.

He took a deep breath and said, "Right. A plan. As I'm sure Kevin told you, Volkov is holed up in that abandoned factory down the street."

"Yes. And I'm assuming the only reason you haven't swallowed your pride and asked Jones to send in a full TAC team to take him out is because you're Derrick Storm and you have to save the world all by yourself."

"No, it's because there are civilians in there."

"Oh. Kevin didn't mention that."

"It's because he doesn't know. He just knows there are warm bodies that show up on the infrared."

"So who are the civilians?"

"Cracker's wife and kids. Volkov kidnapped them. He's using them as leverage to make sure Cracker does as he's told. I worry any large-scale operation—by one of Jones's teams, by the police, by the army, by anyone, no matter how well trained they are—will not end well for them. If Volkov is in charge, his men won't be the type to surrender easily. And they won't show any mercy to their captives. We have to hit them quickly and quietly and incapacitate them before they even know they've been hit."

He shared his thought that the thugs inside would soon split up, and his belief that that would be their best opportunity.

"We just need to get inside the building without being spotted," Storm finished. "The problem is there's so much open land surrounding the factory on all sides. If they have a lookout, we'll be spotted. If the lookout is quick with a rifle, we'll get shot."

The car went quiet for a minute or so. Then Strike said, "We could play it like we did in Sarajevo."

"No good," Storm replied, thinking back on that mission. "There's not enough of a crosswind. And, besides, where are we going to get all the fertilizer we'd need on such short notice? This isn't exactly farm country."

"Good point," she said. They lapsed into silence again. It was interrupted by Strike saying, "I've got flashbangs and gas masks in the van with me. There are enough windows in that place. We launch flashbangs through the windows and then move in."

Storm was shaking his head halfway through. "Too much smoke. Too much confusion. Too much of a chance one of those kids catches a stray bullet."

"Yeah, I guess you're right."

"Do you have night vision goggles?" he asked.

"Sorry," she said. "That's not part of my standard party kit."

Another pause for contemplation. "What we need is some kind of a distraction so we can get inside the building," Storm said. "From there we can pick them off one at a time."

"How about an explosion? I've got some C-4 with me."

"Yeah, but what are we going to blow up?"

A wicked grin spread across Strike's face. "Well, that depends. How attached are you to Becky here?" she said, patting the dashboard.

"You wouldn't."

"I would. Come on."

They didn't need more words than that. In this world, there were two places—and, sadly, only two places—where Storm and Strike were always in perfect sync. One was the bedroom. The other was on a covert operation.

TWENTY MINUTES LATER, THEY HAD WIRED BECKY FOR DETONA-tion and pushed her to a run-down auto repair shop that bordered the factory to the north.

If a lookout saw them, they would just look like a husband and wife pushing their derelict car to a place where it could get fixed. They retreated north, going back to Clara Strike's van.

There, they equipped themselves for the coming confrontation: bulletproof vests; KA-BARs, the combat knives preferred by the Marines; and some extra firepower. Strike went with a .40-caliber Colt and a 9mm Sig Sauer. Storm chose an ankle-holstered Compact Glock G38 with a silencer. It made for a nice complement to his Dirty Harry gun. Plus, he was able to grab several extra magazines. Having a few more bullets suddenly seemed to be a good idea.

"Kevin just sent a schematic to my phone based on the infrared," Strike said, holding out a 3-D image displayed there. "This is their position a half hour ago." She touched the phone and a new image appeared. "And this is their position five minutes ago. Obviously, this is subject to change if Volkov and some of his thugs roll out—as you suspect they will—but at least it tells us a little bit."

Storm studied the second image, went back to the first, then returned to the second. The way Agent Bryan had colored the image, the building itself had been made largely translucent, the walls and floors appearing only as gauzy, blue outlines. Human beings appeared as blazing chunks of orange and red.

The lookouts were in different places in each image, suggesting roving patrols rather than guards at fixed stations. The hostages were on the fourth floor, in a room toward the middle of the building, and they had remained stationary. Two guards were in the room with them in each photo.

There were stairs at either end of the building, but not the middle. Whatever manufacturing the building had been constructed to accommodate had relied on a long stretch of uninterrupted assembly line. Stairs in the middle of the building had been deemed superfluous by some ancient architect. In the building's subsequent uses, before its abandonment, those open floors had been cut up into more discrete spaces. There was now a long, straight hallway bisecting each floor, with rooms of various sizes on either side.

"Obviously we're going to be approaching from below them," Storm said, when he was done analyzing the floor plan. "It probably makes sense for you to take one stairwell and I'll take the other. We'll meet in the middle."

"Sure. You want the north stairwell or the south?"

"North. That's the side the explosion will be on. They'll likely all flock to that side. I'd rather have them coming at me."

"Always the gentleman," Strike said, giving him a coquettish smile and a curtsy.

They departed the van, jogging as they went two streets up, eight blocks south, then two streets back over, allowing them to approach the factory on foot from the opposite side of where Becky was now waiting for her explosive final act.

Without a word, they crossed into the lot immediately to the south of the factory, finding shelter behind a concrete wall—all that was left of what had once been a building.

From there, they each peeked out what had once been a window, taking a brief glance at the approach to the factory—a hundred-yard obstacle course of urban flotsam.

"There?" Storm whispered, nodding at a spot where the bottom of the fence had been pried back, creating a semicircular opening perhaps two feet high, enough for any reasonably flexible person to clamber under.

"Then there," Strike replied in the same hushed tone, using her eyes to point toward a tall pile of asphalt chunks that some paving contractor had dumped there to avoid the tipping fees at the local landfill.

"I'll take the lead," Storm said, gathering his legs underneath him to make the run. "If anyone here is going to get shot, it's going to be me."

"Storm, wait."

"Wait?" he said, because the only noun that wasn't in their shared dictionary was patience.

"Storm, I just . . . ," she started, and he saw she was having difficulty coming up with the words. "In the bar, we didn't really . . . I didn't really get the chance to say some things that have been on my mind, and . . ."

"Is now really the right time for this?" Storm asked, keeping his tone muted. He cast a wary eye toward the building.

"They're not going anywhere for a little while yet. Besides, there's never a right time with us. Our last meeting started with you pointing a gun at me."

"Fair point," he said, relaxing his legs, leaning against the wall, keeping one eye on the building and the other on Strike. "Okay. So what's on your mind?"

"I guess I just . . . Look, I died once and didn't tell you. You died once and didn't tell me. I know I'm still the bad guy, because I'm the one who hit first. But I guess I was hoping we could, I don't know, call it even. You forgive me. I forgive you. Maybe try to start fresh?"

A fresh start. With Clara Strike. Was there really such thing? Or was she the forever spider, with him as the fly?

"Clara, I don't know, I . . . We have all this history, and sometimes it's the best thing about us. Other times it's like this lodestone around our necks. So it's easy to say forget it all and begin again. But, one, I'm not sure I want to forget it all—because if you make yourself forget the bad stuff, you risk forgetting the good stuff. And two . . ."

"Think about it," she said before he could finish. "Just think about it before you answer, okay?"

With that, she disappeared around the wall and ran in a low creep toward the hole in the fence. He knew that he and Clara Strike would likely continue some version of their flawed, volatile relationship, one based on sex and spying and deceit. He would always welcome her back into his bed, always admire her talent as an agent. And she would always understand, better than any private citizen could, the peculiarities of his line of work.

Did that mean they had a real future? Were they too similar to ever work out in the long run? Or were they too different?

He looked down at his left wrist. He was still wearing the SuperSpy EspioTalk Wristwatch Communicator. He knew, eventually, the hurt would dissipate and he would be able to take it off. And he knew he would someday throw away the ridiculous toy, because he didn't have a lifestyle that allowed for the collection of sentimental keepsakes.

He just couldn't do any of that yet. He missed Ling Xi Bang. He wasn't ready to let go. She might have been all the good things that Clara Strike was, but without the lodestone of past sins. Yes, it was a near-impossible relationship—a pair of secret agents for nations whose interests seldom aligned in this way. All he knew was that she had never betrayed him, and he had liked living with a certain version of the future where she never did.

Except now he would never get a chance to know.

Strike had taken her position behind the asphalt and was motioning for Storm to join her. Storm let a large gust of air escape his lungs. It was time to prioritize the mission. He emerged from his hiding place and made a quick, low dash toward her.

He was limping. Just not in a way anyone could see.

. . .

AS TRAINED AGENTS, DERRICK STORM AND CLARA STRIKE COULD
stay like this for hours: coiled, waiting, ready to spring; relaxed,
yet focused; fully deflated, yet one instant away from being fully
pressurized. Two packages bursting with potential energy.

After they had spent approximately forty minutes in this condition, the event Storm had predicted took place. A black SUV
with tinted windows emerged from around the back of the building and exited through one of the missing fence sections. The
darkness and the distance from which they observed the vehicle
made it impossible to tell how many occupants it had. It was large
enough to seat eight, but Storm doubted he was going to get that
lucky.

Storm looked at his watch. They were fifteen minutes from
the designated rendezvous time. Newark Airport was perhaps ten
minutes away. This lent credence to Storm's suspicion: Volkov's
men planned to swoop in, collect Cracker, and return to their
Bayonne base.

There wasn't much time to wait. He nodded at Strike. She
pulled a small detonator out of her pocket and held down two
buttons.

Becky played her part beautifully, creating not one but two per-
cussive explosions in rapid succession. The first was when the C-4
went off. The second was when the gas tank caught and added to
the fireworks.

There was yelling from inside the building—loud, sharp voices
barking orders in Russian. Storm couldn't quite make out the full
sentences, but he did note, with satisfaction, that the words seemed
to express a general sense of confusion.

He held up three fingers, then two, then one. When he dropped
the final finger, he and Strike burst from their hiding place, sprinting toward the building. There were no shouts of alarm, no gun-
shots to greet their approach. All the attention from the Russians
was focused on Becky and her death throes.

Strike disappeared through the south entrance. Storm ran along
the back of the building toward the north entrance, staying close

enough to the brick wall that no one on the fourth floor would be able to see him without sticking his head out of the window.

He paused when he reached the northwest corner of the building, taking a cautious glance around the edge. It was clear. He whirled around the corner, then flattened himself against the brick, stealing toward the entrance with the silenced Glock in his right hand. He didn't know if the Russians would send a man to give the exploded car a closer look, but he didn't intend to be caught unawares.

He was halfway to the door when a man with buzz-cut brown hair appeared and began walking down the short set of brick steps that led from the building to the parking lot. His head was turned away from Storm, toward the burning car.

It was the last thing he ever saw. When the man hit the bottom step—ensuring Storm's satisfaction that there was only one man coming to inspect the car—Storm pulled the trigger twice. The Glock emitted a soft *thwump thwump*. The only other sound was that of the man's body dropping just to the right of the stairs.

Storm scampered quickly to the body, dragging it against the stairs so it would be at least somewhat out of sight. He did not look at the man's face. This was a kind of coping mechanism he had developed years ago. While killing was occasionally a necessary by-product of Storm's work, it was not something he relished. He learned that if he looked at a dead man's face, it stayed with him forever. If he didn't look, there was at least a chance he wouldn't be seeing this Russian in his dreams for the rest of his life.

With the body at least somewhat out of the way, Storm climbed the front stairs and entered the building. It was even darker inside than it had been outside, but Storm could make out the opening to the stairwell on his left. Storm once read that World War II bomber pilots who flew night missions munched carrots to sharpen their night vision. He often did the same, and was now glad for it. It gave him an edge in this murky world.

The shouting voices from the fourth floor had stilled themselves. The only sound was now the distant crackling of a Ford Fiesta burning itself out.

Storm made the left turn and passed through the door frame—if there ever had been a door, it had been busted off its hinges and discarded. He entered the stairwell. It was windowless and made of concrete, which to Storm meant one important thing: It would be like an echo chamber. He holstered the Glock. Even silenced, it would be too loud. He could not risk drawing notice of his arrival. It could spell death for Melissa Cracker or one of her children.

To one side of the stairwell landing, in the corner, Storm could make out the dim outline of a pile of trash, probably left there by a vagrant who had once made that spot home. Storm walked over to it, feeling—and, worse, hearing—the grit of broken glass under his shoes. He crouched and groped gently around until he touched cloth. It was an old T-shirt. Perfect.

He pulled out his KA-BAR and sliced the shirt up the middle. He tied one half around his right foot, one around his left. With the cloth softening his footfalls, he started creeping up the stairs. He counted the treads as he went. It was twelve steps up to a turn in the staircase, then twelve more steps up to the landing for the second floor.

He had just passed that landing and was climbing toward the third floor when his ears told him another Russian was approaching him from above. The man was descending quickly, perhaps going to check on the car, perhaps going somewhere else on patrol. It didn't particularly matter. Point was, he was coming. And fast.

Storm retreated back to the landing. There was a door to the second floor, still on its hinges. Storm couldn't open it without making too much noise. Likewise, he couldn't make it all the way down to the first floor in time. The Russian would overtake him before he got there. Staying mouse quiet was just too slow.

Storm looked around the landing as best he could in the limited light. There was no place to hide. The only concealment he had was the darkness. Storm wedged himself in the corner nearer to the third floor, pressing his back against the wall, trying to make himself part of it. It was not a perfect arrangement by any means. It was merely the best he could do. His hope was that the man would be feeling his way down the stairs in the darkness and looking down at his feet, not at the wall; and that he could jump the man from behind and clamp one hand on his mouth to muffle any screams, while he used his other hand to slit the man's throat with the KA-BAR.

Those hopes were dashed when Storm saw that the man was being preceded by a thin shaft of light that was growing brighter as he approached. He was carrying a flashlight. It was only a matter of seconds until it illuminated Storm. What happened in the seconds that followed would determine the fates of countless people.

Storm stayed still, the KA-BAR firm in his right hand. It was possible the man might not see Storm until he was close enough to attack. That was now the best scenario.

But no. When the man rounded the bend in the stairs between the second and third floors, the flashlight was pointed down at the stair treads, but some of it spilled onto Storm. First the beam struck Storm's feet. Then it climbed up to his shins and knees. When it reached Storm's waist, it stopped, as did the man on the stairs. He was halfway down, a full six stair treads away from Storm.

Storm didn't wait for what came next. He threw the KA-BAR, aiming it just to the left of the flashlight. His thinking was that the Russian likely had the device extended in his right hand, and therefore the middle of the man's chest would be slightly to the left.

It proved to be good thinking. The KA-BAR buried itself, blade first, between the man's ribs, piercing his heart. The small moan that followed was quickly drowned out by the sound of his body tumbling down the stairs. He landed at Storm's feet.

"Corporal, are you okay?" a man said in Russian from somewhere up above. Storm had spent enough time in Russia to recognize the origins of the accent. The man was from Moscow.

Storm summoned his best impersonation of a Muscovite and replied, in Russian, "I stumbled. I'm fine."

"You're as clumsy as an ox," the man said.

Storm replied, "And you're as ugly as one."

The man laughed. Storm pulled his knife out of the dead man's chest, then took his flashlight. It was a full-size Maglite, a big, weighty steel thing, made heavier by the four D-cell batteries that powered it. Thinking quickly, he said, "I think I bent the firing pin on my gun when I fell. I'm going to have to come back up and get another one."

"The general won't like that."

"I will have to offer him my apologies," Storm said.

"No, Corporal. Take one of mine. I've got two."

"Thank you, my friend. If we will be alive, we will not die," Storm said, pleased with himself for hauling out that old Russian saying. It seemed to settle the conversation for the moment.

Storm stripped the T-shirt shreds from his feet. He had to sound like a clumsy Russian who was unconcerned about the noise he was making as he climbed back up. He began trudging noisily upward, to the third floor then up to the fourth.

When he made it to the last bend in the stairwell before he reached the top floor, his flashlight illuminated a pair of dusty black boots. Storm quickly swung the beam upward to the man's face, blinding him. The man reacted by turning away and shielding his eyes with his left hand. His right hand held a gun by its barrel.

"Turn that thing off," he ordered.

"Sorry," Storm said, complying with the order. But by that point the man's night vision was thoroughly ruined.

"Thank you again for the gun," Storm said as he reached the landing.

"You're wel—" the Russian began.

But the words were cut off. Storm had swung the Maglite at the side of his head, connecting with a crushing blow. Storm caught his body before its fall could make a sound. The crack of the Russian's skull had been loud enough.

STORM STAYED AT THE TOP OF THE LANDING FOR A MINUTE, TO SEE if anyone would come to investigate the source of the sound. When he was satisfied no one had heard it—or that it had been dismissed as related to the strange car explosion—Storm tucked the Maglite into his jacket and eased away from the stairwell.

He entered the long hallway that split the two sides of the building. It had doors—or, in some cases, merely door openings—scattered at irregular intervals along both sides. Small amounts of ambient light spilled from those doorways, giving the corridor a gloomy illumination.

Storm thought back to the schematic he had studied on Clara Strike's phone. He did not have a perfect photographic memory, but he could close his eyes for an instant and see it. From where he was standing, the hostages were in the sixth room down on the right. There were also rooms on the left to contend with. Any one of them could have men in it.

He would have to go room by room, clearing them as he went. There was no other way to do it.

He wondered briefly how Clara Strike was doing—what obstacles she was facing, whether she had made it up the staircase yet, how many hostiles she had encountered—then put those thoughts out of his mind. Strike was a big girl. She could handle herself.

He drew the Glock. He inched to the first room on the left, then rounded quickly into the doorway. No one. He crept in. It was empty, save for trash.

He was about to exit when he heard two voices coming from the hallway, talking in Russian. They were heading toward the north stairwell. If they made it there and found their colleague with the crumpled head, they would sound the alarm and this operation would instantly change.

"I hear it's painful," one of them was saying.

"Oh, it's the worst," the other assured him.

"I had a gallstone once," the first said.

"Kidney stone is worse, the only way to—"

The sentence became muffled. They had disappeared behind the door to the room immediately next to Storm's. He had to act fast. He took one glance out into the hallway and, when he saw it was clear, padded silently to the next room.

He paused at the door. It was windowless and made of a cheap wood laminate. It had a piston at the top that kept it closed.

It presented Storm with a conundrum. Waiting for them to reemerge and taking them out in the hallway wasn't much of an option: The hallway ran the length of the building, meaning he— or the bodies he felled—could be spotted from some distance. At the same time, the door ensured there was no way to enter this room without the inhabitants being aware of him.

He pulled his jacket over his head and hunched over, tucking his gun in his gut. He burst through the door, moaning, immediately falling facedown on the floor in a rounded lump as the door closed behind him.

"What the . . . ," one of the guards started to say.

"Ohhhh, my kidney stone," Storm groaned in Russian.

The second guard laughed. The first was less amused.

"Very funny," the man said, walking toward Storm to either kick him or help him up. "Now get u—"

Storm rolled over with the Glock pointed upward and put a bullet between the man's eyes.

The second guard stared dumbly at Storm. The computer in his head was just a little too slow to process what was happening. By the time it clicked in, Storm had rolled to his right and pumped three slugs into the man's face.

They were imperfectly aimed, not the neat kill shot Storm had delivered to the first man. They were enough to drop his target, but Storm wasn't sure if they had completed the job. He leaped on the man like an angry animal, putting a knee on his windpipe and two hands across his mouth to stifle any yell or groan.

None was forthcoming. The shots had not been perfect, but they'd had their intended effect.

Storm got to his feet. The next problem was how to get back out of the room unseen without knowing who might or might not be in the hallway. He silently cursed the invention of solid doors.

Then, suddenly, it became a moot point. The sound of gunfire erupted from the south stairwell. Clara Strike had obviously resorted to doing things more noisily. There was no sneaking up on anyone anymore.

Storm burst out into the hallway, tossing the Glock to the side and yanking out Dirty Harry, happy to have its coercive powers more immediately at his disposal. He was ready to shoot anything he saw, and he didn't have to wait long. A man appeared out of a room roughly fifteen feet away, immediately turning south, toward the noise from the melee and away from Storm.

It was a careless mistake, one the man paid for with his life. Storm pulled the trigger twice. The bullets entered the man's back on either side of his spine. Twin explosions of red burst from his chest. He fell forward, arms splayed.

Storm went to the wall nearest him and crouched, gun still drawn, making himself as small a target as possible. He was ready to drop anyone else who appeared in the hallway. He waited, primed.

A form emerged from the south stairwell. It was too distant— and too dark—for Storm to have a decent shot at it immediately.

He watched how it moved. It wasn't some big, Russian thug. It was Clara Strike. But it wasn't Strike with her normal glide to her. She was hurt.

She moved up the hallway, toward Storm. He started slinking toward her, staying low with his eyes up, his right index finger still poised on the trigger.

But there was nothing more to shoot. Eventually, they worked their way until they met in the middle of the hallway, just outside the room where the Cracker family was holed up.

"Are you hit?" Storm said softly.

"Yeah. The vest took it. But, Jesus, my ribs."

"Broken?"

"I think so," she said.

"How many did you take out?"

"Two. You?"

"Six."

"Show-off," she whispered.

Eight down. So much for the theory that half would go to the airport while half remained here at base. Of the original eleven, there were either one or two left here—depending on whether they had sent one man or two to the airport to scoop up Whitely Cracker.

Storm guessed there were two. It was the safer guess—better to assume you had more resistance and be pleasantly surprised when there was less. More than likely, it was Volkov and one other man inside with the family. They would know that for whatever was happening outside, two armed men barricaded in a room with a closed door would be hard to overcome.

Storm considered his options and decided quickly on a course of action. The door was the issue. The door needed to be dealt with.

"You got any more C-4 left?" he asked.

"Yeah."

"With you?"

She quickly rooted in her flak jacket and came up with a small, rectangular piece of a substance that looked like modeling clay.

"Blasting caps?" he asked. And before he could even ask her to, she was already in the midst of producing those as well.

"Keep me covered," Storm said.

He rose and pinched off small chunks of the C-4, molding them around the door hinges as he did so. He was guessing at how much to use, knowing that too little wouldn't do the job but

289

too much could harm the innocents inside. Just one more thing not to screw up.

He set the blasting caps in the clay, then motioned for Strike to retreat down the hallway with him. There was no sense in either of them taking shrapnel.

He nodded. She pressed two buttons.

The explosion was small, controlled. For a moment, Storm worried he hadn't used enough. But then there was a crash as the door fell inward.

One of the children loosed a muffled scream. A spray of bullets, fired from an automatic weapon, greeted the demise of the door as either Volkov or his thug fired outward at anyone who might be rushing in behind the falling panel. The rounds buried themselves harmlessly in the wall on the other side of the hallway.

Storm nodded at Strike. They began working their way back toward the door, slowly, silently, guns drawn.

More probing gunfire erupted sporadically from the room. The men inside were smart enough to know an invasion was coming. They were just hoping they were lucky enough to guess when.

Storm crouched when he reached the door frame. Strike stayed up.

He held up a fist, then a finger. He wagged the finger to the right. Then he held up two fingers and wagged them to the left. This was a code he and Strike had established long ago. It meant he'd take the assailant on the right, she'd take the one on the left.

Then Storm did a three-two-one countdown with his fingers. When he dropped the last finger, he rolled into the door frame and assumed a shooting position.

His eyes instantly took in the scene. The family was clumped in the middle of the room, huddled against one another, bound and gagged with duct tape. Hovering over them to the right was a man pointing an AK-47. Storm killed him with one shot.

From above him, Storm heard the report from Strike's gun. Then he saw she had taken out her man as well.

The last two men were dead. And that might have been a cause for great celebration, except neither of them was wearing an eye patch.

Volkov wasn't there.

"Fuck," Storm said.

"What's wrong?" Strike asked.

"I should have brought cheese after all."

"Huh?"

"Nothing. Just something my father once shared with me."

"I don't underst—"

"Volkov said he would be at Newark Airport, and he is. For once in his life, he actually told the truth."

CHAPTER 33

NEWARK, New Jersey

They had taken too long. The caution in the stairwell. The steady elimination of the Russian goons. The wiring of the door. It had all been too slow. The time at which Cracker was to present himself at Newark Airport had come and gone. And now Cracker wasn't answering repeated calls to his phone.

This had led Storm to conclusion number one: Volkov had him already.

Any thought Storm had of this ending the easy way was now over. Volkov was no idiot. If he went to the airport alone—and there were ten bodies in a factory in Bayonne testifying to the fact that he had—he would be checking in periodically with his team. They would have reported their distress or just stopped reporting altogether. Either way, he would know they had been compromised. And he would not return to the factory.

Conclusion number two: Volkov was now in the wind. From Newark Airport, he could launch himself anywhere.

So even though Cracker's family was safe, nothing had really been settled. Volkov could go anywhere with Cracker. And, yes, he no longer could hold harm to Cracker's family over the banker's head. But Volkov was resourceful and knew more ways to torture a man than Storm cared to think about. The sadistic bastard would find a way to make Cracker do his bidding.

Conclusion number three: For all his effort, Storm really hadn't done a thing to neutralize the threat.

Volkov was still just as dangerous with those MonEx codes in hand. One way or another, Cracker would do exactly what Volkov told him to do.

Storm had left Strike with the Cracker family. She was in the midst of calling the authorities as he departed. The Bayonne Police would be able to respond within minutes. The FBI would follow shortly thereafter. He no longer worried for their safety. As for the future of Storm and Strike? That would have to sort itself out some other time.

For now, Volkov and Cracker were all that mattered.

As he negotiated the tangle of ramps and roadways that led from the New Jersey Turnpike to Newark Airport, there were two scenarios going through Storm's head.

In one, Volkov had collected Cracker and was now driving. Somewhere. Storm didn't like that scenario. There were probably two hundred thousand black SUVs in the tristate area. Good luck finding the one with Volkov in it.

In the other scenario, Volkov and Cracker were boarding a plane to . . . somewhere. That scenario wasn't much better. But at least it gave Storm something to grab on to. Volkov would surely be traveling under an alias: The man had more fake IDs than a crowd of college freshmen. But he didn't have an alias for Cracker. That's why it had been necessary for the man to bring his passport.

Storm called Bryan.

"What do you want now?" Bryan said in a whisper. "The credit on your Bahrain card is running out, you know."

"I need one of the nerds to check all the airlines to see if they can find Graham Whitely Cracker V on any flights out of Newark Airport."

"Hang on."

While he waited, Storm reached Terminal B. He pulled Strike's van to the curb outside the international departures area and left it there. Let the authorities sort out why a van full of surveillance gadgets and weapons was abandoned there. Maybe they'd do him a favor and shut down the airport.

As he got out, Bryan returned to the line. "He's on Air Venezuela flight nineteen to Caracas."

"When does it depart?"

"It was scheduled to leave Gate 53B two minutes ago. You know Venezuela is out of our—"

Storm knew he didn't have time to listen to the rest. It wasn't news to him. The United States had an extradition treaty with Venezuela that dated back to 1922, but it was shot full of exceptions and oddities. More to the point, the Hugo Chavez government seldom cooperated with extradition requests, particularly when the party to be extradited had the means to pay bribes. As soon as Volkov was out of U.S. airspace, he would be beyond the reach of the U.S. government. Not that the U.S. government was trying to detain him anyway, what with the way Jones was playing things. Maybe Storm could get on the phone with his new buddies at the FBI and convince them Cracker was being kidnapped. But that would take time, something he no longer had.

The fact was, there was no legal or diplomatic mechanism to prevent Gregor Volkov from slipping out of the country; no high-placed phone calls or favors called in or well-reasoned pleading with the right bureaucrat could stop Volkov or his plot. He would slide from Caracas to Moscow, or Brazil, or wherever it was he felt like going to launch a financial meltdown that would consume the world's economies.

There was only one way to stop him now.

Brute force.

Which brought Storm to conclusion number four: He had a plane to catch.

.   .   .

HE STUFFED THE PHONE IN HIS POCKET AND SPRINTED INTO THE terminal. He charged up the stairs, toward the morass of switch-backing humanity that was the security area. The line for crew and airport personnel was on the left side. Without breaking stride, Storm charged past two confused flight attendants, through the metal detector—setting it off in the process—and past a quartet of TSA employees who were so concerned about whether or not people had their shoes on that they didn't immediately react to the most brazen security breach any of them had seen outside a training exercise.

Finally, one of them had the wherewithal to yell, "You! Wait! Stop!"

Storm was already gone. The sign for Gate 53B told him to keep going straight. Arms and legs pumping, he blitzed by curious travelers, all of whom turned to watch this madman's dash through the terminal. Somewhere, well behind, TSA had sounded its alerts.

Gate 53B was at the end of this terminal branch. Storm ran up to a woman who was head down in a computer screen.

"Excuse me," he said, breathlessly. "I'm with the CIA. Did a man wearing an eye patch just board flight nineteen?"

"Yes, sir, but that flight has already closed. If you'd like—"

Storm didn't hear the rest. He was already charging down the Jetway.

"Hey! You can't go down there," the woman called after him, as if that would somehow stop him.

Storm reached the end of the Jetway. There was no airplane there, just an opening at the accordion-like end of the ramp. He dropped down to the tarmac, where he found a man in a jumper with earmuffs still fixed to his head. The man was stowing directional wands in the back of a small motorized cart.

"Excuse me," Storm said. "I'm with the CIA. Did you just direct flight nineteen out of this slot?"

"Yeah." He pointed to a white-and-red Air Venezuela 747 lumbering away in the distance. "That's it right there. But you can't be—"

Storm resumed his sprint. The aircraft had turned right out of its gate but now was heading left toward a runway. It was perhaps four hundred yards away. If Storm went straight, he might be able to catch it.

As he sped toward it, he watched the 747 come to a stop at the head of the runway. There were no other planes ahead of it. It was number one for takeoff. Storm was now three hundred yards away.

Having braked, the pilot was now calling for full power from the four Pratt & Whitney JT9D engines at his command. The plane responded immediately. A 747 was a big, heavy piece of machinery, but those Pratt & Whitneys were capable of pouring out more than fifty thousand pounds of thrust.

Two hundred yards out. Storm was still gaining on the plane, but he could go no faster. The plane, meanwhile, was accelerating. From somewhere behind him, a phalanx of TSA personnel had reached the end of the Jetway that Storm had exited. Storm dared not turn to look. But if he had, he would have seen the guy in the earmuffs pointing toward him.

A hundred yards away. Ten point two seconds of all-out sprinting. Storm was coming in at a nearly perpendicular angle. He picked the point where—he hoped—he and the plane would intersect. He aimed at the front landing gear.

With sixty yards to go he thought he might not make it. The plane was picking up speed too quickly. It was now going faster than him. At forty yards, he adjusted his course and aimed for the back landing gear. It was now his only chance.

At twenty yards, the plane was really starting to pull away. At ten yards, Storm thought his lungs were going to burst.

He closed in, leaping for the strut above the 747's tire. His outstretched hands grasped on to the metal. His body swung to the side of the tire, then slammed into it. The downward force being exerted by the back side of the spinning tire was working to pry Storm off, but it was not yet rolling quickly enough. Storm was able to hoist himself up the strut, then into the landing gear compartment.

The scream of the engines was deafening. Storm hung on against the increasing g-forces as the plane gained speed, then was able to wedge himself against the side of the compartment, hanging on to a pair of pipes that ran along the top. And that's where he still was as the 747 lifted off the ground.

Derrick Storm was now, quite unofficially, the last passenger aboard Air Venezuela flight 19.

THE 747 ASCENDED RAPIDLY, FIRST OVER A PATCH OF JERSEY swampland, then over the suburbs of the Garden State. Storm had found good purchase in the landing gear compartment, but he didn't dare look around—or do anything that might cause him to lose his grip—until the wheels retracted.

When they finally did, Storm retrieved the Maglite from his jacket, turned it on, and assessed his situation. With the wheels up, there was little room for him to move around. But claustrophobia was far from his biggest problem. Climbers who ascended the world's tallest peaks started having serious problems with oxygen deprivation above twenty thousand feet. Above thirty thousand feet, the air would become too thin to breathe and deathly cold. Storm was uncertain whether he would suffocate or freeze to death first, but he wasn't especially keen to find out. He had read news articles about stowaways found dead in wheel wells. He had to get to a pressurized part of the aircraft before it reached that altitude. He guessed he had about twenty minutes.

He looked up at the roof above him. If there was one thing that favored him, it was that airplane engineers preferred lightweight materials, for the simple reason that a lighter plane was easier to get off the ground. Sure enough, there was only a thin layer of sheet metal over his head.

He took out his KA-BAR and thrust it above his head. It punctured the metal, burying itself to the hilt. Storm yanked it out, then thrust again, in a spot just to the right of the first hole he had made. The gash had now doubled in size. He jabbed again.

There would eventually be a mechanic who would wonder what the hell had happened here and have to repair the mess. But Storm knew a small hole in an interior compartment would do nothing to destabilize a 747 in flight.

He could feel the plane turning, perhaps heading south—it was a little hard to have a good sense of direction in a fully enclosed metal box. It was not his concern at the moment. Working steadily over the next five minutes, he continued to perforate the ceiling. When he got about 270 degrees of his way around a jagged circle, he was able to peel a metal flap down and crawl upward through the man-sized hole he had created. He quickly reached a flat metal surface. But this wasn't a ceiling. It was a floor—specifically, the floor to the aft baggage compartment.

Storm sheathed the KA-BAR and hoisted himself into the gap between the bottom of the airplane and the floor of the baggage compartment. Other than the occasional support beam, it was an empty space, the bottom of which curved. At the lowest point of the parabola, there were a few feet in which Storm could crawl.

Storm wriggled into the space, then flipped himself so he was now staring at the underside of the baggage compartment floor. It was made of steel, far more formidable than the aluminum Storm had just carved his way through, and it was resting on metal joists that ran the width of the plane. There would be no cutting through this with the knife. It was too thick. He pushed at it with his hand. It didn't budge. It likely had several hundred pounds of luggage on top of it.

Storm began working his way forward. Baggage compartments were loaded back first. If there was any part of the floor without cargo on it—and Storm prayed that Air Venezuela was one of those airlines that charged a fee for checked luggage—it would be all the way forward.

It was slow going, but he inched his way until he was up against a series of supports that told him he had reached the front of the aft baggage compartment. He looked up and studied the way the floor was attached to the joists. There were steel rivets every two inches. Impossible.

Storm was not the kind of man who panicked. But he did get concerned when the situation warranted. And this was growing into one of those situations. He didn't know, precisely, how much time had passed or how much time he had left before the underbelly of the plane became his coffin. But he knew his ears had popped twice. The plane was gaining altitude fast.

He tried to think rationally. Airplanes needed repairs. There had to be some way for an aircraft maintenance person to reach this part of the plane without carving holes in the superstructure like Storm had. He swept the flashlight on the underside of the floor.

As he did so, he had the strange feeling the plane was no longer climbing. He couldn't tell if that was some kind of a misperception on his part. He knew for sure the aircraft was turning again. And he also knew his ears weren't popping anymore.

Still, it was not his first dilemma. Finding a way out was. Finally, he located a rectangular-shaped hatch on the starboard side of the vessel.

Now a new problem: There was no clear way to open it. Storm recognized that it was meant to be accessed from the other side, then propped open. Still, it was a more vulnerable spot than a solid steel floor. He picked one corner and pounded it with his palm.

The first blow did nothing. So he struck again. Storm was lying on his back. He was able to generate a fair amount of upward force with his pectoral muscles and triceps. They were muscles he used often—Storm could bench press over three hundred pounds.

But after four more tries, he realized it wasn't enough. His bench press wasn't sufficient. Maybe his squat—six hundred and sixty pounds, last time he maxed out—would be better. He positioned himself so his feet were on one corner of the hatch, then gave it all he had.

There was a whoosh of air. The difference between the baggage compartment pressure and the outside pressure was not as great as it would be at cruising altitude, but it was still considerable.

Storm had bent the hatch fifteen degrees upward. It allowed him to see that the hatch was secured into place by several plastic catches. Now that he knew where they were, he could make short work of them. He removed Dirty Harry, slid the gun's grip into the gap he had created, then used the barrel as a lever to pop off the remaining catches, one by one.

He had soon hoisted himself up into the baggage compartment and replaced the hatch, putting some luggage on top of it to keep it down so the plane wouldn't further depressurize.

He shined the flashlight upward to study the next barrier facing him. The ceiling consisted of flimsy looking panels that Storm had no doubt he could punch through one way or another. He just had to get himself up there.

He went to work, perching the Maglite in a place that gave him some illumination yet also allowed him to use both his hands for his task. He began stacking some of the sturdier pieces of luggage on top of one another, creating a pyramid that would allow him to climb up.

He was nearly done when the plane suddenly lurched hard to the right, assuming a steep angle that no commercial airline pilot would ever attempt, sending both Storm and his pile of bags toppling over. Storm landed heavily, bruising his shoulder and slamming his head against something hard and metal—in the darkness, he couldn't tell what.

The plane straightened, allowing Storm to stand for a moment. Then it tilted just as radically to the left. He fell again.

Storm had no idea what was going on. But he could hear the screams from the passengers above him.

LYING ON THE FLOOR OF THE BAGGAGE COMPARTMENT, STORM could taste blood in his mouth and feel more blood leaking from a cut in his scalp. He was woozy and perhaps concussed from the blow to the head he had suffered.

The plane was gaining altitude again, and quickly. Whoever

was now at controls of this aircraft—and Storm had a sinking feeling he knew all too well who it was—wasn't trying to impress anyone with his smooth flying.

Storm got himself to his feet and began rebuilding his luggage ladder. He was working by feel. His flashlight had rolled away and had either broken or buried itself under something. Storm couldn't take the time to go look for it.

His tower completed, he climbed to the top, picked a ceiling tile, and hit it with a powerful upward blow from the butt of his hand. It yielded easily. There was another foot between that ceiling and the floor to the main cabin. Storm retreated back down, hoisted up one more suitcase to give him a little more height, then climbed back up.

He groped around the underside of the cabin floor. He could tell where the seats had been bolted in and, more importantly, where they hadn't been. That was an aisle. And the aisle was where he wanted to be.

He repeated the move he had just used, giving it all his strength. The floor section was thin and no match for Storm. It buckled off the small screws that held it in place. He moved the displaced section to the side, sliding it above one of the other sections. He used the KA-BAR to cut a hole in the carpet, and hoisted himself up.

To the terrified passengers in rows 29 to 45, in the seats along the starboard side of the airplane, it was not a comforting sight: a bloody man with a knife emerging from the floor.

"It's okay," Storm said, reading their faces. "I'm here to save you."

They looked unconvinced. No one spoke. They were ashen-faced.

"I'm with the CIA," he said. "It's what I do."

Finally, a man in a seat near him said, "They probably need you up front."

Storm nodded, parting the curtains on his way into the middle cabin, then proceeded into business class. He kept walking by passengers who appeared both stunned and submissive. The sound of human suffering grew louder with every forward step: moans, wails, groans. As he approached the front of the plane, his ears were joined by his nose in telling him that something was very wrong. He smelled gunpowder. And blood.

It was when he entered first class that he understood why. Storm had seen war zones in his life, and this qualified as one. There was blood splattered against the ceiling, the bulkhead, the seats, the floor. There were at least seven dead passengers, all missing parts of their heads. Several more were lying in the aisle, wounded badly. Flight attendants were hunched over them, attending to their wounds.

A dark-skinned man in pilot's clothes was on the floor, leaning against the door to the cockpit. His close-cropped salt-and-pepper head was caked with blood. He was holding a gauze pad to the right side of his head. His name badge identified him as "Capt. Montgomery."

Storm approached, identified himself, crouched next to the pilot, and asked what had happened.

"It started right after takeoff," he said. "TSA notified flight control that we had a stowaway in the wheel well."

"Yeah, that was me. Sorry about that."

"Well, I still had to follow the flight plan for a while. You can't just pull a U-turn in the busiest airspace in America, you know? So flight control was coming up with a new route. They were going to have me stay low and then make an emergency landing in Philly. In the meantime, they were going to have two F-18s escort me in as a precaution. But it's not like I had squawked a seventy-five hundred or anything."

"A seventy-five hundred?"

"Sorry, that's the hijack code. You squawk a seventy-five hundred on the transponder and the air force knows to send in the cavalry. These were just supposed to be escorts, but not long after they showed up was when I heard the gunshot. My first officer was looking at me like *What the* . . . when one of the flight attendants called me on the intercom. She told me that some guy with an eye patch had blown one of the passenger's heads off with a gun that was made of *wood* of all things. He had told the flight attendant that he was going to shoot one person every thirty seconds unless I opened the door to the cockpit. Regulations say I can't open that door under any circumstances, but goddamn . . . Every thirty seconds I heard another gunshot and I . . . I just couldn't . . ."

The man stopped, needing to compose himself. Storm glanced out the window and saw the blinking lights of an F-18 not far off the 747's wing. Volkov hijacked the plane because he thought he had been caught, never realizing it was actually Storm's actions that had sent the fighter jets flying.

This was not an irony that Storm enjoyed.

Montgomery had regained enough poise to continue: "So we opened the door. He pistol-whipped me and told me to get out of the seat. He told Roger to get out of the seat"—Storm assumed "Roger" was the first officer—"but Roger wouldn't budge. He said something like, 'Who's going to fly the plane?' And the guy just said 'Me' and then he shot him. . . . He shot him. . . ."

Montgomery needed another moment. Storm stood and looked around for Whitely Cracker. He was three rows back in first class, huddled under a vomit-stained blanket, not looking at anyone or anything.

Storm crouched back down.

"I'm armed," Storm said quietly. "If we can get that cabin door back open, I can end this."

"Great. I've got a code that'll open the door."

With great effort, Montgomery stood, turning toward a narrow keypad next to the door.

"You ready?" he asked.

Storm pulled out Dirty Harry. The pilot punched some numbers.

"Okay, here goes," Montgomery said as he hit the pound sign. Then he frowned. Nothing was happening. He typed the code in again. Still nothing. A red light was illuminated.

"Damn it," Montgomery said.

"What?"

"He found the button that allows the pilot to deny access from the inside. We can't get in."

MONTGOMERY HAD SLUMPED BACK DOWN. HE WAS CHECKING HIS blood-soaked gauze pad. His eyes appeared even more sunken than they had been minutes before. He was the picture of defeat.

Derrick Storm knew he could not allow himself to be beaten.

"There has to be some way," Storm said.

"Maybe before 9/11, but not now. Those things are like bank safes."

"Trust me when I say bank safes can be cracked," Storm said. "What kind of lock is it?"

"It's electromagnetic. You're talking about something like twelve hundred pounds of holding force. Not even a moose like you could break that."

"I don't need to break it. Electromagnetic locks require a power supply. I disrupt the power supply, I disrupt the lock."

"You don't think the airlines thought of that?" the pilot said. "There's redundancy upon redundancy in these planes. In addition to the main power supply, there's a battery backup that lasts twelve hours. The battery is in a steel case, imbedded in the door. You'll never get to it."

Storm stared at the door for a long moment, as if he had Superman's heat ray vision. Alas, he did not.

But he suddenly realized he had something that would work just as well.

He looked down at his left wrist. The phrase "Variable Frequency Dial Allows Multi-Channel Communication!" was flashing in his head.

"What frequency is the lock set at?" Storm asked.

"What . . . ? I have no idea."

"No problem. Do the flight attendants have a small tool kit? I'm also going to need a piece of electronics with a nine-volt battery and someone's laptop. Ask around among the passengers."

Montgomery summoned two of the flight attendants, who soon produced the items Storm requested.

He took one last look at the SuperSpy EspioTalk Wristwatch Communicator. "Sorry, Ling. Gotta do it," he said, then pried off the facing.

Inside, he found a circuit board that was, in its basic premise, like the Westinghouse in his father's garage. It was just a lot smaller. He went to work. Changing the toy into a device that would send out an electromagnetic pulse at the proper frequency was just a matter of pirating parts from the laptop, combining them with the transmitter from the wristwatch, and powering it with the nine-volt battery.

It just took time, which, Storm was soon to learn, they were running out of even more quickly than he thought. The problem was no longer leaving U.S. airspace. It was staying in it that could kill them.

"I don't mean to rush you," Captain Montgomery said. "But how's it coming?"

"Just a little longer. Why?"

"Because an old airline pilot like me has an altimeter built into his head. Mine is telling me we're at about eight thousand feet. And I don't think those F-18s just off our wings are going to be very patient. They'll get orders to shoot us down if we get much lower than five thousand feet. One of them just did a head butt."

"A head butt?" Storm asked as he screwed a wire into place.

"It's a maneuver they attempt with a nonresponsive aircraft. They soar vertically upward to within a couple hundred feet of your nose, trying to get you to point it back up."

"I'm almost done," Storm said. "While I'm finishing, I need a favor."

"Anything."

"Get these passengers out of first class," he said. "I don't know what's going to happen when I get that door open. The fewer people to get hit by any stray bullets, the better."

"You got it," Montgomery said, rising to his feet. The man was clearly energized by having a sense of purpose. So Storm added one more thing:

"Oh, and Captain? Don't go far. I'm going to need someone to land this plane after we take back control of it."

"I like your style, Storm," he said.

"Thanks, Captain. By the way, I never got your full name."

"It's Roy. Roy Montgomery."

The men exchanged stiff salutes. Montgomery began herding passengers farther back in the plane, while Storm put his head back down in his task. He wasn't going to tell Montgomery this, but he was only about 50 percent certain his jury-rigged gadget was going to work. The variable frequency dial only operated within a certain range. If the lock was set to a frequency outside that range—which was always possible—it wouldn't respond to the pulse.

Storm finished around the time Montgomery had succeeded in emptying the first class cabin. The captain was slightly out of breath as he approached Storm.

"Okay. That's done. Do you mind if I ask: What's your plan once you get the lock to release?"

"Pretty simple: I open the door and shoot the guy flying the plane."

"How's your aim?" Montgomery asked.

"Pretty good. Why? Is there anything on the instrument panel that can't be shot?"

"Yeah, pretty much all of it."

"Then I guess I better not miss," Storm said.

"Okay. Just remember, these babies all have cameras throughout the front part of the cabin," Montgomery said. "It's another thing we owe to 9/11. It lets the captain know that it's safe to open the door."

"In other words, he's going to know I'm coming."

"Yeah."

"Great. Wish me luck."

"Good luck," Montgomery said. But Storm thought he noticed a small head shake as Montgomery retreated back to business class.

Storm put it out of his mind, concentrating on the tiny dial on the side of the wristwatch. He had reengineered the device so it now had several extra wires coming out of it. Two of them led to the nine-volt battery. He connected the final wire—thus turning the contraption on—switched the dial to the lowest frequency, and focused on the door.

Nothing happened. He began turning up the dial, moving steadily through the multichannel communicator's range of frequencies. He had to go slowly. The connections in his device were far from perfect. He didn't want to risk going too fast past the proper frequency and not delivering a strong enough pulse to trip the lock.

He was midway through the dial, not allowing himself to feel pessimistic, and still wasn't hearing anything.

Then, three-quarters of the way up, he heard a click and a whir.

The magnets holding the lock had been released.

Storm drew Dirty Harry and depressed the handle. The door opened inward, and he pushed against it, using its bulletproof bulk as a shield. The 747 cockpit is one of the largest in the sky, and it has a short, narrow hallway leading to the two front pilot's seats. At first, all Storm could see was the right side of that hallway.

He shoved the door farther in. His vision now extended to the end of the hallway. If they hadn't been in an airplane, he could simply have stuck his gun hand around the crevice and started firing blindly. But, given Captain Montgomery's warnings about the instrument panel, that seemed like a bad idea.

Volkov, on the other hand, would have no such worries. Any bullets he shot from his wooden gun—and Storm was assuming he had plenty of ammunition left—would hit less sensitive parts of the airplane. Storm was expecting to be greeted by gunfire at any moment.

But none came. He opened the door farther. He could now see half of the first officer's seat and part of the corpse that was slumped there.

He kept pushing the door, ready to fire the moment he saw any piece of Volkov. Slowly, steadily, inch by painstaking inch, he pushed until the door was fully open.

There was no one sitting in the pilot seat.

But that didn't mean Volkov wasn't hiding somewhere. Storm crept in, not fully committing himself to entry in a narrow hallway—where he'd be an easy target if Volkov suddenly came at him from around the corner—but giving himself a better view. Still no Volkov.

He allowed himself a baby step. Nothing.

Another step. Still nothing.

After another step, he could now see the entirety of the space: the instrument panel, both pilots' seats, the booster seat for a third pilot, the console, the avionics compartment—all of it.

Storm blinked, unable to believe what he was seeing.

The cockpit was empty.

STORM STAYED PERFECTLY STILL FOR A MOMENT, ALMOST AS IF HE only needed to look hard enough to make Volkov appear. His mind was clicking through possibilities, but none of them made any sense. There was no door in the cockpit other than the one he'd entered through. There was no cubbyhole or space large enough to hide any man, much less one of Volkov's width. There was no way out of the cockpit other than perhaps through the windshield, but that was intact.

Storm watched transfixed the eerie, ghostlike sight of the plane flying itself. The yoke budged itself slightly to the left, making a tiny adjustment in course per the order of the automatic pilot computer.

Storm's reflexes were set on a hair trigger. His gun was still drawn. He reminded himself to relax his grip—holding too tightly actually slowed reaction time—but he didn't dare move anything else.

He was starting to consider other options. Maybe Captain Montgomery had been mistaken. Maybe Volkov hadn't really gone into the cockpit. Storm had been in the belly of the plane when that transaction occurred. Was it possible that Montgomery—who had just watched his first officer get killed and sustained a wicked blow to the head—had missed something?

Storm was working out a new scenario—one involving Volkov somehow loading automatic pilot coordinates into the computer then retreating into the plane—when his peripheral vision registered movement from above him.

It was a human arm.

Storm leaped forward. Some fraction of a second later, Volkov fired.

Had these events happened in reverse order, Storm would have been dead and the world would have been put on a course toward incredible turmoil.

Instead, the bullet, which was aimed for the top of his head, continued traveling in the space where the top of his head should have been. In rapid succession, it passed near his neck, shoulders, back and butt, all body parts that had been removed from harm's way during the course of Storm's lunge. Then it struck one of the body parts that hadn't quite cleared: his left calf.

Storm roared in pain just as Volkov dropped from the ceiling, where he had been splayed ever since Storm started working the dial on the transmitter. Volkov landed square on Storm's back, pinning him to the floor of the cockpit. Storm was aware that his gun, already loose in his hand, had gone flying; and, out of the corner of his eye, he saw it land in the well under the yoke, where the pilot's feet normally go.

Volkov had dropped his own gun like it was of no further use to him—like it was out of wooden bullets? Storm guessed—and wrapped a tree trunk of a right arm around Storm's neck. Then he clasped his right hand with his left and began squeezing with more than enough force to restrict most of the blood flow to Storm's brain.

Storm knew he was in danger. He had perhaps forty-five seconds' worth of consciousness left. He had to make the most of them.

There was no point trying to loosen Volkov's grip. He'd have a better chance of prying open the jaws of a hungry shark. Storm's only advantage was height. Volkov was ten inches shorter.

Storm struggled to his feet, lifting not only his 230 pounds but Volkov's denser 220—and doing it with little help from his damaged left leg. Volkov was now draped on his back like a cape, the extra weight strengthening the chokehold.

Storm started taking backward steps out of the cockpit. He needed some room to maneuver, some runway to get up some speed. Soon, he was backpedaling as fast he could, given his encumbrance, and had cleared into the first class cabin. He finished his back-stagger with a mighty back-dive toward the first row of seats. His aim was to get a hard part of the armrest to connect with the soft part where Volkov's neck connected to his skull.

He just didn't get enough lift with his left leg. So he missed. The backrest connected midway up Volkov's back.

Still, the power of it—450 pounds propelled at a moderate speed from six-plus feet in the air—was enough to momentarily loosen Volkov's grip. Storm adroitly slipped away and the two men faced each other.

Each was in a crouch, ready to spring. Close-in fighting favored the shorter-armed Volkov. Boxing favored the longer-armed Storm. Both men knew this and were sizing each other up, trying to see how they could turn the fight to their advantage.

"I am so pleased you are here, Storm," Volkov snarled.

"Why? You're getting a crush on me? Don't worry. It happens to all the girls."

"No, it's that I realized something when I saw you this morning," Volkov said, then pivoted and executed a sweeping high leg kick. Storm dodged it easily.

"And what's that?"

"I never really paid you back for these," he said, pointing to the scars on his face. "All this time, I thought you were dead, so I figured our score was settled. But now I see you and I know you need to be punished."

Storm grabbed a laptop computer that had been left behind by one of the passengers and threw it at Volkov. The Russian blocked it with one swipe of his paw.

"It won't work, you know. This absurd thing you're trying with Cracker."

"Oh, I beg to disagree, Storm. I have some of the richest men in Russia ready to cash in on the disruptions to the market, and with the money they make, they'll be able to fund an insurrection that would topple even the mightiest government. Those clowns who run Moscow now will have no chance. Mother Russia is meant to be ruled by a strong leader. I am that leader."

"You're twisted."

"You flatter me. It's a shame I have to kill you."

"You're the one who's dying tonight, Volkov."

Volkov's response was to lower his head, emit a banshee yell, and charge. Storm reacted with what was meant to be a devastating right-leg kick to Volkov's rib cage. The only problem was, the launch of it meant he was standing only on his left leg. The moment the majority of his weight transferred to the wounded side, he crumpled.

Volkov, who was aiming for Storm's midsection, ended up overshooting. The entire exchange only resulted in them swapping sides of the small clearing at the head of the first class cabin, where they were facing off.

Storm did not wait for Volkov's next rush. He came at the smaller Russian swinging with his fists. Volkov tried to back away but was not fast enough. He was stung by a roundhouse right, then by the left jab that followed it. Blood flowed from his nose.

Volkov tried to get in underneath the punches so he could bear hug Storm and turn this into the wrestling he preferred, but Storm fended him off with an uppercut that opened a wound over Volkov's eye.

Both men retreated for a moment. Had this been a heavy-weight prizefight, Storm would have scored solid points on all judges' cards. It's just that no scorecard could account for the gunshot wound to Storm's calf.

The men were now on opposite sides of the cabin, each breathing heavily, each struggling with his wounds. Volkov's good eye—the one not patched over—was beginning to swell shut. Storm was losing feeling in his left leg and didn't know how much longer the limb would continue to respond to his commands.

Both knew the fight was coming to an end. Each thought he would be the winner.

Volkov's eyes were darting around. He backed farther away, and Storm thought he was working up room to come at him headlong. Instead, he ran at Storm, then cut quickly to his left down the aisle.

Storm's first thought: He was going for another gun he knew he had hidden in his carry-on luggage.

But then Volkov passed right by the seats where he and Cracker had been sitting.

Storm's second thought: He was fleeing back to the passenger cabins.

But then Volkov stopped short of business class.

Storm was reacting too slowly, thinking too slowly. Both of his thoughts had been wrong and his left leg was now dragging badly behind him.

Volkov was going not for a gun or for a passenger, but for the emergency exit door on the side of the plane. He yanked away the seal around it and then grasped it in both hands.

It came away easily. They were at low enough altitude that the change in pressure was not significant, however the wind was now whipping into the cabin through the opening. Thousands of feet down, the earth sped by.

Storm realized, too slowly, the advantage Volkov now had: a forty-pound steel weapon. He had hefted it so he was gripping the bottom of the door and he was coming fast at Storm.

Storm was trapped midway down the aisle—a sitting duck. If he stood there, he was going to get bashed. And he couldn't retreat fast enough on his gimpy leg to be able to elude Volkov.

He had no choice. He dropped his shoulder and barreled forward.

The move caught Volkov off guard. He brought the door viciously down on Storm but hit only the meaty parts of Storm's back and shoulder. Storm was on him too fast.

The two men landed heavily, rolling on the ground. They hit up against the wet bar in the back of first class, then lurched toward the now-open emergency door. Storm was trying to work his hands into Volkov's face, aiming to further injure his eye. Volkov was reaching for Storm's leg, looking for the gunshot wound, attempting to sink his fingers into it.

Both men were bellowing and snarling, partly because of the pain they were suffering, partly because of the pain they were inflicting, partly because this had become something deeply instinctual. They were two organisms battling for their very survival, calling on the deepest parts of their energy reserves, doing whatever they could to mete out maximum punishment to the other.

They kept switching who was on top, although, to a certain extent, it didn't matter. Neither the top man nor the bottom man seemed to have any advantage, just different ways to gouge, scratch, punch, kick, or grab the other.

Then, suddenly, that changed. Volkov was on top and Storm was so intent on going at the man's eye, he didn't do a good enough job playing defense. Volkov managed to get both his hands around Storm's neck, and the brutal Russian was squeezing with every nanogram of strength he had. Storm realized with sickening certainty that he was going to lose this fight—and his life.

Dots were appearing at the corner of his vision. Then the darkness began closing in. The image—Volkov hunched on top of him, sneering sadistically—was quickly going to become pinprick-sized, then disappear altogether. Storm had mere seconds left.

He did not know exactly where he was on the floor. He sensed he was dangerously close to a whole lot of rushing wind, which meant he was near the edge, but he could no longer be cautious.

With the last ebb of effort he could summon, he heaved himself toward the open door.

As he rolled, his right foot—the one that still had some feeling—hit one side of the opening. Then his right hand the other side. Volkov, whose hands were still clenched tight around his opponent's neck and who had drawn his knees underneath him, was not nearly as wide. He was, in fact, something of a ball.

A ball that Storm had successfully aimed right at the middle of the door opening.

Now it was just a matter of momentum. Storm had something to stop his—the sides of the door. Volkov did not. He was still traveling, only there was no longer an airplane underneath him.

For a brief moment, as his sneer was replaced by a look of sheer terror, he tried to keep his clutch on Storm's neck. But as his body tumbled fully through the opening and started a drop that was as inevitable as gravity, he lost the angle he needed, and therefore lost his grip.

The last thing Storm saw of Volkov was his writhing figure growing small as it plummeted through the night sky to the hard ground many thousands of feet below.

CHAPTER 34

BACAU, Romania

Something had changed. Derrick Storm could see it in the little girl's eyes.

Katya Beckescu was still gripping the same ratty teddy bear. She still wore the same old clothes. But she was a different child than she had been the first time Storm spied her in the courtyard at the Orphanage of the Holy Name. She ran up to him, wrapping her arms around him so fiercely she knocked away the cane that Storm had been using for the last week or so as he recovered from a pesky little gunshot wound to his calf.

Storm had spent the first part of that week in a hospital after a surgery to remove the darndest thing the doctor had ever seen: a bullet made of a wood composite that was harder than lead. In fact, it was so strong, it hadn't shattered on impact like a normal bullet would, meaning the prospects for Storm to recover full function of his leg were quite bright.

He had spent the next part of the week in long meetings with the FAA, the TSA, the FBI, and a whole alphabet of other federal agencies who were trying to sort out what had become known as "the Flight 19 Incident." It took repeated oaths from Captain Roy Montgomery to assure them that, yes, Derrick Storm really had been the hero. Officially, the CIA was—characteristically—quiet about the whole thing.

Storm also visited Jedediah Jones in the cubby, where the head of internal division enforcement assured Storm there really were no hard feelings; and that despite some creative differences during the thick of his last mission, there would be more missions to come. Jones accompanied those assurances with a suitcase full of cash.

Storm spent the final part of the week traveling to Beijing, where he watched Ling Xi Bang be buried with full military honors. Although the circumstances were not explained by the state-controlled Chinese media, she had been awarded the Order of National Glory, the Chinese equivalent of the Medal of Honor. Storm had been the lone Westerner in attendance at the ceremony, and Xi Bang's aging father blinked at him through tears, wondering what an American was doing at his daughter's funeral. But before Storm departed, the man grabbed him gently by the arm and whispered, "Thank you, Mr. Storm, for making sure her death was not in vain."

In other news, "someone" had leaked compromising cell phone photos of Senator Donald Whitmer with a young female Senate staffer to the *Washington Post*. The paper had too much propriety to actually print the pictures. But it wrote a story about their existence, one that identified that Senate staffer only as "an Asian woman in a short, pleated skirt." Within hours, Whitmer was being referred to as "Senator Sleazy" on the Internet. The senator denounced the pictures as being fakes. Then, the next day, he released a short statement explaining he would not be seeking a fifth term, so he could spend more time with his family.

Meanwhile, the Justice Department quietly closed a brief but unfruitful investigation into Whitely Cracker. Although there was no doubt in the assistant U.S. attorney general's mind that Cracker deserved to have charges brought against him, there was a total paucity of evidence with which to bring those charges. No money had passed between Cracker and the assassin he was alleged to have hired. Without the money to follow, there was no case.

It meant that Derrick Storm had to mete out his own justice

on Whitely Cracker, which he was more than happy to do. The first part of it was a personal assurance that if Cracker ever again made another trade—even for bubble gum cards—he would be visited by an avenging angel, either Storm or one of his friends, who would show Cracker no mercy. The second part was the plan Storm had had for Cracker all along, the plan he had first formulated when Carl Storm explained Operation Wafer to his son.

And now here Storm was, trying to pry a five-year-old off his legs.

"What has you so happy, little Katya?" Storm said in Romanian.

"I'm going to be adopted," she gushed. "I'm going to a city in your America called San Francisco."

"What wonderful news," Storm said as she finally released him.

"I kept hoping and hoping and hoping I'd get one mommy," she said, beaming. "Sister Rose tells me now I'm going to get *two*."

Storm just laughed. "Yes, that sounds like San Francisco all right."

Storm bent to pick up his cane just as Sister Rose McAvoy appeared in the main entrance to the abbey. She walked slowly toward him across the courtyard. She had tears in her eyes.

"Well, Derrick Storm, you wouldn't believe the phone call I just got," she said, her brogue coming out choked by emotion.

"Oh?" Storm said.

"It seems some anonymous person from New York has made a fifty-million-dollar donation to the Orphanage of the Holy Name," she continued. "He has requested that five million of it go to purchase the abbey from the diocese and that the remaining forty-five million go into an endowment that the orphanage—and only the orphanage—can draw from. It looks like Holy Name is going to be financially secure for all its days, my boy."

"Is that so?" Storm said, as if this were news to him.

"Now, you wouldn't have had anything to do with this, would you, Derrick Storm?" she said.

Sister Rose had ended her long walk and draped her arms around Storm's thick torso. He could feel her old bones pressing against him through her thin skin. But her hold was still strong.

"I'm sure I didn't," Storm said. "You're always telling me God answers our prayers. He must have answered yours, Sister Rose."

"That He did. That He did. And I think I'm staring at the embodiment of those prayers right now."

She looked up at him, her face tearstained but blissful.

"Does this mean you're not going to be running away with me and marrying me, Sister Rose?"

"I'm afraid not, Derrick my boy. There's work for me to do here at the orphanage."

He sighed. "Too bad."

And then Sister Rose reached around, pinched him on the bottom, and said with a quick, devilish grin: "You are sort of handsome, though. In a rugged way."